Just Another Night on the Beat

She looked through the peephole and unlocked the door. Detective Woodcott looked shaken. "Yes?" She stepped back to let him in.

"You said you were a witch."

"Yes," she said cautiously.

"I was wondering whether there were spells to make somebody invisible, and how difficult they'd be. Off the record. Strictly off the record."

"My old high priestess had a spell that could stop police looking at cars if they were speeding just a little. Not me, of course," she added hastily. "Why?"

"Something a witness said. This case is so bizarre we can't afford not to look into any leads. There's probably a natural explanation," he essayed a smile, "and that probably means our witness was drunk or crazy or on serious drugs. Thanks for your time."

But as he walked back to his car, Woodcott had the feeling it wasn't nearly that simple . . .

"An exciting story with some really original twists. This will entertain you."

—*Science Fiction Chronicle*

Shadows Bite

Stephen Dedman

A Tom Doherty Associates Book / *New York*

SHADOWS BITE

Edited by James Frenkel

A Tor Book
Published by Tom Doherty Associates, LLC
175 Fifth Avenue
New York, NY 10010

www.tor.com

Tor ® is a registered trademark of Tom Doherty Associates, LLC.

Library of Congress Cataloging-in-Publication Data

Dedman, Stephen.
    Shadows bite / Stephen Dedman.
        p. cm.
    "A Tom Doherty Associates book."
    ISBN 0-312-87783-8 (hc)
    ISBN 0-765-30298-5 (tpbk)
    1. Vampires—Fiction. 2. Children of Gangsters—Fiction.
    3. Japanese Americans—Fiction. 4. Photographers—Fiction.
    5. Revenge—Fiction. I. Title.

    PR9619.3.D387 S53 2001
    823'.914—dc21   2001040913

First Hardcover Edition: December 2001
First Trade Paperback Edition: March 2003

Printed in the United States of America

0 9 8 7 6 5 4 3 2 1

To the Saturday Night Immortals:
Sue, John, Elaine, Laurton, Sam, Amanda, Victor, and Alistair

Thanks to my editor, James Frenkel; my agent, Richard Curtis; my wife, Elaine; the Katherine Susannah Prichard Writers Centre; Tanya Schmah; Robin Pen; Sue Isle; Samira Keshavjee; Russell B. Farr; Ralph and Tara Smith; Sally Beasley and Dave Luckett; Keira McKenzie; Ghoti Dalziel; Correyn Tan; Amanda Crossley; Jim Minz; John Klima; Aimee Crump; Jeremy Bloom; Rose Beetem; Rob Sawyer and Carolyn Clink; Alexandra and David Honigsberg; Lillian Butler; and Jonathan Strahan.

Shadows and karma follow one everywhere.

Japanese proverb

Contents

Shadows
Bite

Prologue: 1980

Solomon Tudor picked up a glass and peeled off the protective covering, then helped himself to a miniature of whisky from the bar as though he'd rented the room himself. It had long been his policy to take what comfort he could wherever possible, and it hadn't been many years since the Hilton would have seemed luxurious, even extravagant, to him. "If you'd left town immediately, I might not have found you so soon." His voice, as usual, was quiet; he'd learned that if people *listened* to you, you rarely needed to yell.

Angela fumed. The delay hadn't been her idea, but she had little money of her own. She'd set up wards in the hotel room, to try to avoid detection for a few days, but it had been a vain hope; Tudor was not only a more powerful magician, he had many other ways of obtaining information. "Did you have anything to do with keeping me here?"

Tudor snorted. "If your boyfriend didn't think with his dick, he would have sent you on ahead rather than keeping you here. It's not as though he'd be able to protect you, either way. And no, I had nothing to do with it. I'm not in the movie business anymore, remember?"

Angela didn't comment. Four years before, Tudor had black-mailed her father into buying a screenplay from him and letting him produce it. The film, *Devilspawn*, had bombed, but it had been cheap enough that her father's career had survived. It had been a bad year for the studio; fires and other strange accidents had run up the cost of many films, and formerly healthy execs had suffered heart attacks, nervous problems, and other dis-abling complaints. Angela often wondered how much of this Sol had staged for her father's benefit, and in what coin he'd been paid—apart from the house, an oversized property near Holly-wood Boulevard with an unfortunate reputation. The studio had been glad to unload it as part of Tudor's fee, and the sorcerer had lived there ever since. Until two days ago, so had she.

"He's a weakling," said Tudor, quietly. "He thinks that by rescuing you from me, he can ingratiate himself with your fa-ther—but he doesn't have the willpower to make that sort of decision all by himself." He glanced through the window at the smoggy vista of Los Angeles, saw the sun setting in glorious toxicolor beyond the sprawling mess that was LAX. The City of the Queen of the Angels, he thought with the mental equiv-alent of a snort, had to be one of the most misnamed cities on Earth. Any angels there had either fallen or were still looking for a place to park. If they were ever found, they'd be deported as illegal immigrants.

He smiled. He *loved* the city. "Look at this place," he said, gesturing with the cigarette in his right hand. "It's a sheer man-ifestation of willpower. Or faith, if you prefer. There was no logical reason for it to be here; there wasn't enough fresh water to build a city a fraction of this size in this place—but a few people wanted it, and Lo!, it bloomed." He chuckled. "One day, maybe, the will, the faith, will dry up, and so will the city."

"Don't preach at me," said Angela, wearily. "I've heard it all before, and I'm not sure I believed it then. What do you want, Sol?"

As if on cue, Malachi woke and began crying. "What do I want?" asked the sorcerer. "More than you will let yourself imagine—but I'll settle for my child."

"No!"

"In return, I'll let you go wherever you will. I'm sure that you'd find it much easier without a two-year-old. And you know he'll be safer with me."

"Safer? Like Hell!"

"I have enemies, in and out of Hell, and they know he's my child, and you know I won't see him harmed. Do you think your boyfriend wants him? Or your father? You and I are the only ones who love him, Angie."

He could tell by her expression that *that* had hit home, but she wasn't about to give in that easily. "And if I don't?"

Tudor smiled, stared at the glass in his left hand, and gestured again with the cigarette in his right. The huge ruby in his signet ring glowed, and the alcohol ignited, sending a bright yellow flame a foot into the air. As Angela watched, the pillar of fire slowly shaped itself into a fair likeness of her as she'd been when they'd first met, a nineteen-year-old clad in flared jeans and Nehru jacket. Tudor glanced at this image, which pirouetted prettily above the glass until it faced him. "Your soul," he said, almost sadly. "You signed a pact, remember? I can claim it at any time. As I see it, you have three options, and all of them involve me walking out of here with Malachi. In two of them, your soul is consigned to Hell, and either your boyfriend comes here to find you dead, or I let some demon possess your body, which would be even more distressing to your father and probably fatal for your boyfriend. In the third, you get to live a long and possibly productive life, nothing prevents you having more children, and we all live happily ever after."

"If you could do that," she said, "why did you come here?" The image was probably no more than an illusion, but that was small consolation. She knew she'd been careless enough with her hair and her nail clippings that Tudor could have made an image of her that would enable demons to find her no matter where she hid.

"Because I wanted to give you the third choice," said Tudor, wearily. "I bear you no malice, personally. And because I would still have to come here to collect Malachi in any case, and I want to spare him any distress. It would be difficult to restrain any demon from harming him, impossible to prevent them frightening him, and I'm sure that finding you dead would be an unpleasant experience for him."

"Aren't you supposed to suggest chopping him in half?" said Angela, sarcastically.

"Wrong Solomon," said Tudor, without so much as a smile. "I swear to you, I will not harm him, nor allow him to come to any harm. You must know this, just as you know I will not hesitate to harm anybody else if I must." The flame sculpture in his hand exploded into a fireball that filled the room. Angela could feel the heat, but when she opened her eyes, the room was undamaged, and Solomon and Malachi were gone.

1

Takumo

Plummer climbed up onto the tiny balcony, confident that he'd made almost no sound, then looked with scorn at the locks on the security screen and sliding glass door. He reached into his pocket for his picks, and after less than a minute, slowly inched both doors open a crack. He resisted the urge to chuckle when they moved; Lowe had warned him that the target was supposed to be some sort of eccentric security wizard. An instant later, he heard a drumming, the beat somewhere between military and disco. He blinked, then recognized the tune from his junior high days; "Billy Don't Be a Hero."

A light clicked on above him, and Plummer swore under his breath; he was sure he'd disconnected the power to the apartment. He stared at his shadow on the paper shade, then reached into his jacket for his silenced pistol, turned around, shot out the light, and turned around again, ready to return fire. Nothing. Lowe had warned him that the target liked knives, not guns; fortunately, that seemed to be true. He stayed behind the window as he slid it open, and wondered what to do next. To say that he'd lost the advantage of surprise was a classic understatement, and Lowe had warned him about what would happen if he killed the target without getting the information for which he was being paid. Plummer hunkered down, then burst into the room, going *under* the paper shade rather than through or around.

Something hit him in the back of the neck almost immediately. Dazed, with his eyes not yet adjusted to the darkness of the room, Plummer spun around and received an agonizing burst of pepper spray in the face. His gun was kicked out of his hand a moment later. He heard a voice mutter, "Must be amateur night," then something hit him in the temple, and the pain—and the music—receded into shadow and silence.

Charlie Takumo, who'd been standing motionless in that spot since a few seconds after the power had been cut, exhaled slowly, then knelt and patted down the intruder.

A few minutes later, Plummer tried to open his eyes, which still hurt like hell—even more than his right wrist. No result. He seemed to be lying face up on a floor, with his wrists, thumbs, and ankles bound together. "You bastard," he groaned, "I'm blind! You've blinded me, you—"

"Don't be stupid," said Takumo. "It's just a little home-made pepper spray."

"I can't see a fucking thing!"

"You're in a dark room, with a bandage over your eyes, so don't exaggerate. It should stop hurting in an hour or two. Sorry about your hands; I only meant to dislocate your thumbs and your wrist, but I think I may've broken them. You'd better go see a doctor when you get out of here."

"You're letting me go?"

"In a minute or two. You're going to deliver a message for me, and you can do that much more easily if you're alive. Besides, getting rid of your body is more trouble than it's worth. First things first, though. Who sent you?"

"Get—" Before he could finish, Takumo bent his left little finger backward, and the second word became a gasp.

"Ah, that's better," said Takumo. "A nice clean dislocation.

I must be getting the hang of this *koppojutsu* stuff at last. So. Who're you working for? Nakatani?"

"Who?"

Takumo looked at him, and nodded; the ignorance seemed genuine. "There's nothing in this hovel worth stealing, so someone carrying the sort of gear you had—lockpick, silenced pistol—doesn't break into a dump like this except under orders. So who's your boss?" No answer. "Hegarty? Gacy? Lowe?" A slight flinch. "Thought so; he likes them dumb. You don't know who Lowe works for?"

"Who's Lowe?"

"Can we cut the crap? You were supposed to ask me for information, right?" No answer. "You think you're the first patsy sent here?" Plummer flinched. "Lowe didn't tell you that? I've been averaging one every three months for the past two years. I preferred it when he was sending the women; it's a pity he didn't believe what I told *them*. He really must be scraping the bottom of the barrel by now."

"Get—" He grunted in pain as the little finger on his right hand was bent backward with an audible snap.

"Oops. So sorry," said Takumo, cheerfully. "Look, man, whoever you are, you were sent here to find Magistrale, weren't you? Like all the others were. So I'm going to tell you the same thing I told them; I don't know where he is, and it wouldn't do you any good if I did. Freakin' Hell, if he *was* here when any of you goons came blundering in, you'd know all about it. Or maybe not; he has ways of disposing of corpses that're much more efficient than the pet-food factories. Lowe didn't tell you about *his* body count, either, did he?" He smiled, noticing that the intruder was perspiring more freely. "I didn't think so.

"So. I'm going to let you go. Tell your freakin' boss that I don't know where Magistrale is, and that if he keeps using me as a training exercise for second-rate rent-a-thugs I'm going to start charging; the neighbors have begun complaining. As it is, I'm going to keep those lockpicks and tools, and your ammo; you can keep the gun, though I'd recommend you dump it before you get arrested. You've parked nearby?" No answer.

"You on your own?" No answer, until Takumo grabbed the ring finger of his left hand.

"Yes!"

The stuntman sighed. "Pity. You won't be in any condition to drive for another hour or so. Where are you parked?"

"Two, three blocks away."

"Venice Boulevard?" Plummer nodded. "Okay, I'm going to cut the tape around your legs. Don't try kicking me or anything stupid like that; I'm using a very large, very sharp blade. Okay, now try standing up."

Plummer moved his feet apart, startled to find that he could. He rolled over on to his knees, then stood unsteadily, his wrists still bound before him. "Okay, hold your hands out at arm's length, as far apart as possible, and don't flinch. Yeah, that's fine." This time, Plummer heard—or imagined he heard—a faint whispering sound as the blade swung through the air and slashed through the tape.

"Okay," said Takumo, a moment later. "Take three steps forward . . . that's good, stop, now turn left . . . another two steps . . . left again," Plummer heard a door open. "Now four steps forward. Don't try removing the bandage until you're out-side."

Plummer nodded, and tried to guess his captor's location from the sound of his voice. The pain from his eyes and the broken bones in his hands made concentration almost impossible, but he listened carefully, and on his third step, jabbed with his right elbow at where he expected his target's nose to be. His funny bone hit something hard and unyielding; the explosion of pain almost masked the feeling of a cold metal point prodding him behind the left kidney.

"Don't back up," said Takumo. "Don't turn around. Just take one more step forward, and never come back here again. Ever."

Plummer staggered forward, and felt the door slam behind him an instant later. Using the fingers of his left hand only, he prized the bandage away from his eyes and looked around. It was still dark. He glanced at his watch: 3:58 A.M. The little freak had taken less than twenty minutes to break him; he only hoped his arms worked well enough to let him drive out of here. He was at the bottom of the stairs before he started wondering what he was going to tell Lowe.

Charlie Takumo returned his *ninjato* to its scabbard, and leaned against the kitchen wall. He'd been becoming complacent; the last intruder had broken in less than six weeks before, and he hadn't expected another attack for at least another month. He was just glad that years of film and theatre work, and his mother's unshakable belief that he was the son of Charles Manson, had taught him how to play a tough guy without cracking a smile.

For all his martial arts training and the collection of weapons in his small apartment, Takumo's adult life had been reasonably nonviolent until nearly two years before, when a *rokuro-kubi*— a disembodied head with a murderous pair of hands; a nightmare come to life—had flown into his dorm in a Calgary youth hostel. The rokuro-kubi had intended to attack the room's other occupant, a young photographer named Michelangelo Magistrale, but Takumo was incapable of pretending to be asleep while someone else was in danger a few meters away, and had come to Magistrale's aid. The rokuro-kubi had fled, and the two men had become friends—a friendship that had led to Takumo being poisoned by another monster, fighting and killing two young women trained as ninja, and helping Magistrale break into the Bel Air mansion of Tatsuo Tamenaga, a magician with yakuza connections. Magistrale—Mage to his friends— had killed Tamenaga, then disappeared from L.A. to learn more about the talismans that had given the magician his power. Unfortunately, someone seemed determined to avenge the old man, and their hirelings had visited Takumo's apartment more often in the past year than Magistrale had.

Takumo took a few deep breaths, finding his center, then padded across the tatami—woven straw mats—back to the bedroom. His computer had been bought secondhand a few weeks after Tamenaga's death, and was now almost an antique, but it still did everything Takumo needed it to do; a little word processing, surfing the Web (though with excruciating slowness), and most importantly, sending and receiving e-mail. He logged on, deleted the junk mail that his spambuster hadn't caught, then posted a brief message to alt.fan.dirty-pair.

2

Defender

Kelly Barbet had never liked mornings. She preferred to think of herself as a creature of the night, and the drive from home to her office, especially on a sunny Monday morning, often seemed the worst part of a job she usually regarded as stressful, futile, and about as much fun as trying to eat lunch in a sewer.

She sat in her Range Rover and waited for the gridlock to dissipate. The big four-wheel drive was more car than she needed, and wasn't cheap to run, but it was her favorite souvenir of her divorce and she intended to keep it for as long as possible. Besides, while she rarely drove outside the city, much less off-road, she enjoyed fantasizing that one day she'd just turn the car around and head out of the sprawl to somewhere more civilized. She might have done it now, had she not been boxed in by more cars behind her. She glanced in the mirror, and noticed that the highway patrolman behind her was speaking on the radio; probably calling in to check if the car had been reported stolen. She smiled, and half-turned to show him her profile. Women, she knew from experience, were much less likely to be stopped for the heinous crime of D.W.B.—driving while black.

The traffic inched forward, and she sighed as she moved with it, wondering whether anyone on the freeway actually wanted to *be* where they were bound, or were they all like her?

As always, Kelly made herself a mug of coffee before sitting down at her desk (she knew better than one mug before venturing onto the freeway at rush hour) and reaching for the file at the top of her in-tray. This one was thin and new-looking; a first offender, as good a way as any to start the week. She opened the folder and glanced at the top page, and the contents of her stomach—strong black coffee and low-fat blueberry yogurt—began fighting each other for a chance to escape. She shut her mouth hastily, and clamped her hand over it while she struggled not to vomit.

Kelly prided herself on not being squeamish. She'd seen innumerable crime-scene and autopsy photos before. Her husband had been a keen hunter, and she'd accompanied him on several trips until he'd realized she was a better shot than he was. And she'd once killed a rokuro-kubi by slamming it into her microwave and cooking it until its skull exploded like an eggshell. But this . . .

She closed her eyes and swallowed, despite the sour taste in her mouth, then looked at the color 8 × 10 again. The photo showed a naked boy, with long loops of intestine hanging out of his belly, and ribs showing through incisions from his armpits to the bottom of his breastbone. She forced herself to note details. She didn't know much about children, but she guessed his age at about ten. Skin too pale for him to be anything but white. Hair dark. Eyes red, but that might be a flash effect. The most incredible detail impressed itself upon her last: the boy seemed to be *standing*. The intestines were hanging down, toward his feet.

She studied the rest of the photograph. The picture had obviously been taken with a flash through a window; she could see the glare of the flash on the glass and a thin, almost ghostly reflection of the photographer, a vague shape in a bathrobe, the face mostly hidden by the little camera. It looked as though the boy were standing on a window ledge and hanging on to the edges of the window. The window seemed to be at least one story above the ground. Nothing showed of the room itself except faded tie-dyed curtains at the edges of the photo.

She turned the photo facedown, and looked at the next; another 8 × 10, this one showing strips of film, a—it took her several minutes to remember the term—proof sheet. She studied the twenty-three other images on the sheet, which bore no resemblance to the photo of the boy. The two frames after that shot showed two mostly black cats—probably taken to finish off the roll. Before it were pictures of San Francisco: seals at Fisherman's Wharf with the Golden Gate Bridge in the background; the INDIANS WELCOME—INDIAN LAND graffiti on Alcatraz; an attractive young Asian woman grinning from a Chinatown phone booth; and a series of hastily taken snapshots of people in costumes ranging from latex bodysuits to chainmail bikinis to Band-Aids and boa constrictors, that Kelly guessed showed the Castro Street Fair. She looked at the background of one of the cat pictures. The tie-dyed curtains looked to be the same as those in the photo of the boy, but that didn't prove anything. With a sigh, she covered the first photo with the proof sheet, and read the accompanying report.

The photo of the boy had been noticed by the clerk at a camera shop in Santa Monica, who'd immediately called the LAPD. The cops had been unimpressed, even dismissive, until one had noticed the resemblance to a boy whose body had been stolen from the morgue at St. John's Hospital less than a week before, then found in two pieces in a storm drain downtown. She'd compared the photos, searched the shop's database for the name and phone number of the woman who'd brought the disposable camera in, and called the police. Two detectives had sped over to the woman's walk-up, talked to her neighbors, then rushed to the hospital where she was employed as a licensed practical nurse. The woman had refused to explain about the photo, had been arrested on Sunday evening, and had asked for a lawyer.

Kelly looked at her mug shot, which showed a rather plain young white woman in her mid- or late twenties, still in her nurse's uniform, with long wavy brown hair tied back. Also clipped to the report were laser-printed copies of autopsy photos of the boy—both closeups of his face, one taken before his body had been reported missing, the other after it had been recovered. She stared at these, and at the photo of the boy standing in the window. They were unmistakably the same boy, though in the snapshot his face was snarling—or was it grinning?—while in the earliest photo, it had the sleepy slackness that most people mistook for serenity. In the third, his cheeks were swollen as though with mumps. She shook her head, and looked in the folder for a copy of the autopsy notes. Nothing. Damn.

Kelly sat there for a few minutes, and shook her head. Hell of a way to start the week, she thought, and reached for her car keys.

Without ever intending to, Kelly had acquired a habit of automatically assessing every client as a possible physical threat as soon as she walked into the interview room, regardless of gender, age, race, record, or the crime of which they were accused. Gaye Lind was shorter than her, with arms and shoulders that would have looked at home on a bodybuilder—but this was hardly astonishing; Kelly had spent enough time in hospitals to know that lifting weights was a large part of a nurse's job. On the other hand, she probably wasn't any stronger than Kelly herself, and didn't have her reach, nor probably her training; Kelly, who stood six foot two with her hair cropped short, had devoted much of her limited spare time over the past two years to archery and jujutsu. "Hi," she said. "I'm Kelly Barbet, from the public defender's office. I've been assigned to represent you."

"Hi," replied Lind, politely but without much enthusiasm— nor, Kelly noted, hostility or disappointment. Some clients were obviously distressed to find their defense was being handled by a young woman with skin the color of unsweetened chocolate, but Lind seemed to accept it. Kelly sat down, and looked at her more closely. Though she had a night-shift worker's pallor and obviously hadn't slept well, she was a little more attractive than her mug shot had suggested. "The police want to know about the photo of the little boy that was found in a roll of film that you took in to be developed. They haven't charged you yet, but you're being held on suspicion of being an accessory after the fact to the illegal possession and misuse of a dead body—that's all, so far. The boy in the photograph looks very much like a boy whose body was stolen from the morgue last Tuesday night, and found on Friday morning. Any information you can give them about how the body might have been stolen from the morgue would help—"

"I don't know."

"Have you seen the photo?"

"Yes. They showed it to me."

"Did you take it?" Gaye looked at her, her expression bleak. "The photo," said Kelly, patiently. "Did you take that photo? There's nothing to prove that you did; if someone else could have used your camera to take it, then tell me."

Gaye was silent for nearly a minute. "He was a patient of mine," she said, softly. Kelly nodded; the file hadn't mentioned that, but it made sense. "His name is Nick."

"What was wrong with him?"

"He was starving."

"He'd been starved?"

"No, he . . . We tried feeding him, building him up again, but nothing seemed to work. We tried glucose drips, and iron, we tried giving him blood to replace what he seemed to have lost— which wasn't easy, he's a rare group—and he just kept losing weight. Fading away. It's as though he was being eaten by something. . . ."

"Eaten?"

"The weight didn't seem to *go* anywhere. He didn't seem to be excreting it in any way; he was sweating, but not *that* heavily, and there was nothing unusual about his stool and urine samples; we checked." Kelly nodded, her face still impassive; it was mildly reassuring to know that *someone* had a worse job than she did. "Besides, he was able to put on a little weight during the day, but it always disappeared overnight when he was asleep—and we were keeping him under observation at the end, so it's not as though he was vomiting anything up without us knowing. It's almost as though his blood were turning into water or a gas and he was losing it when he exhaled."

"What? What could cause that?"

"Nothing I've ever heard of. The doctors were baffled, too. They were hoping the autopsy would clear things up, but . . . well, Nick just disappeared."

"Do you know who could have taken him?"

"Not unless it was his family—not his parents, they're in the hospital too, but extended family. They're, I don't know, some Eastern Orthodox religion. Apostolic, I think. They objected to the autopsy, and I don't know whether the hospital persuaded them or just overruled them. I'm just guessing, but I really can't think of anyone else who'd have any reason to take his body— unless it was the CDC or somewhere like that."

Kelly blinked at the idea of the Centers for Disease Control doing anything so clandestine.

"Why are his parents in the hospital?"

"They weren't my patients, but I think they have the same symptoms—the wasting disease. They were admitted a few days after Nick was."

"Nick's body was found again two days later, in a storm drain. Decapitated. Do you think that either his family or the CDC could have done that?"

"No, of course not . . . I really have no idea what could have happened."

"Did you take this photograph of Nick outside your window?" She slid the 8 × 10 across the table.

"I guess I must have," said Gaye, after staring at the picture for a few seconds. Kelly said nothing. "I thought I was having a nightmare, but I must've been thinking clearly enough to take the photo. I wasn't sure, the next morning, how many shots were supposed to be left on the roll, so I finished it off with some pictures of my cats and took it in to be duh-duh-duh . . ." She started to sob, and hid her face in her hands. Kelly reached into her bag for a pack of tissues, and slid it across the table to her, and Gaye took one with a murmur of thanks.

"Developed," she said, finally, after wiping her eyes and blowing her nose. "The next thing I knew, these two cops came into the hospital and were asking me . . . asking what I knew about Nick's body. I hadn't even heard it had been found; the cops told me later."

Kelly nodded. Both the head and body had been taken straight to the L.A. County Coroner's office, not back to St. John's.

"Do you know why someone might stand Nick's body outside your window like that?"

Gaye stared at her, obviously horrified. "No! Jesus, I hadn't even thought of that!"

"What *had* you thought?"

"That it was just a nightmare! I didn't think anything else until the cops showed me that photo and dragged me in here!" She took a deep breath. "Besides, there's no way you could balance a dead body like that on a ledge like mine. It'd have to be—" And she burst into tears again.

Kelly stared at the photo, and silently agreed. It would be difficult even for an agile person to balance on a window ledge that was barely wide enough for a few potted plants, even if he was holding on to the sides. Maybe the body had been . . . what? Superglued to the frame? Hung there like a marionette, controlled from a window above? "Do you have any enemies that you know of?" she asked, gently.

"No."

"No one at the hospital?"

"No!"

"Ex-lovers, anyone with a grudge?"

"I have some exes, but we're friends now." Kelly heard what sounded like a faint hint of pride in her voice, surfacing briefly through the shock. *And why not*, Kelly thought bitterly; *wish I could say the same.* "And none of them would *ever* have done anything like stealing a body from the morgue, let alone . . ."

"I guess you've never dated a pre-med," muttered Kelly. Gaye looked up, startled, then shook her head and did her best to smile. "Okay. The police are waiting for a search warrant, then they want to send some forensic examiners around to your apartment to see if there's any sign that Nick was ever there." Gaye turned slightly pale. "Is there anything in the apartment that you don't . . . ?"

"Just some hash brownies in the freezer," said Gaye, weakly. "If I get busted for those, I'll lose my job."

"I don't think they'll search *that* thoroughly. Nothing else?"

"No. I . . . I didn't let him in."

"Who?"

"Nick." Gaye blinked. "The nightmare. I just remember getting this vibe that he wanted to be let in. But I didn't let him in. The cats were freaking, and . . . I could see he couldn't possibly be alive."

"You say he *spoke* to you?"

"No, I don't think so. I mean, he couldn't have, could he? It was just a . . . an impression. I was mostly asleep, maybe I dreamed that part of it."

Kelly nodded. "What did you do?"

"I grabbed the camera—it was on the bookshelf—and took a photo so I'd know whether it was just a nightmare or . . . well, real. I think the flash must have startled him, because he disappeared."

"Disappeared how?"

"I don't know. Fell, maybe. I didn't really see; I was looking through the viewfinder, and . . . he just wasn't there when I looked again. I couldn't even be sure that he'd been there at all."

Lieutenant Holliday looked up as Kelly hurtled into his office, and looked down again to hide a grimace as she shut the door hard enough to set the thin partition walls vibrating. "Yes, Ms.

Barbet?" he said, his voice neutral. "What can I do for you?"

"For a starter, you can tell me why Homicide is in charge of the Lind investigation."

Holliday looked up, and shrugged. "Sorry. (a) We would've given it to the Grave Robbery Squad, but they were disbanded some time last century." Kelly glared, and Holliday shrugged again. "(b) Because when some poor schmuck found the body, it wasn't identified as the one that'd been reported missing from the morgue until some other poor schmuck found the head. (c) Because even when we'd cleared that up, nobody else wanted the case. (d) All of the above. Pick one."

Kelly, only slightly mollified, nodded curtly.

"That's correct, the answer is (d). So, no, your client isn't suspected of homicide. If she *was* involved in stealing the body from the morgue, of course, there may be an assault charge . . ."

"Assault?"

"Isn't that in the report? The pathologist working on the body was found unconscious next to the slab. The last thing she remembers was making the incision and preparing to remove the organs, and the next thing she knows, she's lying on the floor and the body is gone. It looks like she fainted, though she has no history of it, and it's hard to believe that somebody just happened to be passing by and decided to steal a kid's body because the pathologist's conveniently passed out." He shrugged. "On the other hand, there's no signs of violence or a struggle, and her drug tests came back clear. They're checking her for epilepsy now. Of course, the real fear is that she caught some fast-acting disease from the kid, but that still doesn't explain why somebody would steal the body, or cut off its head and dump the bits in a sewer. Any light your client can shed on this would be helpful."

"My client doesn't know anything about it."

"Pity. I guess we'll have to wait to see what the forensics turn up in her apartment. Let me know if she wants to change her story, okay?"

3

Professionals

Michelangelo Magistrale—Mage to his English-speaking friends—looked intently at the young girl's hands, glad that neither she nor her parents had attempted to cut away the webbing between her fingers. He could remove scars easily, but sometimes there was deeper damage that was more difficult to heal. He glanced at his interpreter, Tida, and asked her to ask the girl to turn her hands over so he could look at her palms. He examined the calluses, nodded, then turned to the interpreter again. "Tell her that the procedure shouldn't hurt, but it's very messy, so I'll need you to blindfold her."

Tida duly translated this, then placed a soft mask over the girl's face and adjusted it. When she'd finished, she looked at Mage and asked dryly, "Coffee?" She knew he didn't like any witnesses while he "operated."

"Yes, and something for the girl. How old is she, by the way?"

"Four, nearly five. Her name's Mali."

Mage nodded. He was slowly learning Thai; his vocabulary was impressive and he'd memorized a few useful phrases, but his grammar was worse than a preschooler's and he suspected his accent was atrocious. "Thanks."

As soon as Tida had left the room, he touched the focus wound about his wrist while he stared at Mali's hands and *saw* them without the webs. He was careful not to make any other changes: he could remove calluses when required, but there was no point in doing so when someone was sure to return to the same sort of work. He'd also erased fingerprints, inadvertently, but he didn't want word of *that* getting out; the clinic was already getting too many visits from Bangkok's underworld figures, despite his efforts to discourage them.

When the webbing was gone, he examined Mali's hands to make sure he hadn't made any unwanted changes. Tida returned a few minutes later, placed his coffee mug on the table beside him, and translated for him as he asked Mali to move her fingers, then warned him that he was going to check her for sensitivity. When Mage was satisfied, he nodded to Tida, who removed Mali's blindfold. The girl opened her eyes, looked nervously at her hands, then let out a squeal of joy.

Mage smiled, and reached for the mug. When his right hand closed on empty air, he turned and looked. The mug was exactly where he remembered putting it down, and his fist was occupying the same space as the handle.

Mage bit his lip to stop himself from swearing—Tida was fluent in English obscenity, and he wouldn't have been astonished if Mali recognized the words—and turned to Tida, keeping his voice and expression as calm as possible while he slowly moved his right hand up to his bearded chin. *That*, at least, felt solid enough. He glanced in the mirror next to the eye chart to see if he'd become translucent, and was relieved to notice that he hadn't. "Have Doi check her out before she goes. Is there anyone else here to see me?"

"Yes—"

"I'll call for you when I'm ready for the next one. I may be a few minutes."

He waited until the room was empty before attempting to

touch anything else. He tugged gently on a lock of his hair, then drummed his fingers on the tabletop, before making another attempt to grab the coffee cup. This time, his hand closed around the handle and he was able to lift the cup normally, if a little shakily. He emitted a soft sigh of relief; *last* time, it had lasted nearly a minute. He slipped the focus off his wrist and pocketed it, and sat with his eyes closed while he counted to a hundred. Then he opened his eyes, looked around the room, walked over to the door, grabbed the handle, and called quietly for Tida.

Tamenaga's bath was a Jacuzzi the size of a backyard pool, bubbling like a witches' cauldron. Tamenaga-sama conducted much of her business there, usually by phone—sometimes with a video link, more often without. Only Shota Nakatani was ever invited to join her, and she suspected that he would cheerfully have forgone the privilege if he'd dared.

Tamenaga was twenty-eight, and looked nearly ten years younger; westerners, she knew, often misjudged the ages of Asian women, and her ancestry was as Japanese as her name suggested. She was short, barely five feet tall with her hair down, but not ethereal or petite; regular sessions in the gym and the dojo had left her well-muscled, and her slender hands could break bricks or bones. Her face was naturally pretty, and could become beautiful when she wished.

She had reverted to using her maiden name immediately before her father's funeral, which had followed her husband's by little more than a week. She'd worn the same black dress to both, but no photographers were admitted to either event, and no one present had commented. Dutifully, she had pretended to believe the story that her late husband had committed suicide, though even then she knew better, and she had eventually extracted the full story from Nakatani. Her father's death had been even more horrific; Tatsuo Tamenaga had been blasted with a shotgun at point-blank range, his carotid had been sliced open with a katana, one of his eyes was gouged out and several of his ribs broken and, at the autopsy, cobra venom was found in his bloodstream. The murder was still officially unsolved; the police had treated it as the work of one of the yakuza clans, but had never named a suspect. Haruko Tamenaga knew better.

It had been Yamada Kazafumi, one of Tamenaga's human bodyguards, who'd found the corpse; Nakatani had wanted to keep his death a secret, *Kagemusha*-style, for as long as possible, but Haruko had refused, insisting on a lavish Buddhist funeral.

"I've heard from Lowe," she told Nakatani, who sat opposite her in the foaming bath. "This one failed also; returned with his right arm, both thumbs, and a finger broken. I suggested to Lowe that he have his other arm broken as well, or maybe a leg, but Lowe said it was difficult enough hiring help as it is. I thought you'd agree," Nakatani nodded, "so I let it drop. We don't seem to be accomplishing anything relying on local talent, and I thought maybe we should try some other method."

"What did you have in mind?" asked Nakatani, warily. He'd spent much of the past two years trying to steer Tamenaga away from the illegal side of her father's empire, which the old man had never intended her to inherit. Like many underworld figures, he'd wanted his child to live as safe and respectable a life as possible. The investments, businesses, and tax shelters he'd set up for her would guarantee her a net income of three to five million a year—about twice what Nakatani was making, which struck him as more than adequate. Both men had also doubted that L.A.'s other crime lords could be held at bay for long by a young, unmarried widow, even if her name was Tamenaga.

Tamenaga had left her father's Bel Air home shortly after his death, and moved to the "open city" of Las Vegas, where people enthusiastically threw away enough money to maintain any number of syndicates. While she received some "rent" and "interest" from the L.A.-based rackets her father had helped establish, Nakatani estimated that between eighty and ninety percent of her income was legally obtained, and the casino successfully laundered the remainder. She had her own bodyguards and security staff, of course, and occasionally sanctioned violence when dealing with competitors or labor problems, but was usually careful not to associate with criminals or know too much about any illegal activity—except when it came to avenging her father.

"A few ideas," she said, "but nothing very concrete yet. Maybe there are *other* people who might know where Magistrale is. All the evidence suggests that Magistrale and Takumo had at least one other person helping them. Who was the man who visited him in jail?"

"His uncle. Dante Mandaglione. He has a good alibi for the time your father was murdered; he returned home to Vegas, soon after Magistrale was released on bail. He's in his forties, and out of shape; if there was a third man involved in the attack, it wasn't him."

"Would he know where Magistrale is?"

"He might, I suppose. We've been watching him, and the rest of Magistrale's family, but Magistrale has only visited them once, for his grandmother's funeral."

Tamenaga felt a brief pang of sour regret that she hadn't arranged for an assassin to be waiting in the cemetery, even though she knew her father would have disapproved.

"And we haven't found anything to indicate where he is," Nakatani continued. "No long-distance phone calls, no return addresses on the postcards he sends occasionally; we don't even know how he heard about the funeral, and he disappeared almost immediately afterward. He must be using the focus to transport himself somehow; the cards he sends his family always come from different locations—usually very large cities in the U.S. and Canada, but with no other discernible pattern. Of course, they may be being relayed by contacts he has in these places, but we don't know who these contacts could be. It's difficult to believe that he could travel so widely without being seen by somebody or leaving some sort of paper trail."

Tamenaga considered this. "Could the focus do that?"

"I don't know. Kazafumi claims that Magistrale used it to transport himself to the top of the stairs, but that was line of sight, very different from instantaneously traveling thousands of miles. It's not something your father ever learned to do, and he was a brilliant man who had the foci for more than fifty years. It seems much more likely that Magistrale has found some way for the focus to make him invisible, undetectable— an illusion. He was a photographer, it's the sort of thing he might think to try, and that would explain his escape and even much of the travel."

"If *you* wanted to keep in touch with somebody like Magistrale, how would you do it?"

"E-mail," replied Nakatani, instantly. "Cheap, fast, and very difficult to establish a physical location, unless you stay online long enough to be traced. It's easy to encrypt, and easy to use code or ciphers for short messages. And it's very popular with travelers. Or you could send coded messages to newsgroups; we suspect that's what Takumo's doing, but we haven't been able to find the hidden messages in any of his posts—if there are any. I'm sure that he knows he's being watched, and that most of them are just jokes, a way of wasting our time. Of course, he may also have other logon IDs that we don't know are him, and we can't spare the manpower to read *all* the garbage that gets posted, so anything could be slipping through."

"What about Mandaglione?"

"He edits a softcore pornographic magazine, which has a website that receives hundreds of hits daily, as well as having an online chat group that isn't archived. I'm sure you could hide messages on that, easily, and he receives more e-mail than we can wade through." He'd had Dante Mandaglione thoroughly investigated after Tamenaga's death, having heard rumors that the murder had been arranged by rival criminal organizations, but found that the man, while streetwise, wasn't connected to any of the mafia families. At least, none of Nakatani's contacts in the families admitted to having any dealings with him, or even to having heard of Michelangelo Magistrale.

"The rest of his family?"

"One of Magistrale's sisters also has an e-mail account. We're watching her, but we've learned nothing useful."

"And his women?"

"Our resources aren't infinite," replied Nakatani, dryly.

"We've been checking the phone records of several, and will occasionally watch their homes, but Magistrale doesn't seem to have contacted any of them. What's even stranger is that we haven't been able to find any women who've begun any sort of relationship with him in the past two years—and such an extended period of celibacy seems completely out of character for him. I hate to admit it, but he may have done a better job of creating at least one false identity for himself, and maintaining it, than we'd thought possible."

Tamenaga was silent for nearly a minute. "Maybe Mr. Mandaglione would be an easier nut to crack than Takumo," she mused.

"Your father always refused to go after a man's family," Nakatani reminded her, a little nervously. "He said that if that were understood, then nobody would attempt to harm you . . ."

"Did I say anything about harm?" said Tamenaga, as innocently as she was able. "Does he have any weaknesses we can exploit? Women? Money? What about blackmail?"

Nakatani relaxed slightly. He'd always preferred bribery to extortion, and was very unhappy that they'd never been able to bribe Takumo. The stuntman seemed uninterested in money or most things that money could buy, legal or illegal, and sending women to seduce him into betraying Magistrale had also been unsuccessful (though one of them had managed a thorough search of his apartment, and established that the foci weren't hidden there). This had disturbed Nakatani, who had long held that all Americans could be bought, if you could only find the right currency.

He'd devoured all the information he could find on Takumo, and had learned a grudging respect for the man. Short, half-Japanese, illegitimate, he'd had to learn to fight while still young, and had become adept at it—yet while he continued to enhance his skills, he'd never been a thug or a bully. Instead, he'd put himself in danger by coming to the rescue of people he'd seen being victimized—including Magistrale. Nakatani knew things about Takumo that Takumo himself had probably forgotten, but he'd come no closer to learning *why* he did what he did. Mandaglione had to be an easier nut to crack. "I'll see what I can find out," he said.

"Good. Bring me a report tomorrow—as much useful information as you can get quickly. Keep the watchers on Takumo; don't let him suspect we might be concentrating our efforts elsewhere. Now, what's the status of our bid for those casinos in Australia? I'd like to acquire as large a share as we can now that their dollar's low. . . ."

Kelly Barbet had requested both of Nick Petrosyan's autopsy reports—the interrupted one, and the one that had been done when the head and body had been brought in. She knew from experience that it might be a month or more before all the tests were finished and cause of death positively established, but any clue as to *why* someone would have stolen the boy's body could be valuable.

Both autopsies had been performed without the permission of the boy's parents; there was nothing in the files to indicate that they'd even been asked. The first autopsy, performed less than six hours after death, had established that Nick showed no signs of *rigor mortis*, causing the pathologist, Dr. Kimball, to proceed with extreme caution. It was rare that autopsy subjects were discovered still to be alive, but not unprecedented. Unable to detect a pulse or heartbeat, she had checked the corpse's temperature (low), thoroughly examined the eyes for any response to light (none), and finally applied a ligature to one finger to see if blood pooled in the tip (it didn't). Kimball had then continued examining the corpse's exterior, had it x-rayed, then proceeded with the Y-shaped incision from each armpit to the bottom of the sternum, then down to the pubis. The last thing she remembered before being revived was preparing to remove the breastbone and front of the rib cage, still half-expecting to see the heart beating.

The only marks on the body had been on the arms, and those could be explained by long courses of injections, intravenous drips, and transfusions. Tests performed while the boy was alive

had been negative for the toxins and viruses that the pathologists had thought to check for.

The second autopsy, though almost as incomplete, was even
more interesting. For one thing, there was still no *rigor mortis*.
The body was mostly drained of blood, with less than a quart
remaining; the coroner had been unable to determine when the
draining had occurred, but there were no bloodstains on the
concrete of the storm drain where head and body had been
found. For another, there was a bulb of garlic in the mouth,
which looked as though it had hastily been sewn shut. The cut
through the neck seemed to have been done at one stroke with
a heavy blade, probably a fire axe. No other body parts had
been removed, though some loops of intestine protruded
through the incision as they had in the photo.

Kelly looked from the report to the photo, then reached for
her cell phone, phoned the Forensic Science Center, and asked
to speak to Dr. Yeoh. Told that he was in the middle of somebody, she grimaced at the well-worn joke, left a message, and
stared at the photo again. She couldn't think of anything else
she could do to help Gaye Lind until the forensic team finished
searching her apartment, which was probably hours away, so
she grabbed the next file—a much thicker, more faded one—
from her in-tray, and opened that. A familiar name and photo,
charges of solicitation and possession. Same old routine; just go
through the motions and pretend it matters. She wondered if
her client felt the same way about *her* job.

Her cell phone rang just over an hour later. "Barbet."

"It's Jim Woodcott," said a voice at the other end. "You
weren't thinking of asking for bail for the Lind woman, were
you?" There was an unmistakable taint of gloat in the voice,
and Kelly resisted the urge to sneer. She'd never been a cop-
hater; nor did she dislike the majority of born-again Christians.
She didn't even hate those cops who also happened to be born-
agains . . . but she couldn't think of a better word to describe
the way she felt whenever she had to deal with Woodcott. She
suspected that he disapproved of her gender more than her race,
but most forms of prejudice irked her—even her own.

"Yes," she replied, refusing to give him the satisfaction of asking for details.

"Well, I wouldn't be in any hurry. You wouldn't believe what we found in here." No answer. "The woman's a satanist," Woodcott continued, after a murderous silence. "We've found pentagrams, a sword, sacrificial knives, rope, candles, Tarot cards, books, and something that looks like blood in the freezer."

Kelly sighed quietly. She suspected that Woodcott saw satanists in every shadow in the same way that Joe McCarthy had claimed to see communists. "Have the forensics team found anything?"

"They're still looking," replied Woodcott, a little too quickly. That, Kelly was sure, meant no.

"Can I talk to one of them?"

"Why?"

"The bail hearing is in three hours. You're obliged to give the defense any information you have that can be used against her."

Woodcott grunted. "Just remember that that cuts both ways . . . Counsellor. Just a minute."

Kelly waited, until a familiar voice asked, "Kelly?"

"Ed?" She relaxed slightly; Ed Douglass, a crime scene officer, wasn't a close friend, but he was always fair, obsessed with accuracy, and unfailingly polite—not just to his fellow blacks, but to everyone, even criminals and public defenders.

"Yes."

"What have you found?"

"No bloodstains. Lots of hairs, but the long ones look like the woman's, and the short ones probably belong to the cats. No evidence yet that the boy was ever in here."

"What about the window ledge?"

"I guess a boy of that age *could* stand on it, but I'd hate to see one try. No bloodstains there, either. There's grass underneath, but no signs of a ladder being used. The ledge has some pretty clear toe prints, one big toe and some partials, all about the right size. I've dusted the window and the walls for fingerprints, as far out as I can reach, but I haven't found anything good."

"What about inside the apartment?"

"Plenty of fingerprints—she's not much of a housekeeper, but you know what hours nurses work." Kelly smiled slightly; both of Douglass's ex-wives were nurses. "None of them are small enough to be the boy's, though."

"Do you think he was ever inside the apartment? In your professional opinion?"

"In my professional opinion? There's no evidence. If he was, he didn't touch anything, which he wouldn't do if he were dead, and he didn't bleed. None of the hairs look like his. That's as much as I'm prepared to say."

"Thanks, Ed."

"Don't mention it. Do you want to speak to Woodcott again?"

"No." Arguing with the detective would accomplish nothing; she would request bail, he would oppose it, the decision would be left to the judge. "Have you seen the photograph?"

"Yes."

"Do you think it's fake?"

"Maybe, but the negative hasn't been interfered with, unless it's a photo of a photo. I'm not qualified to say much more— and if these toe-prints are real, then I'd say the photo's real, too."

Kelly nodded. "Is there a window above that one?"

"Yes. Why?"

"Have you dusted that one for prints?"

"Not yet. The people who live upstairs aren't home—but none of the neighbors Woodcott's spoken to remember seeing anything unusual that night, and I think this would count as unusual."

"I hope so. What about the stuff that Woodcott's found?"

"None of the knives look as though they've been used, though we're taking them in to be tested, and nothing in here could have been used to decapitate the boy. The stuff from the freezer does look a lot like blood, but even if it is, we won't know if it's his until the lab gets it. The library doesn't prove anything; sure, there are books on witchcraft, and I can't see a Bible anywhere, but I don't like the idea of denying someone bail just for what they read. If I were you, I'd speak to someone who knows more about photography than I do."

"Thanks. 'Bye." She placed the phone on the desk, and stared at it for several seconds. Then she sighed, and reached for her Rolodex. The name, number, and address were still there, and she stared at them for a long moment, her arms crossed protectively across her chest, before picking her phone up again.

4

Shadows

Takumo was practicing an aggressive parry and spinning punch *kata* on his Wing Chun dummy when the phone rang. He managed not to flinch, and back-somersaulted away from the dummy and grabbed the receiver. "Hello?"

"Charlie?"

"Yes?"

"It's Kelly Barbet. I was wondering if you could help me." Silence. "I have a client who's being accused of . . . well, I need someone to look at a photo and tell me whether it could have been faked. Can you put me in touch with any special effects people? Or with Mage?"

"I don't know where Mage is," replied Takumo, rather stiffly, "and I can't get in touch with him. Like what sort of photo?"

Kelly hesitated. She hadn't seen Takumo since the murder charge against Magistrale had been dropped nearly two years before, and she suddenly recalled that the last time she'd called him had also been to ask for a favor (only a minor one, she reminded herself; she'd wanted him to recommend a martial-arts style and a dojo). She had never entirely come to terms with her involvement in Tatsuo Tamenaga's death, and disliked being reminded of it. Besides, she and the stuntman had little else in common. "It's pretty gruesome," she replied. "Maybe someone else could help. Do you know anyone who makes horror movies?"

"You didn't see me in *Zombie Cheerleaders*?"

That sounded more like the Charlie she knew; she could almost hear him drawing himself up to his full five foot five. "Sorry, no."

"Lucky you," he said, cheerfully. "I'll see who I can scare up. Can I call you back?"

"Yeah, okay. Thanks, Charlie." She flipped the phone shut, and returned her attention to the autopsy report.

"**A**ll they have is the photograph, the blood, and the toe-prints," said Kelly, as they waited in the corridor outside the courtroom for the bail hearing. "I don't have the results of the blood test yet."

"It's my blood," said Gaye, softly. "I'm A positive. If they want to DNA test me, that's okay."

"They might; Woodcott may well try to make something of it. Do you want to tell me what it's for?"

Gaye hesitated. "I'm a wiccan. We need blood for some rituals, and it beats having to draw some every time."

Kelly tried to look as though she wasn't sorry she'd asked. Gaye seemed to be taking her arrest rather calmly, but the lawyer knew that this wasn't indicative of either guilt or innocence: she'd seen people who were wrongly accused reacting as though they were in shock or with stunned disbelief, as Gaye was, and she'd also seen career criminals put on thoroughly convincing acts of outrage. Some of her colleagues had told her that with time, she'd become better at picking the liars . . . while others had warned her that most lawyers didn't, and if she proved to be an exception, she'd better be prepared to leave her conscience at home before coming to work. "Woodcott will allege that you're satanist, but that's not a—"

"I'm a witch, not a satanist," replied Gaye, mildly. "White magic. There's a big difference."

"Okay, you can explain it to me later. In the meantime, I think we'd better leave religion out of it . . . Are you sure you can't think of anyone else who would pull a stunt like this?"

"I'm sure."

"Okay. The toe-prints are outside the apartment, and that's consistent with the photo, so the police really don't have a case. They're hoping to find someone responsible for stealing the body and assaulting Dr. Kimball, and if you don't know anything about either . . ."

"I don't. How is she?"

"What?"

"The doctor."

"She's fine. We're not even sure she *was* assaulted, and neither is she. You never have any reason to go down to the morgue, do you?"

"No."

"And you didn't on the day that Nick's body was stolen? Tuesday, August twenty-first?"

"No." Gaye shuddered. "I wouldn't want to see anyone cut up like that unless I had to."

"Dr. Kimball blacked out at six fifty-seven P.M. Were you in the hospital at that time?"

"Yes, but nowhere near the morgue."

"How long would it take you to get there?"

"I've never timed it, but it would be several minutes, even if I didn't have to wait for the elevators. I wasn't away from my station for that long."

"Can the other nurses confirm this? Or any of the patients?"

"Sure."

"Okay. I'll make sure the police ask, and time how long it takes to get from your station to the morgue, but no one's accused you of actually stealing Nick's body. They wouldn't be accusing you of *anything* if they had any other suspects—but they don't, and a lot of police tend to fixate on making arrests and getting convictions. If I can't convince the judge to throw this mess out of court for lack of evidence, I should at least be able to keep the bail low enough for you to get a bailbondsman to post bail for you. What do you have in the way of collateral?"

The sun was setting by the time Kelly returned home. She sat in the car listening to one of her favorite songs on the radio until it was finished, then closed the garage door with the remote and walked into the house. Oedipus wasn't waiting for her when she switched the light on, which was unusual and faintly disappointing, but she was sure he'd come running in as soon as he heard or smelled the coffee percolating—the most reliable sign that Kelly was in the kitchen. When that failed, she grabbed a tin of cat food and walked to the back door. Someone was sitting on the back lawn, the cat in his lap; it was too dark for her to see his face clearly, and she was about to slam the door and reach for her cell phone when she noticed the black Kawasaki motorcycle. "Charlie?"

Oedipus leaped out of the stuntman's grasp and trotted toward her, tail held high. "Sorry to disturb you," said Takumo, uncoiling and walking slowly toward her. He was dressed all in a dusty matte black—sneakers, jeans, long-sleeved T-shirt, black gloves and well-traveled leather jacket—and in the near-darkness, he looked disturbingly like a floating head, an escapee from Kelly's least favorite nightmare.

Kelly breathed again. One of these days, she thought, she was going to have to move to a gated community, if she could find one that would admit African Americans. "Do you ever make any goddamn noise?"

"When I want to. What gives with this photograph?"

She stepped back from the doorway, and let him in. "I need a professional opinion on its authenticity, that's all. It's for a client."

"And you thought you'd ask Mage?"

"He's the only photographer I know—well, apart from crime-scene photographers."

Takumo nodded. "No one suggested to you that you ask him?"

"No. I don't think anyone else I know remembers him, much less what he did for a living. Do you want a cup of coffee?"

"Do you have tea?"

"I think so." He followed her into the kitchen as she puttered around, feeding the cat, making coffee, searching for the tea-bags.

"*Someone* remembers him," said Takumo, grimly. "Someone in Tamenaga's old organization, probably Nakatani Shota, is hiring rent-a-thugs from a scumbag named Lowe to hassle me in the hope of finding out where Mage is. I'm pretty sure he's also tapping my phone, and if he's not tapping yours . . . well, you use a cell phone, so he might as well be. And I had to make sure it was you, not some clever impersonator."

"Peter Lowe? Runs an employment agency as cover? Night-club bouncers, strippers, escorts, that sort of thing—mostly il-legal immigrants? A little taller than you, mostly bald, thick glasses?"

"I've never met him."

"You don't want to. He has all the charm of a hyena with rabies."

Takumo smiled slightly. "Sure sounds like the same man; Dante's told me a little about him."

"Dante?"

"Mandaglione. Mage's uncle."

"Have you actually—how do you take your tea?"

"With honey—or one sugar, if you don't have honey."

"Have you actually seen Mage?"

"Not in more than a year . . . I was doing Shakespeare in the Park up in San Francisco last summer, and he was in the au-dience. We had dinner, talked for a while, then he disappeared again. I'm not sure where he's living—somewhere in Canada, most of the time, I think; he's picked up a little of the accent and some of the expressions—but he's keeping busy."

"Doing what?"

"Working in a refugee camp somewhere—he didn't give me

any details—and studying medicine. He's sure that Amanda was able to use the focus to cure her cancer, and he used it to heal the wounds he took fighting Tamenaga and . . . well, you know," he said, noticing that Kelly had crossed her arms over her breast. "He thinks he should be able to use it to cure AIDS, but he doesn't know enough medicine, microbiology, whatever. So he's trying to learn." He shrugged. "How're *you* doing?"

"I'm okay."

He glanced around the house. "Still single."

"Yes. You?"

"Uh-huh. Mika married someone she met in China, and that took it out of me for a while. How's the jujutsu?"

"I made green belt last month."

"Enjoying it?"

"Yes, I just wish I had more time for it."

He nodded. "What's with this photo? I know you wouldn't be asking to see Mage if it wasn't *seriously* important."

"I'll show you the picture."

Takumo looked at the 8 × 10 with barely a flicker of expression. "There has to be a story behind this."

Kelly told him as much of it as she knew. "So," he summarized, "you think someone stole the body, lugged it to this nurse's apartment, and hung it outside the window in the hope that she'd take a photo and incriminate herself?"

"What do *you* think?"

"I'd have to see the actual window. For one thing, I'd need to know how easy it was to get to from the ground, or the apartment above. For another, I'd want to be sure the scale is right. Do you have a photo of the kid when he was alive?"

"You don't think that's him?"

Takumo sipped his tea as he considered this. "I don't know. It would be much easier to use a dummy—much lighter than a corpse, much less embarrassing if you're caught with it, and you don't have the problem of rigor mortis. Or it could be a small stuntman with good makeup."

"But we know someone stole the body . . . why would they go to the trouble of doing this as well?"

"I don't know. Is this the only photo?"

"Yes."

"It's not very clear, but I guess it's good enough for the tabloids." He shrugged. "Maybe I've lived here too long, but I can only think of one reason why anyone would pull something like this, and that's as a publicity stunt. Like for a horror movie, maybe. A stolen corpse, strange goings-on in a hospital, someone trying to terrorize a nurse . . ." He stared at the photo, and shook his head.

"You think that's all it is?"

"Hey, I'm in the movie business myself, remember? Of course, it could be a psycho who *isn't* in showbiz, or who just wants to be. Like someone with a script for a *Halloween* or *Scream* rip-off, or something about kids who rise from the dead. *Preschool Ghoul*, or whatever. How much news time has this gotten?"

"Not a lot. The disappearance of the body was announced after a thorough search of the hospital. The hospital staff weren't enthusiastic, but they were too scared of what might happen if he was a contagion risk. Then, when the body was found, the police decided not to release most of the details; I've probably told you more than I should have. Would someone attack a pathologist in the middle of an autopsy just for a publicity stunt?"

"Unless she's in on it . . . but I've got to admit, that's the weak link. If the incidents aren't related, then some psycho whipped up a very convincing-looking fake in record time. Either way, I think your nurse is being stalked by a *very* sick puppy. When can I see this apartment?"

"Give me a minute, and I'll call her, ask her when's convenient."

"**W**hich window?"

Kelly looked along the row of second-floor apartments, hoping to spot the tie-dyed curtains. "I'm not sure; I haven't been here before. Could you climb up there?"

"For sure—probably faster than you could quick-draw your cell phone." He squatted down to remove his shoes, and Kelly cleared her throat.

"I think we'd better go up and tell her we're here before you scare the living daylights out of her," she suggested.

"Ah. Yes. Good idea."

It had been nearly two years since Valeri Krieg had shot anyone, and more than a month since she'd threatened to break a drunken client's arm, but her reputation hadn't suffered as a result. According to her agent, she was a bodyguard, a highly paid one, and the I.R.S. had been unable to prove otherwise. She was kept on retainer by a large number of people who had good reason to believe their lives were in danger if they left home. She was known for her effectiveness and her inviolable business ethics; none of her clients had ever died while under her protection, though one had suffered a minor cardiac arrest when he heard that the check he'd sent to her agent had failed to arrive on time.

Her sales pitch was simple. If you kept her on retainer as a security consultant, she would guarantee that you were safe from one of the best hired killers in the business. She lived comfortably on these "protection" retainers, but occasionally hired out as a bodyguard or assassin, more for the sake of keeping her reputation alive than for the cash.

Krieg was a handsome but rather colorless woman of thirty-nine, with a faint Rhodesian accent that most Americans mistook for English or Canadian. In a uniform, any uniform, she instantly became anonymous, almost invisible. Her usual costume for work was an efficient-looking business suit, with a Kevlar-lined clipboard to use as a shield, and tinted glasses concealing rearview mirrors. She usually worked with one man larger than her client, who protected his back; her reputation did the rest.

On this night, she was sitting in the Nautilus machine in one of her homes, the penthouse in Miami, watching *Hard Target* on her projection TV when the phone rang—the scrambler phone, the number only her agent was supposed to know. She muted the TV and reached for the receiver. "Yes?"

"I've had an offer for your services," rasped Duncan. "It's . . . interesting."

"Who from?"

"Tamenaga."

"I thought he was dead?"

"Not the old man, his daughter. Used to be Haruko Higuchi."

"I'm listening."

"She wants you to kill the man who killed her father. She says his name's Magistrale."

"Where is he?"

"That's the catch. She doesn't know."

"I'm not a bloodhound."

"She knows that. She wants to work with you to set up an ambush, and for you to drop him as soon as you see him. Apparently this Magistrale can get out of any trap."

"I've never heard of him," she said. Her voice was carefully neutral, but Duncan knew she was intrigued. "Who does he work for?"

"Nobody, at least not under that name. I've never heard of him either, but if he was able to gun down Tamenaga in his own home and escape, he must be *good*. Of course," he added, hastily, "no one's as good as *you*."

"I work for money, not flattery," Krieg reminded him. The statement was mostly true, but Duncan knew as well as she did that her reputation was her greatest asset. Tatsuo Tamenaga had never been a client of hers, so his death didn't reflect on her, but if it were ever widely believed that somebody *was* as good as her, then her income would suffer. "Tell Tamenaga I'll meet her to discuss it, for my usual consultant's fee. Where is she, Tamenaga's place in Bel Air?"

"No, she sold that after the murder, then moved to Las Vegas. She said she didn't feel safe in the house after her father's death."

"Did she have anything to do with that?"

"Not that I've heard, and I can't think of any reason she would have. Does it matter?"

"No. Just curious."

"All right. I'll make the arrangements."

5

Revenants

Gaye answered the door dressed in heavily patched jeans and a Fat Freddy's Cat T-shirt. "The hospital suggested I take a few days off," she said, her mouth twisting slightly as though the euphemism were incredibly sour, "but I thought we might as well do this now. Is the darkness a problem?"

Kelly shook her head, while Takumo grinned and bowed. "Not at all," he said. "Please allow me to introduce myself; Charlie Takumo, freelance ninja."

She raised an eyebrow. "You don't *look* like a turtle."

His grin widened a little. "I'm a master of disguise."

She stepped back and let them in. Her apartment was almost a mirror image of Takumo's, but more colorful, and less tidy. That might have been the fault of the forensics team, but Takumo doubted it; the chaos had an antique flavor. The cats, who Gaye introduced as Isis and Bast, were more likely culprits. The walls were decorated with Susan Seddon Boulet prints, photos of whales and dolphins, and a map of Middle-earth. He glanced at her bookshelves en route to the window, and noticed several books by Starhawk, huge nursing texts, *Sandman* trade paperbacks, and a few *Star Trek* novels. He pulled a tape measure out of his pocket, and measured the window. "How tall was the boy?"

"Four foot three."

Takumo nodded. "Can I have another look at the photo?" He measured the relative proportions of the window and the boy, did the arithmetic, and winced. "Well, that fits, and there aren't many stunt performers that short. Of course, a kid might be able to climb a wall like that. Back in a minute. If you see anything outside the window, it *should* only be me." He removed his sneakers, revealing black *tabi*, split-toed shoe-socks.

Gaye watched as he dashed out. "He's your photographic expert?" she asked.

"No," said Kelly. "I couldn't reach the photographer. Charlie's a . . . a stuntman, and he knows about camera tricks."

"Is that my defense? That this was just a trick, someone's idea of a joke?"

"It should stand up in court, but if you have any other theories, I'd be happy to consider them." Gaye hesitated, then shook her head. "Maybe it isn't directed at you," suggested Kelly. "Do you know anything about the boy's family?"

"Last I heard, both of his parents were still in the hospital with the same disease as he had. He has an older sister, but I haven't seen her, and Nick didn't know where she was. I think she ran away from home." She stared at the window. "His parents must have been horrified when his body was stolen. They'd objected to the autopsy to begin with. I'm sure this has been a nightmare for them, especially the way the body was found again, but even if someone had a grudge against them, why involve *me*?"

"I don't know, but the story must have gone around the hospital by now, and maybe the Petrosyans would have heard it that way. Maybe pulling a stunt like this *in* the hospital would have been too risky. This way—" She blinked, seeing Takumo suddenly appear outside the window, one foot on the ledge, and hanging onto the brickwork with gloved fingers and the toes of the other foot. Isis looked up curiously, then went back to sleep. Takumo paused there for a few seconds, looking up and around, then dropped out of sight.

"Does he do that a lot?" whispered Gaye.

"Sometimes," replied Kelly, trying not to think of the time Magistrale had vanished, even more mysteriously, from her living room. "Do you know Nick's parents' first names?"

"No, but his sister's name is Julia."

"Okay, I'll see if I can find out anything about them. Did you know them before Nick became your patient?"

"No."

"Any other connection that you can think of?"

"No."

Kelly nodded. "Fortunately, I don't *need* to find out who's behind this to clear you—assuming the police can think of anything to charge you with—so I think you'll be okay."

"Aren't you curious?"

She laughed. "One thing I can't afford in this job is curiosity. A lawyer should never try to find out more than she *needs* to know."

"How long have you been a lawyer?"

"About five years. Why?"

"Were you that cynical when you began?"

Kelly sighed. "Pretty much, though not always about the same things. How long've you been a nurse?"

"Seven years."

"Can you remember why you started?"

"Sure."

"You still feel like that?"

"Sometimes. I don't have the same energy, or the same level of faith in medicine or doctors, but I still believe in what I'm doing." There was a knock on the door, and Gaye jumped slightly. "Come in, Charlie."

"It's locked."

Kelly shrugged, and walked over to the door. "Why did you lock it?" she asked.

"Because it might not have been me on the other side," replied Takumo, tersely, "and you're not armed, and locks slow people down, and I suspect you're right, someone's trying to play a very nasty trick on you," he concluded, looking at Gaye. "The wall's easy enough to climb, especially if you have small fingers, as someone that height should have, and bare feet."

"You think that was how it was done?"

"That and some very good makeup; at least, that's the most likely. Is anyone in the building in the movie business, or TV, Gaye?"

"I don't think so. Nat and Tom in 2D are waiters, and I think they've been in a few commercials, but no one else."

"Pity; I was hoping this wasn't directed at you. Of course, it might not be . . ." He turned to Kelly. "The marionette theory has some problems: for one thing, it would be much more likely to be noticed. For another, the photo looks as though the kid was standing on the ledge, not dangling a few inches behind it—"

"The forensics people says they found small toe-prints on the ledge," said Gaye.

"Did they? Have they checked them against the kid's?"

"If they have, I haven't heard the results," replied Kelly, "and the police are supposed to tell me things like that—though they can be a little leisurely about it. But how could they be Nick's?"

Takumo shrugged. "If they are, then either they've been faked, or I'm wrong about the marionette, or the kid walked off the autopsy table under his own power."

"You can't fake fingerprints," protested Kelly.

"If you say so: I can't prove otherwise." He turned to Gaye. "Could I trouble you for a drink? Water would be fine."

"Sure. Put the kettle on if you'd prefer coffee or tea."

Takumo smiled. "Tea would be wonderful. Kelly? Coffee?"

Kelly glanced at her watch. "Is there anything else you need to look at?"

"I don't think so. We've established that this could have been done without anyone inside the apartment being involved . . . Who lives upstairs, by the way?"

"Kim and Emma. Emma does something with computers at UCLA, and Kim works at Tower Records."

"The forensics team searched their apartment," said Kelly. "There's no evidence that a body was ever in there."

"Did they look on the roof, too?"

"Yes. Nothing there, either."

Takumo nodded, as he looked through Gaye's collection of herbal teas for something that contained caffeine. "Do you mind if I give you some advice?"

"What?"

"Go and stay somewhere else for a while."

"Why?"

"Because someone who's crazy enough to steal a kid's body, then mutilate it before throwing it into a storm drain, knows where you live."

Kelly cleared her throat. "Charlie—"

"I'm serious. Look, I work in *Hollywood*, and *I* don't know anyone this sick."

"This might not be the same person who stole and mutilated the body. . . ."

Charlie shook his head. "This makeup job is just too freakin' good; either it was done before the kid died, which I'm not sure I even want to think about, or it was taken from his death mask." He walked into the living room, picked up the photo, and looked at it carefully. "Unless he had a twin brother?"

"No, just an older sister."

"Do you know her?"

"No—not that I know of. I'd never met any of the family before."

Takumo shrugged, then reached into his jacket pocket for his wallet and handed her a business card. "If anything strange happens and you don't think you can call Kelly or the cops, call me. Okay?"

"**D**o you really think she's in that much danger?" asked Kelly, as she started the car.

"She is if she's telling the truth."

"What about?"

"Not knowing what's going on."

"What do you think *is* going on?"

"I have no idea. Like if it's a stunt, it's an expensive one. That makeup job is better than most of the alien autopsy footage around. Unless the photo was somehow faked in the camera, but you'd have to ask a photographic expert about that—and if it was, then Gaye almost has to be lying about how it was taken."

"Do you think she's lying?"

"I don't know. If she is, she's good."

Kelly nodded, then was silent until they'd turned onto the freeway. "How did you know I wasn't carrying a gun?"

"I just notice these things, that's all. Like lots of people do; cops, nightclub bouncers . . ."

"You mean you look for them."

"I used to. Now it's automatic. I meet someone, I check out the body language, how they're dressed, where they could be concealing a weapon. It just takes a glance, less than a second. You *could* be carrying some sort of trick gun, I suppose. A .22 pager, a .32 keychain, in your line of work you could probably get a permit for one . . . but I don't think you are. There isn't a gun in the car, either. Am I right?" Kelly nodded, almost imperceptibly. "So I gather you haven't had any problems?"

"Problems?"

"You haven't been harassed by rent-a-thugs."

"No."

"Lucky you; Nakatani must not know about you. So. I gather you're not interested in solving this case, just in clearing Gaye?"

"That's right," replied Kelly, dryly. "I leave details like that up to the police."

"Would it violate your professional ethics if you told me how it turned out?"

"Why?"

"I like her," said Takumo, simply. "If she's telling us the

truth, and I think she is, then someone she doesn't know is setting her up, and I'd like to help her. So why did you become a public defender, anyway?"

"That's a long story," Kelly replied. She didn't feel the same need Takumo seemed to have to prove that she was on the side of the angels—but then, she hadn't been named after one of California's most notorious criminals or raised by one of his groupies. She considered the request. "I can only tell you what goes into the public record. . . ."

"Okay. And if *I* find out anything . . ."

"I reserve the right to disavow any knowledge of your activities."

"Cool."

Kelly walked out of the courtroom barely managing not to slam the doors, her expression—normally carefully impassive— visibly grim. Her client was trying to avoid his third felony conviction, but the only defense he'd offered was that racist police and the D.A. were persecuting him because he was black. The jury (six whites, three blacks, two Hispanics, and a Korean) had just retired, and Kelly had no doubt that they'd return a guilty verdict within an hour, at which point the prisoner would probably accuse them, the judge, and her of the same prejudice. She'd checked her messages while taking a bathroom break, and saw that Woodcott wanted her to call him. The perfect end to another perfect day, she thought sourly, as she called him and snapped, "Barbet. What do you want?"

"The forensics people have come up with some results from their search of the Lind woman's apartment," gloated Woodcott. "The prints from the balcony are the boy's."

"Balcony?"

"The ledge," Woodcott conceded. "The toes. It's a good match, eighteen points of reference. He was there, all right."

"Nothing from inside the apartment?"

". . . no, but . . ."

"What about the blood?"

"Hers," grunted Woodcott. "Probably menstrual, according to the coroner, but why somebody would keep menstrual blood in their freezer is beyond me."

"That doesn't make it a crime," Kelly pointed out, as sweetly as she was able.

"No, but we may be changing the charges. The kid's mother is dead, and now the pathologist has the same sort of symptoms."

"What symptoms?"

"Anemic anoxia," said Woodcott, obviously reading from his notes. "The mother died early this morning, and the father's condition's been getting worse, too. The pathologist may pull through. . . ."

Kelly chewed her lower lip. Anemic anoxia, she knew, meant that insufficient oxygen was reaching the tissues because of obstructed arteries or, more often, blood loss; she'd often seen it listed as the cause of death for victims of knife attacks. "They have no idea what's causing it?"

"No. The symptoms are consistent with gross internal bleeding, but they can't find any, and there's no reason why three members of the same family should have symptoms like that—unless they've all swallowed ground glass, or something similar, and they haven't."

"Do you have any other information on the Petrosyans—Nick's parents? Whether they have any enemies?"

"What?"

"Never mind. Any news on why Dr. Kimball passed out?"

"If she already had this disease, assuming it is a disease, she probably just blacked out from low blood pressure."

She nodded; that made sense. "What are you going to charge her with?"

"Illegally disposing of a body, for now. If she won't tell us who else was involved, that's her lookout. Maybe somebody should tell her that."

*   *   *

Kelly drove from her office down to Inglewood to work off some of her frustrations in the dojo there, and it was after eleven when she finally returned home. She fed Oedipus, who was complaining loudly, then took a quick shower before slithering into bed. She lay awake for another half an hour, with the feeling that something was wrong nagging at her like a missing tooth, not quite painful, just hollow and uncomfortable. Something someone had said, something she'd read . . . she didn't know.

When she hauled herself out of bed the next morning, the feeling hadn't abated. As soon as she was in her office, she reached for the autopsy reports and scanned both. The first seemed complete enough; cause of death was listed as "unexplained anemic anoxia," which matched what she knew about the other Petrosyans. She turned to the second. It, too, gave cause of death as anemic anoxia, but the space for "Time of Death" had been left blank. She was reading through the report when the phone on her desk rang.

"Barbet."

"Kelly? It's John Yeoh. Sorry it's taken me so long to return your call; what can I do for you?"

"It's about the Nick Petrosyan autopsy. The second one. There's no time of death listed."

She could almost hear Yeoh shrug. "We were still working on it when they positively I.D.ed him, and after that, we just took the time from the first report. You can hardly get a better figure than the one the hospital gives, can you?"

Kelly shook her head. "It's just that some of these indicators . . . putrefaction, for example. There's no green staining on the abdomen. . . ."

"So you're a pathologist now?"

"I had a good teacher," she replied, smoothly (she had, in fact, learned most of what she knew about the subject from Yeoh himself).

"Okay," said Yeoh. He sounded amused rather than flattered. "Yes, I had noticed the lack of putrefaction, and the early state of insect infestation, if you were about to mention that, and it's completely consistent with him being kept in a controlled environment until a few hours before the body was discovered."

"How controlled?"

Yeoh hesitated slightly. "Insect infestation is easily avoided; if the body were taken out of the hospital bagged or wrapped or in a sealed container, and after that simply kept in an insect-free room, that should be enough. If the body and the surroundings are also sterile, you can delay putrefaction—"

"But not autolysis."

"No. That takes cold to slow it down . . . unless whatever killed the kid somehow seriously affected his digestive enzymes, which is possible but not proven. I understand he wasn't able to keep food down for the last few days, and the stomach contents certainly bear that out. One thing I haven't been able to explain yet is the ends of the incisions; they seem to have knitted together, almost as though they'd begun healing. That's not a cold effect; the only thing I can think of that might do it is superglue."

"Superglue?"

"Or some other adhesive. Undertakers use superglue to close small wounds, catheter sites, even eyes, which is why I thought of it. Whoever stole the body may've thought that you could close an incision that size with it, which is insane; they sew them shut with dental floss."

Kelly decided to change the subject. "Do you know what killed him?"

"No, but having his blood drained and head removed couldn't have helped."

Kelly suspected that that was intended as a pathologist's version of humor. "How cold?"

"What?"

"How cold would it have to be to prevent two days of autolysis?"

"A few degrees above zero, Celsius. A domestic refrigerator should do it."

"Would that leave other signs? Some form of skin discoloration, like frostbite?"

"Not if the body wasn't actually frozen. Why?"

"I'm trying to establish what happened to the body between the time it was stolen from the morgue and the time it was rediscovered."

"Okay. He definitely wasn't in that drain for very long before they found him; it got hot early that day, the temperature the day before got up to eighty-seven, and there was a lot of insect activity. He's small enough to fit in a domestic fridge if you remove the shelves, so that's the most likely explanation. Barring miracles, I'd have to say that whoever did it knew quite a lot about preserving a body without embalming it. Of course, this information is widely available if you have access to a library or the Internet, so it needn't be a professional—"

"Would it have to be premeditated?"

"Oh, almost certainly. Stealing a body while the pathologist's actually bending over it? If I didn't know Fran Kimball better, I'd say she was a prime suspect, at least as an accomplice. Hustling the body out of the hospital and into a waiting vehicle . . . I get lost in the hospital myself, and just saying 'waiting vehicle' presupposes premeditation, doesn't it? Not that this is my field, exactly, but yes, someone put a lot of planning into stealing a body. Maybe not *this* body, not specifically, but *a* body, certainly. Does that help?"

"Can you think of any reason why someone would do so?"

"A few, none of which make much sense. I know there's a rumor going around that the body was snatched as a possible plague-carrier by the Centers for Disease Control, not that I believe that for a second; even if they'd wanted to do something like that, they'd have done it in a way that minimized panic, not exacerbated it. If the kid's parents have money, or someone thought they did, they might want to ransom the corpse. Stealing bodies to sell to medical schools isn't done anymore, at least not here; it just doesn't pay well enough. Stealing them so an undertaker can collect a state burial allowance is done sometimes, but by fraud, not violence. Apart from that, all I can think of is that some ghoul wanted some souvenirs, in which case it probably wouldn't just have been thrown away, or that it was meant to scare someone very badly—which I gather it did."

"Yes."

"Is there anything else?"

Kelly scanned the report again. The lack of rigor mortis in both reports, she knew, was consistent with the reported time of death—rigor set in within two to six hours of death, but was gone after forty-eight—as were the body temperature readings. "No, I don't think so."

"If you like, I can test the potassium level in the eyes and determine time of death from that. That's not affected by temperature . . . though I don't really see the point. Do you know Fran?"

"I've met her a few times, mostly professionally, but I don't know her well."

"I've worked with her for years. She wouldn't have opened the boy up if she hadn't been absolutely sure he was dead."

"Thanks."

"For you, any time. Good-bye."

The phone rang again thirty-seven minutes later. "Barbet."

"It's Lieutenant Holliday, Counsellor. Woodcott has asked the uniforms to bring Lind in for further questioning, and she's told them she won't talk without you there. Can you come in? It would save us a lot of time."

Kelly glanced at her watch; 10:12 A.M. "I'm due in court at eleven. What's happened?"

"We've found what may be a link between your client and the Petrosyans," said Holliday. "Have you ever heard of Solomon Tudor?"

"Not that I recall."

"Well, if Lind can't tell you about him, I'm sure Woodcott will. 'Bye."

*   *   *

It had taken Kelly several years to realize why interview rooms reminded her of casinos. It wasn't merely the feeling of gambling, of being in a poker game dependent on luck and bluff, it was the lack of clocks and windows, the sense of being isolated not merely from the rest of the world but even from time. She was surprised that the police never seemed to notice, that they never seemed to realize why she stared at her watch so often.

Gaye Lind looked tired and disheveled, but remarkably calm, while Woodcott had the smug smile of a man with three aces in his hand and two up his sleeve. "Do you know a man named Solomon Tudor?"

"No."

The detective feigned amazement. "You have a large collection of books about magic and witchcraft, yet you've never heard of Solomon Tudor?"

"No."

"For the record," said Kelly, her voice so casual as to almost be a drawl, "neither have I. Who is he?"

"Have you ever heard of the Church of Endless Night?"

Gaye paused, thought for an instant, then shrugged. "I think so, but I've never had anything to do with them, and I don't remember ever hearing of a Solomon Tudor."

"Would you describe yourself as a religious person, Miss Lind?"

"What does that have to do with anything?" snapped Kelly, before Gaye could speak.

"Yes," replied Gaye. "I do."

"And how would you describe yourself?" Woodcott continued. "Religiously, I mean."

"I'm a witch," said Gaye. Kelly managed not to groan audibly.

"Really? Do you happen to know if witches still use parts of dead children for magical purposes? Or if they still keep cats as familiars and feed them on human flesh?"

Gaye sighed. "Yes to the cats, not to the flesh—at least, not to my knowledge."

"I've read the autopsy reports on Nick Petrosyan," added

Kelly, dryly. "You may've noticed that none of his body parts are missing."

"Except for most of his blood," replied Woodcott.

"The blood found in Ms. Lind's freezer was her type, not Nick's," said Kelly. "What does this have to do with Solomon Tudor?"

"You're saying that you've never had any dealings with Solomon Tudor or his so-called church?"

"No."

"Not only friendly dealings," Woodcott persisted. "*Any* sort of association."

"No."

"Would you consider him a colleague?"

"No!"

"A rival? An enemy?"

"A self-styled satanist cult leader? If I've ever considered him at all, I've probably considered him a fraud. All the so-called satanists I've ever met have been in it for the kinky sex; if they call themselves a church, rather than a coven, then it's probably a tax dodge as well."

"Would you expect him to have heard of you?" asked Woodcott, heavily.

"I'd be astonished if he had."

"Did you know that Julia Petrosyan was a member of Tudor's so-called church?"

"No, I've never even met Julia Petrosyan," said Gaye, without hesitation. "Or Solomon Tudor."

Kelly managed not to smile. Woodcott had obviously found a suspect who suited him more than Gaye, but he was still reluctant to give up on his first theory. "Do you have any further questions for my client?" she asked, after the silence had grown a little too thick for comfort.

Woodcott glanced at his partner, then shrugged. "Not at present. You're free to go, for now; thanks for your time."

* * *

"**S**o that's it?" asked Gaye, as Kelly pressed the button for the parking garage and the elevator doors closed.

"It should be. Woodcott may not be convinced that there's no link between you and Tudor—"

"There isn't."

"—but if there really *is* a link between Tudor and the Petrosyans, that gives him a perfect excuse to harass some card-carrying satanists, which should keep him happy, and busy, until the department decides to put the case on the back burner. So, yes, I think that's it, at least for us."

As always, Kelly looked at her notes again before filing them, then shuffled through the rest of the contents of the file to make sure that everything was there. She glanced at the photo that had started the case, then stared at it, her eyes bugging slightly.

The picture now showed only the curtains, the window, and the faint reflection of the photographer and flash. There were two tiny faint red patches that might have been eyes, but even they seemed to fade as she studied the image. Her hands shaking, she reached for the phone.

6

Bodies

Takumo stared at the photo again. "You're sure this is the same shot? Like, not something your forensics people took for comparison, or something like that?"

In answer, Kelly, perched uneasily on a pile of Takumo's cushions, leaned over and handed him the proof sheet. He studied this, then nodded. "I see what you mean. So where are the actual negs?"

"Evidence storeroom. Do you know any way that could be done? A photographic image that becomes invisible like that?"

"You mean, like one of those glasses where the girl's bikini disappears if you pour cold liquid into it?"

"Yes."

"No. Not with an ordinary print, off a photo taken with a disposable. Mage might . . . or Dante. I guess this means Gaye's off the hook?"

Kelly nodded. "Woodcott found out that Nick's sister belonged to a satanist cult, and that was enough for him. When he couldn't establish any link between Gaye and the cult leader, someone named Tudor, he let her go."

"Solomon Tudor?"

"Yes, that's right. Do you know him?"

"Only by reputation. He produced and scripted *Devilspawn*, which has to be one of the worst horror movies of the seventies—a real accomplishment, when you consider the competition. The studio didn't want to release it, but apparently there was something in Tudor's contract that gave him final cut as well as a guaranteed release budget—and this was in the seventies, dig, before there was video to fall back on. It only played for a week or two, though the billboards were around for months after it had closed. Of course, so many other bad movies came out in the seventies that it's now almost completely forgotten, even by horror fans."

"What's wrong with it?"

"The script, mostly. Bad dialogue that even a brilliant cast couldn't have made sound good, plus lots of splatter scenes in the hope that someone was still watching. The cast consisted of a few has-beens, most of whom were probably drunk, a few young TV actors desperate for a big-screen credit, one of whom is still trying to live it down, and a stack of starlets in their underwear, most of whom die on-screen. Fortunately, whatever strings Tudor pulled to get to make it—and there were rumors that he was blackmailing some studio exec—he never pulled them again, and I suspect the only people who still watch the film are his groupies, his so-called cult.

"I don't know much about him, but he might still be capable of this sort of stunt, particularly if Nick's sister knew what was happening to her brother . . . he certainly didn't spare the Karo syrup in *Devilspawn*, so if he still knows some makeup artists, it would probably appeal to him. I don't know how he could make a photo and a proof sheet fade like that, though; easiest way I can think of is to have someone inside your office replace them."

Kelly shifted uncomfortably on the cushions, resolving to buy Charlie some real chairs for Christmas. "It wasn't just makeup," she said. "Those were Nick's toe-prints on the ledge, so whoever it was actually stuck the corpse up there until Gaye came out to see it."

Takumo blinked once, very slowly. "I'll e-mail Dante—don't worry, I won't mention any names—and ask him about the photo. Do you know how many other prints there were, and where they might be?"

"The police would have copies, but I don't know how many."

"See if you can find some, and whether you can get your hands on the negatives. I have a nasty feeling that this shouldn't be possible, unless it's a substitution. . . ."

"I've been carrying this file around with me for days. I left it in my office overnight and occasionally during the day, but security there should be better than that. . . ."

Takumo smiled. "You don't have cleaners? Cleaners can get in almost anywhere, and they're damn near invisible. That's how I'd do it." Kelly looked skeptical. "Don't believe what you see in the movies; ninja only wear black jumpsuits and hoods, *shinobi shozuko*, when they're making a night attack. The costume may even have been invented by the Kabuki theatre for stagehands, then used to represent ninja, then adopted later by the ninja, who've never minded stealing a good idea when they saw one. Of course, I don't know how many Kabuki actors were also ninja, but ninja were taught 'the five ways of going'— peasant farmer, priest, traveling entertainer, merchant, and masseur, all of them beneath any self-respecting samurai's notice.

"The easiest way not to be seen is to be a low-caste individual with a reason to be there—nowadays, that would be a cleaner or security guard at night, a courier during the day. A delivery person with a bunch of flowers or a pizza box can knock on almost any door. A call girl might be remembered, but she can still get into a lot of rooms. A beggar can sit on the street and be ignored by thousands, recognized by no one."

Kelly, who'd grown skilled at ignoring street people, looked uncomfortable.

"Would you rather believe that Tudor cast a spell that made the kid's image vanish?" asked Takumo. "I don't think even Mage could do that to every copy of a photo—the ones he could *see*, for sure, no sweat, but not ones he didn't know about . . ."

Kelly hauled herself to her feet as gracefully as she could. "You'll ask Dante about the photos?"

"For sure."

"Thanks. I'll see you later."

Dante Mandaglione woke a few minutes after sunrise, pleasantly surprised to still find a woman in his bed. He lay there, his eyes half-closed, enjoying the warmth and the smell of sex, until he was alert enough to remember her names (many of the women he met used at least two—one that he wrote on their checks, the other he printed in *Bandit* magazine under their photographs). This one was Rebecca or Becky in private, Rebel in the club and in the magazine. He didn't mind—he did much of his own work under the names Dan T. Mandel and Don Mandeville, and had been published under a variety of house names as well as two other pen names he used for different genres—but he liked to know the real names of the select few he slept with.

Fully awake at last, he slipped out of bed and padded past his office on his way to the kitchen. A message on the monitor told him that he had mail—meaning personal e-mail; letters to the magazine went to another address. He continued on to the kitchen and made himself a cup of coffee before returning to the study.

The letter, from Charlie Takumo, was short and puzzling—rather like the writer, Mandaglione thought fuzzily. *Hi, Charlie,* he typed. *Sorry, don't know of any technique for making an image in a photographic print temporary, though it would've been useful for Stalin, and it's a common theme in ghost and vampire stories, a person whose image fades away after they're laid to rest. Seems much more likely someone's swapped the prints on you.*

"What're you doing?"

He turned around and saw Becky there, wearing one of his Vampirella T-shirts. He smiled, enjoying the way it stretched across her prominent breasts and stopped just below her navel. "Just answering my mail. You want some breakfast?"

She nodded, and yawned. Half an hour later, as she examined the proof sheets of her photo session, she asked, "Whatever happened to that photographer you had *last* time? The tall cute one."

"Mage? I haven't seen him in over a year; he likes to move around a lot, never settles down. Why?"

"Just wondered. I liked him, and I *loved* the shots he took— don't pout like that, he's too young for me, but a friend of mine's coming to work here from New York, and he's her type, I thought I could introduce them."

Mandaglione shrugged his bushy eyebrows. "He e-mails me occasionally, but that usually tells me where he's been, not where he is."

"Uh-huh," she replied, not taking her eyes from the proof sheet. She didn't know why the Sunrise Casino was offering five thousand dollars for information on Magistrale's whereabouts, but guessed it must be a gambling debt—a big one, if the photographer felt he had to keep moving. If that was it, she felt no compunction about claiming the reward; her ex-husband had used her as payment for his own gambling debts, and five grand was only slightly more than he owed her in child support (*he* never stayed in one place for very long, either). "Pity."

Charlie Takumo looked at the e-mail, and nodded. He'd never been convinced by the idea of a corpse being used as a marionette; a body, even a boy's body, was too damn heavy. Wires that were strong enough to support that sort of weight should have shown up on the photograph. And since the boy was naked, attaching them to the body would have been difficult, and even more difficult to hide from the pathologist. The toe-prints merely confirmed it; either the boy had climbed up onto that window-ledge, which was unlikely if Gaye was telling the truth about not having known the family, or . . .

Takumo had only met Gaye once, but he'd liked what he'd

seen. For one thing, she was barely an inch shorter than him, which he regarded as the ideal height for a woman. He liked her taste in music and comics, her simple sense of style, her faded-denim-blue eyes. She wasn't beautiful, but he suspected she'd be stunning when she smiled, if he could only make her smile. Bizarre as details of her story might be, he wanted to believe it—and if that meant considering the possibility that Nick Petrosyan had walked off the operating table with his intestines hanging down to mid-thigh, traveled a few blocks and climbed a wall in his search for one of the last people to see him alive . . . okay, he'd consider it. He'd seen stranger things, and at close quarters.

So. Nick had walked off the table—no, rewind a little. Nick had died of unknown causes, and was taken to the morgue for an autopsy. The pathologist had blacked out and Nick had walked off the table, visited Gaye Lind, leaving his toe-prints on the window-ledge, was photographed and maybe frightened away by the flash, then turned up decapitated and, Takumo hoped, well and truly dead in a storm drain two days later, his mouth stuffed with garlic. His photographic image faded away a few days later.

So. Mandaglione had mentioned vampires. Takumo glanced at his library, and found nothing very useful apart from tapes of *The Lost Boys* and *Vampire Princess Miyu*, paperbacks of *Anno Dracula* and *Sunglasses After Dark*, and two issues of *Swamp Thing*. None of them, he suspected, could be relied upon as textbooks on vampirism, but they seemed to agree on certain points, such as the harmful effects of sunlight on vampire flesh. Only *The Lost Boys* mentioned garlic, and then only to say that it "doesn't work." They also disagreed on how someone *became* a vampire, and how long it took, but they seemed united on the issue of the surest way to kill a vampire— a stake through the heart, something which hadn't been done to Nick. It had been many years since Takumo had read *Dracula*, but he vaguely remembered that the vampires killed in that had also been decapitated, something which struck him as at least as effective as impaling.

He shrugged. Maybe "vampire" was the wrong word, steering him toward the wrong conclusions. Try "revenant," or "shade," or "zombie." Zombies were also undead, weren't they? They lapsed mysteriously into comas, then arose to do the bidding of their *houngans*, the sorcerers who created them. Takumo knew that most of the voodoo in *Zombie Cheerleaders* was pure gibberish, and that "zombies" were actually victims of soporific poisoning. He'd seen the *60 Minutes* episode in which a zombie had been interviewed sitting on his own grave, and sometimes wondered why the process wasn't more widely used by Hollywood. It had to be cheaper than re-animating dead actors by using computer graphics, and he could think of many so-called actors whose performance skills wouldn't be adversely affected.

He shrugged again. Feeding the boy (and his parents?) the zombie drugs might have posed a problem, but maybe Julia Petrosyan had been bringing them in home cooking so they could avoid hospital food. He'd spent enough time as an in-patient to understand that.

Of course, Tudor might have arranged for the theft and the visit to Gaye just to convince his rivals, or his own followers, that he could raise the dead—and then disposed of the body when it became burdensome.

Takumo yawned. Occam's razor didn't strongly favor any of the possibilities, and it was only a matter of intellectual curiosity now. Nick, undead or not, was now simply dead; Tudor was no concern of his; and Gaye would almost certainly be cleared. He resolved to ask her for a date as soon as she'd had time to recover from the shock. He changed into his gi, and worked out with the Wing Chun dummy for half an hour.

After breakfast and a shower, he walked a few blocks up the beach to Small World Books, the only shop he knew with a section set aside for vampire books. He looked through encyclopedias and coffee-table books at pictures of different types of legendary vampires—a tree-dwelling *asasabonsam*, with hook-like feet; a *penanggalan*, a woman's head flying through the air, with its stomach and intestines trailing from her neck;

a batlike *baital*; a birdlike *strige*; Max Schreck and Klaus Kinski as bald, rat-fanged *Nosferatu*. He ended up buying paperbacks of *Blood Is Not Enough, Fevre Dream*, and an autographed *Those Who Hunt the Night*.

The house was surrounded by trees, which in turn were enclosed by a high stone wall, and Woodcott had to wait at the gate, his temper worsening by the minute, until one of Tudor's initiates was prepared to take on the responsibility of letting him in. He parked the car outside the front door; there were no other cars in sight, though two of the three garage doors showed signs of recent use. The third was apparently held shut by the same vines that seemed to be holding the rest of the house together. Woodcott knocked on the door, then glanced around the grounds, noting that the cultists obviously weren't enthusiastic gardeners.

The door was opened by a slight, pale, hollow-eyed man who looked to be in his early twenties. He wore black jeans and a black drawstring shirt, and stood back from the doorway as though avoiding the direct sunlight. "Yes?"

"Detective Woodcott, LAPD Homicide. I'd like to speak to Julia Petrosyan."

The young man stared at him for a moment. "She's not here," he replied, eventually, his voice solemn. "She left us about two weeks ago."

"Do you know where she went?"

"No, I'm afraid I don't."

Woodcott sighed. "Can I come in?"

The man hesitated, then shrugged. "If you wish." He stepped back from the doorway, and led the way down a corridor into a dimly lit living room lined with bookshelves. The furnishing consisted of a large entertainment center in one corner and a variety of chairs of assorted ages and styles. "How many of you live here?" asked Woodcott.

"Seven—I mean six, since Julia . . . six."

Woodcott counted the seats—thirteen—and nodded. "And you are?"

"Malachi."

"Malachi who?"

"Tudor."

Woodcott made a note of this. "Any relation to Solomon Tudor?"

"Yes; he's my father. Look, I've already told you that Julia isn't here. . . ."

"And you have no idea where she might have gone?"

"There's a Greyhound station a few blocks away, on Vine," replied Malachi. "People are free to leave here at any time."

"Do they ever come back?"

"Some do."

"Do you expect Julia Petrosyan to come back?"

"I don't know. I keep telling you, I don't know where she's gone."

"Do you know why she left?"

Malachi hesitated a little too long for Woodcott's liking before answering, uncomfortably, "No."

"What sort of mood was she in before she left?"

"What do you mean?"

"Depressed? Cheerful? Optimistic? Angry?"

"I don't know . . . depressed, I guess. But not angry. What's this about? You said you were from Homicide. . . ."

"I need to speak to Julia."

Malachi seemed to relax slightly. "I was scared you might have found her dead."

Woodcott sat down in a black leatherette armchair. "Had you thought she might be dead?"

"I was worried, yes, not knowing where she was . . ." He stared past, or through, Woodcott, through the walls and the trees and the walls outside. "Queen of the Fallen Angels . . ." he murmured.

"Pardon?"

"It's what my father calls L.A. She eats people, this city."

"All cities do that," said Woodcott. "Exactly when did Julia Petrosyan leave here?"

"What day is this? Thursday?"

"The thirtieth," Woodcott confirmed.

"I think it was Thursday two weeks ago, then. I'm not positive, but I'm pretty sure."

"What time?"

"I don't know when I noticed she was gone. Night time, certainly. Not much happens here during the day." His lips quirked slightly, in what might have been a half-hearted attempt at a smile.

"Can I speak to the others who live here?"

"Only Sindee and Tanith; the others are asleep or at work."

"Then I'll start with them—who are the 'others'?"

"My father, Beth, and Adrian."

"This place can't have been cheap," said Woodcott. "What do you do for money?"

"My father was given this house as part of his fee for producing a movie," replied Malachi, stiffly. "He still writes, and we all work."

"Where do you work?"

"Here. I design software and websites."

"What about the rest of you?"

"Beth's a body artist, Sindee and Tanith are working as dancers, and Adrian's a tour guide."

"Body artist?"

"Skin illustrator and piercer—she designs and makes her own jewelry, too."

Woodcott nodded, his expression sour. "Okay, I'd like to talk to either Tanith or Sindee, but one at a time, and with you out of the room. Is that okay?"

"Yes, of course. I'll go and get one of them for you."

The woman who walked into the room a few minutes later looked more like an opera singer than a dancer. "Voluptuous," "curvaceous," and "pneumatic" were barely adequate to describe her, though "plump" or "chubby" would be ungenerous. In the dim light, her hair looked almost bloodred, and her age was impossible to guess. She wore a scoop-necked red top and leather pants laced loosely up the sides. "Hi," she said, cheerfully. "I'm Tanith."

"What's your real name?"

The woman grimaced slightly. "If you mean the one I was born with, then it's Antoinette, but I don't relate to it."

"Surname?"

A sigh. "Grunwald."

"Malachi tells me you're a dancer."

The grimace became a smile. "He has a nice way with euphemisms, doesn't he? My back's too bad to let me dance much anymore; most of my show is done sitting down. But Sindee dances . . . well, sort of."

"Show?"

"It's mostly talking, a question and answer thing, to a bunch of middle-aged men who remember me from my movies. I never did hardcore—well, not hardcore by today's standards, anyway—but I have fans. Would you believe I turned down a chance to do a Russ Meyer movie so that I could be in *Devilspawn*? My agent thought it would be more respectable, give me a bigger break." She shook her hennaed head. "Jesus, what an idiot. Sol liked me enough to give me a speaking part and put my name on the poster, so when the picture flopped, so did my career. I tried changing my name again and again, but they still remembered me. If Russ had ever finished another movie, I might have been able to start fresh . . . but he didn't. What can I do for you, detective?"

"I'm investigating the death of Julia Petrosyan's brother, and the theft of his body from the morgue. When was the last time you saw Julia Petrosyan?"

"About two weeks ago."

"Can you be more precise?"

She shrugged, and Woodcott caught himself looking down at her breasts. "Not easily," she said, as he blushed. "I didn't really see that much of her, especially before she lost her job. She was working days, I work mostly evenings and nights, doing phone sex when I don't have another gig, so we were rarely here at the same time. Besides, she didn't spend much time with the girls here; when she wasn't with Mal, she was in her room. Writing poetry, I think, or listening to music."

Woodcott looked down at his notepad. "When did she lose the job?"

"About three, four weeks ago."

"Where did she work?"

"Retail Slut."

"*What?*" Involuntarily, he looked up.

"It's a boutique. On Melrose. Goth, fetish, punk, that sort of thing. She was heavily into the goth scene, but she was fired because she kept showing up late."

"When did she join the cult?"

"Cult?" Tanith laughed. "What cult? Sol says he still believes in that sort of thing, he writes his books about magic and does the occasional interview, and heavy metal groups come here for photo opportunities sometimes, borrow some of Sol's stuff as props and pay one of the girls to strip and act as an altar . . . but that hardly makes us a cult. Satanism is really just inverted Christianity, but just as patriarchal, and I find it hard to take either of them seriously. I like the philosophy of 'An It Harm None, Do What Thou Wilt Be the Whole of the Law,' but I don't really worship anyone or anything, and I sure as Hell don't sacrifice animals or virgins or any of that shit."

Woodcott digested this with some difficulty. "Was Julia a satanist?"

"I don't think so. She was on a serious death trip most of the time, and more than a little unhinged, but that's not the same thing. Look, people like Julia come to us because they think God has let them down and they'll be damned if they go to a church for help. Sol turns away the ones he doesn't like, gives the others a place to sleep and maybe helps find them a job so they can either stay in town or go somewhere else, whatever they choose."

"You're a charity?" asked Woodcott, dryly.

Tanith shrugged again, but this time the detective managed to keep his eyes up. "Sol just likes having people around to talk to, especially girls. Besides, the house is sort of empty without them—we can take twice as many as we have at the moment."

"And where do you fit in?"

"Sol and I have lived together, on and off, for years—we started after *Devilspawn* flopped and I couldn't pay my rent. We were never married—well, I was, a few times, but never to him—and never monogamous, but I've always been welcome here. I was the closest thing Mal had to a mother for most of his life—his real mother left when he was two or three."

Woodcott absorbed this slowly. "But you weren't close to Julia?"

"Not particularly. Adrian brought her here, and Mal became smitten with her, but I think she thought we were a bit below her—not that Mal was on top of her as much as he would have liked. And she withdrew into herself even more after she lost her job."

"So you'd say she was depressed when you last saw her?"

"It's hard to tell—she was always a little melodramatic—but yeah, I think I would."

"And she left soon after that?"

"A week or two after. I'm pretty sure it was two Thursdays ago I last saw her, though it might have been Wednesday . . . anyway, it was Friday when Sol told me she'd gone. I hate to say it, but I hadn't actually missed her, and I might not have for a few days. It's a big house."

Sindee Lights—Sandra Halley—was a petite young woman, with a cafe au lait complexion, long dark hair, small breasts, wide hips, and long shapely legs. She wore nothing but a silky black summer robe that ended just below the tops of her thighs. Woodcott guessed her age at about twenty, her height at five foot three, her weight at 105 lbs. When she spoke, however, he looked up and noticed just how pretty her face was. She smiled, showing a gold stud in her tongue. A moment later, Woodcott realized that he'd forgotten what she'd said. "Pardon?"

"Tanith told me you're looking for Julia."

"Yes, that's right. When did you last see her?"

"Two weeks ago? Why, what's happened?"

"Her brother and mother have died, and her father's very sick; that's why we need to find her. He needs transfusions, and they have the same rare blood group. Do you know where she might have gone?"

"No. She never talked to me about having anywhere else to go. I think she was here a long time before I came."

"How long ago was that?"

"Some time in July . . . about two months ago. I'd come to L.A. for an audition, it didn't work out, and then I met Tanith and she told me about this place. I was nearly out of money, it was only a few blocks from where I was working, and my car was nearly dead, so I said yes."

"What did she tell you?"

"That they had empty rooms, and you only had to pay for food and stuff, rent was free if Sol liked you—and Sol likes girls, but he's harmless, and Mal was besotted with Julia and wouldn't be a problem. She was right, and I hit it off with everyone except Julia, so I stayed."

"Why didn't you and Julia hit it off?"

Sindee pouted prettily, and crossed her legs. "She was sort of a snob, and a drag. Always reading Sol's books, and writing stuff; even when she drank, it was to make her some sort of a tragic figure, not for fun. It was like goths weren't supposed to laugh or something—though Beth's just as much a goth as she is, and she's a lot more fun."

"How long had Julia been here?"

"I think it was a few months, but I don't know; we didn't talk much. Ask Mal, or Tanith; Sol's not very good with dates."

Tudor's room was at the back of the house, and its heavy drapes were rarely pulled aside; Tudor had very little interest in the outside world anymore. He sat up in his enormous waterbed in near darkness as his son paced the worn, rather greasy carpet. "A policeman," said Tudor, soothingly. "When have we ever had to concern ourselves about a policeman?"

"He's from Homicide."

"Have we killed anybody?" asked Tudor, not quite mockingly.

"He's looking for Julia."

Tudor shrugged. "I thought he might be. What have you told him?"

"That she left and we don't know where she's gone."

"In a philosophical sense, that's true," murmured the older man. His son glared at him. "Will anybody contradict this?"

"I don't think so. I don't think anybody else has guessed. He's talking to Sindee now." He fumbled his way through the gloom to a chair, and flopped into it. "It's too soon," he worried. "Something must have gone wrong. I hacked into the hospital computer again, her mother's dead but her father's still alive, she hasn't had to feed on anybody else . . . why are Homicide here already?"

"What did he tell you?"

"Not very much; I was afraid to push."

"Maybe they were called in when somebody found the boy's body," suggested Tudor. "That must have looked like a homicide."

"I didn't have time to hide it any better than that," said Malachi. "I'm lucky nobody saw me as it was . . . do you think somebody did?"

"No. That spell doesn't work well in daylight, but it will fool the eyes of anybody who doesn't know you. And if the police had a reason to suspect you, they wouldn't have come here pretending to look for Julia." He shrugged again. "Maybe her father is asking to see her, now that the rest of the family is dead. I don't think we need worry yet."

"What about when her father dies and she has to feed on somebody else?"

"The circle will hold her," said Tudor, "and it should keep others out unless we take them in—"

"*Should?*"

"It prevents anybody from hearing her, or even seeing her

unless they actively look; these concealment spells are never perfect, but they're quite effective, especially when there's no sunlight. Everybody here believes she's not in the house, don't they?
Even the policeman?"

"I think so."

Tudor nodded. "I don't think any of them has enough vision
to be a problem. If we don't slip up, it simply won't occur to
any of them to look down there. And when Julia needs to feed,
we'll find her somebody to feed on."

"What if she turns them?"

"That won't happen unless she drains the body, and she
won't do that overnight—not to an adult. She was gorging herself because she had three family members to feed on, and all
she had to do was gnaw her own flesh to drink their blood. We
found the boy easily enough before he'd turned anybody else,
didn't we?"

"What about the parents? The mother's already dead, she'll
probably turn tonight, and we can't stop Julia from draining
her father. . . ."

Tudor's expression became sour. He had never intended to
create a vampire, but Julia Petrosyan had forced his hand by
attempting to perform the ritual by herself. She'd succeeded in
committing suicide, he granted her that, but had made such a
hash of the preparations that she would merely have died if
Malachi hadn't insisted he intervene.

He wondered if these children would ever realize that the
spells they read in books were almost never complete; he'd even
heard of teenagers attempting to turn themselves with little
more than a few commercially manufactured black candles and
sloppily drawn diagrams, some heavy metal music, and a
knife—or even a shotgun, as though a vampire could regenerate
a head that had been shattered by a blast of buckshot! Some
even tried it by daylight.

Julia had done better than that, using some of his books and
materials; he would have given her a seven out of ten, maybe
an eight . . . but even a minor mistake in a ritual would cause
it to fail. Demons are not capable of forgiveness; few of them

can even grasp the concept, and those that can, think it incredibly funny.

Malachi had found Julia before sunrise, lying in a pool of her own blood but with her body otherwise intact. Tudor had had to redraw the circles hurriedly and repeat the incantations before first light. He wondered, now, if he would have balked if he'd been given time to think, and made some minor error that would prevent a successful turning. It had been years since he'd performed any major magic; sorcery was usually much more trouble than it was worth, and he rarely bothered using it now that he had enough to satisfy him—money, a house, admirers, and a firstborn son he could sacrifice in his own place if a demon demanded his blood and a soul.

He could have sacrificed Julia as a bribe to some petty Hellish aristocrat for a small favor—she wasn't of his blood, and not in any sense a virgin, so her soul was worth little—then reanimated her body well enough to serve as a toy for Malachi . . . but he'd become used to indulging his son, and the thought of the ritual had appealed to his vanity. If only the girl had been an orphan . . .

Tudor closed his eyes. She would be, soon enough. It was simply unfortunate, bad timing, that the autopsy had been performed on her brother while the sun was setting; it was unlikely to happen again. "Her mother may not rise tonight. There are reliable reports of them taking as long as nine days, but it's safest to act as though she will. Find out what you can about the autopsy. See whether they plan to remove the brain; if not, try to put a note on the file requesting it. That will prevent her rising; removing the heart *should*, but it might not, not if the spinal cord is intact. And if the autopsy's not planned for today, flag it as urgent or do whatever you need to do to push it up the waiting list. If we can persuade the hospital to kill her for us, we won't have to go looking for her tomorrow.

"If you can't do that, see if there's any way you can get into the morgue and create some barriers to keep her in her drawer. If she rises . . ." He stared into the darkness. "There'll be a missing body to explain, and the police will be called in. She'll want

to feed, and I don't know whether she'll be able to feed on her
husband the way the children did; if not, she'll probably attack
the first person she sees in the hospital, which will also bring
the police in. We'll have the same problem when the husband
dies, too, which may be as early as tonight, so you'd better get
to work." He didn't add, "I hope you think she's worth it," but
Malachi could almost hear him think it. He nodded stiffly, and
walked out.

Traces

Lamm shuffled his feet slightly as he waited for the door to open. He didn't mind meeting clients personally, he just thought it was time-consuming and not particularly efficient, especially if *he* had to fly out of town to visit *them*. He suspected, too, that Tamenaga was deliberately keeping him waiting outside as a not-so-subtle way of showing him who was the boss. Her father had never bothered with that sort of pettiness; he had treated Lamm with respect, and Lamm respected that. *He* hadn't been born with a samurai sword up his ass.

The door was opened (at last) by Yamada Kazafumi, the only one of old Tamenaga's bodyguards who'd been kept on (Lamm had never been very clear on what had happened to the others). The sumotori bowed, and Lamm bowed in return before being ushered in and steered toward the office. Haruko Tamenaga sat behind a modest, modern workstation, a far cry from the great oaken desk that her father had used. She still managed to dominate the room. "Good afternoon, Mr. Lamm. Thank you for coming at such short notice."

"How can I help you?"

"We're trying to locate a Michelangelo Magistrale. You remember the name?" Lamm nodded. "We have confirmation that he communicates with a relative of his, Dante Mandaglione, by e-mail, and we have reason to believe that he also stays in contact with Charles Takumo by the same means. We need somebody to hack in to their e-mail servers and find a return address for Mr. Magistrale. Better still would be information on when we might expect him to be in a city where we have people who can intercept him—Las Vegas, L.A., or San Francisco. Failing this, I assume it's possible to forge e-mail which might bring him to either of these cities?"

Lamm managed to hide his disappointment; somehow, in the past few years, his hobby of hacking had degenerated into little more than well-paid hackwork. Nothing was a *challenge* anymore. Not that he minded the money—or, more important, what it bought. "Probably. Of course, if he's using some sort of cipher, it will take time to crack—it's tedious rather than difficult—but yes, I can do it."

"Excellent. Here's the information we have already." She opened a drawer, and extracted a floppy disk with no label, and handed it to him. Lamm took it without any show of enthusiasm, or any other emotion. It was only business, after all—not even big business, compared to his other work, but he wasn't sure that it would be safe to turn it down.

He glanced around the room. Tamenaga had kept none of the antiques that her father had collected, and that disturbed him. The old man had always respected good work in any field, and Lamm had always been sure that he'd never have him killed. Crippled, maybe—he could work just as well in a wheelchair, and it wouldn't even affect his social life as long as his spine wasn't damaged—but not killed. The old man wouldn't have made him fly to Vegas just to give him data that he could have sent by e-mail or courier. His daughter, on the other hand . . .

"Let me know when you have something," she said, dismissing him. "Good day."

*   *   *

Woodcott glared at the monitor, and drummed his fingers on the mouse pad. None of Tudor's coven had more than minor offenses recorded, at least under the names they'd given him. Julia Petrosyan, despite her youth, had the longest record, but only for misdemeanors—possession of drugs, but only in small quantities; carrying a concealed weapon (knives, never guns); shoplifting; trespass. Beth Holland also had convictions for shoplifting and carrying a knife, and Adrian Vandermeer for selling amphetamines. Antoinette Grunwald had one conviction from Nevada back in '89, for lewd and dissolute behavior, and nothing but minor traffic offenses—speeding and parking— since.

Even more annoying, both of the Tudors were cleanskins, as was Sandra Halley. And Julia Petrosyan was proving difficult to trace. She didn't have a car, or any credit cards, and nobody had touched her bank account since two days after she'd lost her job. Woodcott had (reluctantly) visited Retail Slut, and the manager had confirmed that she'd been fired for tardiness on August 27th, had given the Tudor house as her forwarding address, and hadn't been back to the shop. None of the nurses at St. John's remembered seeing her visit any member of her family. None of the Jane Does in the morgue matched her description.

The morgue . . .

Woodcott had requested that a police guard be placed on the hospital's morgue and autopsy room, in case whoever stole the Petrosyan kid came after the mother as well, but the request had been denied. Of course, they couldn't prevent him from being there. . . .

The pathologist told him that the "post" was scheduled for three P.M. He arrived a few minutes early. He'd witnessed an autopsy while at the academy, and had taken the precaution of standing next to the sink but not between it and his fellow trainees. This time, too, he kept a respectful distance from the procedure, particularly as the doctors still had no explanation for the deaths.

"What's the news on Dr. Kimball?" he asked, as the pathologist, Dr. Short, was scrubbing.

"Recovering well," muttered Short. "Her b.p.'s almost back to normal, and she hasn't blacked out again, though they're still running tests. It looks as though she scratched her wrist at some time during the post—there's a nick in her glove that corresponds with the bruise—and got infected that way." He pulled on his own gloves as he spoke—three pairs of them, latex, Kevlar, and surgical gloves. "I'm taking every precaution this time around; normally we don't have time."

He donned a waterproof apron over his surgical scrubs, and a visor over his glasses, then checked the tray of instruments: dissecting knife, brain knife, two pairs of scissors, skull key, electric saw. Woodcott was silent as Short made a Y-shaped incision from each armpit to the bottom of the sternum, then down around the navel to the pubis. For the benefit of the microphone over the table, the pathologist commented on the appearance of the internal organs, then removed them individually and weighed them on a hanging scale. Woodcott looked away as the doctor used the skull key, a T-shaped chisel, to remove the skull cap, then after commenting on the appearance of the brain, announced that he was cutting the nerves connecting the brain to the eyes.

Woodcott blinked, then looked again at the metal rim of the sink. The reflection seemed to show three people in the room, one of them in a morgue attendant's coveralls. He slowly turned away from the sink and looked carefully around the room. No one visible but the pathologist—and the corpse on the table, of course. Woodcott hesitated, then looked around the room again for anything else with a mirror finish.

Few of Woodcott's colleagues would have called him broadminded or imaginative, but he was less dismissive of the supernatural than most. Two ideas occurred to him instantly; one, that the third figure in the room was Mrs. Petrosyan's disembodied soul, watching her autopsy and waiting for entrance to the afterlife; the other, that the figure was some variety of angel, faithful or fallen, there to collect Mrs. Petrosyan's soul. He was unsure why either would appear in the outfit of a morgue attendant, but it occurred to him that this might be some form of camouflage.

He looked at the half-silvered window in the door, which showed a broken image that *might* have been a person in a green coverall on either side of the door; an instant later, it seemed to move away. He was almost ready to dismiss it as an illusion, but the feeling that someone else was there was too strong.

Woodcott turned away from the door, and reached into his pocket for his reading glasses, which he held up and tilted until the glass reflected the corner of the room behind him. He had a brief glimpse of a man's pale face, so small as to be almost unrecognizable, but Woodcott was morally sure that he'd seen it before only that afternoon. He turned around and took a step toward the door, which opened seconds before he reached it. Infuriated, he stepped outside as well, looking up and down the corridor. No one in sight. He stood there fuming as the door swung shut behind him, resisting the urge to call out, "Tudor!"— even if he was right, the man was hardly likely to stop—or to draw his gun. He checked the corridor again, drew a deep breath, and stepped back inside.

Short looked up briefly, then returned to his work. "Thought I saw somebody outside," muttered Woodcott.

"Uh-huh," replied the pathologist. "Seeing us remove the brain does that to a lot of people. Even cops. Never really understood why; the stomach and intestines smell a lot worse." He shrugged. "Are you okay now, or do you need to get some fresh air?"

Adrian Vandermeer was too good looking to be anything but an actor, but though he was slim, almost willowy, he lacked the hungry look Woodcott saw on the faces of so many waiters and other would-be screen stars. "Where are you working?" he asked.

"Death Trips," replied Adrian, smiling.

"What?"

Adrian hummed the first few bars of the old Steve Harley and Cockney Rebel song. Woodcott stared blankly at him. "Death Trips," he repeated. "10050 Cielo Drive, 810 Linden Drive, 730 North Bedford Drive . . ." The blank look remained. "I'm a tour bus guide," Adrian explained. "We go past the places where the names have died—not just movie stars, Bugsy Siegel was also killed in Hollywood—and mostly murders or suspicious or just plain gruesome deaths. Marilyn Monroe, Sharon Tate, Ramon Navarro, Thelma Todd, Albert Dekker. And other places like Verdugo Hills, where there was a landslide in the cemetery a few years back, dead bodies everywhere." He grinned and shrugged. "It's a living."

"So you weren't here this afternoon? Between two-thirty and five?"

Adrian shook his head. "Working. Didn't get back until about quarter past six, maybe twenty past. Why?"

"Not important. When was the last time you saw Julia Petrosyan?"

"About two weeks ago. After she lost her job, she kind of retreated into her shell. If she went out at all, it was at night, and by herself. I got her an audition with Death Trips, and she would've been great, she had the look and everything, but she couldn't remember her lines, so they wouldn't even put her on the waiting list. An actor with a memory can get a lot more work than one with just talent."

"Did she want to be an actress?"

"I don't think anyone knows what she wanted to be, least of all Julia."

Woodcott glanced down at his notebook. "How long have you been living here, Mr. Vandermeer?"

"Not long—end of June. I came here for a party, had a great time, and heard there were rooms here and it was a cheap place to stay. The Death Trips gig doesn't pay all that well, and I thought, why not?"

"You know this is supposed to be a satanist church?"

"Oh, that old routine of Solomon's?" scoffed Adrian. "From

what I hear, he does maybe two shows a year, one at Halloween and the other about six months before that. I haven't been here for either, but from what I hear, it's just an excuse for some fat old rich men to dress up in robes and chant nonsense and ogle naked women. Kind of a titty bar for Freemasons. I think Julia did that for him a couple of times; I don't think she had any lines to remember or anything like that. It was probably just stripping and playing dead, and she was good at that. Ooh, that sounded bitchy, didn't it? Sorry."

"What do you mean?"

"She just liked that kind of thing. Posing naked with coffins and in cemeteries. Terminally goth." He looked away; Woodcott guessed he was hiding something, but it took him several seconds to realize what it might be.

"Were the two of you . . ." he ventured.

"Involved? Only a couple of times; once when she first came here, then again when she and Malachi had had a fight and . . . I probably shouldn't have, but you know how it is. I thought she deserved better than him." He shook his head. "I didn't realize just how much she was in control—not of herself, but of him. And she was always on; I just do this for a living." He looked at Woodcott, saw the bafflement on his face. "She was always acting," he explained. "A real drama queen. Even in bed. Every time she left the room, you felt if you applauded she'd come back and do an encore. I almost felt sorry for Mal when they got back together."

"Do you know where she might have gone?"

"To an acting school, I hope. Sorry, did it again. No, no idea; maybe she has some school friends, or maybe she changed her mind about going back home—she grew up around here, as much as anyone ever does."

"Her mother and her brother died in the past week," said Woodcott. "Her father is very sick. That's one reason I need to find her."

Adrian shrugged. "That's all I know. Sorry."

* * *

Beth Holland laughed throatily. Woodcott watched her, slightly unnerved by her appearance. Her lips were dark purple, as was a streak in her long black hair. Her face was almost white, her nails long and black, and her nose, ears, tongue, lower lip, and right eyebrow were pierced. Her black dress had a high collar, and he had no reason to believe that the piercings stopped at her neck. He wondered whether she ever had trouble walking through metal detectors. Behind the adornments, however, she was a moon-faced, pleasant-looking, slightly plump young woman. "A satanist? They'd throw me out of the church!"

"Church?"

"Metropolitan Community Church," she said, still chuckling. "Okay, Julia was interested in magic, and maybe she believed in it—which is more than I think Sol does—but not me."

Woodcott looked more closely at her earrings, noticed small silver crosses as well as double-bladed axes. "When did you last see Julia Petrosyan?"

"Two weeks ago. I'd wondered if she was leaving; she was acting strange, and I thought she might be . . ." She bit her purple lip. "I don't think she'd commit suicide, but she might fake it and go too far. Accidentally. You know?" Woodcott nodded. "But I think if she'd done that, someone would have found her; someone would be meant to find her, preferably while she was still alive. I did my best to keep an eye on her until she got over being fired, but she wouldn't let me watch her all the time, and I have to go to work. . . ."

"Do you know anywhere else she might have gone?"

"No."

"Any old boyfriends?"

"No," she replied, with a faint hint of a grimace.

"How well did you know her?"

"Pretty well. She talked to me more than to the other women here, I even thought she might be on the turn, but she . . ." She looked at Woodcott, noticed his confusion, and shrugged. "She was het—not *straight*, exactly, but het." The confusion only deepened. "Never mind. We were friends, okay? Only friends."

"Detective Woodcott?"

The voice was deep but not loud, and seemed to echo around the huge room like very distant thunder. Woodcott looked up at the doorway, and saw a tall, bald man in a black caftan. "I'm Solomon Tudor," he said, as he entered. "Malachi tells me you wish to speak to me."

"Yes, I . . ." He turned to Beth. "That will be all for now, Miss Holland." He looked up at Tudor again. Apart from the shaven head and the unusual attire, he seemed an ordinary enough man. There was some resemblance to Malachi, mostly in the pale complexion and the dark deep-set eyes. Six foot two, weight unknown (the caftan was loose enough to hide a considerable paunch, but his face and hands suggested that he was slender, even gaunt), age early fifties. His voice was deep, with a tone that suggested that he'd trained as an actor, but Woodcott was used to that, too. "Could you please tell me when you last saw Julia Petrosyan?"

"Several weeks ago," said Tudor, sitting in the director's chair that Beth had just vacated. He reached into one of the caftan's pockets, and fished out a pack of clove cigarettes and a black Zippo lighter. "I know she was living here until two weeks ago," he said, lighting the cigarette, "but we rarely spoke; she was my son's guest, not mine."

"I understood that she was a member of your coven?"

Tudor waved that aside with a flick of his fingers. Woodcott noticed the signet ring on his right hand—gold, with a large red stone. "My Church—my coven, as you call it—holds between two and four services a year, and yes, she attended one of those as a novice. How often do you attend church, Detective?"

"Every week," replied Woodcott, stiffly. "Sometimes I have to work on Sundays, but I attend on other occasions, too."

Another flick. "An exception to prove the rule. Surely you know many who call themselves Christians who rarely or never attend church?"

"Yes."

"As above, so below," said Tudor, smiling. Woodcott looked blank. "Few of our devotees attend services regularly either. Of course, we don't discourage sloth in the way Christians do, so if you're enquiring into our tax status . . ."

"No. I'm from Homicide, not Fraud."

"Oh? Who's been murdered?" His tone and expression were curious rather than concerned, but if he was amused, mocking, he hid it well.

"We hope that nobody has," said Woodcott. "We were investigating what seemed to be a murder, but turned out to be a case of corpse mutilation, the boy having apparently died of natural causes—though this isn't proven, either. What's worrying us is that one of the boy's parents has since died, the other is in a critical condition, and his only other known relative, Julia Petrosyan, seems to have disappeared."

"Disappearing is easy," said Tudor, dismissively. "If you don't have any credit cards, don't own a vehicle, this society regards you as nonexistent already. It's only occasionally they wonder where some of these nonexistent people have gone."

"Do you know where Julia Petrosyan might have gone?"

"No, but should she return, I can call you. Will that satisfy you?"

"I'm afraid not. It's important that we find her before her father dies."

"Has he been asking to see her?"

"No," admitted Woodcott, after a moment's hesitation.

"I thought not. As far as her family is concerned, she ceased to exist years ago—retroactively, I suspect. Who *is* looking for her?"

"The hospital. It may help them discover what's been killing the rest of her family."

"Then I'm sorry that I can't help you, Detective. Is there anything else?"

"You can't look in a crystal ball or something?" asked Woodcott. He regretted it as soon as he'd said it, but Tudor only smiled.

"You don't know anything about magic, do you, Detective?"

"No, but I understand you claim to practice it."

A shrug. "Humans do not perform magic, Detective, they

merely . . . solicit it. The actual magic is done by demons— fallen angels. Our spells are nothing more than prayers, though we have more hope that they will be heard and granted. I'm not a clairvoyant."

"So you couldn't cast a spell to, say, make somebody invisible?"

"Not with any hope of success," replied Tudor, obviously amused. "I wouldn't even try; many demons have very crude ideas of fun. In most cases, they would make somebody invisible by making them too small to see, or vaporizing them, or something equally destructive. Why? Do you think that because you can't find Julia, it must mean I've rendered her invisible?"

"Just an example," replied Woodcott, his cheeks reddening. "If you don't mind, what sort of thing do you do here?"

"And if I do mind?"

"Pardon?"

"I don't see how this is relevant to Julia's disappearance, unless perhaps you think I've turned her into a frog or something equally unpleasant—and I assure you, I haven't."

"I'm not accusing you of anything," said Woodcott, less convincingly than he would have liked. "I'm just asking for your help."

Tudor nodded. "I assure you, we're as concerned about Julia as you are, but you've spoken to everybody who lives here, and we've all told you when we last saw her, and that we don't know where she might have gone. What more can we do?"

Woodcott sat there for a moment, trying to think of something to say, when Tanith walked in, carrying a steaming mug on a tray. "Coffee?" she asked Tudor.

"Thank you," he said, gravely. Woodcott tried not to stare as she bent over to place the mug on the table, her scoop-necked top falling open as she did so. Before he could look away, he was simultaneously hit with powerful waves of lust and terror. It felt, in fact, as he'd long imagined it must feel to be hanged.

"Detective? Would you like something?"

Woodcott opened his mouth to speak, but no words came forth, so he shut it again. He glanced at Tudor, who smiled broadly as he picked up the mug. "Blue Mountain," he said. "You'll never have better."

Woodcott tried again. "N . . . no, th-thank you. I . . . I'd better be going."

Tanith smiled, straightened up, turned around, and walked out. Woodcott watched her leave, then slowly and unsteadily found his feet. His erection was uncomfortable, almost painful; he resisted the urge to look down to see whether he'd done anything else to embarrass himself. Tudor's smile broadened slightly; it was remarkable, he thought, how effective a simple charm could be if you read your victim correctly. "I'm sorry we couldn't be of more help, Detective. I shall let you know if we have any news; come again if you have any more questions."

Woodcott nodded stiffly. "I can find my own way out," he said.

"Of course you can; a fine detective you'd be if you couldn't, eh? Be seeing you."

Gaye was watching *Yellow Submarine* for the thirty-seventh time with both cats in her lap and a half-eaten hash brownie in her hand, when she heard someone walk up to the door and knock. She looked down at the cats, neither of whom showed any inclination to move, then yelled, "Who is it?"

"Detective-Sergeant Woodcott."

"Just a minute." Carefully, she reached for the remote controls for the TV and video, dislodged both cats, hid the brownie in the fridge where it would be safe (the cats were greedy enough without a bad case of munchies), and reached the door nearly a minute later. She peered through the peephole, then undid the bolts and chains that Takumo had recommended. Woodcott looked shaken, even nervous. "Yes?"

"May I come in?"

She stepped back, then shut and bolted the door behind him as he entered. "Okay . . ." She watched as he walked into the center of the room and merely stood there. "Has something happened?" she asked.

"You said you were a witch," said Woodcott, gazing around the room at the posters and her books. Bast looked up at him and dashed off into the bedroom; the more stolid Isis merely yawned and closed her eyes. Gaye realized that he smelled strange; it was a mild day for September, but he'd been perspiring heavily . . . and it was a cold sweat, as though he was sick, but without the smell of a bacterial infection. Fear?

"Yes," she replied, cautiously.

"Do you know any spells to make somebody invisible?"

She blinked, then put her hand over her mouth to prevent herself from laughing. She was only halfway through her second brownie, enough to make her garrulous and a little giggly, but she didn't think she was stoned enough to start mishearing conversation. "Invisible?" she repeated.

"Yes."

"Oh, wow. I don't know. . . ." They looked at each other for several seconds, then both started as the phone rang. "Excuse me."

Woodcott nodded, and she brushed past him to get to the phone. "Hello?"

"Gaye? It's Charlie—Charlie Takumo. How are you?"

"I'm okay," she said, carefully. This close to Woodcott, she thought she could recognize the other smell under the fear: excitement, arousal. She kept her tone light. "Can I call you back in a few minutes? Detective Woodcott is here."

"What does he want?"

Partly because of the brownie, she answered without thought or hesitation. "He wants me to make him invisible."

"*What?*" asked Charlie, as Woodcott winced slightly.

"He asked if I know any spells to make him invisible. I don't, so I shouldn't be long. Can I call you back?"

"For sure. I'm at home, unless you want me to come around. Or call Kelly?"

"Kelly?" She thought for a moment. "No, I don't think so."

"Cool. Call me back when you can. Ciao."

"I don't want you to make *me* invisible," explained Woodcott, as she hung up the phone. "I was wondering whether there were spells to make somebody invisible, and how difficult they'd be. Off the record. Strictly off the record."

Gaye shook her head. "My old high priestess had a spell that could make cars invisible to, uh, cops . . ."

"What?"

"Maybe not invisible, exactly, but . . . not so noticeable. I don't think it worked on radar or cameras or anything like that, but it stopped . . . police looking at them if they were speeding just a little. Not me, of course," she added hastily. "I couldn't speed if I wanted to, not in *my* car."

"Could you cast a spell like that on a person?"

"*I* couldn't, no."

"What about your priestess?"

"I don't know; she died a year ago, and I don't know who taught her. Why?"

Woodcott stared at her for a moment, then said, "Something a witness said."

"Uh-huh."

"This case is so bizarre, we can't afford not to look into any leads. There's probably a natural explanation," he essayed a smile, "and that probably means our witness was drunk or crazy or on serious drugs. Thanks for your time."

"No problem," said Gaye, as she let him out. She locked and bolted the door, retrieved her hash brownie from the fridge, and took a mouthful, wondering whether she was stoned enough to have hallucinated the whole encounter, and if not, what drugs *Woodcott* might be on. She stood there for a moment, chewing, and remembered that someone had phoned during the conversation. Now, if she could only remember who it was . . .

Woodcott woke a few minutes after midnight, his skin clammy. His wife, Patty, a heavy sleeper accustomed to ignoring late night phone calls, didn't even stir as he carefully left the bed and walked to the shower, images of the three women from Tudor's house seeming to hover just outside his peripheral vision. He'd been dreaming of Tudor playing with all three simultaneously, a dream so detailed he could swear that he could have drawn the women's tattoos and jewelry from memory. It had been bad enough when he'd been watching from the outside, but when the viewpoint had shifted and he'd become Tudor and he still hadn't stopped . . .

Woodcott had been married for twenty-two years, and it had been at least ten since he'd felt this aroused. His sex life had been unspectacular even before he'd discovered that he was infertile, and since then, he and Patty had all but stopped trying— but they'd stayed together, partly because neither believed in divorce, but mainly because it felt better than coming home to an empty house night after night.

Woodcott shut and bolted the door behind him, peeled off his pajamas, and stepped into the shower without waiting for the water to warm up. He washed his face and his hands and his groin until they were almost numb, but the visions refused to go away.

Twenty minutes later, wearing a clean pair of pajamas, he sat at the kitchen table with a mug of cocoa, wondering what to do. He'd always been better at avoiding temptation than resisting it, and he had no idea how to resist *this* one. Maybe it was best just to stay away from Tudor's house; there was no evidence of an actual homicide, after all, and nothing to suggest that Julia Petrosyan had met with foul play. . . .

He shuddered, then drained the mug, placed it in the sink, and walked back up the stairs to his bedroom, silently praying for a dreamless sleep.

Takumo woke a few minutes after sunrise, and immediately reached for the knife hidden under the bed. He could hear someone in the apartment, probably the kitchen, yet none of the alarms had been triggered, and the power was still on. Without wasting the seconds it would take to get dressed, he opened the bedroom door, took a quick look into the kitchen, hoping there weren't *two* of . . .

"Morning, Charlie."

Charlie released his breath in an explosive gasp; the man in the kitchen had his back to him, and his hair was ash blond instead of black, but the voice was unmistakeable. "You could have warned me when you were getting here," he grumbled.

"No," replied Mage. "Your message said it was urgent, so I came as soon as I could. Besides, there was always the possibility that it was a trap. Tea?"

8

Mage

"**Thanks,**" said Takumo, turning around and walking back into the bedroom. He reemerged a moment later, wrapping a gi around himself. "Is it my imagination, or have you grown taller?"

"An inch or so, yes."

"Not exactly inconspicuous."

Mage shrugged. "Making myself taller was easier; the important thing is that I shouldn't match any description Nakatani might have circulated. I've changed my eye color too, and made some small changes to my face; I can always change them back if I need to."

Takumo sat down on a cushion. "The beard suits you. I won't ask where you're living, but how's the money holding out?"

"Fine. I can pay you back, if you like, with interest. I have plenty of ways of making money—though *exchanging* it without being noticed is more difficult, sometimes."

"It's cool. It was all Tamenaga's money, anyway." When Mage had been charged with the murder of Amanda Sharmon, Takumo had used the focus to win the money for his bail from

the Sunrise Casino, which Tamenaga had owned. When the
charges against Mage had been dropped, Takumo had insisted
on giving him the bail money. "Aren't you using it to buy food
for people in refugee camps in China, or something?"

"I was. The problem was getting it to them. I tried teleporting
into the camps with it, but I can't carry enough to feed that
many people. And then I started reading up on biochemistry,
and . . . well, I don't *think* the food changes at all when I teleport with it, but I might be wrong."

"Is that why you haven't carried the people out of the
camps?"

"One reason. I've no way of knowing what it might do to
someone until I try it, and I don't want to risk it unless there's
no other way. Besides, it was difficult enough not being noticed
when I was smuggling food; there's no way I could keep a stunt
like *that* secret. Besides, where am I supposed to take them?"
He shrugged. "So, what's your emergency? More trouble with
Nakatani?"

"No—well, nothing I can't handle. This is something weird.
I think there's another magician in L.A., someone powerful
enough to raise the dead, though I'm not sure he can control
them."

"Santeria?"

"Maybe. I don't know much about magic." And he told
Mage as much of the story as he knew, from Nick Petrosyan's
appearance at Gaye's window to Gaye's phone call the previous
evening. When he was finished, Mage sipped at his coffee and
asked, "What do you want me to do?"

"I don't know, but you defeated Tamenaga. . . ."

"I defeated him by killing him," said Mage, grimly. "I'm not
apologizing for that, but it was in self-defense. Okay, maybe
you're right, maybe Tudor is some sort of necromancer or whatever, but I'm not an avenging angel, not a vigilante, not the
Night Stalker—"

"He killed a kid!"

"You don't know that."

"Okay," Takumo admitted, "you're right, I don't *know* that—"

"Do you remember why Amanda stole the focus in the first place?"

"For sure. She had leukemia, and she used the focus to cure it."

Mage nodded again. "I remember when Kelly and I were going over the forensic reports, and she discovered that there was no trace of the cancer in Amanda's body . . . so after Tamenaga was dead, it occurred to me that maybe I could learn to do what she'd done. Cure cancer. And not only cancer, other diseases, like AIDS. Unfortunately, I can't, yet, because I don't know enough about medicine, I don't *understand* the disease process the way Amanda did . . . but I'm studying it and working in a clinic, and maybe someday I *will* understand.

"At the moment, all I'm doing is pretty superficial stuff, though even that can save lives; if I hadn't been able to heal the damage I'd taken in that fight with Tamenaga, I might've bled to death before you and Kelly showed up. I can't restore limbs, but I can heal burns, and lacerations, and erase scars . . . and if I keep working and studying, I may be able to do something *important*."

Takumo nodded. He'd used Amanda's focus himself, and knew that it changed reality according to the user's ability to visualize the world. Tamenaga and Amanda, as mathematicians, had changed it mathematically, altering the fluctuations of the stock market and the spread of cancerous cells; Mage, a photographer with an eye for detail, could make real whatever he could imagine. Takumo had used the focus to open locks and fix poker machines and roulette wheels, but had scared himself badly when he'd tried visualizing himself performing a flying jump kick. "Where are you doing this important work?"

"Everywhere . . . mostly places where they speak English; Italian isn't exactly a universal language, though I've picked up enough Spanish to get by, and a little French. I spend a lot of time in libraries." He shrugged. "And I do some cosmetic work, too. Prettier faces, minor body work, mostly breasts. What the Hell, if they didn't come to me, they'd just go to a plastic surgeon, and I'm safer. I give most of the money away, anyway. I have everything I need, and I don't want to end up like Tamenaga. And there's more. I think this magic costs more than we guessed."

"How?"

"Sometimes, when I've been using it, I . . . I can't touch things. It's like I'm a ghost, a hologram. . . ."

"Insubstantial?"

"Yeah, that's it. My hands pass straight through objects—at least, I've only noticed it happening to my hands."

A quote from *Hamlet*, "O! that this too too solid flesh should melt," came unbidden to Takumo's mind. "And only objects?"

"What? Oh. I can touch my own body, but I haven't tried touching anyone else—I don't want to frighten anyone or weird them out. Besides," he said, wryly, "I don't spend as much time touching other people as I used to."

Man, you have *changed*, thought Takumo. "How often does this happen? Do you have any control over it?"

"Not very often, but always after I've used the focus, especially if I use it to travel." He blinked. "Now that I think of it, I can always touch the focus, too, even when I can't touch anything else. It's as though it was part of me." He shrugged. "And my clothes don't fall through me, or anything like that. It may just be affecting my hands . . . but even so, it's been worrying me for a while. I think I'm developing *some* control, because the . . . problem . . . doesn't seem to last as long now, but it's not becoming any less frequent. A few hours ago, I had it happen after I'd used the focus to help heal someone, and that was a first. It's as though . . ."

"What?"

"I use the focus to change reality to the way I imagine it, right?"

Takumo nodded.

"Okay. What if I'm turning reality into an illusion? What if *I'm* becoming an illusion? What if, every time I make some small adjustment to reality, I'm becoming a little less real? Or what if it's some sort of punishment for killing the people I killed?"

Takumo looked uncertain. "I thought you said you were learning to control it?"

"I think so. I *hope* so. But if I'm going to magic myself out of existence, I want it to be for a good cause. So I'm sorry if I'm not more enthusiastic about your witch-hunt, or whatever it is, but I really feel as though I can do more good at the clinic, and I have no way of knowing how long I'm going to have the power—or the focus. What if Hotei wants it back?"

Takumo thought about this for a moment. Mage had told him a little about the conversation he'd had with Hotei, the Japanese god of gamblers and maker of the foci, but he suspected that he'd also left some things unmentioned. "It took him long enough to get it back from Tamenaga," he ventured. "Like fifty or sixty years, wasn't it? You've had it for two."

"Amanda had it for less than a week."

"She had one focus, Tamenaga still had two. It was nothing to do with Hotei."

"Maybe not, but I can't forget what he said about hoarding luck. I don't want to waste this power. I didn't ask for it, but I can't just give it up or do nothing with it, but I've never wanted to be a hero, either; I'm not a killer, and I'm sure as Hell not turning myself into a target again." He drew a deep breath. "So I apologize for my lack of enthusiasm, Charlie, but . . ."

"You can't come out to play until you've finished your homework?"

"I wouldn't have put it like that, but yes, if you like. If it was personal, maybe, but it isn't." He waited to see if Takumo would contradict him; he didn't. "Have you told Kelly about this magician?"

Takumo squirmed. "Hey, come on, man, you know Kelly. She won't believe it's her *birthday* without forensic evidence."

Mage shrugged slightly. "Then you'd better either find some evidence, or let it go. It sounds as though the only vampire, if it was a vampire, is already dead, anyway. So, what else is happening?"

Takumo made one last try. "Then can I have one of the foci?"

"What?"

"Just until this is over—until *I'm* sure this is over. I won't try to do any serious magic, just . . . I'd feel better if I had it. Please?"

Mage looked at him curiously. "Ok. It'll take me awhile to get it—it's on the moon—but if you're sure . . . I mean, when I offered it to you . . ."

"I said I didn't want that sort of power. Yes, I remember. You'd just beaten Tamenaga, and I thought we were out of danger. Now I'm not so sure. I still don't *want* the power, but I think I may *need* it. Besides, what if something happens to you, like, what if someone takes *your* focus and the others are on the freakin' moon?"

"Okay, okay. I'll get it."

"Thanks."

Julia woke, conscious only of her thirst, unable to remember language or even her name, human in form only. Instinctively, she began chewing on her lips and tongue and then, because these bled too slowly to satisfy her, her hands. Memory slowly returned as the thirst ebbed, until—as she did nearly every night—horrified at her own actions, she stopped biting her flesh. She stared at her fingers, watching the wounds heal in seconds. She licked her lips, now whole, tasting the last drops of blood.

She looked around the windowless room, slowly putting names to the things she saw. The glowing sphere above her head, burning bright in the infrared, was a light . . . electric light, yes. The large, soft box she was lying on was a bed. She could see nothing clearly more than a few feet away—it was as though she was covered by an inverted bowl of smoky glass— but she could hear voices, though she couldn't yet make out the words. She walked toward them, but stopped before she reached the circle drawn around the bed.

"Her father will die soon," warned Tudor, lighting a fresh cigarette. "Maybe tonight, maybe tomorrow; she's drinking only from him, now. If you want to keep her after tonight, you'll have to find a way to feed her."

Malachi shrugged. "If that fool cop comes back . . ." He made the words sound suspiciously like "full cup."

"He won't, and if he does, I'll use a stronger warding. Killing a cop is too big a risk."

"Then there's always the Greyhound station. Plenty of runaways who won't be missed for months, maybe years. Or the hookers down on the boulevard . . . Hell, who'd give a fuck if Adrian disappeared?"

Tudor shook his head, his expression dour. "Think, can't you? Adrian has a job; he'll be missed. We can't afford to draw attention to this area, can't afford to give them any excuse to search this house. If you must go hunting, do it somewhere else—but remember, they'll have to be warm, alive if possible or dead less than three or four minutes, and I'm not going to help you anymore. You've had two weeks with her that you wouldn't otherwise have had."

"You have to help me!" said Malachi, grabbing him.

"No," said his father, grimly. "I don't take orders from you, or anybody. She's your pet, you take care of her."

Malachi scowled as he walked out, though he was careful not to let his father see it. He stared into Julia's eyes, then stepped into the circle.

Gaye woke suddenly, too scared to move, and stared up at the ceiling for a moment until her eyes adapted to the darkness. She was relieved to find herself still in her own bed, not in the hospital, as she'd . . . thought? Remembered? Only dreamed?

She shook her head, then reached for the clock on the nightstand. Four fifty-one; no wonder the cats were still asleep. They

were inclined to wake her, demanding to be fed, as soon as the
sun began shining through her window, but dawn was obviously still some minutes away. She lay there, trying to piece
together the fragments of her nightmare. Two impressions were
strong—one of a death, and the other of . . . Well, something
that wasn't exactly death. Something hungry. And female. She
switched her reading lamp on, then grabbed her dream diary
and a pen, and hastily scribbled every thought, every word, that
came to her. Three pages later, she stopped, then went back and
read what she'd written, trying to make sense of it. Then she
turned the light out, lay down, and tried to go back to sleep.

She arrived at the hospital at eight A.M., and asked where
she could find George Petrosyan. The receptionist looked at her
monitor, then up again, her face a mask. "Are you a relative?"
she asked, sympathetically.

"No," she said, levelly, though she was already sure what
the answer would be. "I'm a nurse; his son was a patient of
mine. What ward is he in, please?"

A heartbeat's hesitation. "I'm afraid Mr. Petrosyan passed
away this morning—"

"*When?*"

"Sorry?"

"When? What time?"

Another glance at the monitor. "Several hours ago, I'm
afraid. Four fifty. Do you know where we could find any of his
relatives?"

"I don't know," replied Gaye. "Maybe." And she walked
away before the receptionist could ask any more questions.

Hollywood Boulevard by day looked more like an abandoned,
largely decrepit back lot than any sort of dream factory. Only
Mann's Chinese Theatre stood out as a recognizable landmark;
the strip shows, costume shops, and souvenir stores made it
look like a cheap copy of Bourbon Street (which hadn't much
impressed Gaye either, the one time she'd been there). She noticed tourists, looking disappointed and faintly bewildered,

walking past the used car lots and gazing down at the stars set into the pavement in search of names they recognized. She turned down Canyon Drive, found the Tudor house, parked outside, and pressed the button at the gate. A few minutes later, Tanith came wandering out of the house, wearing sweat pants and a Minnesota Twins sweatshirt. She stopped at the gate, and looked out rather blearily. "Yes? Can I help you?"

Gaye smiled back as convincingly as she could. "I hope so. I'm looking for Julia Petrosyan."

"You and everyone else," grumbled Tanith. "I'm sorry, she's not here, and we've been told not to answer any questions."

"I'm not a cop," protested Gaye.

Tanith smiled. "I know that, honey; I can spot a cop a block away. You're not a reporter either, but I'm sorry, Solomon's not seeing anyone today. I'm not even supposed to let you in—I would if I could, but it's his house, not mine."

Gaye looked through the gate at the shabbily tended grounds. "But she *was* here?"

"Yes," replied Tanith, after a moment's hesitation. "She lived here until about two weeks ago, but we haven't seen her since, and we don't know where she went. In fact, if you *do* find her, please let us know; I wasn't worried before, but now . . ." She looked at her closely. "How long ago did you know her?"

"I don't," Gaye admitted. "I'm from St. John's. Her father died this morning."

"Shit," said Tanith softly, then, "I'm sorry, I . . . I just don't know what else to say. Look, I'll just go and get you one of my cards; call me if you hear anything. Give me your number, and I'll do the same for you. Please?"

The sun was setting as Takumo returned home, and he stepped onto the balcony for a while to admire the colors. There were times when he considered leaving L.A.—going to New Zealand, maybe, and getting a job on *Xena: Warrior Princess*, being beaten up regularly by Lucy Lawless . . . it had a certain appeal, though he suspected that audiences might eventually wonder

what an Oriental was doing in Ancient Greece, apart from getting the crap kicked out of him every weeknight. He sighed,
shook his head, walked back into the apartment, and noticed
the light on the answering machine. He pressed the "Playback"
button and waited for the tape to rewind.

"Charlie?" He smiled, recognizing the voice as Gaye Lind's.
"Jesus, I hate these machines. I'm sorry I didn't call you back
last night, but things got a bit confused. I'll be home all day
and tonight if you want to call me back."

Charlie smiled, and folded up on a cushion near the phone
before calling. Gaye picked it up after three rings. "Hello?"

"Gaye? Charlie Takumo. How's it going?"

There was a moment's hesitation. "I'm okay," she replied.
"Ahhh . . . can we meet somewhere? I hate talking over the
phone. And not here."

"Dinner?"

"Yeah, okay."

He glanced at the salmon-colored sky. "D'you like sushi? I
know a good place on the Promenade. . . ."

"I'm vegetarian."

"Cool, no problem; I try to be, I just like fish occasionally.
Do you know Lotophagi's? In Westwood?"

"I'll meet you there. Seven o'clock?"

"I'll be counting the seconds."

"What?"

"Nothing." Takumo heard a faint sound of movement behind him, and turned around to see Mage standing in the doorway. Mage took a deep breath with obvious relief, then threw
him one of the foci. Takumo caught it and nodded his thanks;
Mage nodded in return, then disappeared, leaving nothing else
behind except a little moondust on the floor. "Seven is cool,"
said Takumo, managing to keep his voice level. "I'll see you
then."

"**W**here do you and Kelly know each other from?"

Takumo thought for a moment before answering. "She was

defending a friend of mine, and I, ah . . . things became complicated. Like I put up bail for him, but the people who'd set him up were still looking for him, and . . . I'd rather not talk about it. Anyway, it was like a couple of years ago, and I hadn't heard from her in months until she called to show me that photo. . . ." Gaye shivered slightly. "Do you still have a copy?"

"No, the cops took my only copy, and the negatives. Kelly should still have a copy. Why?"

"Not important," replied Takumo, and hastily took a large mouthful of his tofu burger.

"His father died this morning," said Gaye, quietly. Takumo swallowed. "I woke up just as it happened," she continued. "I felt . . . no, *felt* isn't strong enough a word. . . ." She was silent. He waited. "I *knew* he'd just died, and I *knew* that Julia was . . ."

"What?" he asked, after half a minute's silence.

"I knew where she was," she said. "I could feel something flowing between them. I know this sounds crazy, but it wasn't just a dream—not an ordinary dream, anyway."

Takumo considered this. "Where was she?"

"In Tudor's house. In Hollywood. I went there later that morning, but I don't know if she was still there; it didn't *feel* like she was still there, and the woman I spoke to seemed to be telling the truth when she said that she didn't know where Julia was . . . but I'm sure she *was* there, just before sunrise. I just don't know what to do now. They wouldn't even let me in."

Takumo nodded cautiously. "What do you *want* to do?"

"I don't know! I think Nick was trying to warn me, and the dream this morning . . . I just feel that something terribly *wrong* is happening. It's already killed Julia's family, and I don't think that's the end of it, and I want to do *something*, and you seemed like someone I could talk to about something like this. . . ." Takumo didn't answer. "I thought of calling Kelly, but I can't prove anything, and she won't do anything until I can, will she?" Takumo shook his head. Kelly was probably the least superstitious person he'd ever met.

"That detective, Woodcott, came around last night, but I

could tell he was scared, too scared to want to know. So I called you, instead. I hope you don't mind; I know this sounds weird and sort of silly. . . ."

"No," said Takumo, wondering whether he should tell her about the photograph. "No, a friend of mine used to read the *I Ching*, and I remember one time . . . well, she was absolutely right about something she couldn't have known about. And I've seen other things so strange that . . . well, maybe I'll tell you about them some day."

"Could you get into Tudor's house?" she asked, quietly. "Look around, see if she's there?"

If the suggestion startled Takumo, he managed not to show it. He took another bite of his burger to give himself time to think. "I don't even know what she looks like."

Gaye reached into her purse, and removed a folded piece of paper. Takumo looked at it—an enlarged color photocopy of a not-very-clear photograph of Julia, Nick, and their mother in front of a small Christmas tree—and shrugged. "Where did you get this?"

"From the hospital, this morning. After Nick died, and Mrs. Petrosyan realized how sick *she* was, she asked the nurses if they could try to contact Julia. She gave them this photo, and asked them to take copies. It's the best one she had—only about two years old."

Takumo pocketed it. "Are you that sure she's there?"

"I'm sure that she *was*," replied Gaye, "and not long ago. I don't know where she is now."

"Even if I could do it," said Takumo, guardedly, "even if I did . . . if I found something, it wouldn't be, what do they call it, probable cause?" Gaye looked blank. "It wouldn't be admissible as evidence. Like Kelly wouldn't be able to use it to get a warrant. I'm not even sure what crimes have been committed!"

"*Can* you do it?" asked Gaye, eagerly. "I saw the way you climbed up that wall. . . ." She smiled optimistically; it was a beautiful smile, and Takumo felt his resistance crumbling.

"I haven't seen the place," he said. "Let me have a look at it first, then I'll decide."

Unable to meet his father's eye, Malachi rolled over in bed and faced the wall.

"*Idiot!*" the magician snarled. "Am I going to have to shut you away in a circle, like her?"

"Nothing happened last night. . . ." muttered Malachi.

"That was before her father died! She gorged herself draining him—"

"You said she wouldn't feed again for—"

"*Need* to," snarled Tudor. "I told you she wouldn't *need* to feed again so soon, but I also warned you that she'd still thirst, and that thirst is stronger than anything else she feels—"

"She *stopped*," said Malachi. "She didn't *drain* me. . . ."

Tudor snarled, but that, at least, was true. The vampire had fed well since she'd been turned, and though this had not taught her moderation, it had given Julia the strength to recognize Malachi and stop short of killing him. "I'm going to call Ernst, have him look at you."

"What're you going to tell him?"

"As little as possible. And no matter what he says, stay out of the circle until *I* tell you it's safe."

Malachi turned around to face him. "Don't kill her! Please?" Tudor grunted something that might have been a word in some long-dead language. "And don't let her die."

"And who would you recommend I feed to her?" his father asked, with mock sweetness.

"There must be hundreds of wannabes out there who'd love to be bitten by her. . . ."

"And be turned? No, thank you. *One* vampire is trouble enough."

"What about Sindee? Or Beth?"

"I'll think about it. We can't afford any more unexplained disappearances just now." He shook his head. "I'll swear not to let her die if you swear not to go into the circle without my permission again. Do we have a deal?"

Takumo dressed in his usual dusty black, as invisible in the darkness as the best *shinobi shozuko*, and much less conspicuous on the street. Better protection, too; the leather jacket was heavy enough to cushion blows, and he'd sewn thin metal rods into the sleeves to armor his forearms. Under the jacket, he wore a black long-sleeved T-shirt with a hood, black sweat pants, and a black scarf that could be pulled up over his mouth and nose or used as a weapon. He donned black cotton gloves, and changed his socks for black tabi that would enable him to grasp small objects, including knives and shuriken, between his toes. Then he removed his weapons from hiding places around the apartment. The sword and scabbard, though useful, he left behind as being too conspicuous, and too hard to explain away. The *neko-de*, cat's claws, went into his backpack, as did the smoke bombs and his *kyotetsu-shoge*, a knife on a cord that could also be used as a grappling hook. A handful of *tetsubishi*, spikes to be scattered in an enemy's path to discourage pursuit, went into one pocket; eight shuriken, throwing stars, into another. He slipped a spring-loaded collapsible nightstick into his right sleeve, and clipped his favorite sheath knife—slim, all-black, two-edged, chisel-tipped, and balanced for throwing—to his waistband, under the jacket. Other gear—Swiss Army knife, black dust mask, gaffer tape, notebook, camera, pen, pepper spray, a mini-flashlight with a narrow beam, Plummer's lockpicks, and the picture of Julia—went into other pockets. A little nervously, he looped the focus around his left wrist, then pulled his sleeve up over it. He glanced at himself in the mirror, appraisingly; a little lumpy, maybe, but not obviously so, and more important, nothing impeded his movement or made any noise when he walked. He smiled, and murmured, "Ready whenever you are, Mr. de Mille." He felt a little childish, but he could live with that. He grabbed his motorcycle helmet, and walked out.

9

This palace of dim night

The gates were open as he walked toward the house on the other side of the street. He stopped, and looked in cautiously—this was *too* easy—and was almost caught by the headlights of an oncoming car. He vanished behind a tree, and a few seconds later, a dark blue Mercedes drove out and headed toward Hollywood Boulevard. Takumo noted the license plate before it disappeared, then watched the gates close. Slightly reassured, he looked in again and saw no cars, and no lights on that side of the house.

He waited for another twenty minutes—if someone had just left, then there was a good chance that someone else would still be awake in the house—then, after seeing no other signs of movement, crossed the street in the dim moonlight. He took a cautious sniff, but to his relief, there was no evidence of guard dogs. Takumo didn't like dogs, but he didn't like having to kill them, either. He climbed the wall without any difficulty, and took a longer look around the grounds. The grass had not been mown for some time, and was a little more than ankle-high—not deep enough to hide in easily, but enough to conceal traps and obstacles. The trees offered better hiding places, and he sneaked between two of the largest as he approached the house and circled it. No lights showed anywhere. So far, so good.

He found the kitchen door on his first circuit of the house, and checked it for alarms on his second. He took the focus—a loop of braided hair, with a key hanging from it—out of his pocket, and unlocked the door. He slipped inside silently, stood in the room until his eyes adjusted to the near-darkness, then shut the door behind him. The little red light near the ceiling was, as he'd hoped, from a smoke detector.

His plan was simple, if unoriginal; place a smoke bomb in the kitchen, behind the refrigerator, then wait outside to see who evacuated and hope he could recognize Julia Petrosyan in the dark from her old photo. Once inside the house, though, he began to wonder. If he saw Julia come rushing out, cool; if not, they'd gained nothing, and let Tudor know that it wasn't only the police who were interested in him, and then he might improve his security.

He stood there and listened. It was a little after two thirty, so it was hardly surprising that the house was as quiet as it was dark. He looked around the kitchen, saw two more doors, a dusty stove, a large refrigerator, a dishwasher, a percolator, a microwave, an old table, some chairs and stools, and the usual shelves and cupboards. There was a faint aroma of coffee, a fainter one of beer, but it was plain to Takumo that no one had done any real cooking in the room for at least a few days.

After listening to the silence for nearly a minute, he decided to risk using the penlight. The sheaf of papers stuck to the fridge door with assorted magnets proved to be takeout menus, but nothing more personal. He yawned, then cautiously opened the door and looked inside. Jolt Cola, beer, yogurt, diet soda, milk, leftover Chinese, a few rather limp carrots and sticks of celery, a bottle of Karloff vodka, two bottles of black nail varnish, and again, nothing with a name on it. He shut the door again, looked up at the smoke detector, and yawned. He felt like an idiot. Tudor's people had freely admitted that Julia *had* been here, until quite recently, so unless her body was in the freezer, the best he was likely to find in here was corroborative evidence.

He yawned again, and opened one of the interior doors a crack, and peered into the darkness. It took him a few seconds to recognize the clustered, faintly ghostlike shapes for what they were—high-backed chairs covered with dust sheets, around a table. A formal dining room; it smelled a little strange, but that was probably nothing worse than disuse. He yawned, wondering why the freakin' Hell he felt so tired all of a sudden this early in the morning. He looked at his watch, confirming that it was a few minutes shy of three A.M., and sniffed quietly. The air smelled normal, not particularly stuffy, and not—

He blinked, and realized that he'd been leaning against the door frame, with the door open, for several seconds—maybe even a few minutes. He shook his head. He'd never blacked out before, and he shouldn't be tired, he—

Another slow blink. Quickly, but as quietly as possible, he shut the dining-room door, and reached into his backpack for the smoke bombs. He'd thought of exploring the rest of the house, but something was obviously wrong here—either with him, or with the air, and either way, he had to get *out*. He lit the birthday cake candles, knowing they'd take between five and ten minutes to burn down and light the fuses, then knelt down to place the bombs behind the fridge—

He opened his eyes again when a drop of hot wax landed on his finger. The candles had obviously been burning for at least a minute. He put them in position hurriedly, then clambered to his feet and staggered out of the room, hanging on to the table. He was barely able to keep his eyes open as he fumbled with the doorknob, wondering which way to turn it to get the damn thing open—

He snapped out of it as soon as he stepped outside, a moment before the room filled with smoke and the alarm began to wail. He shut the door, without bothering to lock it, then ran back to the trees, sacrificing stealth for speed.

Once under cover, and wide awake, he sneaked around to the tree he'd chosen as a hiding place—it gave him a good view of both doors, as well as shadows to hide in—and glanced at his watch. Three eleven. He waited.

* * *

It took Tudor several seconds to recognize the sound of the alarm for what it was, and nearly a minute before he realized that nobody else was going to wake up and investigate. With unaccustomed haste, he climbed out of bed and stepped outside the protective pentacle inscribed on the floor, pinched out the wicks of his Hand of Glory, grabbed a caftan and a flashlight, and thudded down the stairs toward the sound.

Tudor had made the Hand during his apprenticeship, by inserting wicks into the fingers of a hanged man (fortunately for him, nothing in the grimoires said the donor had to have been hanged legally). It cast a magical sleep over the occupants of the house, and he'd lit it that night to keep the other occupants of the house from blundering about.

He smelled the smoke while he was only halfway down; he knew there was a fire extinguisher somewhere in the house, but . . . ah, yes, in the kitchen. He opened the kitchen door, and was met with a veritable wall of thick black sulfurous-smelling smoke, which collapsed around him as the door opened. Even though there was little heat and no other sign of a fire, he quailed, slamming the door shut and running back up to his room, where he grabbed his book of pacts and tried to organize his thoughts.

He had everything he needed to summon a water elemental, but the ritual would take too long, and asking a fire elemental to stop a fire was pointless. Panting slightly, he ran to Malachi's room, dropped the book on the bed, and tried to shake his son awake.

"Whuh?"

"There's a fire downstairs," Tudor hissed. "We have to get outside. I'll call the fire department, you wake the others. Do you understand?"

Malachi stared at him blankly through half-closed eyes, and Tudor began to worry. Dr. Ernst had assured him that he hadn't lost enough blood to take any serious damage, but Ernst's practice was in plastic surgery, not diagnosis. Unfortunately, he was the only doctor Tudor could absolutely trust to keep secrets. Finally, Malachi blinked. "Downstairs?"

"In the kitchen," said Tudor, but Malachi was already sliding out of bed. "Get the others and—"

"I'm going."

Tudor nodded, grabbed the book, and ran back to his room. He'd just dialed 911 when he heard somebody running down the stairs. He thought for a moment, and cursed silently; of course, his idiot son would think rescuing Julia more important than any of the others. "Operator," said a voice, interrupting his thoughts. "What service, please?"

"Fire," replied Tudor. If he woke Tanith (not easily done, he knew), that left Sindee and Beth and . . . what was his name? Not important, as long as he got out.

Tudor did not consider himself an evil man. A pragmatist, yes, who maintained a good working relationship with demons, certainly, but never evil for the simple sake of being evil. His encounters with evil had convinced him that its influence in the world was greatly exaggerated, and that much more harm was done by stupidity and ignorance.

Malachi thundered down the stairs into the cellar, barely slowing down as he scooped Julia off the narrow bed and swung around to carry her outside. Julia screamed as he carried her through the circle, and he looked down to see her skin turning red and bubbling as though it were melting. She curled up into a fetal position in his arms, trying to protect herself from whatever was hurting her. Malachi looked down, seeing the bubbles—blisters?—bursting, the red fading, as she healed. What the Hell—

The answer slowly dawned on him. The circle was not only a psychological barrier, like the one that kept the residents from looking in the cellar. It prevented Julia from leaving under her own power, but whatever was in its makeup was also actively harmful to her. "It's okay," he murmured, as he carried the still-screaming vampire up the stairs. "You're safe, now."

*   *   *

Takumo watched as the lights appeared in the windows around the front and side of the house, watched the smoke seeping under the kitchen door . . . when the front door opened, he froze, not even moving his eyes, and Malachi emerged, still cradling the naked Julia in his arms. Her face was turned away from Takumo, her hair was noticeably longer and darker than it had been in the photo, and it was difficult to do more than guess her height or weight while she was in that position. Takumo waited, hoping that they'd come close enough that he could get a good look at her face in the moonlight, not so close that they could see him.

Instead, Malachi staggered a few steps away from the door and stopped. Julia looked up just long enough for him to see that the wounds on her face had almost completely healed, and they smiled at each other before she buried her face in his neck. Takumo saw Malachi collapse to his knees, still careful not to drop her despite his weakened state, then folded up completely.

A moment later, a small woman clad in a black summer robe came hurtling out the front door, stopping just short of where Malachi and Julia lay huddled together. She stopped and bent over them, and the vampire looked up. "Julia?"

"Don't look at me!" the vampire shrieked, loudly enough for Takumo to hear. She slithered out of Malachi's grasp, backed away for a few feet, then turned and ran toward the gate.

"Julia!" Sindee yelled.

Takumo, startled, watched as the naked woman veered toward him slightly, then made a running jump onto the top of the wall. She looked back for a moment as Beth and Tanith came running out of the house, then dropped out of sight.

Sindee stared, then looked down at Malachi. Takumo couldn't hear what she said, but the way Tanith immediately dropped to her knees beside him and reached for his throat and his wrist, then placed her ear to his chest, told him more than he wanted to know. He closed his eyes for an instant, quietly

muttered, "Oh, shit," and began looking about for the best escape route.

The phone didn't wake Kelly instantly, but it woke Oedipus,
who immediately leaped onto her chest. Kelly opened her eyes
to see the cat's glowing eyes staring into hers, and let out a gasp
before realizing what was happening. She reached out for the
phone and muttered, "Barbet."

"Kelly? It's Charlie Takumo. Sorry for waking you, but I
think it's an emergency."

Kelly glanced at the clock beside the bed, and inhaled slowly.
"At this hour, Charlie, you'd better be pretty sure it's—are
those sirens I can hear?"

"Uh-huh. Fire engines. But that's not the emergency."

"Oh."

"I think I just screwed up. Badly. Not the fire, that's just a—
anyway, I think I've found Julia Petrosyan."

Kelly hesitated. "I didn't know you were looking for her."

"I'll explain that later. What's important is that last I saw
her she was naked, and running toward Hollywood Boulevard."

Kelly nodded. She suspected she was having a lucid dream,
but after a moment's thought, she decided that the best course
was to act as though she was awake. "What do you want me
to do? Do you think she's a danger to herself?"

To *herself*? wondered Takumo, as he looked around anxiously. "That's one of the things I'm not sure about . . . can you
call the cops, ask them to put out an A.P.B. for her but to
approach with caution? I'll try to find her before anyone else
does."

Tudor carefully placed his book of pacts on the ground as he
crouched beside his son's body, searching for signs of life. "I
couldn't find a pulse," said Sindee, anxiously. "What do you
think it was, suffocation?"

"Looks like a heart attack," suggested Tanith, who'd seen a few. "Can anyone do CPR?"

"I can," said Beth, quietly, her tone suggesting that it was already too late.

Tudor shook his head. "We need to get him to a hospital," he said in his most persuasive tone, and looked up at the group. "I didn't ask them to send an ambulance. I'll need somebody's car."

"When was the last time you drove?" asked Tanith, dubiously. "*I'll* take him."

"I want to stay with him," replied Tudor, stubbornly, hastily thinking of an excuse for taking somebody else. Tanith's antique Corvette was only a two-seater, and Adrian rode a motorbike, which left Sindee's Rabbit and Beth's Subaru as the only other options. "Do either of you have your keys?"

Beth glanced down at her black T-shirt and cotton panties, and grimaced. The young dancer shoved her hands into the pockets of her robe, and fished out keys and her wallet. "Let's go," she said, unhappily.

Takumo rode slowly down Hollywood Boulevard, faster than he thought Julia could run, but slow enough for him to scan both sides of the street for her. None of the women he saw were actually naked, though a few seemed to be working on it. After five blocks, he turned around and rode the other way for another ten blocks without a glimpse of her. He did, however, see enough places where *he* could have hidden to convince him of the hopelessness of his task.

"Hey! Baby!"

Julia slowed her pace to a walk, and looked around. Her hunger sated at last, she was able to think relatively clearly. In a moment, she realized that she was on Hollywood Boulevard, several blocks from Tudor's house, and stark naked. She turned and looked at the car and its driver. He grinned, whistled, and pulled up to the curb, the Offspring's "Pretty Fly (for a White Guy)" blaring from his car's speakers.

"On your way to work?" he asked. She glanced ahead, saw the marquee for a peep show. "Can I give you a ride?"

She stopped, and tilting her face so that her mouth was hidden by shadow, said softly, "Aren't you going the wrong way?"

"For you, I can turn around. Get in."

She did, and he drove into a side street and parked. "How much?" he asked. She stared at him; her eyes wide and black apart from a hint of a red glow where the whites had been.

"Everything," she replied, as she reached for him. A few minutes later, she dumped his body, clad only in leopard-skin bikini briefs, out of the car.

"**R**ight at the next corner," said Tudor, lighting a cigarette.

Sindee looked at him quizzically. "The hospital's—"

"I know a doctor who lives on this street. He'll be able to help."

Sindee didn't speak. She knew enough first aid to be fairly sure that Malachi was already dead, and she was beginning to wonder why Tudor had forbidden anyone to try mouth-to-mouth resuscitation. She was also wondering why everyone had obeyed; granted that Tudor had presence, charisma, call it what you would, none of his orders tonight had made much sense. Despite this, she found herself turning right as he'd commanded.

Dr. Ernst was obviously unhappy to be woken at four A.M., and even more upset when Tudor placed Malachi's lifeless body on his living room couch. He stared at the body through bleary eyes, and ran a hand ineffectually through his ruffled silver hair. "What am I supposed to do?" he whispered. "Write a death certificate?"

Tudor shook his head. "I just need you to keep him here," he said, just as softly. "There are firemen blundering around my house. Keep him in darkness during the day—I know you can do *that*—and I'll be back for him before sunset." He turned to Sindee. "And I'm afraid, my dear, that I'll have to ask you to stay here, as well."

She stared at him for an instant, then muttered, "Fuck *you*," turned on her heel, and prepared to run. Tudor snapped out a few words in a forgotten language and pointed with the cigarette, the ruby in his ring glowed, and the doorway before her was suddenly filled with a wall of flame. As she stared, horrified, the wall became a semicircle, and suddenly transformed into the form of her father, arms outstretched to embrace her. Involuntarily, she took a step back, and Tudor grabbed her arms and lifted her from the ground. She kicked back with all her strength, her foot slamming into his thigh, but he held her firm.

Ernst stared stupidly at them until Tudor barked out his name, then snapped out of his daze and scuttled into the kitchen. Sindee screamed out obscenities and continued to struggle as best she could, using all the tricks she'd been taught to discourage rapists as well as moves learned from her oil-wrestling days, but Tudor shrugged off all her blows.

Ernst reemerged a moment later, holding a filled syringe. Sindee gathered all her strength and attempted to kick it out of his hand, but she was moving too slowly, and he ducked easily. Tudor held her down on the couch, on top of Malachi's corpse, while Ernst lifted up her robe and unceremoniously jabbed the needle into her gluteus maximus. Sindee shrieked in pain, and thought she heard him chuckle.

10

Hunters

The phone woke Takumo from a short sleep filled with horrible dreams. He rolled over and groaned, "Hello?"

"Charlie?"

He recognized the voice as Kelly's, the static suggesting that she was using her cell phone. He opened his eyes, and glanced at the clock: 8:07. He vaguely remembered waiting up to see the sunrise before turning around and coming home. "Yeah."

"I hate to ask this," she said, then, hastily, "but there was a corpse found on LaBrea, a block from Hollywood Boulevard, at four ten A.M. Do you know anything about it?"

"What?" He heard Kelly exhale; fortunately, it sounded more like relief than exasperation. "Was it—was she—?"

"He," replied Kelly, guardedly. "A John Doe, so far; Caucasian, short brown hair, hundred and seventy-four pounds, five eight, nothing on him but underpants and a fake Rolex."

"How did he die?"

"The bruises suggest that he was strangled, by someone with rather small, very strong hands, though until a post is done . . . Did you . . . see anything unusual, when you were out there?"

Where do I begin? thought Takumo. "Was he ex—had he lost any blood?"

"What? Charlie, if you know anything about this—"

"I don't," said Takumo, firmly.

Kelly sighed. "Okay. I was going to go to the dojo this morning for a workout. Do you want to meet me there?"

When she arrived Takumo was working out with her sensei, throwing kick-punch combinations into a padded shield with startling speed and precision. "Sorry I'm late," she said, and bowed to both of them.

" 'S cool," replied Takumo. Neither man looked away from his opponent for an instant. "You sure you want to do this?" the sensei asked her, as Takumo kicked the shield enough to rock him backward. The sensei, Johnny, was a powerfully built Hawaiian, scarcely taller than Takumo but with at least twice his mass. Kelly had seen him sparring with black belts, once taking on five at a time, but she'd never seen him sweat before.

"Yes," she said.

He shook his head. "He hurts you, you sue him, not me. Got it?"

"Yes. Don't worry, he's an old friend."

"Okay. You know where the first-aid kit is. I'll be in my office."

Takumo watched him leave. "Sorry about last night."

Kelly nodded, and ritually bowed, ending on her knees with both hands on the mat. She was wearing her white gi with her green belt; Takumo wore sweat pants and a faded *The Crow* T-shirt. "Where did you make that call from?" she asked.

"A pay phone outside a gas station on Hollywood Boulevard. Why?"

"Do you know where, precisely?"

"I could find it again, if I needed to. Come on, I thought you wanted a workout."

She rose, throwing a punch in the same movement. He dodged it, and she tried a spin kick. He caught her shin easily and helped it on its way, flipping her over. "I see Johnny's taught you how to fall. Why's the gas station important?"

"The body they found," she said, standing, her expression grim. "Hypostasis wasn't visible when they found him at four ten, so he'd been dead less than an hour—"

"Was there enough blood in his body to—" He touched her under the ribs before she could react. She didn't even notice his left hand moving until it stopped; if he hadn't pulled the blow, it would have knocked the wind out of her. She grabbed at it, but it was already gone, and his right tapped her on her collarbone. She leaped back before he could touch her again.

"He was strangled," Kelly said quietly, as Takumo bowed. "Not stabbed. Cause of death was simple asphyxia. They're waiting for the bruises to come up and give a clearer picture of the hand."

"One hand?"

"It looks like it. Long slender fingers."

"Right or left?"

"Charlie—"

"Just curious. No, I don't know anything about it."

Kelly hesitated. "What were you doing in that area at that time of the morning?"

"Looking for Julia."

"Why?"

"Why are the cops looking for her?"

"They're not. Woodcott seems to have given up; no one's officially reported her missing, there's no evidence of a homicide, and they've dropped the charges against the nurse. . . . I think Woodcott still suspects that satanists stole the boy's body for some ritual, but as far as I know, he hasn't even applied for a warrant to search the place. That's where you were, isn't it?"

Takumo was silent for a moment. "I saw her come running out of the house, naked, and jump over a high stone wall. By the time I'd *climbed* over that wall, she was gone. I took a guess at which way, jumped on my bike, and called you a few minutes later. I didn't see her again." He shrugged. "Maybe she murdered your John Doe."

Kelly looked unconvinced. "Why would she?"

"For his clothes? His car? His wallet?"

Kelly nodded. "How high was the wall?"

"About eight feet."

"If she was on serious drugs—PCP, say—could she have jumped it?"

"And been strong enough to strangle someone with one hand? Maybe." She stepped forward, feinted with her left hand and prepared to strike with the right, but Takumo caught both. Sensing that he was about to flip her again, she moved quickly and kissed him on the mouth. He blinked, and she slammed him to the mat and pinned him down with her legs.

"Nice move," he said, an instant later. "Bet it doesn't work next time."

She let go, and stood. She knew better than to help him up. "You know nothing about this man's death? You had nothing to do with it?"

Takumo back-somersaulted onto his feet, and instantly into a defensive stance, then bowed. "All I know is what you've told me. If Julia killed him, then I guess I'm indirectly responsible, but that's all."

"Okay. Because if the cops ever find out that someone called me from that location at that time, I'm going to have to say something. If you need me to defend you, I will, but I won't perjure myself."

Takumo nodded. "I wouldn't ask you to . . . though I think we can help each other."

"To do what?"

"Find Julia."

"Why? What's your interest in this? I know, you like the nurse, but is that all?"

"It was," admitted Takumo, "but not anymore. I think more people are going to die of whatever killed the Petrosyans; I think more bodies are going to turn up, some of them mutilated like Nick's; and I think Tudor's behind it somehow, even if it's now out of his control. And before you ask, the only evidence I have is that photograph of Nick, and I'm not sure what that proves, but I think it's important that we find Julia. Can you trace a license plate for me?"

"What? Why?"

"I saw a car leaving the Tudor house a little after two; it's not much, it may be nothing, but it's the best lead I have." Kelly looked uncertain. "Tell them you're trying to track down a possible witness, or something." Silence. "I can get the information in a couple of hours for forty bucks, no questions asked, and you know it, but I'd rather we worked together."

She hesitated, then nodded. "Okay. Anything else?"

"Anything new about the murder this morning, and any other strange, violent deaths." Kelly raised an eyebrow wryly. "Okay, any that involve exsanguination, decapitation, impaling, or garlic; that should narrow it down to a manageable number. And anything about Tudor or the others in the house."

"I'll see what I can do. If I asked you to stay out of trouble, would I be wasting my breath?"

Takumo grinned, then shouted a *kiai* and leaped at her. She ducked, and he landed beside her; she was still turning around when he tapped her at the base of the spine. She threw a punch, and he caught her wrist and kissed her fist before sweeping her leg out from underneath her. "I promise to be careful," he said, then stepped back and bowed. "That's the best I can do."

Tudor returned home late in the morning, exhausted by the demands of the spells he'd had to cast to prevent Sindee from escaping. He told the others, who were eating breakfast in the dining room, that he and Sindee had taken turns dozing on a bench in the hospital waiting room until Malachi had been removed from the critical list, and that she'd then gone to stay with a friend near the hospital before going to work. He knew it wouldn't take Adrian and Beth long to become suspicious; eventually they'd wonder why she hadn't come back for some clothes.

The news he heard from Tanith did nothing to improve his mood. The firemen had discovered no signs of a fire, only of a smoke bomb set off in the kitchen. The police had been called in, and had questioned Adrian, Tanith, and Beth until apparently convinced of their innocence. Tudor had little doubt that they'd be back to talk to him, too, and to ask after Malachi and Sindee; the only hope was that they'd consider further investigation a waste of time.

There was no sign of a forced entry, either by the firemen or the intruder. The kitchen door was unlocked, and Tudor remembered locking it after he'd lit the Hand of Glory, so it was unlikely that any of the residents had gone out that way. Tudor considered having the lock taken apart and the tumblers examined for scratches, evidence of having been picked, but decided against it; enough people had passed through the house over the years that the intruder might have obtained a copy of a key from a former occupant. Tudor decided to have the lock changed, just in case, and to cast a few protective spells when he had the time and the strength.

He stayed in the house just long enough to pack a bag full of the materials he'd need for a protective talisman, to prevent Malachi from feeding on *him*. He was looking through his grimoires for the appropriate spells when he suddenly remembered Malachi's mother. He had not seen Angela since before her wedding, many years before, but he was fairly sure he would have heard if she'd died. He wondered if she was still living in L.A., and whether he should warn her, and finally decided against it.

He grabbed the bag and walked out, but heard Adrian, Beth, and Tanith still talking as he reached the bottom of the stairs. "But they weren't pissed enough to start a real fire," pointed out Adrian, between mouthfuls of scrambled eggs, "which would've been a lot easier."

"Maybe it's meant as a warning," suggested Beth.

"Warning?" asked Tanith.

"Or a threat."

"Aimed at who?"

"I don't know. All of us, maybe."

"Maybe it was something to do with Julia," said Tanith.

Tudor flinched. He left the bag by the door, and walked quietly toward the dining room. "Maybe she did it," Tanith continued. "She liked melodrama, and she had a key, and . . ."

"I don't see her using smoke bombs, though," said Adrian. "She's more the threatening letter sort."

Beth stared down at her food. "When I was running down the stairs, I thought I heard Sindee shouting something. Did anyone else catch it?" Tanith shrugged, Adrian shook his head. "I thought it sounded like 'Julia' . . ."

Tudor managed not to swear, but he was suddenly very glad that it was Sindee, not Beth, who'd grabbed her car keys. He'd also heard her shout *something* while he was on his way downstairs, but he hadn't made out any words. "Why would she say that?" asked Adrian.

"I don't know; maybe she didn't. Maybe I misheard her. I didn't think to ask."

Another silence, then Adrian said, "Tanith, you've lived here for years; has anything like this ever happened before?"

"Like what?" asked Tanith. "Smoke bombs? No. Threats? Lots of times. People breaking in? Yes."

"Who?"

"Kids, sometimes—probably just hoping to see some naked people—but usually deprogrammers, especially back in the Reagan days, when the media was blaming satanists for everything from child abuse to cattle mutilation. But I think it's more likely the cops are right, and this was just a prank."

Tudor smiled slightly, and began walking away. "Maybe," said Beth. She didn't sound convinced.

Dr. Ernst looked in on his "patients" uneasily. Sindee still seemed to be unconscious, and Malachi still seemed to be dead. *Seemed*, Hell. Ernst had tried most of the standard tests to check for signs of life, without success; Malachi had no pulse or heartbeat that Ernst could detect, his breath didn't fog a cold mirror held over his mouth, his body temperature had dropped to seventy-eight degrees, he didn't flinch when ice water was poured into his ear, his finger didn't redden after a ligature was applied, and it looked as though rigor mortis was beginning to set in.

Ernst stared at them for a few seconds, then closed and locked the darkroom door and walked back downstairs to his den and gazed at the shelves and glass-fronted cabinets full of Barbie dolls. It was one of the best collections in L.A., if you included the costumes and modifications that Mattel had never authorized, and he liked to think of it as his only weakness. Tudor, unfortunately, knew better.

Ernst was not a satanist; he believed in neither God nor Devil. He had attended a Walpurgisnacht ritual at Tudor's temple after being invited there by one of his clients, one of the many porn stars he'd surgically enhanced. He'd found it entertaining enough that he returned six months later, at which point Tudor had offered to pander to his peculiar tastes. He described these in sufficient detail that Ernst had expected to be blackmailed, but Tudor had never asked for money and only occasionally for favors.

Hundreds of pairs of painted eyes smiled at him as he sat in his chair and sweated. He would have liked a drink, but it didn't seem like a good idea, not until after Tudor had left and taken his . . . taken the others with him.

Tudor arrived exactly on time, as always. While most of the rituals he performed were showy fakes, precise timing was so important when dealing with demons that he never allowed himself to slip up. "About time you got here," blustered Ernst, nonetheless.

"Is the girl secure?"

"I'm keeping her sedated. She'll be out until after I get back."

Tudor read his face carefully; he knew that Ernst found women more attractive when unconscious, though he was no necrophile. "Is that safe?"

"It's safer for *me*. All you told me is that you wanted her alive and undamaged."

Tudor nodded. He planned to keep Sindee to feed to Malachi—and to Julia, if he could lure her back to the house. If he could prevent them from draining her, he might be able to keep her alive until he could provide more victims without arousing undue suspicion. He wondered whether she would want to become a vampire, then decided against it; feeding two of them would be difficult enough. Better just to kill her. First, though, he'd need to think of a better excuse to explain her disappearance—and not only from the house, he realized. Tanith would soon find out that Sindee wasn't turning up at work, either. Maybe a staged suicide? And he had to get her car out of Ernst's garage, too . . . maybe sending it off the road and into one of the canyons, with her in it? Maybe then nobody would notice that she'd been all but drained of blood. . . .

"What's so funny?" asked Ernst.

"What?"

"You're smiling."

"I think I've come up with a way out of this mess," said Tudor, and headed up the stairs. Ernst watched him leave. "Yeah?" he muttered. "Who for?"

The ritual to complete the talisman took several hours; tired as he was, Tudor was careful not to make any mistakes. If he had to backtrack, the sun might set before he finished, and Malachi could begin to feed at any time after that. When he emerged, Ernst was waiting, a large cheap crucifix around his neck. Despite his exhaustion, Tudor laughed. "Won't it work?" asked the doctor.

"Only if at least one of you has faith in it," replied the sorcerer. "I wouldn't rely on it."

"What does work, then?"

"That depends on the vampire, and what they believed in life. I was able to confine Julia with a circle of salt, candle-wax, garlic, chalk, eucharistic wafer, and prayer, but *her* background is mostly American pop culture, and cultural background is a major consideration when it comes to deterring vampires. When they're not hungry, they still think much the same way as they did when they were alive, at least at first. The ones that endure gradually learn what can and can't hurt them, and act accordingly."

Ernst nodded. "How did he . . . what happened?"

"The usual: A vampire drank enough of his blood to kill him. It's more complicated than that, of course, but that's all you need to know."

"How do you kill one?" Tudor looked at him sharply, and Ernst paled. "I wouldn't harm your son, you know that, I'd never do anything like that . . . but just in case he turns the girl . . ."

"Sindee?" Tudor smiled thinly. "The only ways to kill a vampire quickly are cremation and decapitation; countries with a tradition of cremation usually have fewer vampire legends than those that don't. Exorcism works, but even if you know the appropriate ritual, it takes time, and the body can not be revived; it soon decays as completely as it would have in the time since it was turned. Burying one, in a concrete grave-liner and under six feet of earth, preferably with roses thrown on top of the coffin, is usually enough to stop one rising, but not from feeding on her family. Starving weakens them, but it doesn't kill until the stomach has rotted away, which takes about a month; until then, they can be revived with as little as a cup of blood. Salt and garlic seem to be distasteful to them, maybe even poisonous, possibly because garlic kills leeches. Sunlight will prevent them healing wounds, and hasten decay so quickly that it can generate heat in some cases, but despite what you've seen in the movies, it won't entirely destroy the body unless it's been dead long enough to have rotted away normally—and in the meantime, the vampire will scream horribly and try to escape. And it has to be direct sunlight, and the clearer the air, the better; there are reports of fresh vampires walking around unharmed before dusk in England and parts of Europe, and less reliable claims of them rising at noon. Even an old vampire can ignore the pain for a time, if it's well-fed, and recover from the damage over his next few feedings—or so the grimoires say, but that information comes from demons and other sorcerers, so it may all be a lie."

"I thought you were supposed to hammer a stake through their hearts?"

"If you pin them to the ground, it immobilizes them and makes them easier to kill, especially if you sever the spine—the heart is inconsequential, and in many countries they aimed for the stomach instead—but it's temporary. If the stake is removed, they can continue as they were, and the wound will heal over eventually. Julia's brother was able to walk, and climb, with his intestines hanging out from the autopsy incision."

Ernst shuddered.

"Piercing the stomach can prevent the vampire taking enough blood to regenerate," Tudor continued, "but the only reasons for choosing staking over decapitation is that the trunk is a larger target than the neck, and that vampire suffers agony until it dies; I suspect it was mostly used by sadists and the misinformed. If you *must* do it, though, use a barbed spear, preferably one with barbs that point both ways—or iron forks, as the Romanians used to recommend—and it works better if you get them in the back. A vampire that's strong enough, one that's fed well recently, can pluck the stake out or even climb up it like a boar on a spear, if there isn't some sort of crossbar to hold it down. That may have contributed to the idea that a cross, or a cross-shaped sword, will hold one at bay, but I wouldn't rely on it."

"Is there something that works *better* than the cross? In case I need to protect myself?"

"Mirrors sometimes work, mostly because they reflect sunlight, and vampires fear things that can hurt them badly enough—at least, when they're not hungry. When they are, they're about as stupid and stubborn as sharks, and as easy to scare. A cross is the equivalent of a . . . a warning sign, neither more nor less. A threat to invoke the power of God. Some vampires can even be scared away with things like St. Christopher medals, and he's not even a real saint anymore. But in your case, it's no more than a bluff; any halfway perceptive vampire would smell your fear and realize that you're no more eager to confront God than it is."

Ernst looked at the cross dubiously. "Is there a God?"

"There are many; millions, I suspect, though many of them go by different names and forms in different cultures, so counting them is impossible. You can call most of them demons, or angels, or spirits, if you prefer, unless you're asking them for help—many of them like to be flattered, even if their sphere of influence is just a little patch of ground somewhere. Sorcery's just a matter of knowing who to ask for what, and how."

"What about—"

"Later." Tudor glanced at his watch. "When do you expect Sindee to come around?"

"In about an hour. I can't be any more precise than that—and I don't want to risk giving her another shot, not just yet. You said you wanted her alive. . . ."

"I do. Vampires don't feed on the dead; there are revenants that do, but they're even worse houseguests than vampires. I'm going to have something to drink, and then I'm going to sit and wait for Malachi to rise. You can watch, or not, as you like, but while you're in the darkroom, do *exactly* what I say. Do you understand?"

Mandaglione looked at his e-mail, and drummed his fingers on the desk. He was used to unusual requests, but this one was strange even for Charlie Takumo.

> Dante,
> I'm looking for any available information on Solomon Tudor, writer/producer of DEVILSPAWN, and High Priest of the Church of Endless Night. Scandal and gossip useful as well as reliable info. Thanks.
> Charlie

Mandaglione shook his head, and reached for the phone. While he depended on e-mail, and frequently used it to stay in touch with friends who lived a few suburbs away, there were times when he felt the need to hear someone's voice. "Charlie? Dante. I can get this stuff for you, but why do you want it?"

There was a silence at the other end of the line, and a horrible thought struck Mandaglione. "He's not making another fucking movie, is he?"

Takumo laughed. "Nothing that scary," he said, unconvincingly. "At least, I don't think so. There's been some weird shit going down, and he may be behind it; like it's probably just a publicity stunt, or some sort of scam, but some people are starting to worry."

"Does this have anything to do with that photo you asked me about a couple of days ago?"

"It might," came the guarded reply. "Anyway, I know how much you know about horror films and B-movie scream queens, and I read some of those articles you wrote about cults. . . . I thought that maybe if you said you were working on a history of horror and exploitation movies, well, you have cred, people would believe you, and they'd tell you stuff they'd never tell me. . . ."

"What exactly has happened?"

"Someone stole a kid's body from an autopsy room, right under the pathologist's nose," said Charlie, quickly. "It was found a couple of days later, decapitated, with the mouth stuffed with garlic."

"Yeah, I heard about that."

"The kid's parents died of some wasting disease, same as the kid; the cops went looking for his sister and found out she was a member of Tudor's coven, living in Tudor's house, but she's disappeared. The photo was of the kid who was decapitated." Takumo wondered whether to tell him anymore, and decided against it.

"*London After Midnight,*" said Mandaglione.

"What?"

"One of Lon Chaney's last films; he plays a detective who plays a vampire to catch a murderer. You've probably seen pictures of Chaney in it; top hat, Marty Feldman eyes, and animal teeth. Directed by Tod Browning, last film they ever did together; Browning remade it with Lugosi a few years later. Tudor would have heard of it, at least . . . you think that's all it is?"

"Yeah," said Takumo, after a moment's hesitation. "It sounds like a good explanation. I think he's trying to scare someone—I'm not sure who, but a friend of mine's gotten mixed up in it. Why? You don't believe in vampires, do you?"

Silence. "No, I guess not, it's just . . . well, it'd make life a little more interesting," he said, with a faintly regretful tone. "Okay, Charlie. I'll see what I can dig up."

Tamenaga walked into Nakatani's office at the Sunrise without being announced—proving to Nakatani that his staff was more afraid of her than they were of him, not that he'd ever doubted that. She had a fax in her hand, and a broad smile on her face. "Have you seen this?" Nakatani looked away from the spreadsheet for long enough to glance at the header on the fax, then shook his head. "It's the latest report on Takumo," Tamenaga enthused. "They've identified two women who he's been seeing recently." Nakatani tried to look impressed, but failed. "Takumo's psychoprofile says that if he has to choose between protecting a male friend or a woman, he'll almost certainly favor the woman—and now we have *three*, including Mika Ward, though she's an unknown quantity. He hasn't seen her since she married, though I suspect he'd still feel honor-bound to try to save her."

"Who are the others?"

"One is Kelly Barbet; she's a lawyer with the public defender's office in L.A. No photo or description as yet—Lamm's seeing what he can find on the Web—but we know she was Magistrale's lawyer. The other is Gaye Lind, a nurse at St. John's Hospital."

"Any idea what the connection between them might be?"

"Barbet is studying martial arts, and Lowe thinks Takumo may be giving her private lessons. We don't know *how* private; Lowe's men are doing their best to shadow him, but it's hard to tail a motorbike through L.A., particularly the way Takumo drives." Nakatani nodded, a faint smile on his face; he hadn't ridden a bike in years, but in his student days at UCLA, there'd been few things he enjoyed more than pushing his Honda to the limit. The only criminal record he had was a string of convictions for speeding; since then, he had never even been arrested. "Lind is a complete unknown. Takumo had dinner with her on Saturday night, returned home, then went out again at two and didn't return until nearly seven. Phone records for the past week show two calls from Barbet, one from Lind, and one to her home number. Maybe it's time to start tapping his phone again."

"If you're sure it won't just make him more cautious," said Nakatani, neutrally. To his way of thinking, the tap had proved to be an unnecessary expense in the past, establishing only that Magistrale never called Takumo at home and vice versa.

Tamenaga considered this. "You're right. We may have enough already. I'll have Lamm and Lowe find out what they can about these women, and pass it on to Krieg. We may be able to use her sooner than I expected." She smiled, and walked out. Nakatani sat back in his chair, wishing it were his bike, and closed his eyes.

11

Out of the Shadows

Malachi opened his eyes—or *something* opened them, at any rate, Tudor thought grimly—and looked around. Tudor had placed Sindee inside the circle next to him; she was conscious, but thoroughly restrained with gaffer's tape. As Malachi sat up, she looked around in alarm and began squirming, trying to crawl out of the circle.

Tudor let her try. He stood leaning against the darkroom's only door, with Ernst's pistol in his pocket.

Malachi scrambled to his feet, took an unsteady step toward him—then, too weak to walk, tottered. One of his hands touched the edge of the circle as he tried to break his fall, and there was a soft sizzling sound and a faint smell of burnt flesh. With a howl, Malachi jerked his hand back and began sucking his blistering fingers. He bit deep into his flesh, and sucked at the blood that spurted out.

Tudor braced himself against the door, but felt none of the weakness or pleasure that came from a vampire's bite; the talismans he'd created to shield himself were obviously effective.

Sindee was working her jaw and rubbing her cheek against her shoulder, trying to dislodge her gaffer tape gag. Tudor yawned, and produced the gun, only a five-shot .25-caliber automatic, but effective enough as a threat. Malachi continued to gorge himself, and Tudor waited for several minutes before the vampire paused. "Malachi," he said, "can you speak?"

The vampire opened its mouth, but no sound issued forth except a strangled hiss.

"You *can* hear me, though. Can you understand what I say?"

The vampire nodded. Its eyes blazed, but there was a hint of awareness there.

"Good. Do you know what's happened to you?"

The vampire opened its mouth again, removing the fingers, and its eyes dulled. A moment later, it moaned "JU-UUULIAAAAA!" Sindee whimpered, and lost control of her bladder.

Tudor ignored her. "Yes," he said. "Julia bit you again, and this time she drained you. Do you know what you are?"

The vampire nodded, as though unable to utter the word.

"Then listen," said Tudor. "When you've finished feeding, and can speak and walk, I'm going to let you out of the circle and take you home. I'll tell the others that you're still sick, so you won't have to say much. If you do exactly as I say, I'll bring Julia back for you," he said, with more confidence than he felt. The vampire stared back at him, its expression sullen, and Tudor turned to Sindee.

"Back into the circle," he snapped, in his most commanding tone. She stared at him through her tears. "I'll shoot you in the leg if I have to," the sorcerer continued. "Both legs. I won't promise not to kill you, but if you do as I say, you may live for another few days, maybe as much as a week, and without any pain. Defy me, and you will suffer more than you can imagine."

Sindee glared at him, then looked back at Malachi, who had managed to stand, though he seemed too unsteady to walk. She rolled back until she was just inside the circle, but it was enough to satisfy Tudor. "Malachi?"

Twenty-five years before, Tudor had fought Angela for custody of his son for the most selfish of motives—he had promised his firstborn's soul, in lieu of his own, to one of the demons with whom he'd made a pact. Over the years, though, almost against his will, he'd developed an affection for his son, taking pride in some of his accomplishments. Though his soul was now lost to him, Tudor found himself reluctant to part with what remained. The vampire stared at him blankly for a moment, then nodded.

"Can you speak?"

Malachi was silent for a moment, then he swallowed. " ' "I always thought they were fabulous monsters!," said the Unicorn.' " he quoted, from his favorite childhood book. " ' "Is it alive?" "It can talk," said Haigha solemnly.' "

Tudor nodded. "What was your mother's name?"

"Angela," said Malachi, after a moment's thought. "I don't remember her very well."

"How old are you?"

"Twenty-two."

Tudor looked at him appraisingly. "I won't bother asking your favorite color . . . what did Aleister Crowley say was the whole of the law?"

" 'An it harm none, do what thou wilt.' "

"Who sang 'Bela Lugosi's Dead'?"

"Bauhaus," replied Malachi, with a ghastly grin.

"Good. Are you feeling strong enough to walk?"

"Yes."

"Strong enough to run, if you needed to?"

"Yes."

Tudor smiled. "Strong enough to hold her down?" he said, with a nod at Sindee. Before the dancer could react, Malachi leaped onto her, pinning her shoulders to the floor. She flailed at him with her joined fists, kicked with her bound feet, with no apparent effect. Malachi laughed.

"Bite her," commanded Tudor, "but don't drain her, just take enough to keep yourself strong for an hour or two."

Malachi snarled at him, then bent his head and bit into her throat. Sindee struggled for another few seconds, then went limp as the rapture hit her. No sex, no drugs, no combination of the two had ever given her as much pleasure as the feeling of him feeding. She fainted from the sheer sensory overload in less than a minute, and lay there motionless, oblivious, as Tudor walked into the circle, forced Malachi back, and dragged her body toward the door. "I'll be back to let you out of here in a minute," he promised his son. "Then we'll see what we can do about finding Julia."

He returned a little more than two minutes later, and set about erasing part of the circle, creating a doorway through which Malachi could walk out—which he did unsteadily, and with some reluctance. Tudor merely shrugged; Tanith, Adrian, and Beth would probably have been even more suspicious if he'd seemed completely healthy. Tudor led the way down to the garage, where Ernst was waiting. "What should I do about the car?" asked the doctor, as they drove away. "The girl's car?"

Tudor swore silently. He'd *seen* the Rabbit in the garage, of course, but he hadn't *noticed* it. "She works in a club on Santa Monica Boulevard," he said, after thinking for a moment. "I don't remember the name. Do you?" He turned to Malachi, but the vampire looked at him blankly. "I'll find out. Probably best if you take it there at night, and leave it, catch a taxi back . . . a place like that, no one looks anybody in the face, nobody remembers anything, you'll be safe. You needn't go inside," he reassured him.

Only Beth was waiting for them when they returned home, and Malachi staggered past her and up the stairs with help from Tudor. He avoided Beth's touch; his flesh was very cold, and she might notice that he wasn't breathing. Tudor returned him to his bed, freshened the protective circle around it, and set to work on his rituals.

He knew of several ways of finding the hiding places of vampires by day, and of luring them into a trap by night, but all were centuries old and he had no way of knowing how effective they'd be in modern L.A. It was after midnight when he finished his work, deciding that the rituals had been a waste of time; demons know and care little for the finer details of geography, and when they'd told him that there were seven vampires in the city, he could only assume that they were either lying to him or had misunderstood his question. He dismissed them, and stomped wearily to bed.

Two hours later, he woke, knowing that somebody was in the room. He opened his eyes, and saw only different degrees of darkness, though there was a faintly human shape at the foot of the bed, with what might have been faintly glowing red eyes. "Surprised to see me?" said something with Julia's voice.

"I wasn't expecting you so soon," Tudor admitted, sitting up in bed and reaching for the lamp on the nightstand. The vampire stood on the far side of his protective circle; she wore a red warmup jacket and baggy jeans, and her skin was pale in the light, but showed no signs of decay. Her eyes were a dull scarlet color, and her lips dark red and wet-looking. "Is this a social call?"

She laughed. "You might say that. I wasn't planning on attacking anybody here. . . ."

"Then what do you want?"

"Sanctuary," she replied. "A hiding place that's safe and permanent, where I can keep a change of clothes, and not smell like shit when I wake; I may not come back to it every night, but it would help if I knew one was there."

"And food?"

She shook her head. "I can find food without your help."

Tudor nodded; that was almost certainly true. The homeless would be easy prey, and she was more alluring than most crack whores, though a few weeks of hiding in storm drains and similar refuges might change that. "And in return?"

She hissed, her eyes growing more lambent, but Tudor didn't flinch. "I can command your son . . ." she replied, darkly.

"You could have done that anyway—and I can protect myself against Malachi almost as easily as I can protect myself against you, though in his case destroying him would be a last resort. Don't try threatening me; you've come here because you're utterly helpless during the day, and you know it. I *can* give you the sanctuary you seek, but I'll want something in return."

"What?"

Tudor smiled sourly. "I may, from time to time, need you to kill some people who might cause us trouble. Apart from that, please try to divert attention *away* from this area when you hunt, not toward it; look for victims in areas where a few more dead bodies won't be noticed, and please be careful not to turn anybody. Anything you do that endangers this house, endangers your sanctuary, and the police have already been here looking for you.

"I won't ask you for a promise—I know how little it would be worth—but I will make you one. If you harm Malachi, I will give you to Hell, where you will receive special attention from all of the demons with whom I've made pacts—and don't think that killing me will save you, or earn you the smallest reprieve. Do we understand each other?"

He watched as she considered this. While tradition had it that some vampires continued to love those they'd loved in life, it was clear that most did not—and it was not a question Tudor could put to any of his demon informants, to whom love was an utterly alien concept. Malachi still seemed to want Julia, but that might not last; tradition also had it that vampires, lacking blood pressure, were impotent. Without sex to distract him, he might come to see her more clearly.

The creature that had been Julia nodded. "I think so. Do I have to sign a pact?"

"Don't flatter yourself. I only sign pacts with the fallen; you've merely slipped a little." She stared at him blankly, but a little anger seeped through the bafflement; as a vampire she might have no sense of humor, but she could still recognize an insult when she heard one. "Your blood is stolen, and your soul would hardly even be a snack. If you want sanctuary here, you will accept my terms. If not, leave now, and never return." He used his most commanding tone, though he doubted it would work on a vampire.

"I'll stay," she said, in a voice like a blister bursting.

Tudor merely nodded. "Malachi is waiting for you in his room."

"I'd prefer my own room."

"It's not as safe." He yawned, then reached for the black
caftan draped over the foot of the bed. "Follow me."

Takumo walked into the apartment, trying to ignore the aches
from his day's labors. Working with actors, rather than other
stuntmen, was the most painful and often the most dangerous
part of his job; few of them had his training in faking or pulling
blows, and he wasn't allowed to dodge or parry unless it was
in the script. He glanced at the answering machine: no messages. He wandered into the bedroom and booted up the computer, logging on and downloading his mail. There was a short
letter from Mandaglione, a longer one from Kelly; he made
himself as comfortable as he could, and clicked on Mandaglione's.

> Charlie,
> Did as you asked, and began looking for people who'd worked on DEVILSPAWN.
> I've found a few who've agreed to be interviewed, but there's a problem with the
> two female leads. Tanith Black is still living with Tudor, and Angela Winslow, who
> was pregnant at the time the film was made and rumored to have had Tudor's
> son, was rushed to Cedars Sinai hospital in L.A. this morning. I called the hospital,
> and she's on the critical list, suffering from blood loss, though they wouldn't give
> me any other details. If this is a hoax, someone's taking it too far. Do YOU have
> any information for ME? Call me.
> Dante.

Takumo read the message and groaned, then opened the file
from Kelly. It contained the name and address of the owner of
the Merc he'd seen leaving Tudor's home on Sunday morning,
and a copy of the autopsy on the John Doe found in Hollywood. The victim—still unidentified—had been strangled with
sufficient strength to break his neck, but hadn't lost any blood.
He read the rest of the report, making what sense he could of
the medical terminology, then returned his attention to the
driver of the Merc. A search of the phone book turned up only
one Dr. Henry Ernst, a plastic surgeon, and the Hollywood

address checked out. So why, Takumo wondered, would a plastic surgeon be making a house call at three A.M.?

A possible explanation occurred to him almost instantly; a plastic surgeon would need to be able to buy blood. It wasn't much of a lead, but watching the house might turn something up—maybe even something that he could tell Mandaglione. First, though, he composed a message, and posted it onto alt.fan.dirty-pair.

The street was lined with trees and bushes; finding a hiding place was easy. He parked the bike a few blocks away, and concealed himself in a tree. He could see grills on the windows, motion sensors on the exterior lights, alarm boxes, and signs warning that the street was patrolled by guards; obviously Ernst took home security seriously. Takumo considered his options as he watched and waited. He could get as far as the house undetected, by hiding in the plentiful shadows and avoiding the motion sensors, but breaking in would be more difficult; the key would open any locks, but there were probably more alarms on the doors and windows.

The place was silent, but lights were visible through the heavy curtains and shutters. Takumo waited until a few minutes after eleven before climbing down from the tree and creeping around the grounds for a look at the back of the house. There were fewer motion detectors, but no other apparent holes in the security measures.

Feeling faintly discouraged and more than a little foolish, he was returning to the front of the house when he heard the garage door opening. He hid behind a bush and waited. To his surprise, the car that left was not the blue Mercedes, but a red VW Rabbit. The exterior lights snapped on as it headed down the driveway, giving him a brief glimpse of the driver and a good look at the license plate. He looked around, aware that he was also visible from several angles, and saw the garage door slowly descending.

Without taking time to think, he scuttled across the lawn

toward the narrowing gap. The gap between door and floor was barely a foot high as he rolled through it. Without pausing to breathe, he scrambled under the Mercedes Benz, waited until the door closed completely, wrote down the Rabbit's license number in his notepad, then performed a hasty inventory, making sure that he hadn't dropped anything on his way in.

Everything was where it should be, though the points of the tetsubishi had been driven through the sides of his pocket and into his flesh when he'd rolled on them. He extracted them, then placed one behind each of the Merc's front tires. If he had time to remove them on the way out, fine; if not, slowing down pursuit might be more important. The door between the garage and the house was dead-bolted, but not fitted with any alarms; he listened for a moment, then set about picking the lock.

The next room was a laundry; the one after that, a well-equipped and immaculate kitchen, which smelled of recent cooking—frying, garlic, and probably chicken. A glimpse in the dishwasher suggested that Ernst had eaten alone; good. There were no bags of blood in the refrigerator, though there were several vials of clear liquid labeled Midazolam. Most of the ground floor was lit, the top floor was dark, and the sound-proofing was excellent. The living room was furnished in gleaming black leather, with one large comfortable chair with controls for a computer TV, facing the large screen; no pictures or objets d'art, and no bookshelves.

The master bedroom had a double bed, but all the clothes in the closet were for a thin man of average height, and all the shoes were the same size. There was a Baby Browning and a half-full box of .25-caliber ammo in the nightstand's top drawer; he emptied the clip into the box, just in case Ernst came home early. The second drawer was locked, but he found nothing of interest there, only a small collection of European porn and old American softcore magazines.

A quick search of the rest of the house revealed two locked internal doors. The one upstairs had a red light outside; a sign on the door proclaiming DARKROOM: DO NOT ENTER. The other was unidentified; an office, maybe? Takumo doubted that Ernst did his own cleaning or gardening, and the house gave a strong impression that he lived alone and rarely if ever entertained at home. The locks were probably meant to keep cleaners out. So, which room to search first?

Takumo glanced at his watch; he'd been in the house for twelve minutes, and had no way of knowing how long Ernst would be gone, but it seemed smarter to check out the ground floor first. He unlocked the door of the den, shut it behind him, and stared around the room, astonished, at Ernst's doll collection. There had to be more than a hundred of them, maybe two hundred—all Barbies or counterfeits, with no Kens. Many were still in their boxes, and these were locked away in the glass-fronted cabinets. The only other item in the room was a reclining chair with an ashtray on one arm, a coaster on the other.

The room looked like a museum, but felt more like a shrine; even the 'Strap-On Barbie' and the framed postcards of Barbies in a still-life lesbian orgy seemed to celebrate different aspects of the plastic goddess. Maybe they served some magical purpose, but Takumo doubted it; he couldn't imagine the collection's owner sticking a pin into any of these dolls. He reached into his pocket for his camera, took five photos of the room, then walked out, closed the door behind him, and ran upstairs.

After the display in the den, Takumo thought he was prepared for anything, but he was still stunned to see a young woman chained to the darkroom's plumbing, naked but for gaffer tape, fur-lined handcuffs, and boxer shorts. She opened her eyes wide when she saw him, and would almost certainly have screamed but for the tape over her mouth.

Takumo pulled down the scarf that covered the lower half of his face, and put a finger to his lips. "It's okay," he said, softly, then froze. Even in the darkness he could tell it wasn't Julia Petrosyan, but what if it were another vampire? She looked sick and weak, and smelled of shit and blood and infection—not exactly traditional for a female vampire, but it was more credible than the idea of an animated corpse looking like Salma Hayak.

Nervously, he switched the main light on, then ripped the

tape off her mouth and looked at her teeth. "Ouch," she said, quietly, then, ungraciously, "Thanks." Her canines looked no larger than normal. He noticed a red welt on her throat, near the carotid, and checked her pulse. Her skin was warmer than room temperature, her heartbeat rather weak but very fast. He gave the welt a short burst of holy water from his squirt ring; she recoiled in surprise, but nothing worse. The welt seemed to fade slightly, but it didn't smoke or bubble. "Jesus," she said, "what was that?"

Takumo hesitated. It seemed unlikely that a vampire could say a holy name, even as a swearword. He wished Mandaglione were with him; if anyone he knew could quickly tell a vampire from a mortal, it was the writer. He flicked another drop of holy water onto her chest; no effect. "Sorry," he said. "It's a— it's good for bites. I hope. Who are you?"

"Sa—Sindee. Who're you?"

"Charlie. You want out of here?"

"Yes!" she said urgently, loudly enough to make Takumo wince slightly.

"Okay. Give me a second." He looked at the handcuffs. The keyhole was too small for the focus, but that wasn't a problem. Sindee stared at him as he removed his keychain from his pocket and quickly found the right key to unlock the cuffs, then cut through the tape with his Swiss Army knife. "Can you walk?"

"I don't know," she said, trying to stand. "He's had me tied up like this for hours, and I think he drugged—" She fell over. "Shit," she said. "I can hardly feel my legs at all. I must have been here for nearly two whole days, and the bastard hasn't fed me."

Takumo grimaced. She was small, but carrying her as far as the bike posed a problem, and if she was too weak to hang on . . . "Looks like you've lost some blood, too."

She looked down at the boxer shorts, and shrugged. "Yeah, well . . . can we get out of here? My car is in the garage—"

"Red Rabbit?"

"Uh-huh."

"Someone—presumably Ernst—just drove away in it. Left his own car here, instead, but I'd rather not take that; it's too obvious, and it probably has all sorts of security gear on it."

"Why would he take *my* car?"

"To dump it, probably, which means he may be planning to do the same to you. I'm going to have to get some help. How long is Ernst likely to be gone?"

"Ernst? The doctor? I don't know."

Takumo nodded. "I'm going downstairs to phone a friend, then I'll be back for you. I don't think I can do much about food just yet, but I may be able to find you some clothes, make you a little less conspicuous."

"Thanks," she repeated, more sincerely, then blinked and began crying. Takumo backed away nervously, watching her carefully until he was past the door, when he made a dash for the bedroom and the phone. He could only think of two people to call for help at this time of night, and he didn't really know Gaye well enough. Kelly would almost certainly make him suffer for it later, but her house was closer, she owned weapons and could use them, and there was no one alive he would rather have trusted with his life in an emergency. Not even Mage.

She answered the phone on the third ring. "Barbet."

"Sorry if I woke you, but I need help, urgently."

"I won't argue with that," Kelly muttered. "What is it this time?"

"I'm in Hollywood, there's a woman here who's been attacked and is in no condition to walk, I only have the bike, and I can't call an ambulance."

"You need me to come and get you?"

"Right on." He gave her the address. "Just do laps of the block, slowly, until I come out. And bring a gun, just in case."

"*What?*"

"Thanks, Kel." He hung up, then, to confound the last-number redial function, punched in the number for a pizza delivery chain. Then he glanced in the closet, and extracted a white silk shirt, black pants, a black frock coat, and a snakeskin belt for Sindee, who was waiting for him at the top of the stairs. "I'm sorry," she said. "Even with the handrail, I don't think I can—"

"That's cool. I hope these are okay."

"Thanks," she said, wriggling into the shirt. "Charlie . . ."

"Yes?"

"What are you doing here?"

"It's a long story, and I don't believe some of it myself, yet."

"Oh."

He picked her up, cradle-fashion, and managed not to laugh.

"What's funny?" she asked.

"I feel like the monster in a fifties B-movie. Never mind." He began walking down the stairs slowly. "Actually, I was hoping you could tell me some of what I missed—of the story, I mean. What are *you* doing here?"

"I drove Sol and Mal here, and they drugged me—Sol and Ernst did. I thought Mal was dead, but he . . ."

"Got better?"

"Uh-huh. The next night," she said, nodding. "And he bit me. I think he thinks he's some sort of vampire."

"He's not the only one who thinks—oh, shit."

"What?"

"The lights just came on out front," he said urgently, his voice low. "Someone's here, and it's too early to be the cavalry." He thought quickly. They were more than halfway down the stairs, and he doubted that he could get back up to the next floor before Ernst opened the door and saw them. Even if they hid, they'd be cornered if he came upstairs after them, and Takumo didn't know how often Kelly would drive around the block without arousing suspicion or giving up. If he hadn't had Sindee in his arms, he would have rushed down and hidden in a corner, staying still enough that there was a good chance that Ernst would walk right past him. . . . With this thought, he hurtled down the stairs and toward the master bedroom.

"What are you—"

"Shh," he murmured, as he laid her on the bed. "If he sees

you, he might not notice me." He dashed back to stand beside the doorway, and flicked the light switch, killing the light. Sindee stared at him, then nodded. They heard the front door close, and listened as someone—Takumo was sure it was only one person, and a lightly built person at that—walked through the deep carpet, hesitated outside the den, then turned toward the bedroom.

Ernst blinked as he saw Sindee lying on the bed, and reached for the light switch. Charlie grabbed his wrist, and threw him into the room. Ernst went sprawling, his head hitting the side of the mattress; he looked up, and Sindee backhanded him across the face, her long nails scratching his cheek. He stumbled backward, and Takumo slid the nightstick out of his sleeve and tapped him on the temple. Ernst hit the floor, stunned; Takumo watched him warily for a moment, then slid the nightstick back into its hiding place.

After a moment's thought, he patted down Ernst for weapons or a cell phone and, finding nothing but his keys (which he pocketed), rolled up the surgeon's trousers, taped his shins and his thumbs together, then unplugged the phone and handed it to Sindee. "Is that going to hold him?" she asked, as he picked her up again.

Takumo merely nodded, wishing he'd kept the handcuffs, but not wanting to go upstairs to retrieve them. Ernst might recover soon, he might even be faking unconsciousness, though Takumo doubted it. On the other hand, he didn't want to risk killing the man, or even permanently injuring him.

On the way out, he had Sindee throw the phone up the stairs, then they left by the front door, locking it behind them and dropping the keys onto the mat. "It'll hold him for long enough," he said, as he carried Sindee across the lawn toward a neatly groomed bush that hid them from view of the road, though not the house. "We only need a few minutes; it'll take him longer than that to get to the phone and call for help. Unless he's thought to keep a spare key *inside* the house, I doubt he can even get out; both the doors and all the windows I saw were dead-bolted." He peered around the bush, hoping to see the lights of Kelly's car. The external lights were still on, making him feel very exposed.

"Do you do a lot of this?"

He laughed, very quietly. "No."

"Who are you working for?"

"Huh? No one."

"So who's coming to pick us up?"

"Just a friend—" He managed not to add "I hope," but he thought it; he'd put the friendship under considerable strain already, and this would certainly damage it. Kelly had a respect for the law that he was unable to comprehend. "Here she is," he said, instead, as he saw headlights a few blocks away. He waited until he could see the Range Rover clearly, then dashed toward the road, keeping low.

Kelly stopped the car and unlocked the doors; even in the darkness, he could see the grim expression on her face, and the small automatic on the seat beside her. He nodded, giving her his most apologetic smile, then ran back across the lawn to pick up Sindee. There was still no sign of movement from the house. Kelly picked up the pistol and slipped it into her ankle holster before leaning across to open the door.

"Hi," said Sindee uncertainly, as Takumo placed her in the front passenger seat.

"Hi," replied Kelly, sourly. Takumo said, "Thanks," opened the rear door, and climbed in. None of them spoke again until the car approached a corner and Kelly snapped, "Where to?"

"A hospital—St. John's, preferably. Sindee may have the same problem as the Petrosyans."

"Petrosyans?" asked Sindee. "Julia's family?"

"Yeah."

"There was a cop around at the house a few days ago, asking about Julia; he said her brother and her mother were dead, and her father was—how did they die? Some disease?"

"We're not sure," said Takumo. "When was the last time you saw Julia?"

"Two nights ago . . . I think. Saturday night, Sunday morning . . . it *is* Monday night, isn't it?"

"Yeah. Where did you see her?"

"If it was her—and I'm pretty sure it was—she was running out of the house like something was after her. Sure, we thought the place was on fire, but no one else went over the wall. I think she was naked, too. Why?"

"We're looking for her."

"So was the cop. I don't know when she came back to the house. Am I going to be okay?" She turned to Kelly. "Are you a doctor?"

"No, just an ambulance driver," said Kelly, heavily. "Okay, Charlie, I'll take you both to the hospital, but *you* can take her in. Tell them whatever you have to, but leave me out of it."

"For sure," replied Takumo, subdued. He considered telling Kelly that he couldn't thank her enough, but decided against it; she'd probably agree with him. He was still trying to think of something harmless to say when they arrived at the hospital, and he discovered that Sindee had fallen asleep. "Can you hang around for, like, twenty minutes while I get her admitted?"

Kelly glared at him, but it didn't look like an outright refusal. "What're you going to say?"

"That I saw her fall over and couldn't find a pulse or bring her around—"

"Where did you see her?"

"What?"

Kelly sighed. "I'll do it. You wait here."

"Thanks!"

"They'll probably be less suspicious if another black woman carries her in, anyway." She switched the engine off, unfastened her seat belt, and walked around to the passenger side. She glanced at her watch; five past midnight. "I shouldn't be long."

It was nearly half past one when he returned home, too weary even to wonder what to do next. Half-asleep, he locked the door behind him, and headed for the bedroom without turning on the light, dropping his backpack on the kitchen table and unzipping his jacket as he walked. The glow of the clock on the VCR was enough for him to see by, even if he hadn't practiced walking around the apartment blindfolded. He glanced at the answering machine—no flickering light, so no messages—and was one step from the bedroom door when he caught a hint of movement at the edge of his peripheral vision.

He looked over his shoulder to see a tall figure standing in the kitchen, masked, wearing a long and heavy-looking coat, and armed with a very large handgun. "Turn around," said an unfamiliar voice—deep, but probably female, and with an odd accent. "Kneel. Hands on top of your head, fingers laced together. Do you understand?"

Takumo nodded, and obeyed. Whoever it was had managed to get past his security systems, so he had no doubt she was competent. "What do you want?"

"Where is Michelangelo Magistrale?"

"He could be anywhere on Earth," replied Takumo, wearily, "and if you find him not there, seek him i' the other place yourself."

Krieg frowned. "Do you think this is a game, little man?"

"No." Takumo wondered how well the intruder could see in the near-darkness; the "mask" he'd glimpsed briefly might have been some type of night-vision goggles. "If it is, I've already lost, because I really don't know where he is."

"Then you have twenty-four hours to find out," said Krieg, flatly. "At the end of that time, I will kill one friend of yours. A female friend. Twenty-four hours after that, if Magistrale is still alive, I will kill another. Unfortunately, we only know how to find three friends of yours, so if we don't find Magistrale within four days, I'll have to kill you instead.

"If you try to warn anybody, I will kill them that much sooner. If we can't locate one of them when their time comes, we will have to kill some strangers instead—a drive-by shooting into a schoolyard in Little Tokyo, maybe, or a bomb in a movie theatre. Now, where is Magistrale?"

12

Daughters of Darkness

"I don't know," said Takumo, through clenched teeth. He wondered if he could reach the knife in his sleeve and throw it before the intruder could aim. It would probably be suicide, but better that than let this monster murder his friends. The vampires he'd been chasing suddenly seemed much more sympathetic than this woman.

"Pity. Do you have some way of finding him? If not, I might as well kill you tonight. I don't much care; I'm being paid for results, not by the hour."

"We send messages to a newsgroup on the net," said Takumo, slowly. "He can read them from any computer with Web access. But even if I tell him to come here urgently, it may be a day or more before he reads it, and he might be anywhere, how long it'll take him to get here . . ."

"What group?"

Takumo sighed, considered lying, and decided against it. "alt.fan.dirty-pair."

"What?"

"It's an anime series."

Krieg looked blank.

"Japanese animation? Like it was my turn to pick a group; we change occasionally."

Krieg nodded. "Send him a message. Tell him to meet you here, but to call you first and tell you when he's arriving."

"What if he needs picking up at the airport?" asked Takumo, trying to keep the excitement out of his voice. Maybe this psychopath didn't know Mage could teleport. . . . "Or Greyhound, or wherever . . ."

Krieg considered this for an instant, then sneered. "He knows you only ride a bike, ay? Nice try, little man. Just send the message. Now."

Takumo led the way into the bedroom, switched the light on, booted up the computer, and logged on. Krieg stood behind him, out of arm's reach, the gun trained at the back of his neck. He went straight to the newsgroup, checked for Mage's logon and, not finding it, began typing a message. "What're you doing?" asked Krieg, pulling her infrared goggles up so that she could read the screen.

"We use a code," said Takumo. "Most of it's in the subject line and the cross-posting; the actual text doesn't matter unless we need to say something we don't already have a code for. The message you've given me is fairly simple, unless you want me to add to it. . . ."

"No, but I want to read the message before you send it."

"For sure." He typed three lines of text, then nodded. "Done. Just press Enter, or the left trackball button, to send it."

"Get on the bed. Facedown, hands on top of your head."

Takumo shrugged, and obeyed. Krieg walked over to the computer desk, and for the first time, looked away from him as she leaned down to read the screen. Takumo eased the knife out of his sleeve, and, as soon as she pressed the 'Enter' key, threw it with all his strength. It *chunked* into her right forearm, between the bones, and bright red arterial blood began spurting out of the wound. Krieg yelled, and her finger tightened on the trigger. A shot rang out, and a bullet buried itself in the wall more than a yard from Takumo's head. Takumo was already rolling across the bed, his spring-loaded nightstick telescoping out to give him extra reach; he lunged forward and smashed it into Krieg's wrist, and another shot went wild, this time into the ceiling. Takumo did a back-flip to kick her in the face with both feet, and she stumbled backward but by the time he had his feet on the floor and was preparing to strike again, she was pointing the gun directly between his eyes.

"Nice try, little man," she said, then tested her teeth for looseness with her tongue. "Now drop the preacher and back off."

Takumo didn't budge. "You're going to kill me anyway, aren't you?"

"Not if we find Magistrale." Suddenly alarmed, she raised her eyebrows, then grabbed the hilt of the knife embedded in her right arm with her left hand. Her face contorted with agony as she extracted it, but her gaze remained fixed on Takumo's face. "Exactly what did that message say, ay?"

There was a faint sound of movement from the living room, a flicker of light so brief that two less alert people might not have noticed it at all—but both Krieg and Takumo glanced at the doorway. Standing in the next room was a tall man; his leather jacket and jeans were almost invisible in the near-darkness, but his face, framed by long blond hair, made an almost perfect target. Takumo winced, and Krieg turned the pistol away from him to fire at Mage, slashing at Takumo with his knife in the same movement. As she squeezed the trigger, the barrel drooped as though it had melted, then the gun exploded in her hand, the slide flying back and narrowly missing her face. Takumo parried the knife with his nightstick, knocking it from her grasp, and Krieg screamed as much in rage as in pain. Her left hand disappeared behind her back for an instant, and before either Mage or Takumo could react, she drew a tiny pocket pistol, then fired twice at Mage, hitting him in the chest and shoulder.

The magician fell, and Krieg, ignoring Takumo, ran into the next room to finish him off.

"Mage! *Get out! NOW!*"

Krieg slowed down and aimed at Mage's face, and Takumo

tackled her from behind, bringing her down. She twisted in his grasp, but not wanting to waste a bullet on him while her target might still be alive, she settled for striking him in the face with her left hand, the muzzle of the gun leaving a gash in his forehead. She turned around to fire at Mage again, but he was gone. Takumo released her and rolled away, reaching into his pocket for his pepper spray. Krieg scrambled to her feet and faced him, the little gun pointed at his navel. "Where did he go?" she asked, as she backed toward the door.

"Who?"

"That was Magistrale, wasn't it? How did he get in? And put your hands where I can see them."

"I don't know what you're talking about," said Takumo, with counterfeit calm. The little gun looked like a derringer, and she'd already fired two shots; either she'd lost count, or she was bluffing. He grabbed the pepper spray, and Krieg fired. Takumo was too startled even to dodge; he staggered when the bullet hit, and collapsed, holding on to his abdomen and watching blood seep out between his fingers.

"Is he still here? Is he coming back?"

"I don't know!"

Krieg glared at him, then looked down at the blood running down her right arm. Standing here and waiting to see who bled to death first didn't seem practical, and Takumo might be more useful scared than dead. "Why did you warn him, ay? I would have let you live. . . ."

She seemed, Takumo noted, genuinely puzzled and more than a little amused. "If you can get proof that Magistrale is dead, in the next twenty-four hours, post an obituary on that newsgroup. If not . . ." She backed up until she reached the door, then pocketed the little gun, gave him a half-mocking salute, and walked out.

Takumo crawled toward the phone, when Mage suddenly reappeared in the room, holding a pump-action shotgun. "She's already gone," croaked the stuntman. "Didn't you get my message?"

"Sure. You said it was an emergency, and—"

"No, the message I sent tonight, like a couple of minutes before you got here . . ." Mage looked blank. "Sorry. I *tried* to warn you, I wasn't deliberately leading you into a trap. . . . Are you okay?"

"I don't know," said Mage, carefully putting the gun down on the floor and kneeling by his wounded friend. "I've stopped the bleeding, but I don't know enough about medicine yet to be sure about internal damage. I couldn't find any exit wounds, so I guess the bullets are still in there, which can't be good, and I think she broke one of my ribs."

Takumo shook his head, and rolled over onto his back. "Can you call me an ambulance? Nothing personal, but I think I'd rather leave this to a professional."

"**O**kay," said Mage, as he finished the bandages. While his medical studies hadn't enabled him to heal all wounds, much less diseases, they had taught him proficiency at basic first aid. "What's our story going to be?"

"What?"

"Who shot you, where, when, why . . ." He glanced at his watch. "The ambulance should be here in a couple of minutes, and the cops are bound to ask."

"Oh . . . yeah. So's my landlord, when he sees the bullet-holes. Shit. Do you think they'd believe me if I said I brought a woman home, someone I met in a bar, and she shot me and—"

"Why?"

"Damned if I know. I've never picked up a woman in a bar in my life, wouldn't know how if I wanted to. I could say she tried to rob me, and wouldn't believe I didn't have anything worth stealing. . . . Maybe she was an addict. The cops would believe that."

"Describe her."

"What?"

"They're going to want a description. They might believe you didn't know her name, but not her—"

"Goth," said Takumo, after a moment's thought. "Dark hair, pale complexion, about five foot five, hundred ten to hundred twenty pounds . . ." Mage raised an eyebrow. "If they pick up Julia Petrosyan for questioning, is that my fault?"

"What was she wearing?"

"Oh. Right. Black jeans and muscle shirt and an ankh?"

"Okay. When did I get here?"

"After she left? Or do you want to tell them she shot you, too?"

Mage shook his head. "I know a clinic where they'll x-ray me and remove the bullets and won't ask any questions when I check myself out early. I've been working there on and off for a few months."

"Can you take me there?"

"It's in Bangkok. I still haven't tried carrying anyone with me when I teleport, and . . ." He looked up at the bullet-hole in the wall. "Maybe I should have tried taking her. Who was she, by the way?"

"I don't know. I'm guessing Nakatani sent her, but she's a lot better than the goons he usually—that's the ambulance."

Mage listened. "Okay. Anything else you want me to do?"

"Yeah. Call Kelly, tell her what happened—the truth as well as the cover story. And . . . no, I'll do that. Just call Kelly."

Tudor sneered as he opened the door, and saw Ernst sitting there, still removing the tape from his ankles. "What happened?" he asked, as Julia closed the door behind her.

"Some guy broke in," said Ernst, wincing as the tape took hair with it. "I didn't see him clearly, but he was dressed all in black. . . ."

"Who isn't?" asked Tudor, dryly. "Did you see his face?"

"No, but he wasn't as tall as I am. It may not even have been a man." He told them the story without any false bravado. He wasn't sure whether Tudor could read minds, though he often acted as though he could, but he knew that he was expert at detecting lies.

Tudor listened silently, without even a smile.

"When I came around, they were both gone," Ernst concluded. "I don't think they took anything unless it was from the darkroom or the garage or the—" He froze for an instant.

Tudor held out the keys. "We'll check those rooms now," he said, almost kindly. Ernst nodded.

The search of the house confirmed Ernst's suspicions; nothing was missing except Sindee and some of his own clothing. Tudor looked at him sourly, wondering whether Ernst might be lying to him. It seemed much more likely that Sindee had seduced or tricked or even overpowered him; Ernst was tall, but slight, and the dancer might well be stronger than he was, particularly her legs. "How did you get those scratches?"

"Sindee," muttered Ernst. "After the other one hit me from behind, she scratched my face."

He seemed sincere, but Tudor had his doubts. He knew the surgeon's weakness well, but he also knew that Sindee had considerable experience in getting men to reveal their fantasies, and in catering to them. Tudor led the way back to the den, with Ernst and Julia following him, then picked a brown Barbie off the shelf. "You're sure you didn't simply let her go, Henry?"

"Why would I do that?" blustered Ernst.

"Why indeed?" He returned the doll to the shelf. "She didn't offer you anything?"

"Offer?"

He picked up another doll, lifted its skirt, and raised an eyebrow. "This one isn't wearing pants. Tsk, tsk."

"That's Teacher Barbie," said Ernst, a faint giggle in his voice. "They sold her without panties; there was quite a scandal about it, and Mattel had to recall them. I managed to buy a few first, Never Removed From Box; that one came without a box, but it was near-mint and cheap. . . ."

"And this one?"

"That's Krista McAuliffe," said Ernst. "They withdrew it after the *Challenger* exploded; it's a real rarity. . . ."

Tudor shook his head. "You have a remarkable collection, Henry. It must give you a lot of pleasure."

"Yes," said Ernst, rather nervously.

The sorcerer glanced at Julia. "A harmless pleasure, at least. Have you fed, my dear?" Ernst looked around, and the vampire grabbed his arms. "Maybe we should show the doctor what real pleasure is," Tudor continued, and Julia smiled and bit into Ernst's throat. The terror and the ecstasy overwhelmed him in the same instant; he closed his eyes, and surrendered to both.

"Don't kill him," warned Tudor. The vampire glared at him, then stopped drinking for long enough to say, "Came here to feed. She's gone. His fault."

"True," the sorcerer conceded, "but he can get blood, give himself transfusions, feed you for years. Can't you, Henry?"

Ernst opened his eyes, and stared blearily at Tudor. "Expensive, I know," Tudor continued, "but you have money, don't you, Henry? And imagine how much you can save on hand lotion, not to mention malpractice insurance. That's *enough*."

Snarling, Julia released him, so suddenly that Ernst fell to the floor. "Still hungry," she sulked. The surgeon lay there, incapable of movement; he was no longer paralyzed with fear, merely stupefied by endorphins. In time, he would get up, clean himself up, and try to come to terms with what had happened, but Tudor saw little point in waiting. Ernst was ashamed enough of his own sexuality that he might well consider this preferable; after all, it didn't require him to undress, or do any more than stand or lie there and be bitten. There was a faint danger that he might commit suicide and leave an incriminating note, but Tudor doubted that. "Leave him," he said. "I know a place where you can feed. They may even be pleased to see you."

It was twenty past two when Kelly walked into the waiting room, to be told that Takumo was still in surgery. She sat down a few seats away from where Mage was staring into space, barely half awake, and they didn't look at each other for more than a minute. "What happened?" she said, finally.

"Some woman who neither of us recognized shot him."

Kelly glared. "What *really* happened?"

"That *is* what really happened. The only details we changed were the woman's description, and the fact that she was waiting for him when he came home. The cops are probably at the apartment now."

"Why? I mean, why did she—"

"She was waiting for me, using Charlie as bait; she didn't know he'd sent me a message warning me to stay away. Fortunately for him, I suspect, I didn't get it in time. I don't know what she would have done if I hadn't showed. I mean, I can guess, but I don't know how long she would have waited."

"What can you tell me about her?"

Mage looked at her blearily, then reached into his jacket pocket for his wallet. He removed a business card, concentrated for a moment, then handed Kelly a small picture of Krieg. "That's the best I can do—I didn't get a good look at her," he apologized. "She's somewhere between five ten and six one. Ambidextrous, very fast—even faster than Charlie—and shoots very well with a gun so small I hardly saw it. I didn't hear her voice." Kelly stared at the photo, then rubbed her eyes and stifled a yawn. "Sorry for getting you out of bed."

"I hadn't been asleep long," she said, and yawned again. "Yours was the second emergency call this morning, and this is my second emergency room. Did Charlie tell you that?"

"No. What happened?"

She summed up the morning's events for him, with a bare minimum of expletives. "I don't know what's going on, but whatever it is, it's killing people, and Charlie is in it up to his neck. What are we going to do about it?" Mage raised an eyebrow. "Come on. If anyone owes him a favor, you do; how many times has he saved *your* life now?"

"I haven't been counting." He sighed. "I thought this was all over, two years ago."

"Yeah, I hoped so too. This woman . . ." She stared at the photo. "I'm sure I've seen her somewhere—not in person, but another photo . . . how do you do that, by the way?"

"Creating the pictures is easy—creating the *paper* is the hard part." He grimaced. "Surfaces, I'm good at."

"You always were," said Kelly, still concentrating on the picture.

"What's *that* supposed to mean?"

"What?" She looked up. "Sorry. I haven't had enough sleep. Forget it."

"The Hell I will."

Kelly sighed. "Charlie asked you for help a few days ago, and you said no—"

"I was busy—"

"I know, but where would you be if, two years ago, Charlie had been too busy to help you? At best, you'd still be in jail for Amanda's murder." Mage scowled. "And what if it'd been a woman who asked you for help—an attractive woman, one who looked like Amanda Sharmon, for example? Would you have said no to her?"

"Are you accusing me of being sexist, or racist?"

Kelly considered this for a few seconds. "Just sexist," she said, finally. "You don't seem any more racist than most people—less than most that I work with. Charlie's told me what you're trying to do, and where you're trying to do it, and I think that's great—but it's no excuse for refusing to help a friend, not when you can be anywhere on Earth in an instant."

"Look, I'm trying to make a difference. I didn't *ask* to be given this power."

"I know."

"And I offered one of the foci to you, and you said no."

Kelly nodded. "And I'd say the same if you offered again. Not that I could use it. I don't have the imagination."

"What?"

"You see things as they are and imagine them being different, you never stop to analyze the situation, and even if you only change them superficially, you *can* change them. I couldn't; I don't think like that. I don't think like Amanda, either—" She turned around as someone else, a young nurse, looked into the waiting room.

"Ms. Barbet?"

"Yes?" The voice sounded familiar, but it was another few seconds before she recognized Gaye Lind. "Hello. You've gone back to work?"

"They were short-staffed in the E.R. I saw you come in. . . . Are you here to see Charlie?"

"Yes. Do you know how he's doing?"

"I'll ask." She turned to Mage. "I'm Gaye Lind."

"Mage," he replied, smiling. "I'm another friend of Charlie's," then he turned to Kelly. "Look, I'd better go." She glared at him. "I'll be back as soon as I can," he promised, and stood, swaying slightly. "Good to meet you," he said to Gaye, who watched him walk out until he'd disappeared into the corridor. Nice buns, she thought, then turned back to Kelly. Mage ducked into the men's room and, finding it empty, *saw* himself back in the clinic in Bangkok.

The Crypt was a small cafe with bad acoustics and a stage barely larger than a queen-size bed, but the rent was low, and it had a loyal clientele whose business paid the bills. Most of the light inside came from the black candles on the black tables and the TV above the bar, which was showing F. W. Murnau's silent film *Nosferatu*. The bare concrete floor, ceiling and brick walls were also painted black, so that the only color in the room came from the bottles behind the bar, and the pictures on the walls—amateur artwork, movie one-sheets and daybills, and a life-size poster of Elvira in a coffin.

Even in the near-darkness, the bartender, Dwight, bore less resemblance to Tom Cruise than he liked to believe, but his costume was a fair copy of Lestat's in *Interview with the Vampire*. He looked up as Julia entered, nodded briefly, and went back to the book he was reading.

Julia had been a regular at the Crypt until recently, frequently showing up for the midnight poetry readings (another feature that scared away most of the curious after only one visit). She sat near the door, and scanned the room. One woman and three men returned her gaze, hints of hope and hunger in their expressions, but none of them moved from their seats. Julia thought for a moment; she had no experience at picking up women, but there was nowhere in the cafe where she could bite a man and not be noticed, and she didn't want to risk taking anybody outside. She walked over to the woman's table, keeping eye contact, then veered away and headed for the ladies' room and waited.

She caught a glimpse of her reflection in the mirror, and looked at it curiously. Unless the mirror lied, she looked human enough to pass, at least at night. She'd fed recently enough that her face was still pink beneath her makeup, and her lips and eyes scarlet. Her teeth and fingernails looked no longer or sharper than they had when she was alive, her eyebrows no bushier . . . her long dark hair was untidy, but it usually had been in life, and it didn't seem to have grown at all. The door opened a moment later, and her intended victim walked in. "Very nice," she drawled.

Julia smiled. "Oh, I'm not that nice," she replied. In the brighter light of the tiny powder room, the woman looked both older and larger, but Julia was stronger and faster. In an instant, she'd grabbed both of the woman's wrists, and pushed her against the graffiti-covered wall. She licked her throat, then sank her teeth into the flesh. She heard the woman moan with pleasure-pain as she drank, and fought to keep control; Tudor had warned her not to leave corpses in places where she might be recognized.

A little less than three mouthfuls later, she realized that somebody else had entered the room, and looked around. A much younger woman, a skinny goth still in her teens, was standing in the doorway with her mouth open in shock. Julia's victim continued to croon as Julia lowered her to the tiled floor. The goth seemed frozen, unable even to scream even when Julia reached out and pulled her into the room. The door creaked shut behind her.

"You're real," whispered the goth. "Aren't you? You're really one of them?"

"Yes."

"And you bit her?"

"Yes."

The goth nodded. "Can you bite me, too? Make me like you?"

"Yes," said Julia, reassuringly. The goth threw her head back, baring her throat, and Julia drank deep.

Haruko Tamenaga and Valeri Krieg appraised each other from opposite sides of Tamenaga's breakfast table. Krieg's carefully tailored jacket hid the bandage on her arm, but her makeup didn't quite conceal the bruising about her face. Despite the early hour, Tamenaga was just as formally attired. "You *saw* Magistrale?" she prompted.

Krieg had insisted on this meeting while one of Lowe's medics tended to her wounds; with her good hand, she'd reached out and grabbed Lowe by the balls, squeezing until he agreed to place the call. Tamenaga wondered idly what would have happened to him if he'd refused.

"Yes, and shot him. It was only a pocket pistol, but I hit him twice, in the chest. I was about to put a third round in his head when he disappeared."

Tamenaga sipped at her tea. "Disappeared?"

"In a second. I don't know how. I checked the apartment out earlier; there shouldn't be any trapdoors or any hiding places big enough for a man that large to hide, but I didn't see him come in, and I didn't see him leave."

"I'm not paying you to wound him," said Tamenaga, coolly. "I want him dead."

Krieg nodded, very slightly. "I'm not asking for more money. I want to know how he does this. Duncan told me that he murdered your father, in his house at Bel Air; is that correct?"

"Yes."

"How good was the security?"

"We've always had the best we could without drawing undue attention to the place. Magistrale came over the wall, killed our guard dogs, and managed to avoid most of our cameras; the first we saw of him was when he walked up to the front door. He slipped past the doorman, the one you saw on your way in." Krieg nodded; Yamada Kazafumi well deserved the title, resembling a door almost as much as he did a man. "Then he killed one of my father's bodyguards and crippled another outside his office. Then, after killing my father, he escaped."

Krieg nodded again. Duncan had told her much the same story, though in a doubting tone; he'd considered it much more likely that the old man's murder was an inside job by his own security staff, and that Magistrale was merely part of their improbable cover story. He'd even hinted that Magistrale might not even exist—not that this was any reason for Krieg to turn down a well-paid job, of course. Krieg had more than half-believed this herself, until now . . . but since Magistrale apparently *did* exist, he was potentially very bad for business. How could she promise to protect a client if Magistrale was able to appear anywhere, shoot, and then vanish again? For the first time since her teens, she felt powerless, something she'd resolved long ago would never happen again.

Krieg had hunted lions and tigers; she was familiar with the concept of 'top predator,' and had long aspired to it. Magistrale was a threat that could not be tolerated.

"If you've seen him, and shot at him, you've accomplished more than anybody else we've hired," said Tamenaga, "but I'll want proof of his death. His body, if possible; if not, his head, and everything he's carrying. He stole possessions of my father's, valuable antiques, and he still may have them, but their sentimental value to me is worth much more than you would get from anybody else. Is there anything else you need to know?"

13

Blood Relations

Doi looked at the X ray as she worked on her strange patient. He'd insisted that they use only a local anaesthetic, and watched intently as she cut into the unmarked flesh in search of the bullets. When she finished, she sewed up the wounds, and helped him into a wheelchair. "You have a broken rib," she said.

"Can I see the X ray?"

She nodded, and handed it to him. He stared at it for more than a minute, then handed it back. "Can you take another?"

"Yes, of course, but—"

He reached for a mirror, looked at the sutures, and *saw* the incision heal. One second the stitches were there, the next the flesh was unmarked again. "Thank you."

Doi nodded. When Mage had first come there as a volunteer, she'd been suspicious of him, but he'd shown himself willing to work. It was several months before he'd started practicing his strange kind of faith healing, offering to give the clinic most of any money he received in exchange for her performing checkups before and after the procedure, to make sure that he wasn't doing any harm. He was good at treating knife wounds and burns and rat bites, but most of his paying clients were Amer-

icans or Europeans who wanted cosmetic work done, and he
was adept at doing that: removing wrinkles and scars and tattoos, enlarging or lifting or reshaping breasts, making slight al-
ternations to noses and ears and cheekbones. He accepted few
of these jobs, profitable as they were, and was obviously frustrated that he couldn't heal more serious wounds—limbs ruined
by land-mines, for example. Lately, the managers of some of
the bars and brothels in Patpong had come to her, demanding
that the healer work on some of their women. He'd accepted
some of these commissions for one-tenth the fee he charged his
foreign clients, and then had given half of the money to the
clinic, the other half back to his patients—but a "businessman"
who'd threatened him a month ago had walked out of their
meeting with both of his arms paralyzed. "I hated doing that,"
Mage had admitted to her afterwards. "I hate doing anything I
don't know I can undo if necessary; I *think* I can fix that, but
only if he believes it too."

"Is that why you didn't kill him?" she asked, her tone im-
plying that it wouldn't have been any loss.

"One of the reasons. I killed a few people in self-defense
before I learned less lethal ways to stop them; the last one was
a man with the same powers I have, who I couldn't have
stopped any other way. I don't want to have to do that again."

The "businessman" had returned several times while Mage
had been away, and offered more money each time. His bodyguards and attendants enabled him to survive without the use
of his arms, but he obviously wasn't absolutely sure of their
loyalty. Doi had never mentioned these visits to Mage; she
wanted to see how high the businessman would go first, and
wouldn't have mourned if he'd died. "What are you going to
do now?" she asked Mage, as she set up the X-ray machine.

"Check to see that my ribs aren't still broken, then go back
to America. I think my friends need my help."

While the focus enabled Mage to travel instantaneously between locations that he could visualize clearly and arrive at

safely, he still had to rely on conventional methods for getting around in L.A., and by the time he returned to the hospital, Takumo was already awake. "You okay?" he asked.

Mage nodded. "Where's Kelly?"

"Gaye said she had to go—due in court—though she was here most of the morning. She seemed to think you'd just run out; you didn't tell her you were wounded, did you?"

"No. I didn't have time, and this didn't seem like the place. . . ."

"Pity; I'd hate to have her pissed at me, and I think this is going to need all of us to deal with it." He glanced over at the only other patient in the room, who was still asleep, and continued, softly, "There's another vampire, probably more than one, and I have a feeling that there'll be more soon. Dante's found a woman in another hospital who has the symptoms of—"

"Are you still on about that? I thought this was about Nak-atani's goons—"

"—I'll get to that—"

"—and you've dragged Dante into it?"

"I didn't have to drag him! I haven't told him what's going on, but he's still helping out. But you're right, we have to do something about Nakatani too. The woman who shot us—she's after you, but she threatened to kill a friend of mine tonight if she didn't find you first. She didn't name anyone, but she said she only knew three friends of mine, and she specified that her first victim would be female. That might mean Kelly, or Gaye— Gaye Lind, she's a nurse here—"

Mage nodded. "Met her last night, while you were in sur-gery. What about that friend of yours who reads the *I Ching*?"

"Elena? She died a few months ago."

"I'm sorry."

"Yeah. Me too, but at least she died in her sleep. So, the only other target I can think of is Mika; we're not exactly friends anymore, though I'd like to be, so I wouldn't want to see her hurt. Anyway, I can't do much to protect Kelly while I'm here, I haven't even been able to warn Gaye yet, and I don't even

have Mika's address—been careful not to find out. Is there anything you can do to protect them?"

Mage was about to speak, when Gaye Lind looked around
the doorway. "Hi!" she said, then, to Takumo, "How're you
feeling?"

"Shot," Takumo replied, cheerfully, "but all the better for
seeing you."

She smiled. "I can't stay long, but can I get you anything?"

Takumo opened his mouth to speak, then closed it again;
something in the way Gaye was looking at Mage suggested that
she was hoping he would answer. He closed his eyes, and suppressed a sigh. The first woman he'd been seriously attracted to
in years, and she'd instantly fallen for Mage. "Charlie?" she
said; he heard concern in her voice, but nothing more. "Are you
okay?"

"I think the painkillers are wearing off," he said, through his
teeth.

"Should I call the doctor?"

"No; I *like* pain. Thanks for dropping in . . . actually, Gaye?
Is there anyplace near here that makes a decent cup of tea? Like
not in a Styrofoam cup?"

"Not in the hospital, I'm afraid. There's a cafe across the
road that might—" She turned to Mage. "I can show you the
way. . . ."

"That'd be great," sighed Takumo. "Mage?"

Mage nodded. "Okay. Whatever you want."

Mandaglione was two-thirds of the way through a sex scene,
the point at which he was wondering whether or not one of the
characters should pause to get a condom, when he heard a
knock on the door. He sighed, hit the save button, and yelled,
"Coming!" He looked through the peephole, and saw Mage
standing outside, a small backpack slung over his shoulders. He
opened the door, and said, "Wondered when you'd be turning
up."

"What?"

"Just a hunch. Come in. Have you heard from Charlie?"

Mage nodded, and shut the door behind him. "Seen him. He's in the hospital."

"Shit." The concern on his uncle's face was instant and sincere. "Accident?"

"No, I'm pretty sure she shot him deliberately. What's he told you?"

"A damn sight more than you ever did," said Mandaglione, easing his bulk into the large once-black leather chair that dominated the small living room. "When did this happen?"

"Last night."

Mandaglione glanced at his watch. "You just flew here?" Mage nodded, almost imperceptibly; it was safer than lying. "Who was it?"

"I don't know."

"Drive-by?"

"No. I didn't see it, got there after it was over."

Mandaglione nodded. "Is he okay?"

"They say he's going to be."

"Good. Jesus." He blinked. "Charlie thinks there are vampires in L.A., doesn't he?"

Mage hesitated. "One vampire, maybe more, but he was on pretty serious medication when I spoke to him . . ."

"You don't believe him?"

"Do you?"

"I haven't decided yet. Sit down! So, who shot him?"

"I don't know."

"Don't bullshit me, Mikey," said Mandaglione, heavily, "and don't insult my intelligence, unless you don't *want* my help, of course. Ever since that mess a couple of years ago, it's been blindingly obvious, at least to people who know you, that you've been trying to keep a secret. I don't know what this secret is, but you seem to think that if it gets out, it'll be dangerous for your family and friends. I know you've been traveling; you never say where you've been, but you have a slightly different accent nearly every time you're here. And a friend of mine saw you in Bangkok a few months ago—and don't try to tell me it wasn't you, Mikey, she's a makeup artist, she never forgets a face any more than you do.

"I was scared that you might be involved in some sort of smuggling, but you don't seem to be on any drugs that I ever heard of, and you don't look like you were spending money on anything else. I'd already heard rumors that there was someone in Bangkok who was using faith healing or hypnosis or something similarly nonsurgical and noninvasive for makeovers and boob jobs, but I didn't start putting two and two together until one of your patients showed up here for a shoot. We got to chatting, and I saw her 'before' photos, and I remembered your ideals of beauty from your photographic work. *And* you'd given her a slight resemblance to Amanda Sharmon. It's not the sort of evidence that would stand up in any court, but she was talking about the guy who'd done it, a tall good-looking American who couldn't possibly be as young as he seemed, and on a hunch, I showed her a photo of you."

"Have you ever considered a career as an independent prosecutor?"

Mandaglione bristled. "No, I do have *some* ethics, and a little pride. But thanks, that's all the confirmation I needed: the woman wasn't sure it was you, but now *I* am."

Mage hesitated, then plunged in. "It's a confidence trick, though faith healing isn't far off. I convince women that they're beautiful, and—"

"And they smile more, dress better, arch their backs more, that sort of thing?"

Mage nodded.

"Like 'Mudd's Women', that *Star Trek* episode? Bullshit. Oh, maybe that's part of it, but this woman damn near went from Nastassia Kinski to Amy Yip. How much kickback do you get from the local boutiques?"

"I don't keep the money. It goes to a free clinic and groups like Amnesty International."

"Good. What else aren't you telling me—apart from how you do it?"

Mage hesitated. "That's the big one."

"What about Tamenaga?"

"What?"

"Two years ago, you asked me about Tatsuo Tamenaga, and a few days later, he was sashimi in his own office. That might've been a coincidence, but if you had anything to do with that, you done good—I wish you'd taken out Aaron Spelling while you were in the neighborhood, but I guess you were in a hurry."

Mage was silent.

"Look, you want my help? All you have to do is ask, you know that—but I think I can help you more if you don't keep me in the dark."

Mage considered this, and nodded. "Okay. Where should I start?"

"**W**hat's this I hear about you not pressing charges?"

Though half-asleep, Takumo didn't need to open his eyes to know who'd just walked into the room; he'd recognized the rhythm of her walk while she was still in the hallway outside. "Hi, Kel."

Kelly, still dressed for work in a severely cut gray business suit, towered over the bed. With her face in shadow and the white wall and ceiling behind her, she looked like a black monolith, an obsidian statue of some fierce African goddess. "Well? Do you want her to just get away with it?"

Takumo sighed, and looked around the room. His only roommate seemed to still be asleep. "She'll get away with it anyway. There was a Homicide cop here this morning, Woodcott, but he lost interest when the doctors told him I was going to live. I don't feel like wasting my time either."

Kelly bristled. "They have good forensic evidence. The bullet they pulled out of you was unusual; a .427-caliber caseless. There aren't many guns that fire that sort of round; it shouldn't be too difficult to trace them all—"

"You won't find her that easily; this woman's a pro. And even if you did, so what? You won't get the asshole who hired her."

The lawyer scowled. "If everyone thought like that—"

"Everyone does," replied Takumo, closing his eyes again. "Including her. The only difference is that the rich think it's fair. So she shot two guys and nearly killed them, but hey, she was protecting some multimillion-dollar invest—"

"*Two* guys?"

"Didn't Mage tell you? She got him, too—twice, in the chest."

Kelly sat down on the bed, her expression softening slightly. "So what are you going to do?"

"Get out of here as soon as I can, and be ready in case she comes back—and I'd advise you to do the same. What if Mage stayed with—"

"No."

"Okay, what if he just looks in on you, like every hour on the hour—"

"No. I'd probably shoot him by mistake. I have a carry permit for the pistol, and I'll keep the shotgun by my bed. I *can* take care of myself, Charlie."

Takumo looked up at her, and decided against arguing. "Cool. So, can you call me, at least—say, three times a day? When you go to bed, when you get up—"

"Okay," she said. "As long as you reconsider reporting this to the cops. They might surprise you."

The Sunrise distinguished itself from the other casinos that surrounded it by a veneer of Japanese-ness, including torii gates, shoji screens, stone lanterns, and a large statue of Hotei, the Japanese God of Gamblers, watching over the tables. The female staff were Asian and wore abbreviated kimonos, the paper umbrellas in the drinks were festooned with Japanese calligraphy, and the restaurant upstairs offered teppanyaki and all-you-could eat sushi.

Mage clad in jeans, leather jacket, and T-shirt and looking more than a little out of place amid the tourists, walked up to the bar and asked to speak to the owner. Within five minutes, he had been flanked by two men with the builds of sumo wrestlers; he repeated the request, and when neither of them replied, he said, clearly, "Please tell Mr. Nakatani that Mr. Magistrale is here to see him. He'll know the name," One guard's mask of puzzlement flickered briefly. "And he *will* want to see me. So I'm going to wait in this crowded room for exactly five minutes, and if Mr. Nakatani hasn't come down to see me by the end of that time, I'll go." He looked up at one of the security cameras, and waved. "Five minutes."

"Can I say what it's about?"

"He knows."

One of the guards walked away quickly, and three minutes later, a woman, slightly older than the waitresses and wearing a much longer skirt, but equally attractive, appeared from the elevator. "Mr. Nakatani will be with you in a few minutes, Mr. Magistrale."

"Thank you."

She hesitated, and looked down at his feet then around the crowded hall. "He asked if you'd rather meet him somewhere more private." Mage raised an eyebrow. "One of the suites upstairs?"

"No, I don't think so."

"We have—"

"I'll discuss that with Mr. Nakatani after he arrives," he said, softly but firmly, and she nodded. Nakatani walked out of an elevator precisely six minutes later. "Mr. Magistrale?" He wore an expensive suit and Italian shoes, a marked contrast to Mage's faded jeans, NASA T-shirt, and well-traveled boots. He didn't offer to shake hands.

"We meet at last," replied Mage. Mandaglione had shown him enough photos of Nakatani for him to recognize the man, unless this was a well-disguised double or another shape-shifter. "One of your people shot a friend of mine this morning."

Nakatani glanced around. No one but the security guard was standing close enough to overhear the quiet conversation, but a few of the less obsessive gamblers were already looking their way with faint curiosity. "I don't know what you're talking about," he said, lowering his voice.

Mage smiled, with mock sympathy. "Okay, you're a busy man, you have people who take care of this sort of thing for you, maybe you don't get reports on time—"

Nakatani took another glance at their audience. "Need we discuss this here? My office is much more private—and more comfortable."

Mage swallowed the smile. "Yeah, okay. Lead the way. . . ." He knew that he might be walking into an ambush, but if he could see Nakatani's office, he could return there at any time. He followed him into an elevator, and stood behind him; Nakatani was three inches too short to make an ideal shield, but it would make any gunman hesitate long enough for Mage to act.

"I don't know where you've gotten the idea that I'm interested in having you killed," said Nakatani, stiffly. "Not that I doubt that *somebody* is, but I'm a little curious. What motive would I have?"

Mage glanced around the elevator; he couldn't see any cameras, but he was sure they were there. "You were a business partner of Tatsuo Tamenaga's. Tamenaga admitted to me that he'd sent people to kill me."

"I had business dealings with Mr. Tamenaga, yes," conceded Nakatani as the elevator door opened at the twenty-fifth floor, "but only business." He stepped out of the elevator, and Mage watched him carefully; if there was anyone waiting out of sight of the doors, Nakatani managed not to acknowledge them in any way. He nodded at the receptionist—the second woman Mage had spoken to downstairs—and asked her to hold his calls. She pressed a button on her desk, and Mage heard a heavy door slide open somewhere out of sight. He took a deep breath, and walked into the anteroom; he smiled at the receptionist, who watched him the way she might have watched a venomous snake through glass.

Nakatani's office was larger than Tamenaga's had been; one wall was adorned with Japanese antiques, the other with TV monitors and a bar. There was a huge window behind the desk, showing a view of the east side of Las Vegas and the desert beyond, but only the one door. A burly Japanese man in a slightly baggy black suit and Raybans sat on one of the black leather chairs and couches near the bar. "You needn't worry about Kojiro," said Nakatani, breezily. "He doesn't understand English, so we can talk safely."

Mage leaned up against the wall, choosing a vantage point where he could watch Kojiro as well as Nakatani, and see the door open before anyone who came in could see him. "Okay," he said. "I don't know whether you're taping this, and I don't really give a fuck because I'm sure neither of us is interested in getting any sort of law involved, but two years ago, I warned Tamenaga to leave my family and my friends alone. I'm giving you the same warning."

Nakatani managed to keep his face impassive, though nervousness and a hint of anger were plain in his voice. "I knew Tamenaga," he said, "and he would never have had your family attacked. Family was sacred to him—his and others. More sacred even than business." Mage conceded the point with a slight nod. "But we were not family, and I have no interest in avenging him. I assume you murdered him, though you haven't had the . . . the guts to say so openly." Mage merely nodded again. "I am not responsible for any attacks on you or your friends. Is that clear?"

Mage grimaced. "I can see you still have some links to the yakuza," he said, glancing at Kojiro, who didn't react. "And I can't think of anyone else who would want me dead. So why should I believe you?"

Nakatani had been turning pink, but this question made him blanch again. Mage waited, but Nakatani only shook his head. Mage realized that while Nakatani was obviously scared of him, he was even more scared of something—or someone—else.

"The attacks had better stop," said Mage, flatly. "If they don't, I will kill you. Do you understand?"

Kojiro moved slightly. Mage didn't pause to wonder whether this was something else Nakatani had lied about, or whether the bodyguard's English vocabulary was limited to that one phrase. Suddenly, Kojiro found himself in the dark. Instead of reaching for his pistol, he grabbed his sunglasses and raised them, relieved to find that he could still see around but not through them. The second thing he noticed was that Mage was gone. He glanced at his boss, and saw that Nakatani was still staring at the spot where Mage had been a moment before. He seemed stunned, but unhurt, and a moment later, he looked back at Kojiro. "Would you recognize that man if you saw him again?" he asked, in Japanese.

"Yes."

"Good. If you see him, kill him. I don't care how or where, as long as you do it immediately. You'll be well rewarded. He murdered Tatsuo Tamenaga, and just threatened me. Do you understand?"

"Yes."

"Good." Nakatani reached for the intercom on his desk, then looked down at his hand and screamed. The little finger on his left hand was now cleanly, bloodlessly, one joint shorter.

The ritual was a simple one, though tedious, and not always reliable. Tudor placed the tetsubishi on the altar, and performed the summoning. He was sure that the spikes had been left in Ernst's garage by the intruder, and hoped that Ernst hadn't contaminated them too badly while removing them from his tires. It was difficult casting magic onto cold iron—many minor demons found the stuff repellent—but at least it had no residual life signs of its own.

Night had fallen before he had an answer, and he was nearly exhausted. He showered and wolfed down a hastily made sandwich before opening the door and confronting his son. Tanith, Beth, and Adrian wandered around the house, behaving almost normally, but with an oddly distracted air as they occasionally strayed too close to the blind spots Tudor had created, areas they found it difficult to even think about.

Malachi had begun gnawing on his fingers almost as soon as

the sun had set, and they now looked like hamburger, while
Julia, lying beside him, glared at Tudor with red-gray eyes.
"When do *I* feed?" she growled, in a voice that her mother
would never have recognized. "Let me out."

"Soon," promised Tudor, standing outside the circle, protected by his talismans. "I need Malachi to do some hacking
first; I need to find some information on Sindee."

"Sindee . . ." The vampire looked blank for an instant.

"The woman he was feeding on—the one who escaped from
Ernst."

The vampire's eyes seemed to flicker. "Don't need her. Can
feed on anybody."

Tudor looked at her, as Malachi began losing his grayish
pallor. "Ernst will be here in an hour," he said, turning on his
heel. "You can feed then." He didn't know what the vampires
would do once Malachi had fed, but he had no wish to watch.

When he returned to the room, forty minutes later, the two
vampires were sitting as far as they could from each other without touching the protective circle. Malachi looked sullen, while
Julia's face was distorted into a bestial mask by her hunger.
"Mal," said Tudor. "I need you to hack into that hospital computer again. Do you think you can do that?"

"Yes," muttered his son.

"Good. I want any information you can get on Sindee—she's
registered as Sandra Halley. I need to know when they expect
to discharge her, and anything you can find out about her ad-
mission. I've made a poppet with her hair, but I don't want to
use it unless I have to; she can identify all of us, people know
she lived here, and while I don't think the cops will believe her,
somebody might." He turned to Julia. "The man who helped
her escape was named Charles Willis Takumo. I've only been
able to find one man of that name in L.A., an actor and stuntman living near Venice Beach. I don't know how he got involved in this, and I don't particularly care, I just want him
dead before sunrise. You may feast on him first, of course," he
said magnanimously.

Ernst arrived shortly before ten, wearing a new leather jacket with a high collar. As Tudor had ordered, he'd brought several bags of blood, which he threw to Julia without entering the circle. Only when she'd drained these and taken the edge off her hunger did he step into the circle and allow himself to be bitten, hoping that she wouldn't take enough to kill him. It was nearly eleven when they left the house, the doctor still unsteady on his feet from the effects of the bite.

"Have you ever thought of getting a less conspicuous car?" the vampire asked, as Ernst searched through the street directory.

"No," the surgeon replied, not looking up. "Is it a problem?"

"It could be."

"I parked out of sight of the club . . ."

"Somebody might still notice you, and remember."

He shrugged one shoulder, then started the car. "Did you tell Solomon about that goth girl you, er . . ."

"No," said Julia, coolly, "and neither will you."

Ernst glanced at her, and decided not to argue. He would have found it difficult to say who now had the greater hold over him; Tudor, who was able to reveal what he'd done to some of his clients while they were under anesthetic, or Julia, to whose bite he was already addicted. He'd waited in the Merc for more than two hours after Julia had disappeared into the Crypt, not realizing that she'd gone home with her willing victim. He'd been shivering with fear when his cell phone had finally rung, and Julia had asked him to come around and pick her up.

"I won't," he said.

She smiled. "Ben Franklin once said that three people could keep a secret, if two of them were dead. I guess he was right." She'd been reluctant to turn Mara; she looked too young, with pimples visible through her goth makeup and mousy roots showing in her black hair, but she was undeniably willing and she'd insisted that she had a car and a place of her own. Julia had told her to wait ten minutes before leaving, then had walked out of the Crypt, half hoping that the young woman would chicken out. She hadn't.

The place turned out to be Mara's father's home, but no one else was there; Mara said that he was out of town on business until Friday, and some instinct told Julia that she was telling the truth. Vampirism had sharpened some of her senses, dulled others; she was more aware of blood flow than any normal human, quick to pick up changes in heart-rate and blood rushing to or from the muscles, and thus better able to detect fear or arousal or deceit. Her new senses also confirmed that either nobody else was home, or the soundproofing was excellent; either way, the risks seemed acceptable. She looked at the young woman, and whispered, "Last chance to change your mind."

Mara shook her head. Her body was shaking too, with as much excitement as nervousness. "Do it," she said, sharply.

"As you wish." Julia kissed her wrist, then bit into the artery and drank. The first taste of fresh, healthy young blood was enough to reawaken the hunger. She heard Mara whimper and felt her try to pull her hand away, and she grabbed her neck and bit into the soft flesh at the side of her throat. Mara screamed, but stopped struggling; a few minutes later, she stopped moving completely. Julia had continued to drink until she was absolutely sure the young woman was dead, then had laid her gently on her bed. If Tudor's grimoires were to be trusted, and nobody disturbed the body during the day, she would almost certainly turn the next night. It seemed a sensible precaution to have allies that Tudor knew nothing about.

Ernst said nothing more until they reached Venice, where he parked outside an all-night cafe. "You have your phone?"

She patted the pocket of her leather jacket. When she'd told him how long it had taken her to find a pay phone after leaving Mara's, Ernst had been so grateful that she'd thought not to call him from the house that he'd bought a cellular phone as soon as the dealership opened. He hated the things himself, drawing the line at a pager and the hands-free phone in the car, but it seemed justified under the circumstances. To his astonishment, Julia leaned over and kissed him on the cheek, not even drawing blood. "You sound just like my father," she said, before disappearing into the night. Ernst had smiled as he walked toward the cafe, and then frozen as he remembered that Julia's father was dead.

Julia was sure even before she knocked on the door that the apartment was empty, but she knocked softly anyway. Still no sound of movement. She knew, without glancing at her watch, that it was slightly after ten, and she wondered whether it was worth waiting for Takumo to come home. She walked quietly but quickly down the stairs and around the building to the other side, then leaped up onto the balcony. She peered through the security screen and the french windows, then at the locks. They looked like dead bolts, so even if she could remove the first screen, breaking the glass and reaching through wouldn't help— besides, there was a barely visible logo on the window saying that the glass was toughened. She took another long, appraising look, then grabbed the handle of the screen and pulled with all of her strength. The metal was slow to bend, but she continued to strain until the locks finally yielded and the screen slid open. The sliding glass door took nearly as long, but finally, with a triumphant sneer, she brushed the paper blind aside and stepped inside the apartment.

An instant later, a light clicked on inside the room, and she heard a slow beat, dum, DUM, dum, DUM, soft, loud, soft, loud . . . Queen's *Another One Bites the Dust*. She looked around; there was nobody in the room, but she realized she had little hope of ambushing Takumo now that she'd set off his alarm. Quickly, she switched to Plan B, and ran through the apartment looking for the bathroom. There was, as she'd hoped, a comb next to the handbasin; she grabbed this, and rushed out of the apartment, leaping down from the balcony and running through the darkness.

There was little Plummer could do with one good arm, so when he'd been offered the job of watching Takumo's apartment, he'd barely hesitated before taking it. It was about as exciting as watching an Andy Warhol movie in slo-mo, and the guy they'd teamed him with snored, but the pay was adequate, and the prospect of seeing the little bastard get his was an added spice.

He'd been watching for nearly two hours without a break while his partner slept on the couch, and he didn't notice the black-clad Julia until she clambered onto the balcony. He blinked, then watched through the telephoto and light-intensifier lenses of the camera as she examined the door. "Joe!" he hissed. His partner continued to snore. Plummer swore, but he didn't dare leave the camera. The figure didn't look like Takumo, though it was difficult to be sure when he could only see her back. The height was about right, the costume was unisex and black—jeans, leather jacket, and sneakers—and the long hair could be faked, but the ass looked wrong. "Joe!" he hissed, more loudly. Still no response.

Plummer took a few photos, without much hope of them revealing anything useful, but didn't do anything more until he saw the figure slide the security screen open. This was weird enough to disturb the boss for, and he reached for the cell phone. Krieg answered after two rings. "Rook to Queen One," he said, wondering who made up these stupid code-names. "There's somebody on the balcony, and I'm not entirely sure, but I don't think it's Elvis." He watched as Julia hauled on the french window.

"It shouldn't be," replied Krieg.

"One of us?"

"No."

"Sh—he's just opened the door, going in—he's set off the alarm—"

"Tell Joe to get over there, see if he can follow him, find out where he came from, who he is—"

"Just a—" He watched the figure, silhouetted through the paper blind, head back toward the window. He waited until he could see a face, then started the motor-drive on the camera. "Leaving now." He dropped the phone, and scrambled across the floor and shook Joe. "Get up! Boss lady wants you! Get up, you lazy bum, or the only thing you're going to be sleeping with is fish! Move!"

Krieg listened at the other end of the line; she couldn't hear the words, but some of the tone was clear. She smiled, and glanced at her watch. Eleven seventeen. Almost time for one of Takumo's friends to die.

Mandaglione looked around the hotel room without any sign of pleasure, then dropped his suitcase and collapsed onto the bed. "Charlie said we could stay at his place," Mage reminded him.

"Sleeping on sofas and floors is for the young and skinny," said Mandaglione grumpily. "I like a big soft bed, some privacy, and my own TV and shower. Thank him for me anyway, but no thanks."

"Okay."

"How the Hell do you do that disappearing trick? It beats the Hell out of Reno Air."

"Magic. I can't explain it any better than that; I just *see* myself in another location, and I'm there. It has to be somewhere I know well enough to visualize accurately and have, I don't know, a feeling for. A sense of where it is; if it were *just* visual, all someone would have to do to keep me out is change some of the furniture."

"Oh."

"I can even teleport up to the Moon, or low Earth orbit—I do it sometimes, mostly for the view. I can't stay long, not without breathing gear, but I can heal the sunburn and any other damage. I've thought of going to Mars, too—the pictures from Viking and Sojourner are clear enough that I think I can *see* myself there—but I don't think it's worth the risk of contaminating the planet."

Mandaglione goggled, but recovered quickly. "What about the space station?"

"Only from the outside. I've thought about going in, but it's probably too heavily monitored. I did visit Mir, a few days before it came down, and retrieved a few things. I'll sell them to a museum if I can come up with a good enough story to explain how I got them."

"Could you take me with you, next time? Not to Mir, but one of—"

"No," said Mage, firmly. "Not until I'm sure it's safe." He glanced at his watch. Four to midnight. "I've got to go."

G aye was walking out of the locker room when she saw Magistrale leaning on the wall outside. "What're you doing here? Visiting hours ended ages ago!"

"I know. I was wondering if you'd like to grab a cup of coffee."

"What?"

Mage shrugged, and started to improvise. "I just got into town this morning, and Charlie's the only person I know here— apart from Kelly, and we don't get on that well—and it's a big city to be alone in, and I don't know my way around very well."

Gaye looked at him doubtfully. "Where are you staying?"

"At Charlie's."

"I have to get home, feed my cats—where does Charlie live? I could probably give you a lift, if it's not too far out of my way. . . ."

"Speedway. Venice Beach."

Gaye smiled. "I think I can manage that. Come on, my car's this way." She stopped at the nurse's station to say good night to a few of her friends, making sure that they had a good look at Mage, then led the way down to the parking garage. "Where are you from? I can't place your accent."

"New York, originally, but I travel a lot."

"I love to travel," she said, a little wistfully. "I get up to San Francisco occasionally, and I've been out to the Grand Canyon and New Orleans and down to Mexico once, but never any further than that. What's the most exciting place you've ever been?"

Mage resisted the urge to say "The Moon." "Depends on what you mean by "exciting." Compared to New York, most places are pretty relaxing, which is fine by me."

"What do you do for a living?"

"I take photographs, and I do other work when I need to. Mostly in hospitals."

"You're a nurse?"

"No, just an orderly, but I'm studying in my spare time."

She nodded, and grabbed her keychain out of her purse as they walked out of the building. Mage noticed a peace symbol, a penlight, and a can of pepper spray on the chain, and was reminded of Charlie. She walked confidently through the parking lot, and stopped at a white Tercel. "You may have to move the seat back," she said, as she opened the driver's side door. "I think the last passenger I had was Bast, in a cat-box." She sat down, and reached across to open his door, then buckled up her seat belt. "So, where do you know Charlie from?"

"We met in Calgary, about two years ago. Both just passing through, but we . . . hit it off pretty quickly, and we're still good friends." He closed the door, and adjusted the seat. She waited until he was strapped in, then turned the key in the ignition.

The car exploded, illuminating the lot and setting off alarms for yards around.

14

Turning

Kelly was enjoying a pleasant dream about a boy she'd dated in her college days; their first kiss was beginning to turn into something more serious, his thigh was between hers, he was gently biting her neck with the obvious intention of descending further, and when the smoke alarm sounded, she accepted it as part of the background music until she realized that she was mostly awake. Oedipus came hurtling into the room just as she opened her eyes. "Yeah, I know," she muttered, and clambered out of bed, grabbed her shotgun, and stumbled toward the noise. She screamed as she saw the burning man rolling around on the living room carpet, and rushed into the kitchen for the fire blanket. He looked up as she covered him with the blanket, and she recognized his face. "Mage?"

"Thanks," he gasped, then grabbed the blanket and *saw* himself back in the parking lot. Kelly stood there, her mouth opened, with only the scream of the alarm and the smoldering carpet to tell her that she hadn't dreamed that, too.

Mage reappeared inside the blazing Tercel, and tried to wrap the fire blanket around Gaye, but discovered that she was still strapped in with her seat belt. The buckle branded his hand as he opened it, but he ignored the pain. He smothered the flames around her as best he could, then *saw* the door open as he lifted her out of the seat. He fell, rather than stepped, out of the car, and staggered away from the flames. He didn't know whether the gas tank was likely to explode, but it seemed like a good idea to put something solid between them and the car. A few yards later, his knees buckled and he fell. He reached for the focus, making sure that it was undamaged, and tightened his fist around it as he unwrapped Gaye. Her face was a blackened and bloody mess of burns and lacerations, her skin barely distinguishable from the smoldering rags that he tried to peel away from it, and blood was pouring from her ears. He touched her throat, hoping against hope for a pulse—and found one, faint but unmistakable.

He heaved a sigh of relief, and began looking at her, remembering her, *seeing* her as she had been less than a minute before. Shock or concussion or internal injuries were beyond his capacity to heal, but he'd had plenty of practice with burns and lacerations and similar flesh wounds. Restoring her face took only an instant, her hands a little longer, but he had never seen her body and had to imagine it, detail by detail. He knew from his first-aid training that burning that destroyed more than seventy percent of the skin was fatal, and the head, neck, and arms together made up less than thirty percent of the body's surface. He was still *seeing* her, flensing away the damaged skin, when a paramedic came running up. "What the Hell?"

He looked up, saw the man recoil, and realized for the first time how badly his own face must have been lacerated and burned. "It exploded," he said, his voice gurgling. "I'm trying to help her—"

"We'll help her," said the paramedic, and Mage looked past him to see other people approaching—more paramedics, nurses, orderlies, and others who he hoped were doctors. "We'll help you, too. Come on."

*   *   *

When Mara opened her eyes, the first thing she saw was her hands, which were covered with bite-marks from her black-lacquered nails down to the scars on her wrists. As she stared, the wounds healed, leaving her hands as beautiful and white as they had been before. It was nearly a minute before she remembered what had happened to her the previous night, and realized that it wasn't merely a wonderful dream. She smiled, and eagerly climbed out of bed. Years ago, she and her best friend Ahna had made each other a promise; if either of them became a vampire, she was to bite and turn the other as soon as possible.

She spent the next few minutes testing her new powers. She was delighted to find that she could *still* see her reflection in a mirror, and safely wear silver; disappointed to find that she could not fly, or transform into mist or any animal form. Maybe there was a trick to it that Julia could teach her, or maybe not; Mara had read widely enough to know that many of the powers and weaknesses attributed to vampires had been fabricated by Bram Stoker, or by screenwriters from Hollywood and Hammer Studios. She glanced at her teeth as she applied her black lipstick, faintly irritated that her canines didn't seem to have grown noticeably longer or sharper. Maybe it took time.

There was a red light flashing on the answering machine as she walked out, and she sighed and rewound the tape. "Tammi?" said her father's voice. "It looks like I'll be here a few days longer than—" She switched the machine off; she'd told him *hundreds* of times that she didn't answer to that name anymore. Maybe she should do something to remind him of who she *really* was. . . .

Krieg was listening in on the police radio bands, waiting for news of the causalities from the car bomb, and she snarled as the phone rang. "Knight to Queen One," said Joe. "The, uh, intruder? The one who broke into, uh, Graceland?"

"Yes."

"Got into a car, a dark blue Mercedes. Didn't get a good look at the driver, but we have a license plate. They've parked on Clarissa Avenue, and she went into a cafe around the corner, the Crypt."

"Stay with the car, see where it goes next," said Krieg. "I'll run a check on the license tomorrow." She hung up, and twisted the volume knob on the radio.

Kelly woke at sunrise, looked around blearily, and realized that she'd fallen asleep on the sofa. The shotgun lay on the coffee table beside her, and her hand still rested on the stock. She'd gotten up twice for coffee since Mage had teleported in and out of the house, and once more to put on a bathrobe in case he returned. She sat up, and grimaced; her mouth tasted like shit, and she suspected she looked and smelled much the same. She was trying to stand up straight in the shower when Mage reappeared, and she came out to find him sitting at the breakfast bar. "You look just like I feel," she said, which was an unjustifiable exaggeration; he looked much worse. "What the hell happened last night?"

He told her in a hundred words or less. "Sorry for busting in on you like that, without any warning; it's a reflex action, like flinching. When I open my eyes again, I'm somewhere safe—not even somewhere I pick consciously. I'm not sure why I came here rather than Charlie's place, or mine. . . ."

"And you immediately jump back into danger."

"I had to help Gaye."

Kelly nodded. "How is she?"

"Unconscious, last I heard, but that was a few hours ago. I think I went into shock—if I wasn't to begin with—but I got out of the hospital as soon as I could, didn't want to answer too many questions. Can I use your bathroom? I want to get these bandages off, and I can heal myself better if I have a mirror."

"Sure."

"Thanks. I owe you."

She nodded again. "A night's sleep, and a hell of a good dream."

"I'll try to make it up to you."

"Yeah?" She watched him stagger toward the bathroom, then glanced at the carpet. He'd already repaired the fire damage. "And that's when I shot him, your Honor," she muttered to Oedipus.

Mage returned a few minutes later; he still looked faintly scruffy, but the bandages were gone, his skin unmarked, his beard trimmed, and his hair—now a paler blonde, and barely down to his shoulders—neatly groomed. "When's your lunch break?" he asked.

"What? One. Why?"

"We're having a meeting at the hospital—in Takumo's room, or maybe in the cafe if there are too many people listening. Dante, Charlie, and I, and we'd all like you there, too, if you can make it."

"Count me in," she said, and immediately wondered why. "Do you want some breakfast?" she asked, to cover her confusion.

"Love some, but I've got to go. Some other time?"

Nakatani was reading a prospectus on one of the legal brothels outside of Reno. The price seemed reasonable, and the owner was willing to fly likely investors out to the brothel for an on-site inspection; rumor had it that he wanted the money to finance his Senate campaign. It would be useful for money-laundering, and for recruiting women for the *Japayuki*; just as important, as Haruko refused to involve herself in any aspect of the sex industry, it would be something of his own. He grinned at the idea of holding it in trust for his son; in the six years since his divorce, he'd given up trying to reconcile with his ex-wife, and was now content with irritating her. Besides . . .

Nakatani had little interest in sex, except the commercial aspects. When out of town, he occasionally hired escorts; always using a false name, always paying cash, and rarely using the same agency twice, no matter how appealing he found the woman. He was far too cautious of his respectable image to indulge this taste while in Vegas, where he was too well known. He suspected that Haruko had tried to seduce him on a few occasions, in the hopes of rendering him even more tractable, but had always resisted.

The fantasy of secretly owning a brothel was so appealing that it was several seconds before he realized that he was no longer alone in the room. He looked over the prospectus to see Mage standing next to the door. He reached for the intercom, and found that it had been replaced by a small cactus. His left hand jerked away from the cactus as his right slid toward the hidden compartment under the desk where he kept his pistol. "Don't," snapped Mage. "Don't move at all."

Nakatani tried to speak, to plead, but discovered that he couldn't open his mouth. Despite Mage's warning, he lifted his right hand up to touch his face, and to his horror, found only smooth, unbroken skin. Unable to gasp, he tried breathing in through his nose, without success.

"Save it," said Mage. "I'm not going to listen to you. I gave you a chance, and you went ahead and tried to kill me, and what's worse, you nearly killed an innocent woman as well. So no more warnings. This ends here and now."

Nakatani stared, his vision already beginning to blur slightly. Moving slowly at first, then urgently, then frantically, he mimed writing on a pad. Mage glared at him, then nodded, relenting. Killing someone in cold blood was even more difficult than he'd imagined. Nakatani grabbed a gold pen from his blotter, and a personalized notepad, and hastily scrawled, "Not me." He slid it across the desk to Mage, who slid it back. "What wasn't you?" he asked.

Blood was pounding in Nakatani's ears as his chest labored ineffectually, trying to suck in air. "Bomb," he wrote.

Mage read this, and smiled venomously. "I didn't mention a bomb," he said.

Nakatani shook his head, and reached across the desk for the pad. "I heard about it this morning!" he scribbled, the pen slipping in his sweaty hands. "I tried to stop her!" Mage snatched up the pad, and looked at it dubiously. Nakatani pitched forward onto his blotter, and Mage grabbed him by the hair and looked into his face. His eyes were closed, and when Mage forced one open, it didn't track.

Mage was unsure how long it would take Nakatani to die from suffocation, and he didn't want to stay in the room to watch. Reluctantly, he restored Nakatani's face, and pushed him back in the chair. Nakatani sucked in a huge breath, and slowly opened his eyes. "Tried to stop who?" asked Mage.

Nakatani opened his mouth to speak, but no words issued forth, only a gurgling noise. Mage threw the pad back onto the blotter. "Who?" he repeated.

Nakatani fumbled for his pen—and hesitated. He'd played enough chess, and watched enough gamblers, to know what it was like to have nothing left to lose. Mage would never trust him enough to let him live. Haruko must already have heard that Mage had escaped from his office yesterday, and that he'd survived Krieg's car-bomb, and she was likely to kill the next person who brought her bad news. He glanced up at Mage, wondering how much he already knew. In a barely legible hand, very unlike his usual neat calligraphy, he wrote what little he knew about Valeri Krieg, then pushed the pad across the desk again.

While Mage looked at the note, Nakatani reached under his desk for his pistol. He was about to fire when Mage glanced up and, without time to think, Mage *saw* him fly through the air and through the window. Nakatani screamed as he fell the twenty stories, but one faintly reassuring thought occurred to him. He had not actually betrayed Haruko, so she would probably let his children live. There was a ghost of a smile on his face as he smashed into the Strip.

Mandaglione looked around the table at the assembled group, all of whom looked as though they'd been fighting demons and losing. Takumo, though still hooked up to an intravenous drip, seemed the healthiest, and certainly the most vital. Kelly had obviously been sleeping badly, if at all; and Mage, though uninjured and immaculately groomed, looked sick, weary, and far older than his twenty-five years.

"I've tried getting in to interview Angela Winslow, but she's not seeing anyone," Mandaglione reported. He sipped at his espresso, and grimaced. "Her doctor thinks it's Munchausen's syndrome—that is, she's faking her symptoms to gain sympathy. Presumably draining blood out of herself somehow—and I have to admit, I've heard of Munchausen's sufferers doing worse. The best I've been able to do is write down a series of interview questions that they've passed on, with a request to see her if she's agreeable. I'm not at all sure she'll know anything useful about Tudor, but she might. He might have taught her a little magic, maybe even something that will protect her from whoever or whatever is draining her—though I doubt it."

"Who would be draining her?" asked Takumo. "Assuming someone is. Tudor?"

Mandaglione shrugged. "Maybe, but I don't think so. I've been swapping e-mails with a writer named Paris, who's an authority on vampire legends; I've never met him, and I only know his net name, but I don't know anyone better at distinguishing the original myths from the Hollywood versions. I suspect he's an academic somewhere, without tenure, who wrote his lit or anthro thesis on vampire legends, but doesn't want his dean finding out he writes erotic horror stories after hours. Anyway, he told me that one of the old German names for vampire is *nachtzerer*, night-waster, and in German and Polish legends, the vampire's first victims are its parents or children. Because it has a genetic connection to them—a bloodline, if you like—it can drain them at a distance, without even leaving its grave. That's how it gains the strength to dig its way out. After that, it usually attacks its old lovers." He shrugged. "You have to remember that while nearly every culture has vampire myths, the myths—and the vampires—are very different. The Malaysian penanggalan appears as a woman's head and neck with nothing but the digestive system attached. A Brazilian *jaracara*—

"So you think it's her son?" asked Kelly.

If Mandaglione was annoyed at being interrupted, he didn't show it; he merely shrugged slightly, then nodded.

"What do you know about him?" asked Mage. It was the first time he'd spoken since the meeting had begun.

"Malachi Tudor is twenty-four years old, a freelance software consultant and website designer, and he uses the same mailing address as his father, so he probably still lives at home. That's all I could find on the Web. I did, however, find a few poems by Julia Petrosyan in different e-zines, and a photo of her at a reading at a place called the Crypt, a hangout for goths and vampire wannabes." He shrugged. "Maybe she met a real vampire there and took something nasty home." He noticed Kelly's skeptical look. "Or maybe not. There are other ways to become a vampire. Suicides are supposed to become vampires, though there must be more to it than that, or the world would be crawling with them."

"So what do we do?" asked Takumo. There was a long silence, which he finally broke. "Okay. I'll probably get out tomorrow. I didn't have any difficulty getting into Tudor's house last time—"

Kelly stood. "I don't think I want to hear this."

"Kel—"

"Do you still think my life's in danger?"

"No," said Mage. "At least, I don't think so. If she knows she's not going to be paid—"

"She may not know that yet," said Takumo.

"I'll be careful," replied Kelly dryly. "Call me when you need a lawyer. That shouldn't be too far in the future."

Mage watched her walk away. "Pity."

"She'll come around," said Takumo, with forced cheerfulness. "So, like I was saying, I think I can get a rough map of the house before I go . . . are you coming with me?"

Mage hesitated, then turned to Mandaglione. "If we're right, and there *are* vampires, how much of a threat are they? Not just to us; are they going to keep killing people, or can they, I don't know, survive by sucking rats?"

"I don't know," replied Mandaglione. "A lot of the old European legends say that vampires attack sheep and cattle, draining them, as well as humans—but I don't really see that as a viable option in L.A. Sure, there are rats and pets, but people will be easier to find and to catch—and I suspect there'd be much less hue and cry if a vampire took a few streetwalkers from Sunset than if it drained a poodle in Pacific Palisades. Paris claims that vampires always *prefer* human blood; if they attacked animals instead, it was because the humans were too well protected, or the vampires were so thirsty they drained the first blood they could find. The legends disagree on how long a vampire's victims take to die—though most of them agree that a baby, at least, can be drained in one night—but they agree that ultimately, many or most *do* die, unless the vampire is killed first."

"And become vampires?"

"I don't know. In the legends I remember, anyone thought to have been the victim of a vampire would be buried or cremated with the appropriate precautions—and remember, history is written by the victors. A village where vampirism wasn't stopped might not have left any stories behind."

"What do you suggest we do?" asked Mage, carefully.

"What I'd *like* you to do is try to capture a vampire alive, if that's the right word. Find out the truth behind the legends, if there is any. Maybe someone will even find a cure—or a way to use vampirism as a cure for other diseases—but even if it just satisfies my curiosity, I think it's worth some risks. I'll come with you, if you think it'd help."

Maybe it was the word "cure" that decided him, but Mage nodded slowly. "Okay," he said. "That sounds good to me. Tomorrow, then."

* * *

Mara and Ahna opened their eyes soon after sunset, and began chewing their hands until living blood flowed from their wounds. They lay close together on the floor of Mara's room, covered with blankets to avoid being burnt by any stray beam of sunlight that might get through the foil on the windows and the heavy drapes. Ahna opened her eyes a few minutes later than Mara, her old self swimming slowly through the dense bloodred miasma of the vampire's satiation. She recognized the room, but had no memory of how she'd come to be there. She rolled over, looked at Mara as she emerged from underneath the blankets, and some memories returned to her. Mara had called her last night, said she had great news and asked if she could see her after she finished work. . . . When the restaurant had shut, her car had been waiting outside, and she'd gotten in, and . . .

"Mara? What am I doing here?"

"It's okay," the vampire crooned. "I brought you here so no one would disturb your body."

"But my parents . . ."

"Probably think you went to school before they were up— you usually do, don't you? You can go home now, if you want, at least for a visit."

"I . . . what time is it?" She glanced at her watch, then at the curtains. "Have I been asleep all *day*?"

Mara threw back her head and laughed loudly. "No, you've been *dead!* Don't you remember?"

"What?"

"We're *vampires!* I *bit* you!"

Ahna stared at her hands, seeing how they healed. "Have I taken something? I do not remember anything. . . ."

"You haven't taken anything," said Mara, impatiently. "Do you remember the promise we made? That if one of us became a vampire, we had to bite the other as soon as possible? There was a vampire at the Crypt the other night—you remember Julia? From Retail Slut?"

Ahna looked at her blankly. "Yes . . ."

"We can go back there tonight. The Crypt. It's going to be wicked."

Ahna blinked. She'd made that promise when they were thirteen or fourteen, after they'd seen Julian Sands in a vampire film. It had seemed like a good idea at the time. "What kind of vampire?"

"What do you mean?"

"A European vampire? A Chinese vampire? A *langsuyar*? A *penanggalan*? What can I do? What can kill me?"

Mara, whose knowledge of vampire lore came mostly from novels and films, looked uncertain. "I don't know yet . . . I guess we'll have to ask Julia, when she comes to the Crypt."

"The Crypt does not open until nine."

Mara shrugged. "Do you want to watch a video? Or go on-line, see what we can find out?"

"I'm supposed to be at work," said Ahna, quietly, as her friend logged on.

Mara turned around. "What?"

". . . nothing."

"Oh. Hey, who do you want to bite first?"

Tudor and Ernst were watching as Julia's eyes began to twitch. The vampire was hungry; it was nearly a week since Julia's father had died, her appetite was still enormous, and all she'd had in the past twenty-four hours was a few mouthfuls of blood from Ernst. The surgeon had taken to wearing high collars and long sleeves; the vampire's saliva enabled their bites to heal nearly as quickly as their own wounds, but sometimes she left bruises. If his nurses had noticed these, they hadn't commented, but he was sure they were gossiping about them while he wasn't listening, and he hated to think what they might suspect him of doing.

Tudor looked at Ernst appraisingly. He didn't know how much longer Angela would last, and Ernst wouldn't survive long if *both* vampires were to feed on him, even though he kept transfusing himself with blood. They needed somebody else to serve as a food source, and Tudor was still reluctant to use Adrian or Beth. The grimoires had also warned him that vampires that drank nonhuman blood were slower to heal and quicker to lose human memories, not something he wanted to happen to Malachi. While he often felt an urge to put an end to this travesty by killing both vampires, he knew that he could never bring himself to do it while there was still some trace of his son remaining. Soon, he realized, he would either have to send him out hunting, or bring a victim back to the house.

The vampire-Julia stood, and Ernst stepped into the circle. As the doctor bared his neck, ready for her bite, Tudor watched dispassionately and repressed an urge to yawn. A few minutes later, Ernst staggered back out of the circle, his eyes glazed; Julia watched him, her face softened into something more nearly human. "Okay," she said to Tudor, "let me out."

"You've fed," said Tudor. "Why do you need to get out?"

The softness in Julia's face disappeared for an instant, then was replaced by a less-than-convincing imitation. "What about Takumo?"

"He's in the hospital," replied Tudor. "Mal did a search last night. I've made a poppet with the hair you brought back, so we can keep him there if we need to. No, I think you're safer where you are."

The vampire hissed. "That wasn't part of our bargain!"

Tudor looked at Malachi. "You can leave tomorrow night, take him with you, teach him to hunt."

The vampire spared Malachi only the briefest of glances. "Better if I teach him tonight, when he's already fed. If his mother dies, he'll wake hungry, difficult to control."

Tudor considered this. The vampire might be telling the truth—not surprising, if the facts suited its purpose. "You've been confined for longer," he said mildly. "I would have thought that would have taught you patience."

"Patience is a virtue," sneered the vampire. "Let me out."

"You're hardly in a position to give orders," said Tudor.

"No?" She turned to Malachi, who was beginning to open his eyes. "Mal," she crooned, "go to my room and get me my velvet gown, please?"

To Tudor's horror, Malachi took two steps toward the door; his foot, bare, stopped when it hit the edge of the circle. He took a half-step back, and then lurched forward again. It was like watching a man try to walk through a wall of shatterproof glass, but worse; every time Malachi's feet, or hands, or face touched the protective circle, the skin instantly turned red and began to blister. Within a few seconds, the skin of his palms and fingers was shredded and oozing, his toes hamburger, his forehead and nose mottled with wounds—and still he continued to press on.

"He'll keep doing this all night if I tell him to," said Julia, calmly.

Tudor watched for a few more seconds, then nodded. "Stop him, and I'll let you go." He reached for the broom leaning against the wall.

"Thank you."

"But he stays here."

She shrugged. "Of course." She waited while he removed a section of the circle barely two feet across, then walked out and grabbed him by the shoulders, pulling him toward her until they were almost nose to nose. "Don't come looking for me," she warned.

He sighed. "I won't unless I need to—but if I may offer you some advice before you go? Choose your hiding places well."

Dwight was reading *Dreams of Decadence* but finding it difficult to concentrate, because he looked up at least twice a page to glance at the clock. Only nine forty, and Julia had said she wouldn't return until just before the cafe closed at three. She would only bite regulars, the real aficionados: "Why should I want to spend eternity with people I wouldn't want to wake up next to?" she'd said, and they'd all agreed—and not take enough to kill them, turn them . . . not yet, anyway. He put the magazine down; reading vampire fiction while waiting for a real vampire to arrive wasn't even a good diversion.

He glanced around the room. Two students, film majors at UCLA, were discussing Val Lewton movies. "It's not a pun," said one.

"*Isle of the Dead*? Of course it is. Look, what was Karloff's best line in *Bride of Frankenstein*? 'I love dead.' If it wasn't meant to be a pun, why didn't he call it *Island of the Dead*?"

Dwight shook his head, and looked at the clock again. Nine fifty. It was going to be a long night. He made himself an espresso, and nearly dropped it when the door opened and Mara walked in with a young, dark-skinned Asian woman whose name he couldn't remember. One glance was enough to tell him that she'd been turned, too—and recently, to judge by her unease. "Evening, ladies," he said, softly, "What'll it be?"

Mara smiled. "We never drink—wine." Dwight smiled politely at the old joke. "Actually, I was wondering if we could speak to you in private."

Dwight looked around the cafe; six customers, none of whom looked likely to try to rob the till or steal the VCR if he turned his back for a moment. "Yeah, okay. My office." He let them behind the counter, and led them into a storeroom barely large enough for the three of them. A filing cabinet was the only piece of office furniture. "I don't think we've been introduced," he said to Ahna. "My name's Dwight."

"Ahna." Her hand was cold, and surprisingly rough.

"We have a deal for you," Mara butted in. "You want to be a vampire, right? Well, we're going to need a place to stay during the days. My father will be home Friday, and Ahna's is probably already looking for her."

Dwight considered this for a moment. He slept much of the day anyway, and there wasn't very much else that he thought he'd miss—his part-time job at the Video Vault was a dead end, and he'd only stuck with it for this long because the Crypt had taken years to start turning a profit. The cafe was also the core of his social life, and what passed for his love life; being undead wouldn't cramp either of these, and might well improve them.

He'd run away from home after his father had found out about his bisexuality, and though he hadn't had sex with men for several years, he hadn't contacted his family in that time either. After nearly a minute of deep thought, he couldn't think of any disadvantages, but he still had doubts. "Tell me what it's like. What can you do?"

"Do?" asked Mara, taking his hand. "We can do *this*," and she bit into his wrist and drank deep. Dwight's knees buckled, and he fell back against the wall, gasping heavily.

Ahna watched for a moment, then whispered, "Don't kill him."

Mara glanced at her, without releasing his wrist, then stopped sucking for long enough to growl, "If you want some too—"

"If he dies, how long will it take him to turn? Tomorrow night? What'll we do tonight? Carry him out the front and prop him up behind the counter and hope no one notices?"

Mara's glare slowly faded until it was merely sullen, and then she dropped Dwight's wrist and put her ear to his heart. "Still alive," she muttered.

Dwight opened his eyes again nearly a minute later, his face pale. "Am I . . ."

"No," said Mara, scowling. "She stopped me. Said to wait until closing time."

Dwight nodded weakly, and was about to lurch out of the storeroom when he looked down. "Uh . . . I'd better clean up here," he said. "Could you girls go out for a minute? I'll be out again soon."

"**A**re you sure that was a good idea?" asked Ernst, as they drove through Hollywood.

"Would you want to sleep with Malachi forever?" asked Julia. "Or be awake with him? Besides, I don't need him anymore."

"What do you need?" asked Ernst, a little nervously.

"The same things I asked Tudor for. A place to keep some

clothes and makeup, mostly. I don't want to end up like Bela Lugosi, wearing the same cape for eternity. A safe place to hide during the day, sometimes—the darkroom would be ideal—but without being confined by any wards. I'll come and go as I please—and in return, I'll bite you at least twice a week. Or would you rather it was more often?"

"Twice a week should be plenty. I can't get blood for a transfusion much more often than that."

She nodded.

"I gather you don't need to be buried in your native soil or anything like that?" he asked, rather weakly.

"Not that I've noticed; I think it's just something else that Stoker invented. Any place that keeps out the sun and predators will do."

"There must be plenty of those."

"Yes, but more of them are taken than you'd think."

"What?" Ernst stared at her, then hastily looked at the road again and jammed on the brakes just in time to avoid going through a red light.

"I think there are other vampires hiding in the city," she said, "or under it, anyway. I didn't actually see any, but the time I first escaped from Tudor's, I wasn't prepared, I didn't have much cash and I didn't want to use the credit cards I—anyway, when morning came, I needed a hiding place, and I found a storm drain and hid there. It didn't occur to me until later that there might be rats, and that rats might think I was dead and eat . . . eat more of me than I could heal, maybe. But by this time, the sun was about to come up, and I didn't want to be caught by it, so I stayed where I was, and then I . . . I don't know. Went to sleep. Died. Whatever. When I came around, I was covered up by a—what do they call those heavy cloth things? Tarpaulins? I don't know who put it there, but they hadn't taken anything of mine . . . and when I left, I was sure there was somebody watching me. Maybe it was just the rats, but I don't think so. That's why I went back to Tudor's."

Ernst nodded. "Do you want me to take you anywhere tonight?"

"I want to go to the Crypt at about three, but I can drive, if you don't mind my borrowing the car."

"No," he said, stifling a yawn. "Not if you bring it back before I have to go to work. I'd better get some sleep tonight." Neither of them spoke again until they arrived home.

"Thanks," she said, leaned over, and kissed him on the cheek.

"What for?" he asked. He opened the car door and stepped out before she could see him blushing.

"For standing up to Tudor."

Ernst shrugged, still embarrassed, and walked into the house without looking at her. "Sol's too scared of you to cause me any trouble. It actually feels pretty good, not being worried that he's going to tell any—" He froze at the sight of a tall blond woman sitting in his favorite chair, aiming a large silenced automatic pistol at his chest. Julia, walking a few feet behind him, also stopped, then smiled at the woman, showing her teeth.

"Good evening," said Valeri Krieg. "Sorry for dropping in on you without warning, but then, you're hardly in a position to complain, ay? You must be Ernst." The surgeon nodded, and Krieg glanced at Julia. "And you're the girl who tried to break into Takumo's apartment? What's your name?"

Julia took a step forward, trying to place herself between Ernst and the gun. "Who are you?"

"Don't move—and I'll ask the questions, if you don't mind. Your name?"

"Julia."

"Julia who?"

"Stoker," she replied, automatically.

"And what's your connection with Charles Takumo?"

"Takumo?"

"You broke into his apartment this morning," said Krieg, dryly, keeping an eye on Ernst. While Julia seemed to be a capable liar, the surgeon was much worse at hiding his reactions.

"Oh. Him." She glanced at Ernst. "*He* broke in *here* first— two or three days ago. I wanted to see if any of the stuff he'd stolen was still at his place. Why? Are you a friend of his?"

"What did he steal, ay? Some of your dolls?"

"Only one," she said. "A valuable one."

"That's quite a collection you have," said Krieg, nodding. "Turn around, both of you, and walk toward the playroom."

"What? Why?"

"Just do as I say, and maybe I won't kill you." She glanced at Julia, who hadn't moved. "Don't be stupid. I can set this to full autofire and shoot both of you before you could breathe."

"I believe you." She glanced at Ernst, who had half-turned toward the den, but who was looking back over his shoulder. "What are you going to do? Lock us in there?"

"Maybe," Krieg replied, as Ernst disappeared into the room. She walked up to Julia, standing just outside kicking range. "Move!"

Julia hesitated, then took a few steps back, toward the door. "He doesn't know anything," she said.

"Really?" said Krieg.

"You don't, do you?" she called to Ernst. Krieg looked toward the playroom for an instant, and Julia leaped. Krieg fired twice, without even turning her head, while the vampire was still in the air. The first bullet punched a hole in Julia's stomach, the second shattered a rib and tore through her left lung, narrowly missing her heart and her spine. The impact knocked her off course, and she hit the floor a few feet away. Krieg kicked her in the ribs, rolling her over onto her back, stared into her face, then walked to the den.

Ernst, pale and drenched with sweat, was standing in a corner of the room, his hands in his jacket pockets. "Your turn," said Krieg. "Where is Michelangelo Magistrale?"

"Who?"

Krieg glanced to one side, and blew the head off Kenyan Barbie. "Don't worry," she said. "I have two more clips. Forty-seven shots before I have to worry about not having a bullet left for you." She fired again, decapitating *X-Files* Barbie. "Forty-six. Now *where is Magistrale?*"

Ernst shrieked, and pulled his pistol out of his pocket, un-
aware that Takumo had emptied the clip. "Drop it," Krieg
barked.

Julia staggered toward the den, and leaned against the door
frame. Though her wounds were already beginning to heal, the
pain was far worse than she'd expected, and she could feel herself weakening. Ernst squeezed the trigger, and Krieg fired once,
hitting him in the neck. Ernst fell backward, blood jetting out
from his wound, and Julia screamed as blackness engulfed her.
Krieg looked down, and the vampire rolled over into a crouch,
its face contorted into a bestial snarl.

"Don't be stupid," said Krieg, managing to keep her voice
calm. "If you're not a friend of Takumo's, we may be on the
same side. We may be able to help each other. I'm looking for
Michelangelo Magistrale." She saw the vampire's eyes turn red,
and aimed the gun between them. "If you know where he is—"

The vampire leaped, and this time, the bullet that smashed
into its chest didn't even slow it down. It grabbed Krieg's gun
hand with one hand, her face with the other, and bit into her
throat. Krieg felt her wrist break as the vampire twisted it, and
for the first time since her childhood, screamed aloud. The vampire tore her carotid open, and feasted on the blood it needed
to heal its wounds. Krieg dropped the silenced automatic and,
with her left hand, reached for her holdout gun. She fired five
rounds into the vampire's chest with the muzzle pressed into its
side, leaving huge exit wounds in its back, but the vampire
didn't even flinch. Krieg drew her head back sharply, breaking
free of the vampire's grasp, then snapped it forward, butting
the vampire in the nose hard enough to spread it unevenly
across that snarling face.

The vampire spat her own blood into Krieg's face, and
squeezed harder on her broken wrist. Though almost blinded
by the pain, Krieg dropped her gun and jabbed her fingers at
the vampire's eyes. It dodged, and bit into her fingers, breaking
one and severing the other. Krieg tried to struggle, to strike at
the vampire with her legs and elbows, but she was weakening
from the pain and the loss of blood, and the blows that landed

worried the vampire not at all. Unconsciousness, when it came
to her, came almost as a relief.

The vampire continued to drink on her blood long after her
heart had ceased to pump it, and its wounds began to heal as
it slowly regained its strength. When the blood was barely seeping out of its wounds, it dropped the body and staggered over
to where Ernst was lying. His heart had stopped, too, but there
was still blood a-plenty to be sucked from his veins and licked
from the floor.

Finally, with its own wounds almost closed and its hunger
bearable, the vampire sat back and examined Ernst's corpse.
The bullet had not only nicked his carotid, it had damaged two
vertebrae, a wound that she suspected might never heal if he
were turned. Krieg's body, on the other hand, had fewer serious
wounds than Julia's. The broken wrist and missing finger might
prove a problem, but they would heal in time; apart from that,
hers was an excellent host body, and her memories and person-
ality should be an asset, not a weakness.

The vampire carried Krieg's body up to the darkroom and
then, not really understanding why, propped Ernst's up in the
chair in the den so that the dolls could watch over him. Then
it went out, looking for more prey.

15

House Calls

Hartmann, the morgue attendant, lifted the sheet to glance at the woman's face, then looked at the chart. Angela Winslow, age forty-four, approximate time of death three A.M., cause of death left blank, religion: none. He lifted the sheet again, and shook his head. Unusual for a professed atheist to wear a cross around her neck. Handsome woman, too. He glanced at the chart again, and found the entry for next of kin: David Green, husband. Someone would have to contact him, to ask his permission for an autopsy, and Hartmann thanked the gods that that wasn't *his* job. He'd never understood why it was necessary, either; after all, the bodies were already dead, it wasn't as though you could hurt them anymore. Ah, well, living people are crazy, he told Angela, and he closed the drawer and glanced at his watch. Just over an hour before shift change—the sun must already be up. He yawned.

In the hour before dawn, the vampires returned to their shelters—Ernst's darkroom, Mara's bedroom, the storeroom at the

Crypt, and other hiding places where they were protected from sunlight and predators—and waited for darkness.

"They're letting me out this afternoon," said Sindee, relief plain in her voice. "Tomorrow at the latest. They say my condition's been stable for a day already, but they wanted to keep me under observation for a little longer because I healed too fast! There's no pleasing some people." She looked around the cafe. "Thanks for rescuing me."

"No problem."

"I don't just mean from the ward, though that's bad enough; it feels like I've been here for years. Thanks for . . . well, you know."

Takumo smiled. "I'm getting out today, too. I . . . can you do me a favor?"

"For sure," she said, without hesitation.

"I'm going back to Tudor's house to look for Julia. Can you draw me a rough map of the place?"

"Okay, but I don't think Julia's there anymore."

"What about Malachi?" He slid a notepad and a pencil across the table toward her.

"Maybe," she said. "Wouldn't it be better to leave this up to the cops?"

"You told me the cops had already been there."

"One cop, yeah. A homicide detective—Woodcock?, or something like that. He didn't come back. I guess there wasn't any evidence, right?" Takumo nodded. "What if I accused them of abduction? Ernst and Tudor, I . . . oh." It was difficult for a blush to show against her dark complexion, but Takumo saw the color appear in her cheeks before she looked down at the map she was drawing. "I'd have to explain how I was rescued, wouldn't I?"

"I think they'd be curious, yeah," said Takumo. "And it'd just be your word against theirs, and while I doubt that Tudor's is worth much, Ernst . . ."

"Is rich. Right. Besides, you're having too much fun doing this yourself."

"What?"

"You are, aren't you? Not this part, not being hospitalized, but the rest of it. Being a hero. You get off on it. The adrenaline rush; it gives you a buzz, gets you high."

Takumo thought for a moment, then shrugged. "I suppose so."

"I thought so. That's cool. Most of the men I meet enjoy things that're . . ." She shrugged, and slid the map back across the table. "Let me know if you can't read my handwriting."

"No, it's fine." He studied her drawings, then tapped a finger at a scribbled-in box. "What's this?"

"That? It's a staircase."

"Where does it go?"

Sindee blinked. "It goes to . . ." she began, then hesitated. "Maybe there isn't a staircase there."

"It's on the ground floor," said Takumo, "and it doesn't lead upstairs. Is there a cellar?"

"A cellar?" Sindee thought about it, and her eyes became slightly glazed. "I . . . I don't think so. I don't remember there being a cellar."

"Just a staircase going down?"

Sindee stared at him, her face ashen, her expression confused. "Maybe there isn't a staircase. . . ."

"But there *is* a door?" She looked bewildered. "It's okay. You've been a great help; I think I know where to look for Julia. You want another drink?"

Sindee shook her head. "I hadn't thought of this before, but I've just realized that I don't have anywhere to stay when they let me out. I can't go back to Tudor's place, can I?"

Takumo was quiet. "Do you have stuff there you need? Or want?"

"Some clothes, stuff like that, yes, but I—"

"We'll come with you," said Takumo, trying not to sound too eager. "It'll give us a chance to look at the place. Or if you really don't want to go back, write us a letter that we can show

Tudor, to say that we have your permission to collect your stuff. We'll go in the day, so it should be safe enough."

"We?"

"Mage and I—I'll introduce you later. Okay?"

She hesitated, then nodded. "The other people there—Beth, Tanith, and Adrian—they're okay. I mean, they always treated me okay. So did Sol, until a few days ago; I used to think the satanist thing was just an act. Maybe they're all vampires now, or some sort of monster, but if they're not, can you just get them out of there?"

"We'll try. Even if there are vampires there, we're going to try to take one alive, see if we can find a cure."

She looked down at her plan of the house. "I hadn't thought about this before . . . hadn't realized that I was going to have to move out. I don't have any other place to go, and I never was any good at saving . . . Is it safe for me to go back to work? I feel well enough, and if I did that, I could afford to stay in a hotel until I found somewhere else. . . ."

"That's up to you, but if you need a place to stay . . . well, my pad's pretty small, but it should be safe, and you could have the bed. . . ."

"I'd hate to put you out, but thanks for the offer. I'll think about it."

Mandaglione shook his head as they drove past Mann's Chinese Theatre, and began whistling one of his favorite Billy Joel songs. "Thanks for the ride," said Takumo.

"No problem. Always interested in meeting a cinema legend. Besides, what were you going to do otherwise—carry her stuff on the back of your bike, or take a bus?"

Takumo shrugged, and glanced at his watch. Sindee had phoned the house just before they'd left and spoken to Tanith, giving Tudor less than half an hour's warning of their arrival. She'd been careful not to mention any of their names, or to tell Tanith where she was staying. He wondered whether she was safer back in his apartment than she would have been coming with them . . . and decided that she probably was, as long as they returned before dusk. "How much do you know about black magic?" he asked Mandaglione.

"I've read a lot about it, but how much is *true*, I couldn't begin to guess. Why?"

"Just curious."

"Curiosity is good," said Mandaglione, nodding. "Are you armed?"

"Yes. You?"

"Hell, no. Only combat skill I ever learned was running, and that was thirty pounds ago. Mikey?"

"I can get a shotgun if I need one."

"How quickly?"

"Couple of seconds."

"Can you use it?"

"Yes."

"*Have* you used it? Against a—"

"Yes, unfortunately."

"Okay." He parked outside the house, and they walked up to the gate. " 'Abandon hope, all ye who—' " Mage rolled his eyes. "Sorry." He pressed the button.

Tanith appeared a moment later, wearing the low-cut red top and her leather pants. Mandaglione smiled appreciatively as she walked up to the gate. "You're Sindee's friends?" she asked.

"I am," said Takumo, bowing, then handing over the letter. "These are friends of mine. She just asked us to pick up some of her stuff."

"Where do you know her from?" asked Tanith, looking up from the letter. "Work?"

Takumo smiled. "Kind of. I met her at an audition, oh, must have been a couple of years ago now. I didn't even know what she was doing these days, until I saw her at the hospital."

"You're an actor?" she said, with a faint sigh.

He shrugged. "Well, I work in the hospital, sometimes, doing data entry."

"Uh-huh. Okay, come in." She pressed a button in the pillar, and the gate swung open.

"Thank you," said Mandaglione. "You're Tanith Black, aren't you?"

"Yeah," she said, not looking back as she led the way to the house. "And you are?"

"Don. Don Mandel."

"You're an actor too?"

"Not since college. I'm a writer, but I remember you in *Devilspawn*."

"Oh. I'm sorry."

"It's okay—it wasn't *your* fault it bombed. What've you been doing since?"

"Hiding, like most of us who were in that turkey. Why?"

"Could I interview you sometime?"

"What for?"

"I've been doing a series on scream queens for a couple of different magazines, hoping to get enough for a book."

Tanith shrugged, then opened the door. "I'm not exactly Natasha Henstridge . . . I don't think my name's going to sell many copies, and my photo . . . well, it'd have to be an old one."

"That's up to you, of course," said Mandaglione, "but Mikey here takes great glamour photos—"

"Glamour, huh?" she said, as they walked in, then looked up at Mage. "What're you going to do, use low-calorie film?"

"Tell me how you want to look," he replied, "and I'll do what I can. This is an amazing place; how many of you live here?"

"Just the—" She hesitated slightly as she climbed the stairs; they could almost hear her running through a list of names in her head. "Six of us, now, but only Sol and . . . and Mal and I are home. . . ." She seemed uncertain. "Is Sindee okay?"

"She's out of the hospital," said Takumo, after an uncomfortable silence, then, blandly, "They say there won't even be a scar."

"Did she say why she was moving out?"

"Not to me. What did she say when she called?"

"Just that she was going to stay with a friend for a while."

"Sol," said Mandaglione, after another silence. "You mean Solomon Tudor? This is his house?"

"It was part of his fee for the movie—the studio owned it, and they couldn't sell it to anyone else. Why?"

As though on cue, a door opened on the landing, and Tudor emerged. He stared down the staircase at them, reminding Takumo uncomfortably of the "Night on Bald Mountain" sequence from *Fantasia*. "They're here to collect Sindee's clothes," explained Tanith, in reply to his raised eyebrows.

Tudor blinked, then nodded. "Of course," he said.

"Don, this is Solomon Tudor. Don wants to interview me," she said, as she led the way to Sindee's door. "About *Devilspawn*."

"Does he indeed?" asked Tudor, dryly. "Well, you were one of the film's high points—you, and the lack of sequels. I don't recall any others."

Mandaglione smiled. "What about Angela Winslow?"

"What about her?"

"I'd be interested in interviewing her, too—if you know where she is."

"I haven't heard from Angela in more than twenty years," said Tudor, "when she left me literally holding the baby. I didn't even hear *of* her until a few years ago, when her father died, and I sent her my condolences. She didn't reply. But I bear her no malice. I understand she married, and has been quite successful as a studio accountant, or something similar. Why?"

"Just curious—wondering what she might have to say about the film."

"I doubt she would remember it with any enthusiasm," replied Tudor. He watched as Mage opened the door with Sindee's key, then took a step back toward his own room. "If you will excuse me, gentlemen?"

Takumo looked into the untidy room. The walls were a pale peach, the carpet tiles brown, and there was a beaten path from door to bed to closet to door. An orange vinyl beanbag slumped in one corner, and an antique lava lamp bubbled on the black dresser. The only obviously new items were a boombox, a CD

case on the nightstand, and some of the soft toys on the bed.
"Oh, man," he muttered.

"How long did you say she'd lived here?" asked Mage, picking up a teddy bear in a deerstalker hat and Inverness cape, and a toy orangutan that looked as though it had lived a long, hard life.

"A couple of months. I don't know how long she was planning on staying, but she told me she likes to travel light."

Mage nodded, then pulled his backup camera, a tiny Canon Elph, out of his pocket and took a few shots. Takumo walked to the closet, removed the suitcase, opened it, and began bundling clothes into it. "You'd better go get the other case; there's more stuff in the dresser."

"On my way." He grabbed the boombox and the CDs on his way out, and saw Mandaglione at the top of the stairs, still talking to Tanith. "Just getting another bag," he said. They nodded. He ran down the stairs, looked up, then ducked into the kitchen. The door to the cellar was locked, but that didn't even slow him down.

The cellar turned out to be unremarkable, with bare brick walls and a concrete floor, and empty apart from a pile of folding chairs, a folding bed, a folding table, and a padlocked metal trunk that looked large enough to hold a smallish human body. Mage flicked the light switch, then shut the door and walked cautiously down the stairs. The room smelled musty and there were spiderwebs along the ceiling, but he could tell that the floor had been swept and scrubbed recently. A little nervously, he opened the trunk. It contained hooded black robes, black-hilted sheath knives, a large black cloth, assorted skulls—one of them human, the others from horned animals—and large candles of various colors. He closed and locked the trunk and headed back upstairs and out to the car. "What kept you?" asked Takumo, when he returned with a suitcase and a clothing bag.

"I checked out the cellar. It's clean, suspiciously clean, in fact—"

"You went in there *alone*?"

"The sun's still up, isn't it? And if anything had gone wrong, which of us would you say was better at getting *out* of trouble?"

"The sun's still up, for sure, but there could still have been traps—and for all we know, vampires may be able to move about during the daytime, as long as they stay out of the light."

"Look," said Mage, "I'm much better at saving my own skin than I am anyone else's; it's just the way the magic works. I thought you wanted to check this place out as thoroughly as possible beforehand, so that's what I've done, and I didn't find any vampires in the cellar."

"Cool. Shall we get out of—where's, uh, Don?"

"Still trying to chat up—was it Danni?"

"Tanith."

Mage nodded, and picked up the two of the cases. "Uncle Don? We're going now."

Mandaglione glanced away from Tanith, and blinked, as though suddenly reminded of where he was and why. "Okay." He turned his attention back to Tanith. "I'll send you a copy of the questions, and if you decide you want to do it, next time I'm in town we can—"

Takumo coughed. "Sorry," he said, when Tanith looked around. "Allergies."

"Okay," said Tanith, smiling. "Send me your questions, and I'll think about it. Nice to meet you."

"I don't believe it," said Takumo, when they were outside. "I hope you didn't tell her your real name, too? Or ours? Or where you're staying?"

"Of course not," replied Mandaglione, huffily, hoping that he hadn't. "I don't think I told her anything. Besides, she's—"

"Tudor's partner," said Takumo, balancing on one leg and pressing the button to the gate with the toe of his boot. "They've been together for twenty years."

"Well, yeah, but I don't think she's . . ." He shook his head as he opened the car door. "Did you see their body language? Did they look like a couple to you? Anyway, I was trying to get information out of her, too, and I think Tudor's keeping her in the dark."

"Like the vampires?" asked Mage.

"She's not a vampire."

Takumo shrugged. "Tudor can still learn as much about us through her as we can about him. Did she ask where Sindee was staying?"

"Yes, and I said I'd have to check with her before giving out her address, and to hold on to her mail until then. If Tanith knows what happened to her, then she's a much better actress than anyone's ever given her credit for. Personally, I think Tudor's given her some sort of mental block, so that there are things she simply doesn't think about."

"A blind spot," said Takumo. "Like Sindee and the cellar."

"Exactly."

They were silent for a moment, then Takumo murmured, "An invisibility spell."

"What?"

"I called Gaye a few days ago, and she said she couldn't talk because there was a cop there asking her about invisibility spells. She didn't ring back, and I forgot about it. I don't know what it was about, but I'd guess that creating this sort of blind spot is a trick that Tudor tends to overuse—and one we may be able to turn against him."

"How?" asked Mage.

"Did you have any problem finding the cellar door?"

"No, but I knew it was there."

"Then either he's only cast the spell on the people who live in the house, or he cast it on the door and has since removed it. Last time I was there, I'm pretty sure I saw two doors, but I didn't look in the cellar, and it didn't occur to me that I should have done so until now. Do you remember what the cellar door looked like?"

"Sure. Just a plain door."

"Color?"

"White, with dark brown showing through in places."

"Panels?"

"Two horizontal across the top, three vertical—"

"And Sindee's door?"

"Same pattern, but stained dark, almost black, and with a gold star, five-pointed, in the middle of the second panel—"

"And Malachi's?"

Mage hesitated. "I don't know."

"Would you remember where it was—don't think of the map, think of the house."

Mage shook his head. "I know it was on the other side of the house, I didn't see it close up. I remember seeing a few doors, but they were all pretty dark. How does this help us?"

"If the other people in the house have a blind spot where that room is, they won't notice anything while we're in there."

"Except for Tudor," said Mandaglione.

Takumo conceded the point. "So unless we're wrong about vampires having to rest during the day, we'll only have Tudor to worry about. I can live with that."

"So you're going ahead with it?"

"For sure," said Takumo, before Mage could speak. "Tomorrow. First thing after sunrise."

It had been a quiet morning, and Hartmann had just sat down and poured himself a cup of coffee to prevent himself from nodding off, when the thumping started. He looked around, and went to the door. No one was there. He looked up and down the corridor, to see if anyone was knocking at any of the other doors, and saw no one. Puzzled, he closed the door, turned around, and stared at the refrigerators. He'd been working in the morgue for seven years, and none of the corpses had ever disturbed him before. In fact, that was one of the things he liked about the job; it was much less stressful than being a teacher, especially in South Central L.A.

Nervously but quickly, he walked along the row of drawers, trying to locate the source of the sound. Two possibilities occurred to him; one was that it was a prank by medical students, and the other was that someone had been pronounced dead by mistake—a rare event, but hardly an unprecedented one. While the thought of leaving a prankster in the refrigerator for a little longer was an appealing one, he realized that he might never find the right drawer if he waited and the banging stopped.

He opened one drawer, found the body inside completely motionless, then opened the drawer above that. The woman inside twisted around and looked up at him, her previously handsome face haggard, her eyes blazing red. Hartmann took a step back. In all the recent cases he knew of people reviving on the autopsy table or in funeral homes, the signs of life had been faint, easy to miss. "Jesus," he said. "What the—"

She reached out for his hand, squeezing it tightly. "It's okay," he said. "I'll go get a doctor—"

The vampire pulled his hand toward her face. Her flesh was cold, but that didn't surprise Hartmann; the refrigerators were kept at a few degrees above freezing. But he *was* surprised when she bit into his wrist, drawing blood, and more surprised still when the pleasure hit him so that the terror became almost, but not quite, unimportant.

Julia's slap wasn't quite hard enough to break Mara's neck, but the sound of it echoed through the Crypt like a gunshot. "You *idiot!*" she shrieked. "I was keeping him alive for a *reason*; who will look after us during the daylight *now?*" Mara didn't reply. "Your father will be looking for you soon, *her* parents must be looking for her already, we need a place to hide. . . ." She stared at Mara in disgust, while Ahna and Dwight looked away. Krieg stood behind her, as imposing in her stillness as Julia was in her rage.

"There are places we can hide. . . ." said Mara.

"Oh? And how will we know how safe they are during the day?"

Mara didn't answer, but to her surprise, Krieg did. "There are plenty of places where no one will disturb you, if you pay. I have money, and experience with safehouses."

"And when the money runs out?"

"It won't—not any time soon," said Krieg, "and I can get most of it without leaving the city or needing to go into a bank, and I have ways of making more. I can hire people to run errands for us during the day, if necessary, and we don't need houses. One of those U-Store-It places would do, as long as we could get in at night."

"More than one would be better," suggested Dwight, as Julia considered this suggestion. "Dracula kept ten hiding places around London, and that was much smaller then than L.A. is now. If we had a few, we could hunt in different places and always be close to shelter, and we wouldn't have to go back to the same place every night; we'd be harder to find that way."

"We could all keep a few changes of clothes in each hideout," added Mara. "It's not glam, but neither was all of us staying here."

"Nobody is perfectly safe anywhere," said Krieg. "Locks, alarms, guards, dogs . . . there are people who can get past any of them. Even a good security system only stops the amateurs and slows the professionals down."

Julia looked at them, her expression grim, but she couldn't find any flaws in their argument. "That's okay as a stopgap, but in the longer term . . ." She turned to Krieg. "Is there anything you can do before sunrise?"

"I can get some cash," she replied. "A few thousand dollars. If you have Web access here, I can transfer some more money and check out some places where we could stay tomorrow. I can't do much more than that in two hours."

Julia nodded, and turned to Mara. "How secure is your place?"

"My father won't be home until after dark tomorrow night; we'll be safe there until then, at least."

She glanced at Ahna. "What if your parents come there looking for you?"

"They've already phoned," said Mara. "They left a dozen messages on my voicemail. I called back tonight, told them I don't know where she is. Even if they try coming around, they won't break in, they're too law-abiding for something like that." She glared at Ahna. "It'd help if *you* called them, too, and told them you'd run away or whatever. I bet they've already told the cops you've been murdered."

"We left Malaysia because of the police and the courts," said Ahna, quietly. "My brother had been arrested for sodomy, and my father had been accused of criticizing the prime minister. Even if your police are different, I do not think he would go to them willingly."

Julia looked at her appraisingly, then nodded. "Go with her. We'll meet here tomorrow, after midnight." Krieg watched them leave, then asked, "Would we be safer if her parents died?"

Julia blinked, startled, then shook her head. "They'll die soon. She may not know it, but she's draining them every night, without even needing to see them. Are your parents . . . ?"

"My father is dead already," said Krieg impassively. "My mother lives in Australia."

"Any children?"

"No."

She turned to Dwight. "You?"

"Both alive, last I heard. No kids. Will they turn?"

"Maybe," said Julia, carelessly. "It depends on what happens to their bodies. Do they live near here?"

"They don't live near *anywhere*," snorted Dwight. "They have a farm in Idaho."

"Then it's not our problem." She turned to Krieg. "What were you saying about making more money?"

"There's a man named Michelangelo Magistrale," she replied. "He's a friend of Charles Takumo's, whose apartment you broke into, and he's worth sixty thousand dollars. All we have to do is find him and kill him."

It was four thirty A.M. when Mage woke, an hour he regarded in much the same way he thought of sharks, venomous snakes, and landlords—namely, he admitted that they served a useful purpose, even a necessary one, but he felt no desire to ever associate with them. He looked blearily at Takumo, then at his watch, and muttered, "What the—"

"Shh. I don't want to wake Sindee."

Mage looked around the apartment, saw Takumo's sleeping bag lying a few meters away. "Jesus. Look, this may have slipped past you, but I can get to where we're going in a second—"

"I know. That's why I let you sleep in; I've been up for a quarter hour already. I just wanted to make sure you were awake before I left. Coffee?"

Mage opened his eyes a little wider. Takumo was already dressed in his leather jacket and black pants, and was busily checking his collection of weapons. "Yeah. Thanks," said Mage, watching as he dropped two cans of insect spray into his backpack. "What're those for?"

"Flame-throwers. Not much range, but just in case." He dropped two railroad flares in after them, a few smoke bombs, and his kyotetsu-shoge. "Can you take this for me?" He handed him his ninjato, sheathed. Mage slipped his arms out of the sleeping bag, and grabbed the mug with one hand, the sword with the other. "I could strap it to the bike, if I removed the tsuba, but it's still sort of conspicuous, and I think we might need it. I know some of the legends say you're supposed to use a gravedigger's shovel, but I don't know if gravediggers even use shovels anymore, and a backhoe is a little cumbersome. The way I see it, decapitated is decapitated. Sorry I don't have a spare, but I can lend you a knife if you want one."

"It's okay." Mage sipped his coffee, and looked at the sword uneasily. "I thought we were supposed to be looking for a *cure*."

"For sure, if the vampires *want* to be cured. If they *like* being vampires and are prepared to fight for that right, I want to be prepared. *You* don't have to worry too much about defending yourself if it comes down to deciding who has the better claim to your blood; you can always escape. Even if they take over the city, you can always escape. Hell, if they take over the freakin' *world*, you can spend all your time on the sunny side. The rest of us can't."

"And?"

"And?"

"And you want to kill some monsters?"

Takumo grimaced. "I prefer to think of it as saving lives, but I see where you're coming from. Sure, there are too many monsters in the world. Are vampires any worse than the ones who sell drugs to kids—and I include tobacco and alcohol in that—or make antipersonnel landmines? The ones who calculate that it'd be more profitable to deal with lawsuits from a few hundred people incinerated in their cars than to recall the cars and make them safer? The ones who start pointless wars as an advertisement for their weapon shops, then sell these toys to genocidal dictators and call it defending democracy? The ones who—"

"Quiet. You'll wake Sindee."

Takumo took a deep breath, and continued, more softly, "Jesus, compared to some of the monsters we're supposed to regard as the pillars of society, vampires look positively cuddly. They only kill because they need to to survive, not just so they can be richer than all the other monsters. Hell, maybe they don't need to kill at all, or maybe they do *now*, but they can be cured. Maybe we could all just agree to just get on with each other—hey, I'll give everyone that chance. I've never started a fight with anyone." He shrugged. "If we can stop the killing without hurting anyone, vampire or living, then that's cool. But maybe vampires aren't like the other monsters. Maybe they don't have a choice, maybe they can't stop, maybe they need someone else to stop them—and to stop there being any more of them." He picked up the backpack and his helmet. "Drink your coffee; I think Tudor casts some sort of sleep spell over the house. It's probably to keep the other occupants from wandering around at night, but I could barely stay awake last time. I'll see you there."

Mage put down the sword, finished his coffee, then shed the sleeping bag and walked toward the bathroom. He showered, shaved, flossed and brushed his teeth, and dressed, then picked up the ninjato and *saw* himself standing inside the gates of Tudor's property. Takumo arrived three minutes later, just as the sun was rising. "What kept you?" asked Mage, and reached for the button to open the gate.

"Don't bother," said Takumo, climbing over the wall. "It might ring a bell, or something, inside. Let's roll."

Mage handed him the ninjato, which he slipped into a loop on the side of his backpack, and they entered the house by the kitchen door. The place was quiet, and Takumo winced slightly at the sound of Mage's footsteps, but no one confronted them as they climbed the dark staircase to the second floor. The door to Julia's room was locked, but the key on Takumo's focus opened it easily. The two friends stared inside. The walls and the floorboards were painted black, though the high ceiling was a dirty white, and the curtains a dark wine red. The queen-size bed was covered with a yellowed lace bedspread that resembled the cobwebs that adorned the corners and the chandelier. There was a large bookshelf beside the closet, a desk near the curtains, and a chest of drawers topped with a huge mirror in the far corner. Mage looked in the closet, Takumo under the bed. "Not here," he reported. "Not unless she can transform into dust."

"There's not enough clothes in here, either," said Mage, shutting the closet door. "She's gone."

Takumo glanced around the room, and satisfied himself that there was nowhere else where a body could be hidden. "She left her books."

"That doesn't necessarily mean she's coming back."

"True." They walked out, and tried Malachi's door. That was also locked, and just as easy to open. The room was illuminated by the glow of the computer monitor on the workstation; the seti@home screensaver was running. The walls were lined with shelves packed with books, DVDs, and disc boxes, and the only window, in the east wall, was covered with heavy curtains. An *Arcade* Virtual Fox calendar hung on the closet door. The floorboards were varnished, and there was a circle of gray powder around the futon bed, on which a naked man lay motionless. One of his eyes was open, but it didn't seem to be tracking. Mage and Takumo looked at each other, but neither moved for several seconds, until Takumo took a deep breath and stepped inside. Mage followed him, then quietly shut the door behind them. "Only one," he breathed. "What do we do?"

Takumo walked carefully up to the circle, judged the distance carefully, then cautiously reached over and squirted the sole of Malachi's foot with holy water. The results were more spectacular than he could have imagined; Malachi jerked his foot away as though it had been zapped with a cattle prod, and Takumo stared as a blood-colored blister appeared on his sole. It quickly swelled to the size of a gumdrop before bursting, leaving a brown puddle and releasing a stench of decay. Mage turned pale, and Takumo clapped his hand to his mouth, and willed himself not to throw up. Malachi sat up, opened his other eye, looked straight at Takumo, and bared his teeth in a snarl.

Takumo backed up until he was well outside the circle, and drew his sword. The vampire continued to stare, but neither moved nor spoke. "It's okay," said Takumo. "We're here to help you, not harm you. Are you Malachi Tudor?"

No reply, not even a flicker of recognition or a blank look of puzzlement. "Do you speak English?" asked Mage. The vampire glanced at him, but made no sound.

"So what do we do now?" asked Takumo, looking at the horrific wound on Malachi's foot.

"I don't know," said Mage. "Is that circle meant to keep us out, or him in?"

Slowly, Takumo lowered himself into a crouch, then quickly jabbed his hand into the circle and immediately withdrew it. "I think it keeps him in—or maybe other vampires out. Assuming he *is* a vampire, and not a zombie or something like that." He looked Malachi in the face. "Nothing personal, man, but if you don't say something, I'm going to open the window and let the sun shine in." No reply. "Cool."

Carefully circumnavigating the protective circle, he walked to the window and tugged at the curtain. The window behind it was covered with aluminum foil, which Takumo began tearing away in strips. When a beam of sunlight fell across Malachi's shins, he jerked both of his legs up to his chest in a fetal position, out of the light, and uttered a thin keening wail.

The door opened a few seconds later, and Tudor strode into the room. "What—" He looked around, then pointed at Takumo with his right hand, the one holding the cigarette. *"Get away from there!"*

Takumo stepped away from the window as though the light were burning him, too, then stared at Malachi. There was already a broad band of scarlet across the white-gray flesh of his shins. He looked levelly at Tudor, who nodded slightly. "Charles Takumo, I presume?"

Takumo, a trained actor, did his best to look innocent, or at least inscrutable, but Tudor merely glanced at Mage and read the answer in his startled expression. "And you are?" he asked, and when Mage didn't reply, he merely shrugged. "You're right, it doesn't matter," he said, languidly. "They can identify anybody with dental records. What are you doing here?"

"We're looking for Julia," replied Mage.

Tudor looked him in the eye for a moment, then nodded. "She's not here," he said. "Oh, she *was* here; a few days ago, you would have found her in this very room, but Julia is . . . flighty, shall we say?" He smiled. "I don't actually know where she is, though if I had to find her, I would look in Ernst's house first—you know where that is, don't you, Mr. Takumo?"

Takumo didn't reply. "We don't want to harm her," said Mage. "Or your son. We want to find a cure."

Tudor stared at him, then laughed—loudly and sincerely. "A *cure?* The only *cure* for vampirism is death, and a violent and painful death at that. Do you believe that if there were another cure, however difficult or costly, that I wouldn't already have tried it? He's my *son.*" He shook his head, and chuckled. "Thank you, young man, whoever you are. I thought I'd lost my sense of humor decades ago. What sort of cure were you going to try, now that sunlight and—is that holy water I smell?—have failed? Blood transfusions? Antibiotics? Or were you going to go straight to the stake through the heart?"

"We were going to take him—her, if we'd found Julia—to a pathologist for examination."

"That might be interesting," conceded Tudor, taking a drag on his cigarette. "Of course, they show no life signs during the day, and he's too fresh to decay very much in only a few hours, and I doubt you could persuade even a well-fed vampire to submit to much testing at night. . . . A pity that you didn't find Julia instead of coming here." He yawned, then gestured with his cigarette. The ember swelled into a fireball the size of a fist, which instantly hurtled toward Takumo. The ninja dodged to one side, and the ball splattered against the curtains, setting them alight. As Mage watched in horror, a stream of fire ran up the curtains, taking on a serpentine shape, which then flew through the air toward Takumo.

"Charlie!"

Takumo looked over his shoulder for an instant, then leaped forward onto the bed. The elemental hit him in the back in midflight, and wrapped itself around him like a sash. His hair and clothes were alight before he hit the bed; he beat at the flames with his hands for a few seconds, then grabbed the bed-sheet and tried wrapping it around himself. When this failed to smother the flames, he hurriedly shrugged off his smoldering backpack and, leaving it on the bed, rolled off onto the floor, still trying unsuccessfully to extinguish the flames engulfing him. His leather jacket was giving him some protection, but his legs and hands and head were already badly burnt, and the elemental continued to slither around his body. Malachi, who was already huddled against the headboard to avoid the sunlight, tried to make himself smaller still as the flames spread across the bed.

Tudor turned to Mage as he summoned another elemental, and was stunned to find him gone. He blinked, and Mage reappeared a few feet away, brandishing the small fire extinguisher from the kitchen. He ran closer to Takumo and began dousing the flames, but unwittingly stepped into the circle. The vampire sprang at him, grabbing his arm and pulling him out of the light. Mage swung the fire extinguisher around into the side of Malachi's head, but the vampire didn't relax his grip; he merely opened his mouth and emitted a rattling sound that might have been a chuckle.

Mage jackknifed and rolled off the bed, dragging Malachi with him. The vampire grabbed at the side of the bed, but it had little of the strength or speed it possessed at night; its wounds had weakened it further, and its desperate lunge at Mage had all but exhausted it. It let go hurriedly as Mage stumbled back outside the circle—but too slowly to prevent its hand from crossing the barrier. Its skin blistered from fingertips to wrist, and it screamed again. Mage looked at it for an instant, then at Takumo, who was still writhing on the floor. He blasted him again with the fire extinguisher, smothering him with foam, but the flames continued to dance. Mage persisted until the extinguisher was empty, then turned to Tudor and growled, "Get it off him."

The sorcerer looked badly shaken, but he managed a superior smirk. "Or?"

Mage hurled the empty extinguisher at the window, shattering it. The tattered foil held some of the glass in the frame for a few seconds, then it twisted and fell away, letting a wide shaft of dusty light into the room. Malachi recoiled further, squashing himself into a compact ball near the headboard. Tudor shook his head, and glanced at Takumo. The ninja had been burned almost beyond recognition, his exposed flesh the same greasy blackish brown as his charred clothing. He gestured with the cigarette, and the elemental snaked through the air and struck at Mage. He smiled as the younger man was also engulfed in flame, then gaped as he vanished altogether.

Cautiously, he advanced to where he'd been standing, wondering whether the intruder had disappeared or merely become invisible, and whether he was likely to return. He looked down at Takumo—who had stopped moving, but still seemed to be fighting for breath—and then at Malachi. The vampire was still huddled near the headboard, unable to heal itself, and unable to cross the barrier of its own volition, even though the flames were rapidly spreading toward it. Tudor had no means close to hand of extinguishing the fire—a fire elemental would be enraged if asked to *stop* a fire, and he doubted he had the strength to control one if it went berserk. He'd performed a ritual to conjure an undine, a water elemental, after the incident with the smoke alarm, and it would only need a brief incantation to bring it forth, but he'd have to be in his own room for it to succeed. Then, when he'd extinguished the flames, he could break the circle—it had been compromised anyway—and let the vampire out. Takumo's body was probably still hot enough to badly burn any human who touched it, but after it cooled, Malachi might be able to feed and begin to heal.

Tudor glanced at the curtains. One had already burnt away, the other had caught, and he could see the rising sun between them. Even if he covered the window, it would only be a temporary measure; moving the vampire to Julia's room would be much safer. There was little more he could do with what he had in the room, so he hurried back to his own.

It took a few seconds to complete the ritual, and then his waterbed erupted into a waterspout which punched through the plastic like a spear, then collapsed itself into a rough, vaguely human shape, like a five-foot-tall Willendorf Venus made from jellyfish. "Come," Tudor ordered the undine, in a language older than writing. "I have need of your services; there's a fire to be quenched."

Mage *saw* himself back on the moon, near the Apollo 17 landing site in the Littrow region. The cold and the near-vacuum extinguished the flames in an instant. He then *saw* himself in Sindee's room, uninjured. He could feel blood pulsing in his ears, and it didn't feel like decompression. He opened the door, and raced down the corridor to Malachi's room, his fury red-hot. He was startled, and disappointed, not to find Tudor there, but after a few seconds, he cooled down enough to realize that this could be an advantage.

The vampire didn't seem eager to move out of its shadowed

corner, and Mage scrambled over to where Takumo was lying. The stuntman was still breathing, though unevenly and with difficulty, and his leather jacket had protected nearly half of his body from the flames. Mage concentrated hard, *seeing* him uninjured. He knew Takumo must have inhaled hot smoke, damaging his lungs and throat, but there was nothing he could do about that now. The only thing that mattered was to get help; he could come back for Tudor and the vampire later.

He looked up as Tudor walked into the room, carrying a heavy blanket. The two magicians stared at each other for a moment, then Tudor's cigarette—the fire he needed to summon the elementals—went flying from his mouth and landed on the blazing bed. "Don't you think it's time you quit?" said Mage, softly.

Tudor glanced around the room, seeing how the flames were spreading. "Maybe you're right," he conceded. "Isn't there a saying about only fools fighting in a burning house?"

Mage looked at him warily, and saw the water elemental stomp up to stand behind the sorcerer. Tudor stepped aside, into the room, and barked out an order, and the elemental's arm shot out across the bedroom and hit Mage like a water-cannon, knocking him from his feet. He was still trying to pick himself up off the floor when the flares in Takumo's backpack ignited from the heat, and the spray cans exploded, shredding the pack and sending burning debris and fragments flying across the room. The sword, still in its scabbard with a large chunk of burning nylon hanging from it, shot over Mage's head, missing him by little more than an inch, and smaller scraps rained down on him a moment later, like burning snowflakes.

Malachi, sitting only a few feet away, was blown off the bed and outside the circle by the blast. Small fragments embedded themselves in his arms and shins, and a sharp-edged metal shard all but amputated one hand, leaving it hanging on by a shred of flesh, and carried through to his face, slicing his cheek open from his mouth almost to his ear.

Mage opened his eyes, and realized that he was still in Malachi's room, surrounded by small fires. Tudor was still standing in the doorway, his face a pale gray, with a cut on his forehead oozing blood down into his eyebrow; a drop splashed onto his cheek, and then onto the floor, as Mage watched. He muttered something that Mage, still deafened by the blast, was unable to hear, and the undine began spraying water around the room, trying to douse the fires. The air was thick with steam and smoke, and seeing clearly was becoming more and more difficult. Mage picked up Takumo and ran for the doorway, and hit the elemental as though it were made of soft concrete.

The water engulfed Mage, squeezing him like an enormous powerful hand; he tried to force his way through it, and found himself lifted off his feet, with no purchase, as though bowled over by a powerful wave. He tried swimming, with no better results; he was already running short of breath, and he wondered how much water Takumo had already inhaled. He could hear something that sounded like laughter, and he managed to twist around and stare through the turbulent water at the room. He could see a vague black-and-gray shape that might have been Tudor only a few yards away, but everything beyond that was merely a blur, a van Gogh nightmare.

He closed his stinging eyes, trying to remember how the room had looked a moment before. He remembered Takumo's ninjato lying on the floor, and held off the blackness for long enough to *see* it slide from its sheath and fly through the air toward Tudor. A second later, he fell to the floor, gasping for breath and wetter than he had ever been.

He opened his eyes and saw Tudor lying on the ground nearby, with more than a foot of Takumo's sword protruding from his chest. He was also gasping, and his eyes were closed. The undine loomed over the three of them, then reached down and picked Tudor up. It spun him around like a leaf in a whirlpool, then hurled him into the bookshelves against the far wall.

Tudor fell to the floor amid a shower of planks and books and DVDs, and didn't move. The elemental stood there for a moment longer, then collapsed into a puddle spreading across the floor.

Mage took a breath of the thick air in the room, and painfully hauled himself to his feet, picked Takumo up, and staggered out into the corridor. Once he was clear of the door, he lay Takumo on the ground and began mouth-to-mouth resuscitation. Takumo coughed up several mouthfuls of dirty water, but didn't open his eyes.

Mage looked around the house. There were no signs of movement; early as it was, he would have expected the explosion to wake *someone*, unless they were all vampires. He shrugged, then picked Takumo up and began walking quietly down the stairs, fighting off the urge to collapse in a heap and never move again. He felt a little better when he stepped outside into the sunlight, feeble as it still was, and staggered to the gate. He lay Takumo under a tree, hoping the shadows would hide him until he could return, and then *saw* himself in Mandaglione's hotel room. A rattling snore told him his uncle was still asleep. He sighed, switched the lights on, pulled the curtains open, and when that failed, yelled, *"Dante!"*

Mandaglione jumped, then rolled over and opened one eye. "Huh? Mikey?" The other eye opened. "Jesus, what happened to you? You look like something the cat dragged in and was told to drag out again."

"That's roughly how I feel," said Mage, reading his lips; his ears were still ringing from the explosion, "but at least I'm still standing. I need you to come and get Charlie."

Mandaglione groaned, but he sat up. "What happened?"

"I'll explain later," he said, as Mandaglione hauled his bulk out of the bed and retrieved his clothes from the floor. "I didn't find Julia, and I think Tudor is dead. Don't know about Malachi, or the others in the house. I left Charlie just inside the gate; I'll meet you there."

"What good will that do? Tell me about it in the car. I'd offer you some dry clothes, if I thought they'd fit."

Mage looked down at himself, stepped into the bathroom, and emerged a few seconds later with his clothes and hair clean, dry and undamaged, though his expression was still haggard, his face gray, and his eyes red. Mandaglione, now dressed, merely nodded. "Let's go."

* * *

"**H**ave you tried teleporting out of a speeding car?" he asked, a few minutes later. "All the rules say you'll keep the momentum."

"It doesn't work like that," said Mage.

"Just as well. Let's see, you go from here to the moon, differences in velocity and direction would mean—Jesus, you'd be moving at—"

"Don't say it!" snapped Mage. "If I visualize myself arriving safely, I arrive safely; if I visualize myself hitting the place like a meteor, it might just happen, and I'd rather not find out."

"You probably wouldn't—at least, you wouldn't know it. Is this why you can't carry someone with you when you do it?"

Mage shrugged. "The way I understand it, I re-create myself when I do it—usually unhurt, if I can block my mind to the pain. Sometimes I can't. I don't know if I'm also recreating the place where I arrive, by seeing it as it was rather than as it is, but I haven't noticed any major changes. Of course, because it's all . . ."

"An observer effect? Heisenbergian?"

"I think the word I was after was 'subjective', but 'observer effect' will do. I think places are shaped, at least a little, by people's perceptions of them, and if I do change them when I 'port, other people change them back. But the risk of re-creating other people, as I think they are or should be . . . I don't want to do that. Look, I remember Amanda Sharmon, the woman who gave me this focus, well enough that I could probably create someone who moved like her, maybe even talked like I remember Amanda talking—but she wouldn't *be* Amanda, she'd be my idea of her, my fantasy. I wouldn't be saving her life; I'm not even sure that what I created would *have* a life while I wasn't watching. Or say I teleported Charlie now, while he's unconscious. Would he stay unconscious? And if he did, is that because I teleported him? I don't want to take that risk."

" 'That's not an office for a friend, my lord.' "

"What?"

"*Julius Caesar*. It sounds like something you should try on your enemies first, though I can see that that'd be risky, too. Someone you were afraid of might become even more frightening, even more powerful . . . how old are the foci?"

"I don't know—a few centuries, at least. Why?"

"I was just wondering if that was how vampires and other monsters were created; someone with an item like that, their nightmares becoming reality . . . what? You okay?"

"Just remembering something someone said to me, once," said Mage, weakly. He'd never told anyone, not even Takumo, that Hotei had warned him that he might one day become a god. He took a deep breath. "If you meant that literally, I'm pretty sure the focus has never created anything out of my dreams, or I wouldn't be waking up alone as often as I do. Besides, if that's where the vampires came from, where did the *foci* come from?"

Mandaglione smiled. "Good point. I used to bug the nuns with that one when I was in school; using God to explain the origin of the universe doesn't explain anything, because then you have to explain the origin of God. None of them ever came up with a good answer to that one—well, not a rational answer, and damn few nonviolent ones. I always was a troublemaker." He parked the car across the street from Tudor's house. "How're you going to get him over the wall?"

"I'm not. I'm going to press the button to open the gate, carry him back to the car, then go back in. Don't wait for me; take Charlie to a doctor. Tell them he—well, you're the writer, you make something up."

"How long do you expect to be?"

"As long as it takes. I'm pretty sure Tudor's dead, but there may still be some vampires inside," and he vanished from the car before Mandaglione could speak.

Mage *saw* himself in Sindee's room, and stood there silently for a moment, listening in vain for any other sound of movement. It struck him as strange that no one had come running at the sound of the explosion, but he remembered what Takumo had said about sleep spells. He opened the door, looked around, then walked quietly toward Malachi's room.

The air was still hazy with smoke and steam, but not thick enough to stop him seeing the far wall. Neither the vampire nor his father were visible from the doorway, and Mage hesitated, wishing he'd thought to bring a weapon. After a moment's consideration, he took a step inside. The closet door opened as he walked past it, and the vampire stumbled out, tottering on its wounded feet, and reaching for him with his good hand. Mage half-turned, ducked under the arm, and drove his elbow into the vampire's chest hard enough to send it stumbling back.

Mage finished his turn, and stared at the vampire, who bore little resemblance to the Malachi Tudor who had died a few days before. Its eyes, apart from large black pupils, were completely red. Most of its skin, back and front, was either badly burnt or tinged green with decay. Most of its hair had also burnt away, and what remained was thick with ash or matted with pus from his wounds. Its right hand hung from its wrist, limply. A huge gash extended from the right corner of its mouth almost to its ear, and debris stuck from its legs and arms like thorns.

It stood there frozen for a moment, screaming in pain and reeking of burnt flesh and putrescence, its daystruck brain trying to choose between attack and flight—and then, driven by hunger, it lashed out again. Mage grabbed the closet door and slammed it shut. It closed on the vampire's arm, and Mage heard the distinctive snap of bone breaking. He leaned on the door with all his weight and strength, and wondered what to do next. He stared around the room, looking for a weapon while the vampire tried to pull its arm back into the darkness.

Unable to see any sign of Takumo's sword amid the heap of books and planks where Tudor had fallen, he settled for the broom that was leaning against the far wall, seeing it sliding across the floor toward him. He broke the stick over his knee, and concentrated on the broken end until it was sharpened to a point. He glanced at the hand, which didn't seem to have decayed any further in the past few seconds, then stepped away from the door and spun around. The vampire opened the door, and Mage thrust with the stake, driving it through his chest.

Mage watched, expecting it to fall; instead, it reached up, grabbed the stake, and plucked it out. Then it leaped toward him, lunging with the stake. Mage ducked backward, and the point scraped against his leather jacket but didn't penetrate. Mage stepped back again, and when the vampire lurched toward him, he kicked the stake from its rotting hand. Okay, he thought, grimly. Stakes don't work. Sunlight takes time. The fire obviously wasn't hot enough. They don't bleed, and breaking their bones hardly even slows them down. What else kills vampires?

The vampire raked at his face with its fingers. Mage caught it by the wrist, forced it to its knees, and twisted its arm behind its back. The vampire stared out the window for an instant, straight into the sun, and recoiled, screaming even more intensely. It whipped its head from side to side, trying to avoid the light, and Mage pushed it closer to the window. After a few seconds, the scream was suddenly cut off and the vampire ceased to struggle. Mage hesitated, suspecting a ruse. He thought for a moment, then *saw* himself in Death Valley, still holding the vampire. He opened his eyes; the vampire still showed no signs of movement, and he dropped it on the sand.

He looked around, and saw the shack where he and Takumo had tried hiding from Tamenaga two years before. It was still standing, two or three hundred meters away, and there was no shade between it and the vampire. He blinked, and teleported toward it. Leaning up against the wall, faded almost to the same dusty gray, was the old spade Takumo had used to dig a mass grave. He picked it up, examined the edge, and shrugged.

The vampire hadn't moved when he teleported back, though a greenish stain had spread from its abdomen to its chest and thighs, and there were already flies landing on it to feed. Mage stared at it for a moment before driving the spade through its neck, decapitating it. He stood there a moment longer, won-

dering whether or not to bury the body, then shook his head
and *saw* himself back in Malachi's room.

A glance at the chaos convinced him that it would be impossible to remove all evidence of his and Takumo's presence
there, but he could collect some of the more incriminating items.
Cautiously, he shifted the shelves until he found Tudor's body,
and then the hilt of the ninjato. He extracted it, then collected
the scabbard from where it had fallen. The house was still silent
as he walked to the sorcerer's room and looked around.

Mage had no background in the occult, and few of the items
made any sense to him. There were candles of various shapes
and colors, including one shaped like a hand with burning fingers, and a rack of swords and knives. Books—some ancient
and leatherbound, some battered paperbacks—shared the
shelves with jars of different herbs and liquids and some oddly
shaped glassware. There was another circle of powder on the
floor around the punctured waterbed, and inside that, a com-
plex multicolored pentagram studded with nails. He looked in
the closet, and found a few clothes—mostly black caftans,
though there was also an ancient tuxedo and a few dark suits
that had been fashionable in the seventies—but no vampires.

He was examining some of the books, hoping for some useful
information about vampires, when he heard a door open on the
other side of the house. He froze. It seemed unlikely that a
vampire would be venturing out of its room at this time of day,
but even a living occupant of the house could cause trouble,
especially if they got a good look at his face. He grabbed the
large book on the table next to Tudor's bed, inside the pentagram; it was sealed with a locked clasp, so it was obviously
important to him, and even if it was only his diary, it might still
tell them something about Julia. He *saw* himself back in Takumo's apartment, and collapsed onto the cushions, exhausted.

The bedroom door opened a few minutes later, and Sindee
emerged, wearing one of Takumo's *Sandman* T-shirts. "Morning," she said, sleepily but cheerfully, and walked to the window to open the blind. "Where's Charlie?"

Mage glanced at the mirror-imaged clock on the wall, then yawned. "He went out early, but he should be back soon."

"Uh-huh." She glanced at the book, which he'd dropped onto the floor nearby. "Where did you get that?"

"What?"

"It's Sol's, isn't it?" Mage hesitated, wondering how much to tell her, then nodded. "I thought so. I saw him with it the night he grabbed me; it was the only thing he bothered taking from the house, so it must be valuable. What is it, a grimoire?"

"Grimmer?"

"Book of magic. Isn't that what they call them?"

"I wouldn't know."

"Uh-huh. You want some coffee?"

Takumo returned home less than an hour later, with Mandaglione hovering over him anxiously. "I'm okay," he said, between wracking coughs. "My mouth and throat feel pretty raw, but I don't want to go back to the hospital. Are *you* okay?"

Mage filled him in as concisely as he could, while Mandaglione leaned against the breakfast bar and absorbed every word. "The stake didn't affect him?"

"Didn't even slow him down. What was it, the wrong sort of wood?"

"Possibly. I'll e-mail Paris, and see what he can tell me."

"What do we do now?" asked Mage.

"We try to find Julia," said Takumo. "Ernst's place first. After that, I don't know. Where would a vampire hide?" They both looked at Mandaglione.

"What? How should I know? I don't even live in this city!"

"If *you* were a vampire, where would you hide?"

"There must be thousands of places," said Mandaglione, after a moment's thought. "Basements. Warehouses, storerooms. Some S and M freak's dungeon. Fallout shelters. The subway. The sewers. The trunk of a car. Why not a movie theatre? No sunlight there."

Takumo shook his head. "What about by night? Where would they hunt?"

"That'd depend on the vampire—looks, gender, apparent age . . . A vampire who looked like Max Schreck or Klaus Kinski's Nosferatu couldn't do much but feed on derelicts downtown and maybe pick up some hookers in Hollywood, but if this woman still looks the way she did when she was alive, she could be hitting the singles bars . . . male vampires might find better pickings at the bathhouses. Hell, if they were organized, they could be working as escorts, or delivering pizzas, and attacking their victims at home or in their hotels. They'd probably be easier to find by day. And safer." He rubbed his chin. "Or we could do what they do in a couple of novels, and burn the whole town. It's not as though anyone would miss it." Takumo glared at him. "Just a thought."

The stuntman sighed. "Okay. Give me a minute to get dressed and—where's Sindee?"

"Went out to pick up her car from the impound yard," said Mage. "Said she was going to look for some work and a place to stay, too; said she didn't feel right having your bed while you slept on the floor. I asked her to let us know where she went, and she promised to call." He stood, stretched, then knelt down and picked up Takumo's sword. "Are you sure you're okay?"

"Yeah, I'm—"

"Ernst's place is patrolled, isn't it? And fitted with alarms?"

"Yeah, that's what makes it such a great hiding place—"

"Can you get in without being seen? During the day? Because these vampires don't collapse into dust—at least, not quickly. Malachi just smelled bad and turned green. Julia hasn't been dead for that much longer. If someone sees you go in, or come out, the cops might come looking for you. You took photos of Ernst's place, didn't you? Of the inside?"

"For sure—"

"Because if I can see those, I can get to Ernst's in a second, and be out instantly if there's any trouble, without anyone outside seeing me."

Takumo considered it. As much as he hated to admit it, it made sense. "Okay," he said. "But take some holy water, and the sword. Just in case."

Tudor opened his eyes, and saw a blur in shades of near-darkness. He was conscious of pain, but after taking a moment to collect his thoughts, he decided that he probably wasn't in Hell; the agony wasn't quite intense enough. He took stock of his limbs—all four hurt, but seemed capable of movement—and then tried to move.

It took more than a minute to dislodge the shelves and free his arms, and nearly a minute more to clear the fallen books away from his face so that he could see. The angle at which the sunlight was coming in through the window suggested that it was still morning, and fairly early. He squirmed and clawed his way out of the debris, and looked down at his body. There was a wound in his chest, more than an inch wide, and he soon discovered a matching wound on his back. The last thing he remembered was the intruders, Takumo and the tall blond magician, engulfed in the water elemental, and then—then he'd blacked out. He must have lost control of the undine, and freed elementals tend to take revenge on those who summoned them.

He shuddered, glad that the magician had somehow dispelled the fire elemental; they were even more unhappy at being brought from their own fiery plane into what they considered bitter cold, and caused far greater destruction if uncontrolled. Tudor winced as he stumbled toward the door, but there was a hint of a smile on his face; none of his bones seemed to be broken, so he'd gotten off relatively lightly.

Twenty-six years before, Tudor had made a bargain with a demon for a hundred years of life, but he knew that a hot enough fire could still destroy his body as surely as it would destroy a vampire. He could survive decapitation, but only as a disembodied head. With Malachi undead, he couldn't even steal his son's body to replace his own, as he'd once planned. The pacts hadn't mentioned injury or pain, and he was well aware that it would appeal to the demon's sense of fun if he spent most of that century paralyzed and writhing in agony. Still, it would keep him out of the clutches of Hell for another seventy-four years.

Tudor had nearly reached the door before he thought to wonder what had happened to Malachi and the intruders. He searched every hiding place in the room that was large enough to hide a body, but found no trace of his son. He sat down, leaning against a bookshelf, and gritted his teeth; had he remembered how, he would have wept.

After two minutes of sitting in silence, he stood and staggered into his own room. The ritual to discover what had happened to Malachi was a simple one, that required no fasting and little preparation, and could be performed at almost any time, even during daylight. He was gathering the materials he needed for the spell when he noticed that his book of pacts was gone from the table, and then he woke Adrian and Tanith with his scream of rage and fear.

16

Blood Groups

Mage stared at Ernst's body from as far away as he could without leaving the den, and wondered what to do. The hole in the surgeon's neck looked as though it'd been made by a bullet, not teeth; there were also bullet holes in the walls, but none in the chair, making it clear that the body had been moved. That didn't prove that it hadn't been done by a vampire, but it didn't seem likely. He looked at the wound again, and at the small automatic lying on the floor near the corner of the room; he guessed that it was possible that the wound had been self-inflicted and the body moved later, but that didn't seem likely either. He stepped closer and squirted Ernst's eye with holy water, and the drops merely ran down his cheek like tears, doing no harm.

Mage left him where he was, and searched the rest of the house. When it became clear that no vampires were hiding there, he took a last look at Ernst, then went into the kitchen and cracked the window with the hilt of the sword. The alarm sounded immediately, and Mage *saw* himself back in Takumo's apartment.

* * *

"**W**oody!"

Detective Woodcott was reading the report on the theft of
Angela Winslow's body from the morgue; he looked up, startled, and the lieutenant waved a fax at him. "Got a stiff with a
gunshot wound, at home. Security guard found him a few
minutes ago when something set the alarm off. Uniforms have
secured the premises, and the pathologist's on his way. Do you
think you can handle it?"

Woodcott's cheeks burned. When a body had been found a
few blocks from the Tudor house on Sunday morning, he'd gotten lost and arrived late. The other cops had noticed how jumpy
he was at the time, and since he'd been unable to offer any
explanation, they had been kidding him about it all week. The
disturbing dreams had stopped a few nights ago, but he was
still a little shaky. "Sure," he said, dropping the report on the
desk, then wished he hadn't sounded quite so meek.

He arrived to find Ed Douglass already there. "It's a weird
one," Douglass said, as the photographer took closeups of the
bullet holes around the room. "No sign of forced entry, though
someone broke a window from the *in*side. No sign of robbery.
No suicide note. We found a little pistol in the corner, a Browning, .25 caliber, but the clip was empty; we haven't tested it yet,
but I don't think it's been fired recently. We've found five nine-
millimeter Parabellum cartridges, and the holes in the walls, and
in Ernst, look more like nine mil than .25. There's no sign of
tattooing around the wound, so I'm pretty sure it wasn't self-
inflicted, but that's the pathologist's call."

"When did he die?"

"Some time last night, probably before midnight; none of the
neighbors heard anything, but the soundproofing is pretty
good."

Woodcott stared around the room. "What's with the dolls?"

"He must have collected them. We've spoken to his cleaning
service and they said that they'd never seen any sign that anyone

else lived here—though someone might have last week, because I've found hairs here that weren't his, and last Monday the occupant rang to cancel the cleaners. No complaints, no explanation, he just didn't want them to come around until further notice. But if you think this room is strange, you should see the refrigerator."

"The refrigerator?"

Douglass looked around to see Dr. Yeoh walk in, accompanied by a uniformed cop. "I always check the fridge as soon as I can," he explained, with a smile. "It's a good source of fingerprints, and I like to get to it before some rookie gets hungry. This time around, it paid off. There's a bag of blood in there, and a vial of Midazolam."

"Human blood?"

"According to the label, yeah. Type O."

Woodcott made a note of that. "And the vial?"

"Midazolam's a general anesthetic," said Yeoh. "You're right, that is strange." He nodded at the body. "Who is he?"

Douglass shrugged. "If this is the occupant, and it looks like him, he's Henry Ernst, M.D. No criminal record. Phone book says he's a plastic surgeon. We've called his office, and his receptionist says he didn't come in this morning; she's been working for him for six years, and has never heard him mention his family or any close friends, so she's going through his Rolodex. If she doesn't come up with something, we'll have to ask her to ID the body."

Ernst looked at Yeoh. "Time of death?"

"Approximately twelve hours ago; whoever did this has had plenty of time to get away. I can be more precise once I get him to the morgue; I'll fax you my report as soon as it's done."

Beth was autoclaving her instruments while her latest client stuck out her tongue and admired her handiwork in the mirror for a few minutes. Beth helped her pack her bra with sterile dressings, made her a cup of tea, and gave her her instructions on post-piercing care, finishing with, "Don't remove the tongue stud, rise your mouth after every meal, and no licking any carpet for at least a day." The woman looked blank, and Beth suppressed a sigh; there were few things more frustrating than a woman who was both gorgeous and straight.

"Here's some bonjella for the nipples," she said. "Call me if there's any problems." She checked her diary when the woman left, saw that she had no appointments scheduled until two, and sat down with a book. She looked up when the door opened a few minutes later, and saw Adrian walk in. "Hi," she said, curiously. "What's up?"

Adrian sat down. "I'm moving out. Something's going on in that house, and I don't like it. If I were you, I'd do the same."

"What do you mean?"

"I woke up this morning, after you'd left, because Solomon was screaming. Malachi's room looked like the aftermath of a wrap party for a Tarantino movie, though Solomon shut the door pretty quickly when he saw I was up. There was no sign of Malachi, or Julia; maybe they were in Julia's room, but I'd defy anyone to've slept through the racket Solomon was making. I don't know what the fuck is going on, but I've had enough. I can't think as clearly when I'm there, I'm always tired . . . is it just me?"

Beth thought for a moment. "No, you're right. I haven't felt the same about the place since . . . well, with Sindee gone, it's just too quiet. House of Usher-ish, almost. Maybe that's why I haven't felt like doing anything except going to bed as soon as I've eaten . . . when was the last time you even *thought* of bringing anyone home?"

Adrian blinked, and thought hard for several seconds. "A couple of weeks . . ."

"Me too. Have you found a place, yet?"

"Not really; haven't had time to look. I'm staying in a motel near Farmer's Market."

"Do you want to use this place as a mailing address until you settle down?"

"Thanks. Are you going to do it, too?"

"Yes, as soon as I can, but I feel sorry for Tanith."

Adrian shrugged. "She's a big girl; she can leave Sol if she wants to. Besides, I'm sure it won't be too long before someone else moves in."

Woodcott returned to the house just before sunset, when Douglass and the photographer had finished. He could have relied on their report, with its maps and pictures, but he liked to think there might be some important detail that only he would notice—a smell, maybe, or a feeling, or the way things looked or sounded at another hour of the day.

He wandered into the bedroom, knowing that all documents had already been collected and catalogued, and the sheets taken to be searched for hairs and other traces. He walked around to the far side of the bed, and almost tripped over a stack of books. Donning his gloves, he bent down and examined the titles. All of them were about vampires, and all looked new. Absent-mindedly, Woodcott sat down on the bed as he pondered. Vampire books by the bed, blood in the refrigerator . . . a coincidence, maybe, or just an eccentricity of Ernst's, no reason for concern. What worried him more was that he'd been reading reports of bodies disappearing from the morgue, and the word "vampire" had never even entered his mind. And something else was nagging at him . . . he looked around, remembered where he was, and stood up hurriedly. A glint under the bed caught his eye, and he dropped to his knees and stared into the shadows. A large, ornate crucifix lay on the carpet, within easy reach of the edge of the bed.

Woodcott hurried back to his car, and drove back to the station. He flicked through the report on the attack on a morgue attendant at Cedars Sinai Hospital, found the record of the woman whose body had disappeared, and pored over it. Her husband was listed as next of kin, but there were also a son and an ex-husband mentioned; Malachi and Solomon Tudor.

Woodcott smiled, reassured by the weight of his pistol in his shoulder holster and the Bible in his pocket. If it was only vampires, then he was ready.

* * *

Plummer was watching Takumo's apartment through the infrared scope and wondering when he'd last had such a boring job. The time he'd hidden in a shopping mall crawlspace for thirteen hours seemed almost thrilling by comparison, though he could've done without the Muzak. The phone caught him in mid-yawn. "Queen to Queen Rook One," said Krieg.

"Elvis has entered the building," replied Plummer. "With two visitors."

"Describe them."

"One man, white, blond hair, early twenties, about six-one, a hundred and sixty pounds. Another man, white, gray hair, mid-forties, about five-eleven and two hundred. There was a woman who opened the blind early this morning—Hispanic or part black, dark hair, early twenties, five-three, a hundred pounds, nobody on your list—but she left about an hour later and I haven't seen her come back."

Krieg made a note of this; nearly a foot too short to be Kelly Barbet, but worth investigating.

"Elvis closed the blind again a little after three, but nobody's left the apartment."

"Are you sure?"

"The front door hasn't opened, nobody's come over the balcony, and there are still three warm bodies, the right size and shape, inside. Is the tall guy the one you're after?"

"It sounds like him," replied Krieg, cautiously. "Call me on the cell phone if he goes anywhere; I'll be there as soon as I can. How did they arrive?"

"A car—Chevy Geo. Shall I run a check on the plates?"

"Yes." The older man matched the description Tamenaga had given her of Dante Mandaglione, but confirmation might be useful. She hung up, and walked back from the booth to the motel room. "Magistrate is at Takumo's apartment," she told Julia, who was just stepping out of the shower. "Shall we go?"

"What were you planning to do?" asked Julia, languidly.

"I have a silenced sniper rifle with an infrared scope; with that, I can shoot through the blind. With him dead, the others will be easy prey. It shouldn't take more than a few minutes."

"We have that appointment with the real estate agent at seven," Julia pointed out, "and I don't want to stay in *here* any longer than I have to." She looked around the motel room with distaste; she'd chosen a cheap motel that advertised in-house adult movies simply because she was sure she could trust the room to be dark, and now she regretted it. It smelled of too many emotions, few of them pleasant. "It can wait until after that."

Krieg nodded, to hide her sour expression. She was a little resentful that Julia had forbidden her to attack Kelly Barbet; apart from it looking as though she'd broken her word, she'd taken a rare, almost instantaneous dislike to the woman, just from reading the bio Tamenaga's people had prepared. She disliked anybody who called themselves African American without even having been to Africa; Krieg had been born in Rhodesia, and had lived there until white rule had ended. She considered herself a *real* African, and was fiercely proud of her pale skin and blond hair. But she was unable to defy the vampire who'd turned her. "Do you need to feed now?"

Julia finished drying herself. They'd drunk deeply on willing victims at the Crypt, but that had been before sunrise, and while the thirst was mild enough that she could think, she suspected she'd be better able to deal with the real estate agent if she fed first. "What did you have in mind? It's rather early."

Krieg smiled. "Somebody whistled at me as I was walking through the car park. I told him if he was interested in a three-some, to check in to Room Twelve and wait. Shall we see if he's there?"

"Isn't that risky?"

She shrugged. "The maid'll find him tomorrow, lying in the bath with his wrists slit. Do you think his family's going to want the cops to investigate? Or the manager? Besides, we'll already have checked out. Come on."

*   *   *

"**O**kay," said Takumo, "where is the *last* place you'd expect to find a vampire?" Mage and Mandaglione looked at him wearily. "Because that's exactly where a smart vampire would hide."

"Disneyland?" suggested Mage.

"A church," said Mandaglione, after a moment's thought. "One of those shops that sells Bibles and crucifixes and china figurines. Or a garlic farm."

"A tanning parlor," said Mage, suddenly inspired.

Takumo nodded, impressed. "I hadn't thought of that; I was going to say a nude beach, but I agree a tanning parlor would make a better hiding place. Would sun lamps harm a vampire?"

Mandaglione glanced at the bookshelves, then laughed. "Do you have a web browser?"

"You're going to run a search for 'vampires'?"

"Not exactly. You know 'The Purloined Letter'?"

Mage snorted. "Even *I* know 'The Purloined Letter'. He hides the letter by disguising it as a letter, which is the last place the cops . . . oh."

"So what did you have in mind?" asked Takumo. "Holly-wood Wax Museum, or the Movie Monsters show at Universal Studios?"

"Neither. There's a hangout for vampire wannabes, called the Crypt; Julia Petrosyan used to read her poetry there. Maybe she still does. The details should be on the Web."

Mage and Takumo looked at each other, then shrugged. "Beats sitting around here," said Takumo. "Let's check it out."

The bar was near the Forensic Science Center, so the staff were used to overhearing some strange shop talk, but Yeoh, as usual, kept his voice low. "How bad is it?" asked Kelly.

"Four dead," Yeoh replied, "assuming the Winslow woman at Sinai had the same thing. We may never know, unless *her* body turns up, too. I've e-mailed as many internists and admit-ting physicians as I can reach; of course, most of them will be way behind on their mail, but I've already had eight responses.

A woman went to her doctor with the same symptoms yesterday; she put it down to stress, because her daughter disappeared recently, but the doctor was smart enough to check her husband, who was refusing to admit he was sick. He was, of course. And today, *seven* replies from different doctors around the city. Apart from one, a three-year-old kid, they're all fairly mild cases, so there's hope. Fran Kimball seems fully recovered, and Hartmann, the morgue attendant who passed out when Winslow disappeared, is stable."

"Could it be psychosomatic?"

Yeoh shook his head. "Stress may make it worse, but I think there's more to it than that. We used to believe stomach ulcers were caused by stress and diet; now we know that they're started by a bacterial infection. I haven't found any evidence of an infective agent in these cases, but it looks more as though the kids have brought home a new disease which spreads to the parents, presumably through contact. I don't know where Winslow caught it—her only kid is an adult, and her husband seems to be unaffected. In both of the other cases, it's affected both parents, which all but rules out a genetic problem."

"Didn't the Petrosyans have a rare blood group?"

"Only the father and the children, but yes, it was rare. When the boy needed surgery last year, they had to use blood from the father and the girl. I've asked for blood types to be taken for all other cases, but all the ones I've seen have been ordinary enough. It was when I looked at their medical records that . . ." He was silent for a moment. "I was working in New York when the first AIDS cases were being autopsied—young men with Kaposi's sarcoma. And I remember how long it took us to realize that AIDS was being transmitted through blood transfusions, and thinking, my God, if only this had occurred to us sooner. . . ."

Kelly nodded. She'd been fascinated by the case of the French politicians charged with manslaughter for perceived delays in implementing tests to screen blood for AIDS in the hope of using a French test rather than an American one, then infuriated when the one person convicted had been given no sentence, the judge ruling that fifteen years of public criticism constituted punishment enough.

". . . and I wondered, what if this disease were transmitted the same way? Four of the seven people who have this problem have had surgery in the past year. That could be a coincidence, it's too small a sample to be meaningful, but it worries me."

Kelly sipped her soda while she thought about it. "How likely is it?"

"I don't know. I don't even know for sure whether it's viral, I don't have any idea of the incubation period, and I rather hope it's as *difficult* to transmit as AIDS. The couple who were admitted yesterday run a restaurant in Chinatown. I don't want to be premature, or risk starting a panic, but I don't want to be too late, either. I called you," he said, in response to her unasked question, "because you know something about this case already, because you were a good student, and because you know much more about politics than I do." Kelly didn't reply, but she certainly didn't disagree. Yeoh stared into his scotch, which he hadn't even tasted. "And because I know I can trust you to do what you think is right, not just what's best for you. I can't say that about everyone. So what do you think I should do?"

Kelly sat silently for nearly a minute, wondering how to answer that. "How many people do you think might be affected?"

"I've no way of knowing *that*, either. A city this size, the number of people who've received transfusions of blood or blood products over the past . . . year? Maybe several years? You're counting back, aren't you?"

Kelly grimaced. She'd last had major surgery nearly five years ago. "I'll need more information," she said.

"Of course."

She stood. "Will you excuse me for a moment? I need to make a phone call."

They listened in silence until Kelly had finished speaking, then Mage said, "The vampires can drain anyone who had a transfusion of their blood *before* they became vampires? That makes no sense at all."

Mandaglione shook his head. "Not scientifically, but it does symbolically, and a lot of magic depends on symbol. It's what they call the principle of contagion; it's why magicians are supposed to be careful never to let their enemies get hold of their hair or their nail clippings. Blood would create an even stronger bond. That may be how *nachtzerers* drain their parents and children, too; as the saying goes, they're their own flesh and blood."

"How do you know—"

"Dante writes horror stories," said Mage. "That's why he knows all this weird stuff."

"Not exactly," said Mandaglione, with a slight cough. "I've been reading weird stuff since I was a kid, and that's why I write horror stories. There's not a lot else you can do with that sort of information."

"There is now," said Takumo. "What did Paris say about the stakes?"

"He said the choice of wood isn't important—iron works just as well, for that matter—but it only works if you either break the spine or pierce the stomach, and even then, it's slow. Decapitation and burning are much more effective."

"What about guns?" asked Kelly.

"All but useless, unless they're powerful enough to do damage that a vampire can't heal—and they can heal anything a human can, but much faster. They can't regenerate limbs, for example. And he says there's nothing in folklore to say that silver would work any better—though incendiaries probably would. Or tracers, or white phosphorus shotgun rounds—"

"And where would I get *those*?"

"I haven't a clue. Everything I know about guns, I learned from books and movies." He looked at her curiously. "Charlie told me you don't believe in vampires."

"I don't," she replied, "but sometimes I'm wrong. What do we do now?"

* * *

"**R**ook to Queen One. They've gone—all of them—and taken both cars, the Range Rover and the Geo." Plummer hesitated. "Joe followed the Geo, but it looks like Elvis and the tall guy are in the Rover."

Krieg, who was driving, looked balefully at Julia. The Geo, she knew, was a rental, registered to Magistrale's uncle. "You're sure they're not still at the apartment?" she asked.

"Not according to the infrared, but they might not be in the Rover, either. Elvis's bike is still in its bay, but they might have slipped out some other way."

Krieg fumed. "I'll call you back." She turned to Julia. "They've gone."

"Magistrale and his friends?" said Julia, her voice suggesting that she would have yawned if she still needed to breathe. "The apartment was more important, especially with that man in the room next door. We have enough money for a few months, don't we?"

"Yes."

"Then a few hours more won't make very much difference." She glanced at the digital clock on the dashboard; nine fifteen. "They'll have to come back some time, won't they?"

"Magistrale might not—"

"Why don't you wait for him there? Drop me off at the Crypt; I'll call you when I need you." She supressed the urge to sigh. Krieg was useful, but so were accountancy and birth control; that didn't stop any of them from being boring. She glanced through the window at a billboard for Century City, which read "Vampires Hate it Here," and laughed. "Little do they know," she said.

Krieg said nothing. She was sure that Julia and her wannabe followers were being far too reckless, turning too many of their victims, ignoring their enemies, not making enough effort to cover their tracks. . . . And the trash Julia, Mara, and Dwight chose to turn! Students and clerks, most of them; teens and twenty-somethings, bored with life and less scared of death than they were of growing up to become like their parents. Kittens playing at being leopards, sharp-toothed but weak, dependent on her to protect them and bring home her prey until she could teach them to hunt and kill; deluded children, more concerned with fashion than power. They were wasting their abilities, and that frustrated her. Nothing she'd done since being turned had tested her strength or her invulnerability.

She allowed herself a faint smile. After she'd killed Magistrale, she could indulge herself with his friends. Or better still, she thought, she could kill the others, but turn Takumo! If his loyalty to her could be assured, he would be a much more useful aide than anybody Julia had turned. And while she could not disobey Julia herself, much less attack her, one of her own victims—her "get," as Julia called them—might, and then she'd be free.

She looked around at the city with faint distaste. It was better than most as a place to make a reputation for herself, but scarcely somewhere she wanted to spend the next few centuries. Better to find some smaller country where the secret police would appreciate her abilities and those of her underlings, pay her well, and not restrict her unduly. Given her choice of soldiers to turn, she might create a uniquely effective strike force.

Her smile become a little wider. In time, after a few assassinations, she might even be able to go home again.

17

Down Among the Dead

They drove to Kelly's house, and placed the less concealable weapons—Takumo's ninjato and Kelly's pump-action 12 gauge—in the back of the Range Rover, under a blanket. Mage spent a few minutes practicing teleporting into the car and grabbing them, then teleporting out again. "Five seconds exactly," said Takumo, fast-drawing the sword as he clicked the stopwatch. "Can we live with that?"

"We can," said Kelly, turning to Mage, "as long as you remember to come back to where you leave from, and not back here."

"If you let me go in alone—" Mage began.

"No way," said Takumo. "We don't know how many vampires there may be, by now, or what they can do at night. What if they have some sort of hypnotic powers? What if they can move faster than you can blink yourself out of there? What if—"

"Then all three of us die," said Mage. "Not just one of me."

Kelly shook her head. "He's right," she told Mage. "If we all go in, watch each other's backs, then we stand a much better chance—not just to survive, but to stop the plague, which is much more important."

"I already have Tamenaga's blood on my hands, and Tudor's, and two women whose names I've never known," snapped Mage. "I don't want any more. Especially not yours."

"And what about the vampire's victims? Would you rather be responsible for them?"

Mage reached inside his shirt for the focus, and removed it from around his neck. "I didn't ask for this," he snapped. "I've tried to do the best I can with it, tried to use it to save lives; Hell, I tried to give the others to you, two years ago, and neither of you would take one. So how am I more responsible than anyone else?"

"Because you have more power to change things," said Takumo, softly. "You tried to share the power two years ago, and we both said no, partly because we thought we didn't need them but mostly because we didn't want that responsibility." Kelly hesitated, then nodded agreement. "So maybe we were wrong. Maybe we could have learned to use them then, but we didn't. Come on. The more time we waste arguing, the more of them there are likely to be."

Mage looked at both of them, then grabbed the sword and the shotgun. "Let's see if I can get it down to under five."

Dwight was watching an old sci-fi vampire movie with the sound turned off when the three warms walked in. He assumed the look of bland affability he reserved for newcomers as he watched them. Both men were dressed in black jeans and battered leather jackets, while the woman wore loose blue jeans, sneakers, and a gray sweatshirt, none of which did anything for her. Dwight watched her appraisingly as they chose a booth. Someone who went to that much trouble to conceal her body probably had something worth hiding. He wandered over, took their orders: tea for the little Asian guy, Coke for the other man, espresso for the woman, and returned to the bar. He stopped the tape—the last good nude scene had ended, and there was no point in watching further, even if everyone in the cafe hadn't all seen it before—and replaced it with *Vamp*, trying to imagine the woman in Grace Jones's makeup and costume of copper coils. "Poetry reading begins at midnight," he said when he returned with their drinks, trying not to make it sound like a threat.

"Thanks," said Takumo. He looked past Dwight at the two young women walking down the stairs. The goth was pretty enough, and knew it, but the woman behind her had almond-shaped eyes, a dark golden complexion, and one of the most beautiful faces he'd ever seen.

Dwight noticed his reaction, and glanced over his shoulder. "Your first time here?"

"Yes," said Kelly, before Takumo could speak. Dwight waited for her to say more, but when she didn't, he walked away again.

"I know it's dark, but I can't see anything but strange costumes and heavy makeup," she said softly, glancing at an over-muscled man wearing a black sleeveless 'Got Blood?' T-shirt, ripped jeans, and an unconvincing tan. "Can you?"

"No," said Takumo, just as quietly, "but what did you expect? Nine-inch fangs?"

"I wasn't expecting anything," replied Kelly, a little more sharply.

Mage sipped at his Coke, and looked around the cafe. "Do vampires breathe?" he asked, after a few minutes.

Takumo considered this. "I don't know," he replied. "Most legends say they have halitosis, and the Chinese vampire, the Ch'ing Shih, is supposed to have poisonous breath, but whether they actually need to inhale. . . . It depends who you want to believe. Why?"

"The woman in the corset and the low-cut dress, sitting at the table in the corner. Her chest hasn't moved at all."

Takumo waited before looking around casually, and managed not to do a double take. He turned back to Mage, and said softly, "I think it's her."

"Her?"

"Julia," he said, even more quietly; he knew how easily people can pick their own name out of background noise.

"Are you sure?"

"No. She's wearing a damn sight more than Julia was last time I saw her, including more makeup. What do you want me to do? Get close enough to take her pulse? Or just squirt her with holy water?"

"Maybe if she goes to the bathroom, you could follow her," Mage suggested to Kelly. "The light must be better in there."

"I'm not sure vampires need bathrooms," said Takumo, blinking.

"They must need mirrors," said Kelly, uncertainly, "for their makeup, if not their hair. Or do they have to do each other?"

"Damn," said Takumo. "I knew there was something I forgot to bring. Did you?"

Kelly reached into her handbag, and removed a makeup mirror. A few seconds later, she replaced it in the bag, and shook her head slightly. "Everyone I can see still has a reflection, and I don't think that's just their makeup. What do we do now?"

"Did you see anyone else who doesn't seem to be breathing?" Takumo asked Mage.

"No, but I haven't looked too closely. That one *expects* to be stared at."

"Maybe you should go over?"

Mage seemed taken aback by this suggestion from Kelly, then nodded. "Yeah. Maybe I should." He picked up his Coke and stood, then walked across the floor. The woman looked up, unsmiling. "Yes?"

"I was wondering if I could buy you a drink."

She looked him up and down. "No, thanks," she said, giving him a quick glimpse of her teeth.

He placed his glass on the table. "Well, may I sit down, or are you waiting for someone?"

"You're new here, aren't you?"

Mage felt several people staring at him, but ignored it. "Yes, I am. If you're spoken for, then someone is incredibly fortunate, and if I'm out of line, I apologize. My name's Michael, by the way."

"Julia." He pulled up a chair and sat. "I thought you were with her," she said, nodding at Kelly.

"No; they're just friends of mine. I'm staying with them while I'm in town. I asked them to show me what the nightlife was like in L.A., and they brought me here."

She looked at him warily. "How long are you staying?"

"As long as I want to."

"Do you have a job here?"

"Not yet."

The corners of her mouth quirked slightly. "You're an actor?"

"Photographer."

"What type of photographer?"

"Whatever type they pay me to be. You're an actress?"

"No."

"Model?"

"No. I used to work in a boutique, but I was fired. I'm not at my best in the morning."

"Who is?"

"Don't you wish you could just sleep through the whole day?"

"Sometimes," replied Mage. "I think I'd miss the sun, though."

Julia smiled slightly. Maybe this one would make a good protector. She could feed on him later, take just enough to get him hooked on the bite, maybe even mix it with some sex. She'd let Malachi fuck her once since her death; he'd been unable to arouse her, but he hadn't been particularly adept at that when she was warm. Now, to her surprise, she discovered that she missed those feelings. Suddenly, Dwight stepped onto the Crypt's tiny stage, and shouted, *"It's showtime, folks!"*

She winced.

"I'm Dwight, your host, and it's time for the Preachers of the Night. The Bards of Ill Omen. The Undead Poets Society. And to open, we have the Lady Julia."

Julia glared at him, then turned to Mage. She seemed slightly embarrassed, though there was no hint of a blush on her pale skin. "Excuse me for a moment."

"Certainly." He watched as she walked to the stage. "I haven't written anything new in more than a week," she said, "and this isn't exactly a vampire poem, but I haven't read it here before. It's called 'Interregnum.' " She glanced around the room, and began. She read at breakneck speed, never pausing for breath:

> Contortions and abortions and beginnings you let slide
> come to haunt you: hear them taunt you, making
>   weapons of your pride.
> You're afraid to move; afraid to prove you've chosen the
> wrong way,
>   and although you hate the silence, you don't want to
> hear them say
> They predicted this would happen, any day.
>
> Are you waiting, hesitating, or just drifting off to sleep?
> Hear the dying throes of dominoes, felled by entropic
> creep.
> You think you're stuck? You're out of luck: you knew it
> had to be.
> Or did you? Would you rather it remained a mystery,
> and let other people talk of destiny?
>
> You shut your ears to all your fears, although you know
> they're right.
> You missed your turn, and will not learn you've no re-
> course but flight.
> Just carry on: tomorrow's gone, and yesterday as well.
> Your only consolation in defeat will be to tell
> an apathetic world to go to Hell.

There was some scattered applause when she finished, and she read two more poems, both of them even worse, though they obviously pleased her followers. While she read, she looked around the room, and realized that there were too few warms to satisfy the eight vampires present. The addicts—Damien, Jeremy, and Nina—had been bitten too recently; taking more of their blood might kill them. She might be able to persuade the others to spare Michael, leaving him as an addict, but his friends would probably be drained. Only Mara and Todd were her own get; Mara had turned Ahna, Dwight, and April; Dwight had turned Lalena . . . but Garrett, the bodybuilder, was Krieg's, and Krieg wasn't here to control him. As she stepped off the stage, she saw Lalena head up the stairs to shut the door. Mara and April sat down in the booth, blocking Kelly and Takumo in. Julia slipped past Dwight, who was walking toward her, and hurried toward Mage.

"Wait!" she said, and leaned over the table. "Michael, don't say anything, please, and I'll make sure no one hurts you." She realized as she said it that she could have put it more diplomatically, but Mage didn't seem offended. "What's going on?" he asked.

"Why did your friends pick *this* place? For a laugh?"

"No," he replied, softly.

"Do they want to be vampires? Do you?"

"No."

She winced slightly. "I'm a vampire. *Don't* just nod like that, *don't* patronize—"

"I wasn't. I believe you."

"—me . . . you do?"

"And I want to help."

"Help?" She glanced over her shoulder. Everybody in the room was watching them. "What do you mean, help?" she asked, hopefully.

"Do you know how many people are dying because of you?" He didn't raise his voice, but most of the vampires in the room were able to hear him clearly. "Not just those you attack. Not just your parents, or any children you may have." None of the crowd, whose ages seemed to range from late teens to early twenties, responded to that. "If any of you have ever given blood, you may be killing people who've had transfusions of your blood—that's how your brother died," he told Julia, gently.

She stared at him. "And how do you intend to help?" asked Dwight. "Apart from feeding us for tonight?"

"He's mine," said Julia, without turning away. "Michael . . ." She reached for his hand; he snatched it away. "I won't kill you," she said, and smiled thinly, showing her canines. They were only slightly longer than they'd been when she was warm, but they looked sharp, and were. "I'll just take a little. It'll feel good; you'll want to come back for more. Just ask *them*," and she nodded at the addicts. "You may even be able to help us."

"I don't trust him," growled Dwight.

"If you want my help," said Mage, loudly and clearly enough that even Lalena, thirty feet away, heard him, "you'll have to stop killing people."

"And how do we do that?" asked Mara.

"I don't know. Do your victims have to be human?" Julia's expression turned cold. "There are doctors, scientists, who'd be fascinated to see you. Maybe they could cure—" He stopped as he felt the hostility intensify; none of the vampires uttered a sound, but the air suddenly seemed to have become poisonous.

"We don't need a *cure*," said Mara. "We *chose* to become what we are. We *like* it."

There was a murmur of assent from all the vampires except Ahna, who looked uncertain and slightly queasy.

"What do you have to offer us that's better?" asked Todd.

Mage looked around the room, and tried to think of an answer that most of them—even a few of them—would believe. "Sorry," he said. He pushed his chair back and stood, and when Julia grabbed at him, he *saw* himself back in the Range Rover.

Mara reached for Takumo, and he squeezed on his squirt ring; the holy water caught her under the chin and ran down her neck, and she screamed as she backed out of the booth hurriedly, her skin already cracking and turning red where the fluid had touched her.

April lunged at Kelly, and found herself staring into the muzzle of a little automatic. "Back off," said Kelly, softly. The vampire merely laughed, and grabbed her wrist. Kelly fired into her left eye at point-blank range. April screamed, but she didn't release her grip. Takumo tried to squirt her with the holy water, but the bulb was all but empty; a thin trickle dripped onto the table, falling far short. Takumo slid his knife out of his sleeve, preparing to throw it at April, and saw Dwight reach behind the bar and bring out a snub-nosed revolver. Takumo flicked his wrist, and the knife flew across the room and hit the bartender in the shoulder. Dwight flinched, and the pistol flew from his hand and landed on the floor behind the bar.

Mage reappeared at the end of the table, and both Takumo and Kelly grabbed at the weapons offered them. An instant later, Takumo realized that he was holding the shotgun, and Kelly the ninjato; either Mage had grabbed the weapons with the wrong hands, or they'd been sitting in the wrong positions. Rather than waste time wondering about it, he pointed the shotgun at Dwight, one-handed, and squeezed the trigger. The recoil was fierce, and the shot passed over Dwight's head, shattering bottles behind the bar and showering him with spirits and broken glass.

The vampire, who was pulling the knife from the bloodless wound in his arm, stared at him, then vaulted the bar before Takumo could take aim. The ninja swung the gun and pointed it at April's good eye. April released Kelly's wrist and slid out of the booth. Takumo and Kelly glanced at each other, then exchanged weapons. Kelly pumped another round into the shotgun's chamber, using her forearm to work the slide rather than drop her pistol, then slowly eased out of the booth.

Julia stared at Mage, her eyes a lambent red. "Todd! Garrett!" The two vampires hurried toward the booth, and Todd flung himself at Mage. Mage stepped aside, and the vampire ran into the edge of the table. Takumo chopped down with the ninjato, slicing through his neck, and Julia shrieked at the shock and pain of losing one of her get. Takumo wrestled the blade free, then turned to Mage. "Do we have a plan?" he asked.

"Not anymore," replied Mage, grimly.

"Do you have a weapon for yourself?"

"No . . ." He stared at Julia. "If you let us walk out of here . . ."

Julia seemed frozen. After the shock had passed, the residual pain of losing one of her get was less than that of a pulled tooth, an ache and a faint feeling of something being missing, but the urge to avenge the insult was strong. "Nobody will get hurt?" she finished for him, her voice thick and dry as a scab, then shook her head. "It's not that simple, Michael. Suppose we did let you go? We'd still need to feed, and besides, you might follow us to our hiding places. On the other hand, how many rounds are in that gun?"

"Six at most," growled Garrett. "Maybe only two. Another four or five in the pistol."

"I think you have more to fear from us," said Julia, smiling. Dwight poked his head up above the bar, then brought the pistol up and fired without taking time to aim. The first round missed Mage by more than a yard; he moved the gun a few degrees right and fired again, and his next shot hit Nina in the back. She screamed as she hit the floor, facedown, and April and Garrett took advantage of the distraction; he leaped at Mage, blindsiding him, and she lunged at Kelly again.

Garrett grabbed Mage from behind, pinning his arms to his sides and squeezing until Mage's ribs creaked. Mage struggled, but the vampire's grip was much too strong for him to escape. He whipped his head back, hoping to butt the vampire in the nose, but connected with his chin instead. Kelly fired the shotgun into April's chest at point-blank range, the hot gases and powder setting her silk shirt aflame around the wound. April staggered back, trying to beat out the small blaze with her hands, and Mage *saw* himself engulfed in flame again.

Garrett, who'd been about to sink his teeth into Mage's neck, released his grasp hastily and backed away with a yelp of pain and fright. His short beard and the hairs on his arms were blazing, and the flames were spreading quickly. Mage stared, and the vampire was enveloped in a pillar of fire. The others backed away from him, watching in horror as he fell, rolled over the floor a few times, and then ceased to move. Flames continued to lick across the black husk, which still had the outline of a human body, the arms protecting the face like a boxer with his fists up, the skin of the face burnt away to reveal the teeth.

"Open the door!" Mage yelled over the shriek of the smoke alarms. He *saw* himself whole and uninjured, but because he didn't dare extinguish the inferno that surrounded him, his skin soon began to blister and crack again. He tried to speak, but had to shut his mouth and grit his teeth to prevent a scream of agony escaping. He *saw* himself whole again, and bellowed, stopping every second or so to heal his wounds, *"Open the— door and—let us out—or—by—God—I will burn—this place— and every—damned—one—of you!"* He opened his eyes briefly and stared through the flames that engulfed his face, hoping to see whether the command would be obeyed.

Lalena, at the top of the stairs, didn't hesitate; the door was open in an instant, and she was on the other side of it. Damien was the next to break, and he ran for his life, with Jeremy only a few steps behind him. Dwight ducked back behind the bar, and the others turned to Julia. She stood her ground for a moment, then turned away and began walking, slowly and with exaggerated dignity, toward the stairs. Before she was halfway up, Mara began running after her, then Ahna. Mage walked briskly toward the stairs, with Takumo and Kelly following a safe distance behind him, protecting his back.

Dwight popped up from behind the bar again and took a moment to aim at Mage, who was busy looking up at the door-way. Takumo saw him, and yelled, "Dwight!"

The bartender flinched slightly, looking away from Mage, and Mage immediately turned around and looked at the bar. Dwight's shirt, soaked with spirits, burst into flames. "Fry," snapped Takumo, watching him burn. Dwight tightened his grip on the gun, and a bullet smashed into the wall between Mage and Kelly before he fell to the floor.

Mage looked back, to see April slowly walking toward the stairs, her hands empty, one eye red, the other a deep bloody hole; Kelly was tracking her, both guns pointed at her face. Everyone else in the room seemed utterly dead. Mage *saw* himself on the other side of the street, in case the other vampires were waiting in ambush outside the door; seeing no one, he extinguished the flames that still enveloped him, and teleported back. "Clear," he barked.

"Movin' right along," replied Takumo, breaking into a run. Kelly followed at a more cautious pace, not letting April out of her sight until she was standing on the sidewalk. They looked up and down the street. "Well, that could've gone better," said Takumo, mildly.

Kelly shook her head, her eyes gleaming, her expression fierce. "Three of them dead, none of us injured . . ." she said, holstering her pistol in her shoulder bag. "It could've gone a Hell of a lot worse. What do we do now?"

"Charlie's right," said Mage, healing himself as best he could without a mirror and shaking the ashes out of his hair. "We shouldn't have let them get away like that." He stared along the street. "Where have they all gone?"

Takumo looked in the other direction. "How did they get here?"

"What?"

"This is L.A.," he pointed out. "The only way to get around at night is to drive. They must have at least one car parked around here . . . and if they get to it, they have five hours before sunrise to go looking for a hideaway." He glanced up at the rooftops of the buildings opposite. "Mage, can you fly?"

"*What?*"

"Can you see yourself flying? Teleport up into the air and stay there? Or onto that roof?"

Mage looked up. "I think so, but why?"

"So you can see further."

"It'd better be the roof, then," said Mage. "I won't have to concentrate on not falling. Back in a second." And he vanished.

Kelly shook her head. "If we're so determined not to let the vampires get away, to stop them feeding, what're we going to do about the one in there? The one with one eye?" Takumo blinked, and the lawyer sighed, turned around, and opened the door. Before Takumo could react, she'd stepped inside, and closed the door behind her; the thick wood muffled the sound of the shotgun, but to Takumo it sounded like the end of the world. He was still pale when Kelly emerged, but Mage reappeared before he could speak. "Around the next corner," he said, pointing, and teleported away again. Takumo and Kelly glanced at each other, and set out at a run.

"Is it just me," said Takumo, "or do you feel a little conspicuous, too?"

Kelly glanced at the gun, and shrugged. "I'll worry about that later—*Mage!*"

Lalena had been asthmatic since early childhood and had never learned how to run, and though she was pleased to discover that being dead meant that she no longer needed to breathe, her head start over the others soon diminished and Jeremy and Damien passed her before she reached the corner. Neither of them looked back, even when she tried to bark out orders as she'd heard Julia do, or when she tried pleading instead. She kept going until she reached the corner, then looked behind her to see that Julia, Mara, and Ahna were heading the other way.

"The car's that way," shouted Mara.

"We can come back for it later," said Julia. "I know a place where we can hide."

The Camaro hurtled past Lalena as she plodded along. Jeremy spared her the briefest glance, instantly rejecting the idea of picking her up. After being caught in the crossfire between vampires and vampire hunters, he decided that neither side could be trusted as allies. When Mage suddenly appeared on the sidewalk near the corner ahead, he steered the car toward him and floored the accelerator. The magician disappeared when the car was less than a yard away, and Jeremy hastily stomped on the brake. The car skidded to a stop across two lanes at the inter-

section. Jeremy looked around, and saw Kelly and Takumo running toward the car. After nearly a second of indecision, he
turned the Camaro toward them and accelerated. "Jesus, man!"
Damien shouted, still fumbling with his seat belt. "Just get us
the fuck out of here, okay?"

Jeremy ignored him, but when Kelly raised the shotgun, Damien grabbed the steering wheel and tried to take control of the
car. A blast of shot shattered the windscreen, but little of it
penetrated, and Jeremy hardly even flinched. Takumo threw
himself at Kelly, knocking her out of the car's path. The Camaro sideswiped a lamppost before smashing into a store window, setting off alarms. Damien was flung forward, cracking
his head on the roof of the car, and slumped back into his seat,
dazed. Jeremy glared at him, then looked out the back window
to see Kelly pick herself up. He threw the car into reverse, running over the tetsubishi Takumo had just flung behind his
wheels. He swore as his back tires blew and the car fishtailed,
and Takumo, kneeling on the roof and hanging on with one
hand, lunged with his ninjato until the point pricked Jeremy
just above the heart—and stopped. "Turn off the engine," the
stuntman commanded, "and get out of the car. Both of you."

"My friend's unconscious!" shrieked Jeremy.

Takumo bent down and glanced through the hole in the
windshield. After a moment, he nodded, and pulled the sword
back a few inches. "Throw the keys out, then get out. Slowly."

"I'm not a vampire!" Jeremy protested, as he obeyed. "Neither is he! We're just—"

"Just what?"

Jeremy turned around, to see Kelly standing barely six feet
away, which put the muzzle of the shotgun only *four* feet away.
"We let them bite us, sure," he said, almost crying, "but we're
not dead. We don't drink blood. We haven't killed anybody. . . ."

Takumo and Kelly exchanged glances, then Kelly said, "I
think he's telling the truth."

"Why?"

"He's sweating. None of the vampires did that, even when the place was on fire."

Takumo hesitated, and regarded the two men closely. It was hard to be sure in the streetlight, but the blood welling out of the wound on Jeremy's chest and Damien's forehead looked bright red, while none of the vampires in the bar had bled at all. Even when he'd decapitated Todd, there'd been almost no blood; he looked at the black blade of his sword, which seemed much too clean.

"Do you know where they've gone?" asked Kelly, as Takumo wiped the blade.

"One of them went around the corner there," said Jeremy, quickly. "I haven't seen the others; maybe they turned into bats or something. . . ."

"Have you seen them do that?"

"No! I thought they were just kidding around until one of them bit me. I never wanted to be one of them! Who the fuck *are* you guys?"

"We're the Ordained of the Elder Gods," said Takumo, solemnly. "Vampires cannot harm us. Even if these bodies could be destroyed, we're only borrowing them, and we can always find new hosts; when the sun rises, these mortal forms will forget everything that has happened tonight. I advise you to do the same."

"Yeah. Sure. Anything."

"This has only been a nightmare," hissed Takumo. "You went to bed early. Your car was stolen and trashed while you were asleep. If you ever talk about this, we will find you, though we may not have these bodies. Do you understand?" Jeremy nodded. "Then go."

Kelly watched as Jeremy drove away, the car riding low on its shredded rear tires. "You have a nice line of bullshit," she said, unsmiling.

"Thanks," said Takumo. "My grandmother always wanted me to be a lawyer. Shall we go and see how Mage is doing?"

* * *

Lalena had seen Mage disappear as Jeremy's car swerved toward him, but she hadn't expected to find him standing in front of her when she turned around. "Where are the others?" he demanded. "Where did they go?"

She stared at him, then threw her head back and laughed. "Or what?" she asked. "You'll kill me? You're going to do that anyway, aren't you?" She looked him in the face, careful to keep eye contact; it might not hypnotize him, but at least it might make him hesitate about killing her.

"Can you stop killing?"

"Oh, yes," she said softly. "I'm sure I can."

"And how will you . . . feed?"

"I'll find a way," she said, edging closer. "Not draining people—not drinking so much that it kills anybody. I'm sure I can do it." She was almost in arm's reach now. "Why don't you join us? Live forever . . ."

"Are you enjoying your life so much?"

She hesitated. She hadn't fed yet that night, and the thirst was already making it difficult to think. "What?"

"What's the best thing about the way you live now? What gives you the most pleasure?"

The thirst was almost an ache, now; she could see the warmth of his blood where it flowed close to the skin, smell it, hear his pulse. . . . There was only one true answer to his question, but she knew she shouldn't give it. "What do you mean?"

"What do you love?"

"What?"

"*Do* you love?"

She thought back to her life. She couldn't remember loving anybody then, or being loved. She hadn't loved her job, or her home, or the city. . . . She looked up. "I could love you," she whispered. She reached up to touch his face, and when he grabbed her wrist, she sprang at him.

Mage *saw* both of them back inside the Crypt. There was a roaring fire behind the bar where the spilled alcohol had been set alight, and the room was filing with smoke. As Lalena's teeth grazed his neck, he *saw* both of them engulfed in the flames.

Fire caressed Lalena, then consumed her; she writhed and screamed as the pain, more intense than any she had ever known before, obliterated all other sensation, and then all memory. Mage released her, and *saw* himself back on the street. He was still healing his fresh wounds when Kelly and Takumo came running around the corner a moment later, Takumo's breath rasping. "Where are the others?" he gasped.

"I don't know," said Mage. "I only saw the three of them come this way, two men and a woman." He looked at their weapons. "You'd better get back to the car. I'll come and get you."

"What—?" Takumo shut his mouth when he realized that he was talking to himself; Mage had already *seen* himself back on Vermont Street, and disappeared again a moment later, teleporting form corner to rooftop to corner, looking down side streets and alleys. A hint of movement caught his eye, and he teleported down to hear a manhole cover clang down. He stared at it for a moment, then *saw* himself back in Kelly's Range Rover.

"**S**top!" Takumo puffed. He bent over near a red Hyundai, and Kelly turned around anxiously. "Are you okay?"

"I'm not breathing well," admitted Takumo, coughing. "Smoke damage, I guess. But that's not why I stopped. Look at these stickers."

"What?" Kelly glanced at them, then did a double take. The larger sticker read "Carpe Noctem." She looked more closely at the smaller, a fish, and saw that it had fangs and was inscribed "Vampire", not "Jesus" as she'd assumed. Takumo produced his penlight from one of his pockets, then looked through the rear window. Vampire books and magazines lay on the back seat. "Can you run a check on the license plate?" he asked.

"Yes, but not quickly, not at this hour," said Kelly, taking a note of the number anyway. She glanced over at the Range

Rover half a block away. "Should we stake this out—" He winced. "What? Oh. Sorry. I mean, do you think they'll come back here?"

"Whoever owns it might—it may not be Julia's—but I think it's worth trying." He glanced at the Range Rover, half a block away, and waved the flashlight. Mage appeared beside him an instant later. "Find anything?" he asked.

Mage told them what he'd seen, and they looked at each other uncertainly. Takumo tried to imagine Julia, in her velvet dress, wading through a sewer; it wasn't an image that came readily to mind. "So what do we do?" he asked. "Try following them, or wait for them to come back here?"

"I vote for waiting," said Kelly. "You're sure you saw them go down there?"

"I didn't see them, but I'm sure I heard the cover close," said Mage. "At least one of them went that way."

Takumo nodded. "It might be a diversion, even a trap . . . but what else can we do? If they *don't* come back for the car, we've lost them again; they could hide down there all day, and surface anywhere. On the other hand, if we're still blundering around down there when they come back for the car," He turned to Kelly. "Why don't you stay here, follow their car if they come back, find out where they're hiding?"

"Why me?" asked Kelly, angrily.

"Because it's your car, and you can drive it better than we can."

Kelly considered this, then shrugged. "I can't really argue with that, can I?" She looked at Takumo. "Maybe you should stay here, too."

"What? Why?"

"If you start coughing the way you did when on the way here, Charlie—"

"I won't," snapped Takumo. "I *know* how to be quiet—"

"Coughing?" asked Mage.

"Smoke inhalation damage," said Kelly. "And the air down there won't be good for his health, either."

Mage nodded as he considered this. "Okay. If I get lost, or it's a trap, I can always get out more easily alone—"

"Unless it kills you instantly," retorted Takumo.

"I'll take that chance," said Mage.

"Wait!" snapped Takumo, realizing that he was about to disappear. He drew a deep breath. "Okay, I'll stay here. But in case the shit—ah, in case anything goes wrong . . . thanks."

"What for?"

"For coming when I asked you to," he said. "For putting yourself in danger when you didn't need to. And for all the times you've saved my neck—particularly with Dwight."

"Dwight? I didn't do anything to Dwight."

"Sure you did. He was the bartender; you—"

Mage shook his head. "No. It must have been you—you're wearing a focus, aren't you?"

"Yeah, but . . . freakin' Hell, I'm no magician!"

"Yes, you are. You're the one who taught me to use the key, remember? The magic probably helps keep your sword sharp, too; I remember Tamenaga chopping his desk in half with a katana, which shouldn't be—"

"Yeah, but—are you serious? You really didn't do it?"

"I'm serious," said Mage. "When I see someone threaten me with a gun, *I* take care of the gun first." Takumo considered this, and realized it was true. "You can do it when you need to—and thanks. He could've shot any one of us—"

"Except the one he was aiming at," muttered Kelly.

"Maybe, but I'm not much good with bullet wounds; they're much more difficult than burns. I'll see you both later. By the way, are there supposed to be alligators in your sewers? The climate would suit them better than New York's."

Takumo shook his head. "The giant ants must have eaten them all."

"Thanks—I think."

"Shouldn't you take a weapon?" asked Takumo. "Just in case?" He reached into a pocket, drew his balisong knife, unfolded the handle, and offered it to Mage.

Mage looked at the five-inch blade dubiously, then took it. "Do you think that's going to be much good against a vampire?"

"It's a bit short," agreed Takumo, "but—" Both he and Kelly stared as Mage looked at the blade, *seeing* it lengthen. Five inches became seven, nine, a foot . . . Mage finally stopped when the blade reached eighteen inches. "Thanks," he said. "Later."

"So I'm a magician," murmured Takumo, after Mage vanished. "Oh, *shit*."

Mara looked down at the ankle-deep sludge at the bottom of the sewer, trying not to think about how much her shoes had cost. She'd managed to remove her fishnet dress and bundle it up under one arm, and was walking around in her underwear and pantyhose. The wound on her throat and chin still burned, though not as badly as it had, and she wondered how long it would take to heal. If Stoker was right, it would last until Julia was killed—a horrifying prospect. She wondered if she could cover it with makeup.

Ahna had rolled her jeans up to above her knees; Julia's velvet dress only reached down to mid-thigh, and the tops of her boots were higher than the muck, though they weren't entirely waterproof. Mara's heel caught on something in the murk, and she fell backward, splattering the others. She screamed, and Julia growled at her. "Sorry," Mara whimpered. The smell would have been bad while she was alive; with her keener vampiric sense, it was almost overpowering. Julia quickened her pace, and Ahna fell back, maintaining a greater distance between them.

Rats chittered around them in the darkness, but none came too close. Mara suppressed the urge to ask Julia if she knew where she was going, and then she became aware of another presence. Somebody ahead in the darkness. Somebody watching them. Somebody without a pulse, somebody who didn't breathe. Julia looked back at her, passed a finger across her throat, commanding silence. They advanced for another twenty yards, thirty, and then Julia said softly, "Show yourself."

The vampire crept forward hesitantly—almost timidly, Mara thought. He was cold enough to be almost invisible in infrared, but when he stepped into a weak beam of electric light from a grate overhead, she saw a bald head, a pointed chin, and two incisors grown into fangs. His flesh was almost white, with a faint tinge of green, and the soft parts of his ears and nose had been eaten away. Mara managed not to scream. "What. . . ."

Julia laughed harshly. "I wish Michael could see this; he wanted to know what would happen if we stopped feeding on humans. I think this is the answer."

Ahna stared, horrified. "This?" The vampire winced, and extended a hand. A bleeding rat writhed in its bony grasp, and this time Mara *did* scream.

"Nosferatu," said Ahna. "They eat rats . . . is that why they look like them?"

"Maybe," said Julia. "The legends say they can control them, too, and you know how people come to resemble their pets. They bring the rats, the rats bring the fleas, the fleas bring the plague . . . or they used to, at least."

Ahna looked at the creature more closely. He wore the gray tattered remains of coveralls that might have been of any age. "How long have you been down here?" she asked. The creature looked at her, but didn't reply. "Do you speak English?" The nosferatu was silent. "Do you understand me?" A hesitant nod. "How many of you are there?"

The monster stared, then backed away and scurried into the darkness. "I guess he was some sort of maintenance worker who blundered into a vampire down here," suggested Julia.

"Did you know he was here?" asked Mara.

"I knew there were vampires or ghouls or *something* living in the sewers; one covered me up when I hid in a storm drain, protecting me from the rats and flies, a few days ago. But I didn't know they looked like *that*."

"If nosferatu are real," said Ahna, slowly, "then what about other sorts of vampires . . ."

"I don't know."

"Are we going to turn into *them*?" asked Mara.

"I don't know that either. I haven't seen any other old vampires. But maybe if we live on humans, and *among* humans, we'll continue to look human."

Mara gasped softly as the nosferatu returned, leading a small figure by the hand. It was too fat and dirty for its gender to be obvious, but the rags it wore had once been a pink dress. Its fangs were less pronounced than the larger creature's, its eyes larger, its ears and nose less ravaged, and long pale hairs still clung to the back of its skull. "Do you speak—"

It nodded, and hissed something that might have been a yes.

"What happened to you?" asked Ahna, gently. "How long have you been down here?"

"Later," said Julia. "If anybody followed us down here, that scream's going to lead them to us in a minute. Can you take us somewhere we can hide?"

The bloated creature looked up at them, then hissed something at the larger nosferatu. It let go her hand and disappeared back into the shadows. "Come," she said; it sounded more like a gulp, but her intention was clear.

After they'd followed her for a few minutes, she began telling her story. Few of her words were recognizable, at first, but her English slowly improved. She told them that her name was Karen, and recounted how her parents had taken her to Disneyland one day, and she'd sneaked out of the house that night to return there and become lost. She'd met a man who'd looked a bit like a cartoon character, with big teeth and ears, and he'd told her that he knew a tunnel that would get her into the Magic Kingdom free. He'd shown her his pets first, and then he'd asked if he could kiss her, and she'd been here ever since.

"How long ago was that?" asked Mara, anxiously. Karen didn't know.

"What was your favorite TV show?" asked Ahna, after a moment's thought.

"*The Mickey Mouse Club*. I was a Mouseketeer."

"Shit, how long ago was *that*?" asked Mara. "The sixties?"

"I think so," said Julia. "Sesame Street is more than thirty years old—do you remember Sesame Street?" she asked the nosferatu, who looked back at her blankly. "Big Bird? Cookie Monster? The Count?" A faint shake of the head. "The man you met—was that him, back there?"

"Max? No," she replied, almost proudly. "He's mine."

"What do you live on, down here? What do you eat?"

"What we find. What we can. People taste best, but they're hard to catch. When Max gets one, he lets me drink first." Julia nodded. She guessed that Karen drank more human blood than her get, because he gave her his share, or maybe she needed less because she was smaller. Either way, she looked more human even though she'd been down here longer—unless she was lying. It had become easy for her to tell when humans were lying, but not vampires; they didn't sweat, and their hearts didn't beat. "If he catches the man who's chasing you, I get him first," she said, in the imperious, childish tone of one who's always had adult help to rely on. "That's a nice dress. Can I look at it?"

Tudor was reading his grimoires, his face tight. He dared not call on any major demons while his book of pacts was missing, and that left few spells that were worth casting. He could still summon elementals, but most elementals were too stupid and impulsive to remember an order and obey it once out of his sight. He could summon a succubus and send it after Takumo, but succubi had to be invited in, and he doubted that Takumo was that trusting. Besides, he was more interested in finding the other intruder, the magician, and only Takumo could lead Tudor to him; obtaining reliable information from Hell was difficult in the best of circumstances, especially when he had nothing of the magician's that could identify him, not even a *name*. Without his book of pacts, the best he could hope for was that some demon might also have a grudge against the magician. . . .

He blinked. Who was the older man who'd come in to help collect Sindee's things? The one who'd been so entranced by Tanith? Hadn't she introduced him?

He looked up as the door opened, and froze when he recognized Angela. "Hi, honey," she said. "I'm home."

Tudor hesitated, then drew a deep breath. "What do you want?" he asked.

"Our son is dead," she replied, grimly. "I want to know who's responsible."

"You're sure he's dead?" asked Tudor, cautiously. "I knew he'd disappeared, but I thought he might be hiding—"

"He's *dead*," snapped Angela. "I didn't feel him die, but I woke up tonight and knew he was gone. Did you kill him?"

"My own son—my *only* son? Of course not."

Angela looked at him appraisingly. He seemed sincere, even hurt, but she knew he was an accomplished liar. "Do you know who did?"

"Not exactly," said Tudor. "I've seen the man most likely to have done it, and fought him, but I don't know his name. He's incredibly powerful, magically; he may even be a power himself." Angela raised an eyebrow. "He can teleport, levitate objects, heal himself instantly, but he doesn't summon spirits. As far as I can tell, he has no training whatsoever; he stole my book of pacts, which would be useless to him—"

"Except that it weakens you."

Tudor shrugged. "True, but then, why hasn't he destroyed it? Or ransomed it? I don't think he knows what it is, what it's worth." He shook his head. "Some of his power seems to come from a talisman he wears around his neck, but I don't think that's all. He may be an avatar, a new incarnation who's still holding on to his old body—not that he's old. He looks impossibly young, in fact, about Malachi's age, and while I'm sure some of that's glamour, he *moves* like a young man. He has an—an apprentice, I suppose—of about the same age, who wears a similar talisman, but prefers to rely on sharp swords and blunt instruments. I know *his* name, and his address, I even have enough of his hair to cast a spell on him if I had my book, but I'd rather let him lead me to his teacher." He thought for a moment. "And there was a third man who accompanied them when they first visited here, an older man, who said he was the magician's uncle, and spent his time trying to impress Tanith. He said he wanted to interview her, and you too."

"Did he give his name?"

"Don Mandel, but he didn't leave any contact details."

"Somebody came to see me while I was in the hospital," said Angela. "I was too sick to speak to him, but he left me some interview questions. . . . I remember his first name was Dante; his surname was longer than Mandel, but I think it started with an M, and it ended with a vowel . . . he left an address and a phone number, too, but I don't remember them, and I don't know what the hospital would have done with the letter."

Tudor nodded. He'd never tried to hypnotize a vampire, but he didn't see why it wouldn't work. "I think I may be able to help you remember," he said.

18

After Midnight

Mage walked gingerly through the sewers, stumbling often but always managing to recover his balance before he fell. The vampires, he guessed, probably had better night vision than he did, which gave them an unfair advantage. He considered teleporting back up to street level to ask if Takumo could lend him a flashlight, but quickly realized that this would help the vampires to see him long before he could see them. He kept walking, and was heading in the wrong direction until he heard Mara's scream. Then he turned and walked quickly toward the sound.

Max waited until he could see his target splashing along the tunnel, a clear target for his infrared vision, before summoning the rats with an ultrasonic squeal. The rats swarmed out of the pipes by the dozen, swimming toward Mage, jumping at him from narrow ledges, climbing up his clothes. . . . One leaped at his face, hanging onto his hair; Mage barely managed to grab it before it went for his eyes, and held it away from his face, tearing some of his hair out in the process, but it was only one of many, and other rats swarmed up to take its place, the short-sword in his hand no deterrent.

Mage closed his eyes, but felt teeth sink into his nose, his

ears, his cheeks, his fingers; desperately, he *saw* himself
shrouded in flame again, and was rewarded with the sound of
outraged squeaks. Blazing rats fell away into the foul water,
and kept their distance. A few attacked his sneakers, his socks,
or held onto the wet cuffs of his jeans, but even they were discouraged when he lifted his feet and stomped down.

Mage looked around through the enveloping flames; Max
tried to retreat from the firelight into the shadows, but he
had already been spotted, and a moment later he, too, was engulfed in fire. Like his rats, he dived into the sewage and rolled
around until the fire was extinguished, then scrambled to his
feet. Too wet to burn, he hurled himself at Mage, but the sludge
slowed him down, and Mage swung his sword with all his
strength. The nosferatu's head fell into the muck, faceup. The
eyes stared up at Mage for an instant, protruding as the face
swelled; Mage looked away, saw the rats scatter back into the
darkness, and after healing himself—glad, for once, about how
much practice he'd had treating rat-bites—he continued on his
way. As soon as he was gone, the rats swarmed over Max's
bloated corpse, and began to feed on the rotting flesh. Within
minutes, nothing remained but his bones.

Karen was pouring dirty water out of a child's teapot into
assorted cups, when she suddenly winced. "Max is dead," she
announced, and handed a cup to Julia.

"What about the man who's chasing us?"

"I don't know," she said, pouting. "Shall I pour a cup for
him, too?"

Julia and Mara glanced at each other. "I think we'd better
be going," Julia told Karen.

"You *can't* go!" said Karen. She stamped her foot, splattering
herself with more waste. "You *can't!*" Julia stood. "It's *your*
fault Max is dead," the nosferatu wailed. "You have to stay
and look after me, like he did." She looked at Ahna. "*One* of
you, at least."

"I'm sorry," said Julia.

"He won't find you here," said Karen.

"No," said Mara, grimly. "Not if we're not here to be found." She turned to Julia. "And I'd rather fight him than stay here and turn into . . ." She shuddered.

Karen looked at them slyly. "I'll show you a way out, but one of you has to stay here," she said, looking pointedly at Ahna.

Mara, the only one of the vampires who'd never had a younger sibling, reached out and grabbed her by the throat before Julia could speak. "How long would I have to hold your head under before you drowned?"

"Forever, I should think," said Julia, tartly. "Leave her. We're going."

Mandaglione was dreaming about Tanith, images from old movies merged with more recent memories, when the knock on the door woke him. It took him a few seconds to realize that this wasn't part of his dream (he was used to his subconscious punning at him), and he sat up and reached for his bathrobe, tying it around himself as he lurched toward the door. Probably Charlie, he thought fuzzily; Mage no longer pretended to need to open doors. He opened it as far as the chain allowed. The woman standing outside was handsome, close to his own age, and looked vaguely familiar. "Yes?"

"Mr. Mandaglione? Sorry it's so late, but you left a message saying you wanted to speak to me. My name's Angela. Can I come in?"

He looked at her blearily, and went to close the door so that he could unfasten the chain. She shoved at the door, tugging the bracket from the wall, and hurtled into the room. Mandaglione staggered backward, and she grabbed him by the elbows and lifted his ninety kilos from the floor. Tudor walked in, and closed the door behind him. It took Mandaglione a few seconds to recognize him, and then he turned pale. "I don't remember inviting you in. . . ."

"I'm not a vampire," said Tudor, leaning on the door.

Mandaglione nodded. "But you are?" he asked Angela.

"Yes," she hissed. "We're looking for the man who killed our son."

"I don't know what you're talking about," said Mandaglione, as bravely as he could. He was suddenly glad that he'd taken a leak before going to bed. "I thought a vampire—"

"The young man who was with you when you visited the house on Thursday," said Tudor, loudly. "The taller one, not Mr. Takumo; the one you said was your nephew. We need to know his name, and where we can find him."

Mandaglione hesitated. "You're a writer, aren't you?" asked Angela. "How well will you write if I break both of your arms? I could do it with just a little squeeze. . . ."

Mandaglione looked into her eyes, and looked away. "He told me he was going to a place called the Crypt," he said. "Takumo was going there too. You might catch them there, if you hurry."

Tudor looked at him skeptically. "He's telling the truth," said Angela, but she didn't release him.

"Are you sure?"

"Yes. Now, what's his name?"

"Mikey."

"Mikey what?" asked Angela.

"Mandaglione. Same as mine." He shrieked in pain as both the bones of his forearm snapped, less than an inch from his elbow.

"Try again," she said. "I'll know if you lie—and don't think saying nothing is an option. I can break your other arm, both hands, your legs, and then I'll start on the soft parts." Mandaglione was too scared to get even a glimmer of hope out of that. "And I'll leave the tongue until last. Now, what's his name?" Silence. "Three . . . two . . . one—"

"Mage!" shouted Mandaglione.

Angela looked at him uncertainly, then nodded. "Thank you," she said, and glanced at Tudor. The sorcerer was looking around the shadowy room, and seemed to be sniffing. Suddenly he grinned, and made a beeline for his book of pacts, which was sitting on the chest of drawers. "And did he give you this?" Mandaglione stared at him, then nodded.

"Thank you for returning it to me," said the sorcerer, cheerfully, then, to Angela, "Don't kill him. Feed if you want to, but leave him alive; we may need him again later." He produced a small roll of duct tape from his pocket, then reached behind him and removed the "Do Not Disturb" sign from the doorknob. Angela pulled Mandaglione close, and sank her teeth into his throat, drinking deep.

Three vampires emerged from a manhole near the corner of Bates and Sunset, and two looked around to get their bearings while the other donned her filthy fishnet dress. "I think the car's that way," said Ahna.

Julia shrugged, as she reached into her purse for her phone. "You can walk if you like; I'm going to call Valeri, and have her come collect me."

"Where shall we meet, if the Crypt's not safe?"

Julia thought for a moment. "Outside Retail Slut," she said. "At ten."

"We'll be there," said Mara, looking down at her ruined skirt. "See you then."

They walked back to Mara's car, Mara staring down to prevent anyone from looking at her neck, and both of them staying as far away as possible from other pedestrians, knowing that it would be impossible for them to hunt until they'd changed their clothes and washed. They drove away, not speaking, with the sound track of *The Lost Boys* blasting out of the speakers. Despite their more acute senses, they were only a few blocks from Mara's home when Ahna noticed they were being followed. "It's them, isn't it?" Mara asked, looking in the rearview mirror.

"I think so. What should we do?"

"We have hours before sunrise; maybe we can lose them. Or maybe . . ." She glanced around, and turned a corner, heading away from her house.

"What're you looking for?"

"A place to park. I'd rather face them now than during the day."

Takumo and Kelly watched as the Hyundai pulled into the parking lot. "What would vampires want from a Stop-and-Rob?" asked Takumo, as they drove past, then answered his own question. "A Big Gulp, maybe?"

Kelly didn't answer for a moment, but she turned left at the next corner without appreciably slowing down, then left again at the next. "It could be their hideout, but I don't want to risk it. Did you notice any other cars outside?"

"No."

"Do you think they saw us?"

"Yes, but only a few blocks ago."

Kelly snarled as she rounded the corner. "They'll see the car if we park right outside, and a black woman carrying a shotgun in the street, in this neighborhood . . . And if I walk in and they haven't attacked, the clerk's going to try to shoot *me*—"

Takumo shrugged. "If we wait for the fuzz, the clerk will probably die. If you go in unarmed, you'll probably die. Or worse. It's up to you." Almost as soon as Kelly parked, he was out of the car, his sword drawn, the scabbard in his other hand.

He ran toward the store without hesitating, walked around the sensor to open the automatic doors, and glanced through the glass. The clerk, a pimply kid in his late teens, was watching the concave mirror in the far corner; Takumo craned his neck, but he couldn't see it. Mara appeared from behind one shelf, and started looking at the magazines. After a moment, she glanced over her shoulder and looked straight at Takumo, smiling, then walked toward the counter. There was no sign of Ahna, but he didn't wait; he sheathed his sword, then stepped back to open the door, and ran in. The clerk looked at him, and then at the sword; nervously, he began easing toward the alarm. Ahna leaped at Takumo from her hiding place between the shelves, and the stuntman swung around, unsheathing the sword and striking in one motion. Ahna recoiled, and the blade merely left a long, narrow wound across her throat. Mara grabbed the clerk's hand before he could do more than flinch, and sank her teeth into the major artery at his wrist. The clerk fainted, collapsing onto the counter.

Takumo swung around as Ahna leaped toward him again, and kicked her under the chin. The flesh of her neck tore and her head flew up into the air, with her digestive tract still connected. As Takumo watched in horror, her stomach and intestines followed, until her body collapsed on the ground. He brought the sword to bear—an instant too late.

The head swooped down from the ceiling, blindsiding him, and bit him on the neck. Takumo tried to continue fighting, but everything went dark as the sensation overwhelmed all his other senses. He didn't even notice as the door opened again and Kelly came in, shotgun at the ready.

Mara looked up, and Kelly shot her in the stomach. Mara recoiled, releasing the clerk's hand, and Kelly pumped the shotgun and fired again. Mara staggered back as the shot tore into her chest, and the clerk, dazed, collapsed into a heap behind the counter as though boneless.

Kelly hesitated. When the clerk recovered, he was certain to go for the alarm, if not for a gun. She fired one more round at Mara, then looked at Takumo, who also had fallen to the floor and was draped with Ahna's writhing entrails. Realizing that she couldn't shoot at Ahna without endangering Takumo, she grabbed him and hauled him back toward the car. The doors closed on Ahna's trailing intestines, and she jerked back, losing her grip on Takumo's neck.

Kelly ran back to the Range Rover, and reached it just as the shop doors opened and Mara came running out. She dropped Takumo onto the hood while she fumbled in her pocket for her keys and remote, and the stuntman opened his eyes and stared ahead. He was on his feet an instant later, and slashed at Ahna with the sword as she flew toward him. "It's unlocked!" snapped Kelly, as she opened her own door and slid behind the wheel. "Get in!"

Takumo reached behind him for the door handle, and backed in. Kelly floored the accelerator, and Ahna barely managed to duck before the door swung shut on her. Takumo dropped the sword and fumbled for his seat belt as Kelly drove away at top speed, leaving the vampires behind them. "What the hell was *that*?" she demanded.

"Some sort of Malaysian vampire," panted Takumo. "I don't remember what it's called—Dante might know—"

"We can ask him later. Are you okay?"

"I'm still alive," said Takumo, gingerly touching the jagged wound on his throat. He took his pulse, just in case. "I don't know how much she took. . . ."

"I'll take you to a hospital."

"I don't think it's that bad," said Takumo, plaintively. "The hole will probably have gone away by the time we get there, anyway, so it won't be easy to explain, and I don't feel like cutting a new one . . . I think I'll be okay." He reached into his backpack for his flask of holy water, and splashed it on the wound. It stung, but not unbearably.

"Charlie . . ."

"I *hate* hospitals, okay? If I'm still alive when the sun rises, I should be fine. Then we can run a check on their license plate, and look for them during the day." He looked around.

"They're not following us," Kelly reassured him.

"I was looking for the cops. *You* have a reputation to worry about." He looked at her curiously. "What made you change your mind, and join us?"

Kelly was silent while she chose her words. "I still thought you were probably wrong, that it was much more likely that the whole thing was a hoax, and that if I went with you, I could show you that you were wrong. I didn't have any evidence to the contrary until I talked to Yeoh this afternoon." She shrugged. "What do you think the cops will think when they find the bodies in the Crypt? What do you think will happen to us if they link us to those killings? They won't believe in vampires without good evidence—either forensic evidence, or the evidence of their own eyes. Neither will a jury.

"And even if you *were* right, I didn't think the people who you thought might be vampires posed enough of a threat that they should be hunted down and killed." She shrugged. "I don't like to prejudge people. Everyone is supposed to be innocent until proven guilty, right?"

Takumo, rightly suspecting that this was a rhetorical question, didn't answer.

"Your grandparents were living in America during the second World War, weren't they?"

"Yes."

"Were they sent to an internment camp? Just because they were Japanese?"

Takumo nodded.

"How many men do you think get arrested, jailed, even beaten up by cops, mainly because they're black or Hispanic? How many do you think get jailed for crimes for which whites would get probation, or executed for crimes for which whites would get jail?"

"I don't know," said Takumo, wearily.

"But the main reason I joined you? If you were right, I thought you might need my help."

"Thanks."

She shrugged. "And while I still haven't completely forgiven him, I think that what Mage is doing is important."

"Looking for an AIDS cure?"

"My brother is HIV positive."

Takumo was silent for a moment. "I'm sorry."

"I don't know how he caught it, and I don't care. Sharing needles? Unsafe sex? He's probably done both a hundred times, but he's still my brother." Another shrug. "Not that preventing a plague of vampires isn't important, but the sooner Mage can learn to become a healer, not just another killer, the better. So here I am."

Tudor looked around the Crypt, examining each body. Few of them were recognizable; the only two with undamaged faces, a man who'd been decapitated and a woman who'd been shot in the back, were complete strangers to him, and to Angela. None of them bore much resemblance to Mage or Takumo, and most seemed to have been dead for a day or two, not just a few hours. The fire that had consumed most of the bar hadn't spread to any of the other furniture and had all but gone out by the time he'd arrived, but the air in the cafe was foul and filthy with smoke. He sniffed cautiously, and detected a faint odor of decay. He peeled Todd's lips back to examine the teeth; they'd returned to normal size. "It looks as though he was telling the truth, at least," he said, mildly. "They probably *were* here; this certainly looks like their work—what's up?"

Angela was looking up the stairs. "Somebody's upstairs. Cars. Several of them." She began running, but the door opened before she reached the top. Tudor stared at the uniforms, and thought quickly. If Mandaglione had been freed, then he might have tipped the cops off, but it was at least as likely that somebody had heard the gunshots or the smoke alarms. He didn't know the cafe well enough to know where the escape routes were, or where they emerged, but neither flight nor a pitched battle seemed practical. Given a little time, he could have cast a minor glamour and convinced the uniforms that he and Angela were detectives, but it was too late. "Good evening, officers," he said, mildly.

The first cop through the door looked down at him dubiously, then counted the corpses. Angela smiled tightly, not showing her teeth. "Mornin'," said the cop. "Don't move, don't touch anything, and keep your hands where I can see them—please?" Tudor obeyed, and Angela, after a moment's hesitation, followed suit. "Names, please?"

Tudor considered lying, but the cop would almost certainly ask to see his wallet. "Solomon Tudor," he said, "and this is my—" He faltered for an instant, "friend, Pamela. She was kind enough to give me a lift—"

"Pamela what?" asked the cop.

"Winter," replied Angela.

The cop nodded. "And can you tell me what happened?"

"I'm afraid not," replied Tudor. "We'd only just arrived ourselves. I came here looking for my son; he'd told me he was coming here, but when he hadn't returned by two, I called the place. There was no reply, so I came by—"

"Where do you live?"

"Canyon Drive."

"Your son's name?"

"Malachi."

The cop looked at him. "No offense, Mr. Tudor, but you seem pretty calm for a man who's standing in a room with five corpses—"

"Seven—" said Tudor, automatically.

"Seven?"

"There are two behind the bar. Very badly burnt. I, uh, put the fire out with that extinguisher."

"Are any of them your son?"

"None of them seem—" Tudor began, then blinked, as he saw Detective Woodcott walk carefully down the narrow staircase to stand beside the tall officer.

"Mr. Tudor."

"Detective," replied Tudor, with a slight nod.

Woodcott stared around the room. "He says there are seven bodies," said the officer. "Two behind the bar that I can't see from here. Says he only just got here himself."

"And you don't know how this happened, I suppose?" asked Woodcott.

"I'm afraid not—"

"I didn't think so." He looked at Angela, and turned pale as he recognized her from her photo. "Your name, please?"

"Pamela Winter."

"Do you have any ID?"

A longer hesitation. "No."

"And what's your relationship to Mr. Tudor?"

"I'm a friend," she parroted. "I gave him a lift here."

Woodcott nodded. "Where's your car?"

"I'm sorry?"

"You gave him a lift; where's your car? Outside?"

"Yes—"

"Could you describe it, please?"

Tudor realized where this was going before she did, and winced, but there was nothing he could say. "A blue BMW."

Woodcott turned to one of the cops behind him, and after a brief, quiet conversation, read out a license plate number. "That it?"

"Yes."

He nodded. "That car is listed as stolen. Bobby, take them both down to the station. I'll talk to them later."

Angela looked shocked; the car had been registered in her name, and it hadn't occurred to her that her husband would have reported it missing. Tudor groaned, but he didn't resist, even when he realized that he'd left his book of pacts in the BMW. The cops milling outside included two SWAT officers armed with M-16s, while two of the patrolmen carried shotguns. He knew they couldn't kill him, but they could certainly wound him badly enough to foil his escape. He allowed himself to be pushed into the back of a patrol car, and did nothing until they were out of sight of the Crypt. "I can explain this," he said, wearily, through the speaker grille in the partition. "It's her husband's car; she didn't tell him she was going out—"

"Explain it to the detective."

"How long will we have to wait?"

"I don't know. They can hold you for seventy-two hours."

"Three days?"

"Yeah, that's right."

Angela absorbed this, and nodded very slightly. A block later, she began making retching noises. "I'm going to be sick," she moaned.

The cops stared at each other as Angela bent over, her head disappearing from view beneath the back of the seat. "Probably a delayed reaction to seeing those bodies," said Tudor, so quietly it was almost subliminal. The driver pulled over to the curb, stepped out of the car, and opened Angela's door. She staggered out, grabbed hold of his hand, and bit his wrist. The cop swayed, leaning back against the car, and the vampire took his gun.

"Bob?" called his partner. "Are you okay?" When there was

no reply, he opened his door and ran around the car. Angela, not having had time to drain the first cop, snapped his neck and laid him on the sidewalk. She looked up as the second cop appeared; he saw the blood around her mouth, and reached for his gun. She fired first, without aiming, hitting him in the thigh. He staggered backward, and she leaped at him. He fired as she descended, hitting her in the chest, but she grabbed the wrist of his gun hand and squeezed, shattering both bones. He yelled in pain, and then in fear, then the yell was cut off as suddenly as it began.

Tudor emerged from the car a moment later, and surveyed the scene. "Throw the bodies in the trunk," he said. "We'll dump them, and the car, later, but the tall one looks to be about my size; his uniform might be useful."

"Where are we going?" asked Angela, lifting the body easily. "Mandaglione's?"

"No. I need to collect some things from the house before the cops get a search warrant, and then I'll need to get you a safe place before sunrise."

"I have a place," said Angela. "A beachhouse. It belongs to the studio, and I have a key. It's dark enough with the shutters closed."

"Fine," he said, popping the trunk. His book of pacts, he decided, would be safe enough in a police evidence storeroom, at least temporarily. He could stay with Angela until after sunrise, and then make his plans. He had cash hidden in the house, as well as a disguise kit in case he didn't have time to cast a glamour. He had contacts who could provide him with false passports and other ID; he could be in Mexico with a new identity before sunset. With the cops looking for him, it wasn't safe to stay in the city any longer—especially with two dead cops to explain. He could imagine the demons with whom he'd signed pacts laughing at the idea of him being sentenced to life without possibility of parole, and spending more than seventy years in prison.

There was a risk that Angela might try following him, but that was easily solved. He could decapitate her while she slept, or just cast a circle around her and open the shutters.

This man Mage posed more of a problem—distance might mean nothing to someone who could . . . travel . . . as he apparently could. Tudor was still musing about this when they arrived at his house and he began dividing his possessions into essentials and trifles; there just wasn't room in the police car for all of it *and* two corpses. He chuckled as he remembered a story he'd heard about a group of FBI agents who'd tried to impound a tyrannosaur's skeleton, expecting to carry it away in the trunks of their cars.

He looked at the Hand of Glory, wondering whether taking it was worth the risk of waking Tanith, and decided that the resale value justified it. The same with his tarot deck, once owned by Aleister Crowley. He handed one of his caftans to Angela. "Put this on; if we're stopped, it'll hide the bullet hole. I'd offer you something of Tanith's, but it wouldn't fit."

"Are you just going to leave her here?"

"Yes, I think so," he said, after a moment's thought. "She can have the house—I left it to Malachi, but if he's dead, it goes to her. I don't know if he wrote a will, so she may not be able to sell it until the lawyers work out who predeceased who, but she won't starve."

Angela nodded. "After putting up with you for all these years, that's the least she deserves."

"You're probably right," said Tudor, adding the poppet of Takumo to the "essentials" stack, then smiled. "Lucky we don't all get what we deserve, isn't it, hon?"

Krieg was furious at being called away from her sniper's nest, and her mood didn't improve when Julia described the trio who'd wreaked such havoc at the Crypt. "That was Magistrale," she hissed, "and you let him get away."

"We're lucky *he* let *us* get away," retorted Julia. "He and his friends killed four of us—Todd, Garrett, April and Dwight—and one of the nosferatu we found."

Krieg nodded; she'd felt Garrett die. It suddenly occurred to her that she could have sent Joe to collect Julia, and stayed watching Takumo's window, and this made her even more angry. "We won't be safe until he's dead. He can appear anywhere, survive any wound that doesn't kill him instantly—"

"He set himself on fire, and wasn't even hurt," said Julia, "and cremated Todd and Dwight just by looking at them. But how do we *find* him? Or do we wait for him to find us?"

"We can find his friends," said Krieg, "and we can use them to bait a trap. If that fails, at least we'll have killed two of his allies. It won't be easy with only four of us, but I don't think we can afford to waste any more time."

As soon as she returned to the apartment, she picked up the sniper rifle and stared through the infrared sight, lying in wait until the sky began to turn pink, but no one returned. Sunlight was glinting off the window, burning her eyes, when she finally put the rifle down and retreated into the apartment's bedroom, warning Plummer under pain of dismemberment not to disturb her until she emerged.

Tudor looked down at the cards, and swore under his breath. The Tower. Death. The Devil. *Again.*

All of his readings had shown him two possible futures. In one, Mage died within the next twenty-four hours. In the other, *he* did. He stared at the cards, then at his watch. The shutters over the windows blocked out all sunlight, as Angela had said, but he had a faint feeling that the sun must have risen already. The watch told him it was six A.M.

Two possible futures, and nothing to say how to bring about either one. He could try another reading later, but he doubted the outcome would be any different. Should he run, hide, try breaking into the police's evidence storeroom to recover his book of pacts, or go hunting for the man who'd killed his son?

If he had less than twenty-four hours to live, what better way to spend it?

19

Shadows and Karma

The vampire hunters met again at eleven, in Mandaglione's hotel room. Mage arrived first, found his uncle still bound to the chair, and freed one of his hands before hesitating. He then backed away from the chair and pulled the drapes open; Mandaglione blinked and recoiled slightly, but when it was clear that the sunlight did him no harm, Mage cut him loose and did what he could to heal him. There was a rather tentative knock on the door a minute later. "Sorry," said Kelly, as Mage let her in, with Takumo right behind her. "The sign said 'Do Not Disturb,' and I thought . . ."

Mandaglione explained, as quickly as he could, and Kelly whistled. "Then they'd be the two people arrested at the scene."

"What scene?" asked Mandaglione.

"The cops arrested two people at the Crypt this morning, but—don't laugh, this isn't funny. *That's* been all over the news all morning, but there's a rumor going around, based on stuff picked up from police band radio, that neither of them ever turned up at the station, and neither did the cops who were taking them there. And it's been seven hours."

"What're the cops saying?"

" 'No comment.' "

"Shit. Okay, tell me the rest of it."

They did, concluding with Mage's profitless search of the sewers and Takumo's escape from Ahna. "What the hell was that?"

"A penanggalan," said Mandaglione. "Malaysian vampire. It—or she, they're all supposed to be female—returns to her body before sunrise, if she can find it, and lives during the day as a normal person."

Kelly shrugged. "There's been no report of a headless body being found in a Stop-and-Rob. Or a murder, either—I guess the kid survived."

"How do you kill one?" asked Mage.

"The traditional way is to set up thorn-bushes around your house so they'll get their intestines caught, then kill them by daylight, but I guess the methods you've been using on the other vampires would work." He shrugged. "So what's the plan now?"

"I have to go back to Bangkok," said Mage. "I just checked my e-mail; there's a bad fire in a backpacker hostel near the clinic, a lot of people seriously burned. I may be the only one who can help them. I'll be back as soon as I can."

"Could it be a trap?"

"I don't think so. The message was from Doi, and the local news radio services are carrying the story, though details are sketchy. The yakuza are well established in Bangkok, so Nakatani might have been able to arrange a fire, but with him dead . . . no, I think this is just another disaster. Besides, even if it *is* a trap, what choice do I have?"

Kelly nodded. "You're right. Okay. I've traced the license plate of that car, and have an address. I suggest Charlie and I look there, see if we can get any of them while they're sleeping. I'd still like to hand one over to Dr. Yeoh intact, if possible."

"And if they're not there?" asked Mandaglione.

"I don't know. I suppose we try looking for them in other places where they might hide, or hunt—but I want to get some sleep first. And we'd better get you out of here, in case they come back. Do you need a doctor? I can't persuade this idiot to get himself looked at."

"I guess it wouldn't hurt," admitted Mandaglione, trying to stand. "But I'm going to need help getting there; I've been sitting in this chair most of the morning. And the bathroom. Mikey, can you give me a hand?"

Mage and Kelly took an arm each and walked him into the bathroom. "Shut the door," he said softly, as they lowered him onto the toilet.

"I intended to," said Kelly, dryly.

Mandaglione shook his head, and Kelly pushed the door shut and leaned against it. "What?" she asked.

"There's something else about the penanggalan," said Mandaglione, "that I didn't want to say while Charlie was listening. According to the legend, they also carry diseases, like most other vampires, and whoever has their blood sucked by one is sure to die. They don't say how soon, and that's true of all of us, and legends tend to grow in the telling—but I thought I'd better warn you. Just in case."

Despite her injuries, and the aftertaste in her mouth from the hospital's attempt at a vegetarian breakfast, Gaye grinned as Takumo walked into the room. "Charlie! Hi! What's happening?"

Takumo sat down on the bed, handed her the bunch of flowers, and wondered what to say. Could he tell her that he'd spent the night hunting vampires, or that he'd tried to decapitate a beautiful girl only to have her turn into a penanggalan and bite him, that Mage and Kelly had sat vigil on him in Kelly's house until after sunrise, ready to cremate his body if he died, or that he'd just returned from breaking into someone's home on an unsuccessful quest for a sleeping vampire to autopsy, or that Mage had just teleported to Bangkok to perform some emergency surgery? He said nothing, and smiled.

"You look terrible," Gaye said. "Haven't you been sleeping?"

"Not much, no." Another long silence.

"What's that around your neck?"

"What?" He reached for the place where Ahna had bitten him—he'd thought the wound had disappeared—and touched the focus. Gaye nodded.

"Mage wears one of those, too, doesn't he? What is it? Someone's hair?" She reached up to touch it, and Takumo suddenly felt as though something had sucked all his fatigue poisons out and replaced them with fresh blood. His lungs and throat felt cleaner than they had in his entire life, as clean as if he'd never even heard of L.A. He stared at Gaye, his eyes wide open and bright, and she murmured, "Oh, wow . . ."

"What did you . . ."

"It's magic, isn't it? Some sort of talisman?"

"What?"

"It is, isn't it?"

"*What did you just do?*"

"Just a healing," she said. "Kind of like reiki—you know reiki?" He nodded. "I use it on patients, sometimes, but I've never had results like *that*."

He grabbed the focus, handed it to her. "Can you do that to yourself?"

"I don't know," she said, hesitantly. "I don't think so—I mean, it's really my energy. Besides, the doctors tell me I breathed in a lot of hot smoke, I was just lucky Mage got me out of—"

"Try it," he said, urgently. "Just *try*."

Woodcott read through the preliminary forensic report with disbelief. All but one of the bodies recovered from the Crypt— the young woman who'd been shot in the back—had clean lungs and no trace of carbon monoxide in the blood, indicating that they'd died *before* any fires had started, and the patterns of blistering on their bodies confirmed this. Establishing a cause of death for any of the burnt bodies was proving difficult; none of the pathologists involved had reached any conclusions.

Woodcott continued reading. It didn't help. The time of death for the woman who'd been shot in the back had been fairly definitely established as between midnight and one A.M., but the male body behind the bar showed signs of having been dead for *four days*—yet the bullet recovered from the woman's body seemed to match the revolver he was holding in a death grip ("cadaveric spasm," in the words of the autopsy report), and which tests confirmed had been fired less than twelve hours before the investigating officer had arrived. A knife that matched the wound in the dead man's arm had been found on the floor, and the only clear fingerprints on it matched those on fragments of bottles found behind the bar, which might have been his own, though his fingers were too badly charred for anyone to be sure; that wound, too, had apparently been inflicted after death. The other bodies had apparently been dead for approximately twenty-four hours, with a six-hour margin of error.

There was nothing in any of the reports to implicate Solomon Tudor. Even if Woodcott accepted the suggestion that most of the bodies had been killed elsewhere, then arranged in the cafe as a gruesome tableau, the car in which Tudor had apparently arrived showed no signs of being used to carry corpses. Furthermore, the satanist had been unarmed, and it was clear that one of the women found dead had been shot at point-blank range with both a shotgun and a pistol—shell casings had been found that seemed to confirm that—yet Tudor and his partner had been unarmed, and neither weapon had been found on or near the scene, or in the car. If the cops had brought them back to the police station for paraffin testing, the forensics could have established whether either had fired a gun recently—but the unit carrying them had disappeared, along with two officers and both suspects.

It didn't make sense, Woodcott thought. Not just the forensic evidence, but Tudor's actions. If the satanist *had* turned up after the slaughter, as the evidence seemed to bear out, then all they had on him was a count of grand theft auto. Not that Woodcott didn't have doubts about *that*, too; the woman who called herself Pamela Winter had born a close resemblance to photos of Angela Winslow, the car's owner. Of course, Winslow had been declared dead (though her body had since disappeared), but since it *was* her car, he wondered what a lawyer might make of *that*.

Woodcott had an ambivalent attitude toward science. He was ready to rely on it when it supported his beliefs, decry it when it didn't. He regarded all evidence for evolution and an ancient universe as suspect—the claims of some physicists that some stars were billions of years older than the universe struck him as the best possible proof that God was playing the scientists for fools and the age of the universe might only be a few thousand years—yet "creation science" had always struck him as inconsistent at best, hypocritical and often fraudulent at worst. Yet he relied too heavily on forensic science to want to believe that the L.A. County Forensic Science Center could be so far wrong in establishing a time of death; if that was true, then many people whose guilt he'd helped prove to juries might be innocent. Yet what was the alternative? That a man four days dead could still shoot a woman in the back? He thought of Angela Winslow, and the Petrosyan boy, and shuddered.

In a huge Ziploc bag on his desk was an item found in Winslow's car; a large, locked, leatherbound book. Woodcott doubted that it was evidence of anything, but he'd had a strange feeling about it ever since he'd first seen it. He stared at it again, then walked to the window.

The sun was setting over the Pacific; he watched as the sky shaded from red to charcoal gray, and shuddered again. He returned to his desk, and phoned home, telling his wife that he wouldn't be home until morning. Too much work. Make sure you lock all the doors and windows, and set the alarms, he told her. I'll be home in time to take you to church in the morning. Love you. He didn't need to remind her to include him in her prayers, and didn't—couldn't—say that he was scared of the dark, too scared to venture outside until after sunrise. His hands shaking, he looked at the book again, wondering why he had the feeling that it was looking back at him.

* * *

Krieg was the first to rise, and immediately returned to her position watching Takumo's window. "There's somebody in there," confirmed Plummer, "somebody his size, but he's had no visitors today. He came in about half an hour after you went to bed, and had a shower and changed his clothes, then went out again, came back at about four. Worked out with a dummy for a while, then went for a run and a swim, came back and had a rest." He shrugged. "And the explosives and detonators you ordered have arrived."

"Excellent," said Krieg.

Angela woke, and emerged from the bedroom to find a cop sitting in the living room, smoking a cigarette. She did a double take, and realized that it was Solomon, wearing the uniform of one of the cops she'd killed the night before, further disguised by a dark blond wig, mustache, and a minor glamour spell. "Get dressed," he said. "Places to go, people to kill."

"Where are we going?"

"I have one more lead—another friend of Mage's. Charlie Takumo." He picked up the poppet on the table, and blew smoke into its face. "We should be able to trick him into letting us in, and then you're going to bite him. Turn him. If Mage doesn't return tonight, his friend can kill him some other time. A satisfactory revenge, don't you think?"

"Adequate," growled Angela.

Tudor sighed. Vampires didn't appreciate irony, especially not when they were hungry. He stood, with some difficulty; he'd spent the daylight hours overindulging in almost-forgotten pleasures, just in case this night *was* his last. "Shall we go?"

Takumo blinked, his eyes suddenly sore. He looked around the room, peering at posters, trying to read fine print, then shook his head. He'd spent the afternoon trying to use the focus to boost skills he'd learned the hard way: taijutsu, running, swimming, and stealth. He'd also tried body control tricks his grandfather had told him ninja had once known—slowing his breathing, even his heart rate.

He wasn't sure that any of it had been successful. Every time he'd thought his pulse had stopped for more than a few seconds, he'd become nervous or excited and it had immediately sped up again. Obviously it took practice, and if the way his eyes were stinging was any indication, he'd already been practicing too hard.

He closed his eyes and tried to relax. He had been lying there for several minutes when someone knocked on the door. He walked to the door, his vision still blurred, and stopped en route to grab his largest kitchen knife. He peered through the peephole, saw a police uniform and a squareish chin. "Yes?"

"Charles Takumo? LAPD. Can we come in, please?"

"What's it about?"

"I have some questions for you about an incident this morning."

Oh, *shit*, he thought. "Just a second," he said, and placed the knife on top of the refrigerator. He opened the door, and looked up into the cop's face. Tudor brought his nightstick up into Takumo's groin sharply; Takumo, caught by surprise, staggered backward, gasping. Angela pushed past the sorcerer and grabbed the stuntman's arms. "Where is Mage?" she hissed.

"I don't know."

"You're lying!"

Takumo headbutted her, but he might as well have tried smashing his forehead into a rock; she merely laughed, and held him at arm's length. He kicked her under the ribs, hard enough to kill a living person; she barely even flinched. "Where?" she asked, tightening her grasp. "Tell me, or I'll break your arm."

"Bangkok," he groaned.

Angela hesitated, and looked back at Tudor, who was shutting the door behind him. "I think he's telling the truth," she said, puzzled.

"It's possible," said Tudor, nodding. "If Mage can teleport . . ."

"It's where he *told* me he was going," said Takumo.

"Can you call him?"

"No."

"When will he be back here?"

"I don't know," Takumo replied, trying to keep his heartrate and breathing steady. Angela looked at Tudor again. "Is he lying?" he asked.

"Not about calling him," she said. "About him coming back . . . I don't think so, but I'm not sure."

"Try rephrasing the question," suggested Tudor. "Are you expecting him back tonight?"

Takumo hesitated, then, "Yes."

Tudor raised an eyebrow, and Angela shook her head. "I think that was a lie."

"You're not sure?" The magician looked at Takumo's face, then shrugged. "He's an actor, after all; maybe he's just too good at lying. Bite him. At least that way, we can be sure he tells us the truth *tomorrow* night. But try not to do any damage that he can't heal."

Takumo spat at him, and struggled against Angela as she pushed him up against a wall, ignoring his kicks and holding fast as he tried to writhe out of her grasp. He tried to remember how he'd conjured the flames that had destroyed Dwight, but nothing seemed to happen except that his eyes hurt even more than they had before. He glanced over at Tudor, and saw him take something out of his jacket pocket, something roughly human-shaped, with dark hair at one end.

Tudor squeezed the hairy end between thumb and forefinger, and Takumo was struck by a blinding headache. The next thing he felt was Angela's bite; there had been no warning breath on his neck, no warmth of lips, just teeth sinking into his flesh and a burst of darkness. He barely heard the door open.

Tudor looked around as Krieg burst in; before he could move, he too was pushed up against a wall, a silencer pressed up under his chin. Krieg stared into his face, then backed up. "Sorry," she said. "Thought you were somebody else."

Tudor stared at her, then dared to smile. "You're looking for Mage, I assume?"

"Magistrale? Yes. Do you know where he is?"

"This one—" He nodded at Takumo, who was trying to concentrate, to will himself into a trance, slowing his breathing, his heartbeat. "—said Thailand. I don't know whether or not to believe him. Who are you?"

"She's with me," said a voice from behind her, and Tudor looked around to see Julia walk in and close the door behind her. "What are you doing here, Sol?"

"I'm hunting the vampire hunters, as I suspect you are. Am I right?" Julia nodded. "Maybe we should work together?"

"What was your plan?"

Tudor explained it as concisely as he could, and Krieg nodded. "Much the same as ours," she admitted, grudgingly, "but we were going to booby-trap the room with explosives, too. Plastique with ball-bearings, with heat-sensitive triggers, in case Magistrale tried setting himself on fire, the way he did at the Crypt this morning. And one of Julia's useful idiots in the room, with a dead-man switch." There was a thud as Angela dropped Takumo. "I like the uniform," Krieg continued. "Nice touch."

"Thank you." He glanced over at Takumo's body, then turned to Julia. "As we all seem to be on the same side—or at least, *against* the same side—shall we join forces? At least until Mage—Magistrale, you say?—is dead?" Which should be before sunrise, he thought, keeping his smile polite. "Swear not to attack each other in that time and, oh, until twenty-four hours afterward?"

Julia looked at him, realized that he was—for once—sincere, and nodded. "Tell him the rest of the plan."

Kelly had spent most of her Saturday nights over the past three years either alone or working, thinking of it as just another evening, and this was the first time since New Year's that it had bothered her. She'd even called Charlie, to see if he was okay, and left a message on his machine, and the fact that he hadn't called back yet made her more uneasy than she cared to admit. It was getting late—nearly half past ten—but she'd slept during the day and drunk too much coffee since. Maybe, despite the hour, she should go to the dojo and work out, even if it meant turning her cell phone off for a few moments. She jumped when she heard a knock at the front door, and pocketed her pistol before getting up to answer it. There was a uniformed cop at the door, blond with a mustache, no one she knew. "Yes?"

"Counsellor? May I come in?"

"What's happened?" She heard Oedipus behind her going berserk, and hushed him.

"There's been an incident in a house three doors down. We're just seeing if anybody noticed anything."

Kelly hesitated. "No, I'm afraid not. I've been working all evening."

"You didn't hear anything unusual?"

"No, I'm—shut *up*, cat!—I'm afraid not—" She turned around, in time to see a beautiful face trailing a red, snakelike mess of guts. She managed to draw her pistol and fire as it struck, shooting the penanggalan through the stomach before the blackness overpowered her.

When she opened her eyes again, she was lying on her bed, her hands cuffed to the headboard. She tried moving her feet, and discovered that they were cuffed together, though not fastened to anything else. Krieg, Julia, Ahna, and Tudor—minus his wig, cap, and mustache—watched her from the other side of the room. "Ah, good," said Tudor. "There are some questions we'd like to ask you, Counsellor. About Mr. Magistrale."

"I don't know any—"

"Don't waste our time by lying," said Julia. "You were with him last night—you and the late Mr. Takumo."

The news of Takumo's death hit Kelly like a blow to the stomach. "*You're* lying," she said.

"Are we?" asked Julia, cheerfully. "I suppose that depends on where you draw the line between life and death. Are we alive? Are we dead?"

Tudor smiled as the blood drained away from Kelly's face. "If you go looking for Takumo now, you'll find him dead, but tomorrow night—ah, tomorrow night, *he* may find *you*. Now, where might *we* find Mr. Magistrale?"

"I don't know. He left L.A. this morning, and I don't know when he's coming back."

Tudor glanced at the vampires. Julia shrugged, and Ahna looked blank, but Krieg and Angela nodded slightly. "When he does, where will he go first?"

"I don't know."

"Takumo's apartment? Will he go there?"

"Maybe."

"Here?"

"I don't know. I doubt it."

"Do you know how to contact him?"

"No."

Tudor glanced at the vampires; they all nodded. "That's a pity," he said. "If I were you, I'd think of something before sunrise." He turned back to the vampires. "Do any of you want to turn her, or should we just kill her?"

Kelly saw Krieg grimace, but Julia looked at her appraisingly. "She may be useful," she said, casually.

"Let me up and I'll show you how useful I can be," said Kelly, softly, looking straight at Krieg. "Just me against her. One on one."

Julia raised her eyebrows at that. "That might be entertaining . . . briefly."

Tudor shook his head. "I don't think so."

"No . . ." said Julia, after a moment's consideration. "You're probably right. Ahna, watch her. Excuse us, please, Counsellor."

* * *

Mara waited, bored, the dead-man switch in her hand, the TV remote in the other. Krieg had assured her that the explosives set up around the apartment wouldn't kill her, and that she'd set a timer that would cut off power to the detonator at five A.M., allowing her to get to safety before sunrise. Mara suspected that she'd been lied to, but Julia had commanded her to grab hold of the switch, and she couldn't resist an order from the vampire who'd turned her—not while she was in the room, anyway. She was just glad that she didn't have to take bathroom breaks any longer, and during a commercial break that seemed to last forever, she pondered the fashion potential of this—clothes that wouldn't need to be removed so quickly, jeans or skirts that could be sewn shut instead of zipped . . . With the TV blaring, she didn't hear the slow, faint beating of Takumo's heart, even as it gradually returned to normal.

Takumo opened one eye cautiously, then the other. Both still stung, but he could see clearly enough. Moving his head very slightly, he took in his surroundings. There were no weapons within reach, apart from the knife in his belt buckle, which was too small to be effective against a vampire and not balanced for throwing. All of his other weapons were in his backpack, the pockets of his jacket, or their hiding places behind or under various items of furniture. Even his squirt ring was in the bedroom with his other clothes. He looked around the room, tracing the wires that led from the dead-man switch in Mara's right hand to the detonators. Krieg and Plummer hadn't made any particular effort to make the system difficult to defuse; all he had to do was disconnect the battery, which would only take a few seconds. Of course, releasing the switch would take even less time.

Takumo wasn't an explosives expert; all he knew about the subject was what he'd picked up working in action movies. He wasn't sure whether slashing the wires connecting the dead-man switch to the rest of the system would prevent an explosion or trigger one, and wasn't eager to bet his life on a guess. He knew where to hit a nerve in the forearm to make the thumb retract, and lock in that position for the few seconds he needed . . . but vampires seemed able to disregard levels of pain that would have incapacitated the living, and he wasn't sure enough that pressure-point techniques would work against them. He considered grabbing her hand and holding the switch closed . . . but even if he had the strength, that would mean hanging on for hours, or until Mage arrived, whichever happened first. He thought for a moment, then began edging toward the battery, dragging his body along a fraction of an inch at a time with his shoulders, elbows, hips, and feet.

He was nearly there when Mara finally looked around. "Wait!" he snapped, his voice toned to make her freeze for an instant, like a samurai screaming out a kiai. "Think for a moment. Maybe you have the guts to let go of that switch—and if you do, they'll be spread over the room, because the shrapnel in that plastique is going to pulverize everything in here. Maybe you'll survive, maybe you won't, maybe you'll just have some wounds that never heal—missing limbs, holes that never close, that sort of thing. I don't know."

"It'll kill you," said Mara. "That's—"

"Completely irrelevant," interjected Takumo, hurriedly. "They left you here to kill Magistrale, not me. Right?" Mara glared at him, but she realized that he was telling the truth. He could sense her frustration growing as she tried to puzzle out the situation. "So. If you're going to kill me, you'd better hope it *does* kill you too, because I'd hate to have to imagine what they're going to do to you if they find out you've let Mage get away." He sat up, yawned, and stretched. "Pardon me," he said, and leaned back, reclining on his hands. "So," he continued, his hands edging closer to the battery, "if I were you, I'd just let me walk on out of here—"

"No!" she snapped. "Stay where you are, or I'll . . ."

Takumo hesitated. "You won't do it," he said, letting a faint hint of nervousness creep into his own voice. "You can't even say it." He made sure she kept looking into his face as his hands found the terminals, and kept talking to cover the sound as he disconnected one wire, and then the other. He disguised his sigh of relief as another yawn. "Look, do you mind if I get a drink? My mouth feels like something died in there—no offense." He stood, then began walking to the kitchen, still watching her carefully. Ignoring her command to stop, he opened the refrigerator. "You want something?" he said, palming the small plastic bottle of holy water he'd been using to fill his squirt ring, then grabbing a bottle of apple juice.

"If you try to leave—"

"Last thing on my mind," he said, pouring himself a glass of the juice and downing it in two swallows. "If I leave, and Mage comes here, you're going to kill him, and I can't allow that." He poured himself another glass, downed that, then turned his back on Mara and emptied the bottle of holy water into the glass. He walked back into the living room, and squatted down opposite her. "I'd let you go, but then you'd just kill more people, and I can't allow that, either. So I'm sorry, but unless you kill me first, I'm going to have to kill you."

She showed her teeth in a snarl, and he threw the water in her face. She screamed as it burned, and he back-somersaulted into the bedroom, and grabbed his sword. He saw Mara let go of the dead-man switch, and flinched despite himself. Then, when nothing exploded, he shouted a kiai and ran back into the living room. Mara leaped up from the chair and met him halfway across the room.

He swung the sword, aiming at her neck, but she caught the blade in her right hand before the blow landed. It sliced into her dead fingers, but she held on grimly, the pain in her hand minor compared to the burning where the holy water was eating away the flesh of her face down to the bone. Her free hand clawed at Takumo, who ducked underneath it and put all his strength into a kick to her chest. He felt her ribs crack, and she staggered backward, but she didn't release the sword; instead, she grabbed the pommel with her left hand.

Takumo tried to sweep her legs out from underneath her with another kick, but only succeeded in hurting his shin. She twisted the sword around, attempting to drive the point through his face, and Takumo released his grip and leaped back toward the bedroom. Mara threw the sword aside and charged, and he stepped aside, grabbed her arm as she hurtled toward him, and threw her into the wall. Without looking back, he dashed into the living room, and leaped toward the sword.

Mara turned around, and caught sight of her ruined face in the mirror on the wall. Her skull showed through a hole in her forehead where a gigantic blister had burst. Other blisters, some larger than quarters, dotted her forehead and cheek and ran down toward her chin. The skin between them was a grayish green. She turned away from the mirror, and saw Takumo standing in the living room, sword at the ready. She nodded slightly, then ran toward him with a piercing scream. He stepped aside and swung his sword, and her head flew though the air as her body collapsed near his feet.

Takumo stared at the corpse for a moment, then ran back into the bedroom, grabbed the phone, called Mandaglione's hotel, and asked the switchboard operator to put him through to his room. "Dante?" "It's Charlie. Is Mage there?"

"No, I haven't seen him. Are you okay? You sound—"

"Are you expecting him?"

Mandaglione laughed dryly. "He doesn't usually give me much warning."

"Okay. They're waiting for him at Kelly's. All of them—well, all expect one of the young women. She's . . ."

"Is there anything I can do?"

"Can you come and get me? I'm not in any shape to drive. I'd like to swing by St. John's on the way, too. Thanks. See you soon."

When Mandaglione arrived, nearly twenty minutes later, Takumo had washed his wounds with holy water, armed himself, and covered the corpse with an old blanket. Mandaglione looked at his face, then at the mess in the room, and decided not to ask.

Gaye woke up to see Takumo sitting beside her bed, while Mandaglione argued with nurses in the corridor outside. "Charlie?"

"I need your help," he said, softly but urgently. "Are you well enough to leave? Just for tonight?"

"I think so," she said, sleepily. "The doctors say I've made a remarkable recovery, and they were going to discharge me tomorrow. . . . What's happening?"

"I'll explain in the car; we don't have much time. I need healing, and I'm pretty sure that some friends of mine will need even more before sunrise. Can you come with me?"

"Sure," she said, blinking, as though surprised that he would doubt it. She grabbed her overnight bag, and, clad only in panties and T-shirt, followed him out of the room. She pulled her jeans on while they were in the elevator, her sneakers when she was in the car. They both held onto the focus while she touched the wound in his neck, his bruised forehead, even his still-tender genitals. He recounted as much of the history of the focus as he knew, then answered her questions about vampires as best he could until they were a block from Kelly's house. "Okay," he said, "I'm going in alone; I want you both to wait out here, and if you see anyone come out of the house, unless it's Kelly or Mage or me, then *go*, go as fast as you can, and don't come back until after sunrise. Get it?"

"Got it," replied Mandaglione.

"Good." He turned to Gaye, and she leaned over and kissed him. "Good luck," she said.

He ran toward the house, his ninjato in his hand, and opened the door with the key on the focus. He stepped inside, closed the door, and looked up to see Julia, Tudor, Krieg, and Angela sitting on the sofa, staring at him. "It's showtime," he said.

20

Blood and Judgment

Doi stared at the back of the ambulance as the doors slammed shut, brushed her gray hair out of her eyes, then turned toward the smoldering wreckage of the hostel. "Do they know what started it?" asked Mage. He knew the backpackers' hostel well—it was almost directly behind the clinic, and he'd frequently gone to its Internet cafe to check for messages and to schmooze with travelers. Unfortunately, he'd never seen any of the dorms, and hadn't been able to *see* himself inside to help rescue any of the people who were trapped. He'd done his best to fight his way through the fire, knowing that he could heal himself, but the fire crews had stopped him, so he'd had to settle for helping Doi tend to the burns victims who were waiting for ambulances.

"I don't know. If it started in there, it was probably just an electrical fault or a kitchen fire."

Mage nodded, wondering whether the yakuza had somehow traced him to the place and set the fire hoping to catch him there. It seemed unlikely. He looked at Doi, who'd been outside on the street since before the ambulances had begun arriving, and had stayed until the last of them had left. "You look exhausted," she said, a second before Mage was about to say the same.

"I'm okay. I just wish I'd gotten here earlier."

Doi snorted. "You can't be everywhere all of the time, Michael; you can't make the world safe for everyone. You're not the patron saint of travelers. Tida may think you're a saint, or maybe a god, but even she knows there are some things you can't do."

"I'm not a saint."

"I know. And even if you *had* got here earlier, what more could you have done? Now if you were an electrician and you'd been in there *yesterday*, you could've done more to save those people in a few minutes than all the firemen and medics have managed—but you aren't and you weren't. So you do what you can, and the rest is karma." Stiffly, she unbent from her squat, reluctantly allowing him to help her up. "How long has it been since you slept? As your doctor, I can tell you it's been too long."

"Are you okay?"

"Just old and tired. I've been running on adrenaline for too long too, and now that there's nothing more that I can do, I'm going to—what's the expression? Smash?"

"Crash." He picked up her bag and walked with her as she staggered back to the clinic.

"Thanks. You should maybe do the same."

"No," he said, quietly. "There are still things I have to do."

None of the vampires moved for a moment, and only Tudor breathed. Julia was the first to speak. "How . . . you were dead . . . I felt Mara die, I thought . . ."

"Oh, Mara's dead," said Takumo, trying to watch all four of them. He decided that Krieg, who was sitting on the right, posed the most danger, but that didn't mean the others weren't a threat. "Where's Kelly?"

"Where's Magistrale?" countered Tudor.

"I asked you first."

"Kelly's here," replied Julia. "Still alive. Still safe. Where is—"

"Mage? He had *important* work to do," said Takumo, without even a hint of irony. He glanced at where Angela had been a moment before, sitting at Tudor's left, then looked around in time to see her come running toward him in almost complete silence. Without time to plan, he lunged toward her, impaling her through the chest with his ninjato. He swept her around just as Krieg drew both her pistols and fired, and six hollow-point bullets smashed into Angela's back.

Angela tried to recover her footing, and found that her legs no longer obeyed her commands. With a snarl and scream of hatred, she reached for Takumo, but he danced away from her, extracted his sword, and struck her head off as she fell.

Julia closed with him almost immediately, and he leaped back as she struck at him, another bullet passing between them as he did so. With his free hand, Takumo reached into one of his pockets and removed the cap from a loaded syringe. When Julia leaped and seized him, he rammed the point of the syringe through his jacket and into her flesh, then pressed the plunger. Julia screamed in pain as ten cubic centimeters of holy water jetted into her stomach, and she recoiled, staggering away from him.

Tudor and Krieg watched in horror as she fell to the floor, writhing in agony, and Takumo made a dash toward Kelly's bedroom. Krieg turned when he was still seven feet away from it, and he dived for the floor just as she fired both pistols again. He looked around, seeing no cover that he could reach, and smiled. "What say you lose the guns and I lose the sword and we settle this in a civilized fashion?"

Krieg bared her teeth in a smile, and sounded genuinely amused as she said, "But this *is* a civilized fashion, little man. Guns and civilization have *always* gone together. Why, if you had a gun now, you could be standing up like a civilized person, and not lying on the floor waiting to die like an animal."

Takumo shook his head. "It's guns that have made you Westerners weak."

"Weak?" Krieg raised an eyebrow, and snorted, then aimed the gun. "Nice try, little man, but I don't need to prove myself to anybody, so why should I fight you?"

Takumo looked over at where Julia lay groaning. "I lose the sword, you lose the guns, you try to bite me, drain me, I try to stop you. You win, I'm your slave until one of us dies, right?"

Krieg considered this. Takumo had already killed three vampires that night, two the night before; somebody with his skills and ingenuity would be a useful addition to her planned strike force. "And if *you* win?"

"If I can stay alive until sunrise, Kelly and I get out of here."

"Don't listen to him," said Tudor, standing behind her. "It's a trick. He—"

Without even looking at him, Krieg turned her holdout pistol and fired the last shot into Tudor's chest. "You're beginning to irritate me," she said mildly, as the sorcerer slumped back into the chair. Then she dropped the holdout gun, still keeping the larger pistol aimed at Takumo. "Okay, little man," she said. "Now *you* lose the sword."

Takumo stared at Krieg, then threw the ninjato into the corner. "Now the ring, and the jacket," she said. "No tricks."

Slowly, he unzipped his jacket, and shrugged it off. "Stand up," she said. Tudor groaned, and Krieg, without turning around, fired another two bullets into his chest before throwing the gun across the room. "Now, little man, show me how strong you are."

Takumo advanced cautiously, aware that the best he could do was play for time—until the sun rose, if possible. Nothing he could do was likely to harm the vampire. They circled each other for several seconds, and Krieg threw the first punch; Takumo parried it successfully, striking at her forearm with the side of his hand. Krieg showed no signs of having felt the blow, and immediately jabbed with her left, catching him in the belly. Takumo jumped back as she planted her foot for a spinning kick. He grabbed her ankle as it went past, and helped it on its way, throwing her across the room. She hit the far wall, hard, and fell to the floor, but immediately leaped back to her feet. "Savate?" he guessed.

"Bronze gloves," she affirmed, obviously pleased despite herself. She came running at him, then leaped, feetfirst. Both feet caught Takumo in the chest; he rolled with the blow as best he could, and they both fell down. He breathed in slowly, suspecting that she'd broken some of his ribs. She was back on her feet first, and Takumo barely managed to dodge another kick to the ribs as he stood.

He stepped toward her before she could recover her balance, and clapped his hands over both her ears. It left him open to her next attack, a powerful punch to the abdomen which sent him staggering back again, but from the way she shook her head, he decided that he might have deafened her for a moment. He dodged another kick, staying on the defensive, waiting for an opening that would enable him to strike at her eyes.

She was at least as fast as he was, and so much stronger that no pins or holds were likely to work, but if he could blind her temporarily, he might have a chance to find Kelly and get both of them out. . . . He tried to parry another kick with his left hand, but misjudged slightly, and the toe of her boot slammed into his forearm just above the wrist. He spun around, and kicked her in the teeth hard enough to loosen them. He fell to the floor, and she raised her foot to stamp on him, but he kicked the leg on which she was standing out from underneath her. She fell, and he scrambled to his feet and back-somersaulted over the sofa.

Krieg jumped over it and kicked out, and he grabbed a cushion and threw it at her face. She landed on the glass coffee table, shattering it, but rolled off and picked herself up immediately. To Takumo's amazement, she began laughing.

"Getting tired, little man?" she taunted. "We still have *hours* before sunrise." She grabbed at him, and Takumo leaped back over to the other side of the sofa. She saw him look toward the door, saw his eyes dilate and a smile flicker across his face, but suspecting a trick, she resisted the impulse to turn around and look. Mage, standing in the hallway, stared at the carnage around him. "Sorry I'm late," he said, softly.

"**D**id you mean what you said about a cure?"

Kelly, who'd been trying to squeeze her hands through the cuffs without any appreciable success, stared up at the penanggalan's face. "What?"

"What the tall one was saying last night," said Ahna. "About a cure. Can you do it? Can you cure us?"

"I don't know," said Kelly, after a moment's thought. "Why?"

"I want to save my parents," said Ahna. "If it's not too late. Mara, who turned me, is dead, I felt her die, and now I . . . If you can't cure me, can you kill me? While my parents are still alive? Please?"

"I can't do anything while I'm chained up here like this," said Kelly, "and you don't look as though you can set me free . . . but if I *can* save your parents, I will. Okay?"

Krieg kicked the sofa, sending it rolling across the floor and pinning Charlie underneath it, then took a step toward Mage. He teleported into her path, sword at the ready. "Where's Kelly?" he asked.

"Julia said she's still alive," said Takumo, as he squirmed out from under the sofa. "I haven't seen her, so she may have been lying. Don't ask her; I don't think she can hear too well."

Mage stared at Krieg, who stared back, neither of them moving. "Are you okay?"

"No, but I can still walk. Run, even."

"See if you can find Kelly, get her out of here."

"For sure." Takumo managed to stand, then tottered toward Kelly's room. Krieg, her ears still ringing, glanced at him as he opened the door, and Mage swung the sword at her neck. She reacted with incredible speed, ducking low and kicking at his hand, so that the sword flew through the air and landed behind her. She grabbed his right wrist and squeezed until the bones of his forearm splintered. Mage *saw* her engulfed in flame, burning brightly, but she began laughing again.

"Is that all you can do?" she said, between chuckles. "Haven't you ever heard of a flame-proof suit? The sort Grand Prix drivers wear? I'm wearing one now. Did you think we were all amateurs like you?" She spread her arms wide. "Oh, sure, it *hurts*, but that won't kill me. It *will* kill your friends if I set the house on fire with them still in it." Mage nodded wearily, and the flames died down. "Now," said Krieg, grabbing the front of his jacket and ripping it open, "where's this thing you stole from Tamenaga?"

"Tamenaga's dead . . ." said Mage.

"Yes, I know," crooned Krieg, "but his daughter wants this back, and she's prepared to pay handsomely for it—even more than she'll pay for your head." She stared at the focus. "That's it, isn't it? That's where your power comes from." She snatched at it, but Mage *saw* himself back on the other side of the room. He picked up the fallen sword, and Tudor sat up and shot him in the back with Krieg's gun. Mage staggered, and Tudor stood and continued firing until the clip was empty. Krieg stared at him. "I'm not that easy to kill either," said the sorcerer, coolly.

Krieg merely nodded, shed her smoldering jacket, and walked over to where Mage was lying. She rolled the body over onto its back, then grabbed the focus, pulled it over Mage's head, stared at it for a moment, and pocketed it.

Takumo staggered into the bedroom, saw the penanggalan, and reached for the knife in his belt. "Leave her," snapped Kelly. "Just get me out of here. What the hell is *happening* out there?"

"Mage is here," said Takumo. Still looking uneasily at the penanggalan, he removed his keychain from his jeans pocket, and fumbled for the handcuff key. He'd freed Kelly's feet and one of her hands when they heard the shots. Kelly grabbed her shotgun from under the bed and rushed out right behind him.

They were in time to see Krieg pick Mage up and shake him. "Did you *have* to shoot him?" she asked Tudor, who had walked over to stand beside her. "There are supposed to be three of those things, and she wants all of them."

Mage opened his eyes. "Hidden," he groaned. "Only I can get there; no other way in."

"You're not going anywhere," Krieg growled. "Not any-more." Mage's vital signs were too weak for her to tell whether or not he was lying; she was about to drop the body in disgust when she glanced over her shoulder and saw Kelly and Takumo. "Tell me," she said, "and I'll let them live."

Kelly raised the shotgun, and lowered it again; at that range, she was almost certain to hit Mage as well, and much more likely to kill him than she was to inflict any harm on Krieg. Takumo hurtled toward them, and Krieg half-turned and knocked him down with a slap across the face. "Drop the gun," she commanded Kelly, placing her foot on Takumo's neck. "Drop it, or he dies."

Kelly hesitated, then tossed the gun aside. "I know where another of the foci is," she said.

Krieg stared at her; she seemed to be telling the truth. "Is it somewhere I can find it?"

"*No!*" screamed Takumo. Krieg didn't even glance at him. "Is it?" she asked.

"Yes," said Kelly. "It's in this house."

Another truth. "Tell me, or I'll kill him."

"No," said Kelly, backing away. "Get away from them, now."

"Don't tell *me* what to do," snapped Krieg, but she removed her foot from Takumo's neck.

"*No!*" yelled Takumo, again. "Kel, what the Hell are you doing?"

"Which is worth more?" Kelly asked Krieg. "The focus, or him? Let him go, and I'll tell you where it is."

Krieg shook her head. "Bring it to me, and I'll let them go."

"No."

Krieg took a step toward her, and Takumo suddenly realized what Kelly was doing. He covered his face with his hands and turned away from both Krieg and Tudor, huddled into a near fetal position—and slipped the focus off from around his neck and palmed it. He glanced up at Tudor, who was watching the women with obvious amusement, then turned toward Mage and pressed the focus into his hand. The magician opened his eyes, looked at the focus, wound it around his fingers, and nodded slightly.

"Bring it to me," barked Krieg, "or I'll kill you all." Kelly didn't move, and the vampire leaped at her, grabbing her by the shoulders and snarling into her face. *"Where is it?"*

Kelly smiled at her, then, with startling speed, leaned forward and kissed Krieg on the mouth. The vampire recoiled, releasing her grip, and Kelly pushed her back further with a powerful kick. Krieg stumbled back toward Mage, who suddenly reached out to grab one of her ankles, and in the same instant, one of Tudor's. His insubstantial hands passed through them as though they were shadows.

Krieg glanced down, then raised her foot and stamped down hard on Mage's wrist. Kelly winced at the sound of a bone snapping, and Mage roared as he realized that his arm was solid again. He grabbed Tudor's leg, clutched the side of Krieg's boot, and *saw* all three of them in low Earth orbit.

Tudor looked down and screamed, but in the vacuum of space, no one heard him. Mage released him, giving him a slight push toward the Earth below them, then turned his attention to Krieg. She glared at him, her eyes blazing red, and kicked at his face with her free leg—and then they passed over the terminator into the full glare of the sun, unfiltered by any atmosphere. Krieg covered her eyes to protect them from the light, and Mage watched as the skin of her hands seemed to melt away like wax. He reached into her pocket for the focus, grabbed it, and *saw* himself back in Kelly's house.

He looked up to see Kelly bending over him, her expression anxious. "Where are they?" she asked.

"Gone," he said. "Neither of them is going to be coming

back, except maybe as a meteorite. Can you call me an ambulance? I don't think I can heal this much damage."

"No need," said Takumo, painfully picking himself up off the floor. "I've found something better. Do you have my focus?"

Epilogue

Woodcott woke up from the worst nightmare in his life, and looked over at the book a few inches from his face. It took him a few moments to remember where he was, and even longer to remember why he was there at a quarter past five on a Sunday morning. He looked at the book again, Tudor's book; he had the uncomfortable feeling that not only had it caused the nightmares, horrific visions of Hell, but that now it was *laughing* at him. He pushed his desk chair back, shook his head, and stumbled over to the water cooler.

Woodcott had never performed an exorcism before, and wasn't entirely sure how to go about it, but he settled for blessing some water, opening the plastic bag that held the book, and then drawing a cross on it with a finger dipped in the water, while quietly invoking the Trinity. Suddenly, he felt the building lurch, and ducked under the desk, scared that the long-overdue Big One might finally have hit the city. He stayed there for several minutes, but there were no more shocks, and eventually he emerged, shaken but unhurt. He stared at the book, which now seemed to be nothing more than a book, silent and solid.

He drew a deep breath, then walked to the window and waited for dawn.

Tudor had traveled around the world twice, and already he was bored with the view—especially as it included the desiccated husk that had once been Krieg. He suspected that he didn't look much better, but Hell had kept up its end of the bargain; he was still alive, and if the tarot had told him the truth, that meant Magistrale was dead. It was small consolation for the prospect of spending the next seventy-four years drifting through space, but it was better than nothing.

He blinked. He was floating over the dark side of the Earth, and with the moon eclipsed, there was no light except that of the stars—and they seemed to have suddenly dimmed, as though a shadow had passed between him and them. He looked around, and saw the shadows break up into vague shapes; saw three-faced heads, long claws, huge wings.

Every demon with whom he'd ever made a pact was there—and each one grabbed a piece of his body, and pulled, before flying off in different directions.

"Don't tell me you've never been in a plane before," said Gaye.

Mage looked out the window as they flew over the Pacific. "Not since I was a kid," he admitted. "My parents took me to Italy when I was twelve, but that was the last time. It's still hard to believe that something this heavy can just stay up in the air."

"You could have taken me with you when you . . ." She smiled, and reached up to touch the focus she wore around her neck. "You know."

"Maybe," said Mage, "but I still think this is safer." He looked out the window again. "I hope so, anyway."

Her smile became a little wider. After she'd managed to heal Mage, Takumo, and even Ahna, Mage had suggested she come to Bangkok to work at the clinic there, at least temporarily. She'd accepted with pleasure, left Isis and Bast with Kelly, and packed her bags before he could change his mind.

Mage stood. "Excuse me," he said, squeezing past her to the aisle. He walked to the bathroom, closed the door, and *saw* himself in Nakatani's office.

Haruko Tamenaga looked up, and immediately reached for the gun in the drawer. "Don't worry," said Mage, sitting on the sofa opposite her. "I just wanted to see who had this office now. Did anyone ever tell you that you have your father's eyes?"

"What do you want?"

"A truce," he said, blandly. "Your promise that I can live my life without having to look over my shoulder for your goons, and that the same goes for my friends. I promise you the same in return."

"You killed my father, you killed Nakatani—"

He nodded. "And a few people who were working for them—or for you—but how many people did your father have killed? I'm sure *he* knew, but he was good with numbers; do *you* have any idea?" He waited, but she didn't answer. "If I killed you, would whoever took over this office try sending someone to kill me too?"

Tamenaga moved her hand away from the gun, and smiled. "You won't kill me," she said. "I know too much about you. You won't kill an unarmed woman—you're just not capable of it."

Mage shrugged. "How do I know you're unarmed?"

Tamenaga pushed her chair back from her desk, stood, and slowly removed her jacket. She dropped the jacket onto the floor—Mage heard the faint thud of her cell phone landing on the carpet—then walked out from behind the desk and turned around, her hands clasped behind her head. "Satisfied?"

"Not quite."

She smiled scornfully, and unzipped her skirt, letting it fall around her feet. Standing there in a raw silk blouse, panties, pantyhose and shoes, she took a step toward him. "Do you really expect me to be frightened of you?" she asked.

"Lose the jewelry," he said.

"What?" She rolled her eyes. "Look, if this is a robbery, I can get you as many unmarked bills as you like from downstairs, if you wait a minute. Or are you looking for a job?"

"I thought some of it might have sentimental value."

"Do I look like the sentimental sort?"

He shrugged, and her watch vanished. Startled, she looked down at her bare wrist, and her eyes widened. "What are you doing?"

He stood and reached for her hands. "It's my turn to show you something," he said quietly, and *saw* the two of them standing in a dark and dirty shower cubicle. Tamenaga broke free of his grasp and hit him in the solar plexus and throat—an instant too late. She took a step away from Mage and looked around, letting her eyes adapt to the darkness. "Where . . . how . . . ?"

Mage, winded, tried to speak, but could only shake his head. Tamenaga faced him, prepared to hit him again, and waited until he'd recovered his voice. "China . . ." he croaked.

"What?" She shivered, and suddenly realized that she was cold as well as frightened. She wrapped her arms around herself, and was startled to find the fabric of her blouse rougher and heavier than she'd expected. Her fingers were bare of jewelry, and hardened with calluses. *"What have you done?"*

"Quiet," he wheezed. "You'll bring the guards, and they won't be happy."

"Guards? Where are we?"

"In China. In a refugee camp near the Korean border, to be precise."

"What?"

"You were right," he said, as he leaned against the corrugated steel wall and tried to breathe normally. "I can't kill you, but I *can* make you poor—and I have. I'm sure that *eventually* you'll get out of here and maybe find someone who'll smuggle you back to America . . . but how long it'll take, and how much of your empire you'll still have when you get back there . . ."

Tamenaga turned pale. "You . . ."

"You still have your voice, your face, your memory. . . . I can't vouch for your fingerprints, and I had to make sure you didn't have a phone or any papers or anything on you that you could sell, but you won't be any worse off than millions of other people around the world, and maybe you'll learn some empathy while you're here. And one more thing . . ."

"What?"

"If I have any reason to think you're a menace to me or my friends . . . well, there are plenty of places like this and some worse, and I can do this as often as I need to." Tamenaga threw herself at him, but he was already back in the bathroom on the plane.

He sat on the commode until he could walk and breathe without wincing, then staggered back to his seat, to find Gaye grinning. "What's so funny?" he asked.

"Just remembering Charlie at the farewell party—the way Ahna kept dragging him one way, and Sindee dragging him another . . ." She chuckled. "Are you okay?"

"I'm fine," he said. "In fact, I think everything's going to be fine."

About the Author

Stephen Dedman is the author of the Stoker Award–nominated novel, *The Art of Arrow Cutting*, and *Foreign Bodies*. His award-nominated short fiction has appeared in most of the major genre magazines, including *The Magazine of Fantasy and Science Fiction*, *Asimov's SF*, and *Science Fiction Age*, and in such highly regarded anthologies as *Little Deaths*, *The Year's Best Fantasy and Horror*, *The Year's Best Science Fiction*, *Dreaming Down-Under*, and *Centaurus*, and has been collected in *The Lady of Situations*. He lives in Perth, Australia.